COLLECTED STORIES

Janice Galloway's first novel, *The Trick is to Keep Breathing*, now widely regarded as a Scottish contemporary classic, was published in 1990 and won the MIND/Allan Lane Book of the Year. Her second novel, *Foreign Parts*, won the American Academy of Arts and Letters EM Forster Award while her third, *Clara*, about the tempestuous life of nineteenth-century pianist Clara Wieck Schumann, won the Saltire Award in 2002. Collaborative texts include an opera with Sally Beamish and three cross-discipline works with Anne Bevan, the Orcadian sculptor. Her 'anti-memoir', *This is not about me*, was published by Granta in September 2008 to universal critical acclaim. She lives in Lanarkshire.

ALSO BY JANICE GALLOWAY

JANICE GALLOWAY

Collected Stories

VINTAGE BOOKS
London

Published by Vintage 2009

2 4 6 8 10 9 7 5 3 1

The stories in this book were originally published in the following: *Blood*: 'Blood',
'Scenes from the Life No. 23: Paternal Advice', 'Love in a changing environment',
'Frostbite', 'Scenes from the Life No. 29: Dianne', 'it was', 'David', 'two fragments',
'Scenes from the Life No. 26: The Community and the Senior Citizen', 'Into the
Roots', 'Breaking Through', 'Fair Ellen and the Wanderer Returned', 'Scenes from
the Life No. 24: Bikers', 'Need for Restraint', 'Plastering the Cracks', *'later he would
open his eyes in a strange place, wondering where she'*, 'The meat', 'Fearless',
'Scenes from the Life No. 27: Living In', 'Nightdriving', 'things he said', 'A Week
with Uncle Felix'; *Where You Find It*: 'valentine', 'where you find it', 'sonata form',
'a night in', 'test', 'after the rains', 'waiting for marilyn', 'hope', 'bisex', 'peeping
tom', 'babysitting', 'someone had to', 'a proper respect', 'the bridge', 'tourists
from the south arrive in the independent state', 'he dreams of pleasing his mother',
'last thing', 'not flu', 'proposal', 'six horses'

This collection first published in Great Britain in 2009 by Vintage

Blood first published in Great Britain in 1991 by Martin Secker & Warburg

Where You Find It first published in Great Britain in 1996 by Jonathan Cape

Vintage

Random House, 20 Vauxhall Bridge Road, London SW1V 2SA

www.vintage-books.co.uk

Addresses for companies within The Random House Group Limited can be found
at: www.randomhouse.co.uk/offices.htm

The Random House Group Limited Reg. No. 954009

A CIP catalogue record for this book
is available from the British Library

ISBN 9780099540397

The Random House Group Limited supports The Forest Stewardship Council (FSC),
the leading international forest certification organisation. All our titles that are
printed on Greenpeace approved FSC certified paper carry the FSC logo. Our paper
procurement policy can be found at www.rbooks.co.uk/environment

Printed and bound in Great Britain by
CPI Cox & Wyman, Reading RG1 8EX

TO PETER K.

Contents

Blood

He put his knee up on her chest getting ready to pull,
tilting the pliers. Sorry, he said. Sorry. She couldn't see his
face. The pores on the backs of his fingers sprouted hairs,
single black wires curling onto the bleached skin of the
wrist, the veins showing through. She saw an artery move
under the surface as he slackened the grip momentarily,
catching his breath; his cheeks a kind of mauve colour,
twisting at something inside her mouth. The bones in his
hand were bruising her lip. And that sound of the gum
tugging back from what he was doing, the jaw creaking.
Her jaw. If you closed your eyes it made you feel dizzy,
imagining it, and this through the four jags of anaesthetic,
that needle as big as a power drill. Better to keep her eyes
open, trying to focus past the blur of knuckles to the cracked
ceiling. She was trying to see a pattern, make the lines into
something she could recognise, when her mouth started to
do something she hadn't given it permission for. A kind of
suction. There was a moment of nothing while he steadied
his hand, as if she had only imagined the give. She heard
herself swallow and stop breathing. Then her spine lifting,
arching from the seat, the gum parting with a sound like
uprooting potatoes, a coolness in her mouth and he was

holding something up in the metal clamp; great bloody lump of it, white trying to surface through the red. He was pleased.

There you go eh? Never seen one like that before. The root of the problem ha ha.

All his fillings showed when he laughed, holding the thing out, wanting her to look. Blood made a pool under her tongue, lapping at the back of her throat and she had to keep the head back instead. Her lips were too numb to trust: it would have run down the front of her blazer.

Rinse, he said. Cough and spit.

When she sat up he was holding the tooth out on a tissue, roots like a yellow clawhammer at the end, one point wrapping the other.

See the twist? Unusual to see something like that. Little twist in the roots.

Like a deformed parsnip. And there was a bit of flesh, a piece of gum or something nipped off between the crossed tips of bone.

Little rascal, he said.

Her mouth was filling up, she turned to the metal basin before he started singing again. *She's leaving now cos I just heard the slamming of the door* then humming. He didn't really know the words. She spat dark red and thick into the basin. When she resurfaced, he was looking at her and wiping his hands on something like a dishtowel.

Expect it'll bleed for a while, bound to be messy after that bother. Just take your time getting up. Take your time there. No rush.

She had slid to the edge of the chair, dunting the hooks and probes with having to hold on. The metal noise made her teeth sore. Her stomach felt terrible and she had to sit still, waiting to see straight.

Fine in a minute, he said. Wee walk in the fresh air. Wee walk back to school.

He finished wiping his hands and grinned, holding something out. A hard thing inside tissue. The tooth.

You made it, you have it haha. There you go. How's the jaw?

She nodded, and pointed to her mouth. This almost audible sound of a tank filling, a rising tide over the edges of the tongue.

Bleed for a while like I say. Don't worry though. Redheads always bleed worse than other folk. Haha. Sandra'll get you something: stop you making a mess of yourself.

Sandra was already away. He turned to rearrange the instruments she had knocked out of their neat arrangement on the green cloth.

Redheads, see. *Don't take your love to town.*

Maybe it was a joke. She tried to smile back till the blood started silting again. He walked over to the window as Sandra came back with a white pad in her hand. The pad had gauze over the top, very thick with a blue stripe down one side. Loops. A sanitary towel. The dentist was still turned away, looking out of the window and wiping his specs and talking. It took a minute to realise he was talking to her. It should stop in about an hour or so he was saying. Maybe three at the outside. Sandra pushed the pad out for her to take. If not by six o'clock let him know and they could give her a shot of something ok? Looking out the whole time. She tried to listen, tucking the loops at the ends of the towel in where they wouldn't be obvious, blushing when she put it up to her mouth. It was impossible to tell if they were being serious or not. The dentist turned back, grinning at the spectacles he was holding between his hands.

Sandra given you a wee special there. Least said haha. Redheads eh? *Oh Roooobeee,* not looking, wiping the same lens over and over with a cloth.

The fresh air was good. Two deep lungfuls before she wrapped her scarf round the white pad at her mouth and walked. The best way from the surgery was past the flats with bay windows and gardens. Some had trees, crocuses and bits of cane. Better than up by the building site, full of those shouting men. One of them always shouted things, whistled loud enough to make the whole street turn and look. Bad enough at the best of times. Today would have been awful. This way was longer but prettier and there was nothing to stop her taking her time. She had permission. No need to worry about getting there for some particular ring of some particular bell. Permission made all the difference. The smell of bacon rolls at the cafe fetched her nose: coffee and chocolate. They spoiled when they reached her mouth, heaped up with sanitary towel and the blood still coming. Her tongue wormed towards the soft place, the dip where the tooth had been, then back between tongue root and the backs of her teeth. Thick fluid. A man was crossing the road, a greyhound on a thin lead, a woman with a pram coming past the phone box. Besides, girls didn't spit in the street. School wasn't that far though, not if she walked fast. She clutched the tooth tight in her pocket and walked, head down. The pram was there before she expected it; sudden metal spokes too near her shoes before she looked up, eyes and nose over the white rim of gauze. The woman not even noticing but keeping on, ploughing up the road while she waited at the kerb with her eyes on the gutter, trying hard not to swallow. Six streets and a park to go. Six streets.

The school had no gate, just a gap in the wall with pillars on either side that led into the playground. The blacked-out window was the staff room; the others showed occasional heads, some white faces watching. The Music block was nearest. Quarter to twelve. It would be possible to wait in the practice rooms till the dinner bell in fifteen minutes and

not shift till the afternoon. She was in no mood, though, not
even for that. Not even for the music. It wouldn't be
possible to play well. But there was no point in going home
either because everything would have to be explained in
triplicate when the mother got in and she never believed you
anyway. It was all impossible. The pad round her mouth
was slimy already, the wet going cold further at the far
sides. She could go over and ask Mrs McNiven for another
towel and just go anyway, have a lie-down or something
but that meant going over to the other block, all the way
across the playground again and the faces looking out
knowing where you were going because it was the only time
senior girls went there. And this thing round her mouth.
Her stomach felt terrible too. She suddenly wanted to be in
the music rooms, soothing herself with music. Something
peaceful. Going there made her feel better just because of
where it was. Not like at home. You could just go and play
to your heart's content. That would be nice now, right now
this minute, going up there and playing something: the
Mozart she'd been working on, something fresh and clean.
Turning, letting the glass door close, she felt her throat
thicken, closing over with film. And that fullness that said
the blood was still coming. A sigh into the towel stung her
eyes. The girls' toilets were on the next landing.

Yellow. The light, the sheen off the mirrors. It was always
horrible coming here. She could usually manage to get
through the days without having to, waiting till she got
home and drinking nothing. Most of the girls did the same,
even just to avoid the felt-tip drawings on the girls' door –
mostly things like split melons only they weren't. All that
pretending you couldn't see them on the way in and what
went with them, GIRLS ARE A BUNCH OF CUNTS still
visible under the diagonal scores of the cleaners' Vim.
Impossible to argue against so you made out it wasn't there,

swanning past the word CUNTS though it radiated like a
black sun all the way from the other end of the corridor.
Terrible. And inside, the yellow lights always on, nearly all
the mirrors with cracks or warps. Her own face reflected
yellow over the nearside row of sinks. She clamped her
mouth tight and reached for the towel loops. Its peeling
away made her mouth suddenly cold. In her hand, the pad
had creased up the centre, ridged where it had settled
between her lips and smeared with crimson on the one side.
Not as bad as she had thought, but the idea of putting it
back wasn't good. She wrapped it in three paper towels
instead and stuffed it to the bottom of the wire bin under
the rest, bits of paper and God knows what, then leaned
over the sinks, rubbing at the numbness in her jaw, rinsing
out. Big, red drips when she tried to open her mouth. And
something else. She watched the slow trail of red on the
white enamel, concentrating. Something slithered in her
stomach, a slow dullness that made it difficult to straighten
up again. Then a twinge in her back, a recognisable contrac-
tion. That's what the sweating was, then, the churning in
her gut. It wasn't just not feeling well with the swallowing
and imagining things. Christ. It wasn't supposed to be due
for a week yet. She'd have to use that horrible toilet paper
and it would get sore and slip about all day. Better that than
asking Mrs McNiven for two towels, though, anything was
better than asking Mrs McNiven. The cold tap spat water
along the length of one blazer arm. She was turning it the
wrong way. For a frightening moment, she couldn't think
how to turn it off then managed, breathing out, tilting
forward. It would be good to get out of here, get to
something fresh and clean, Mozart and the white room
upstairs. She would patch something together and just
pretend she wasn't bleeding so much, wash her hands and
be fit for things. The white keys. She pressed her forehead
against the cool concrete of the facing wall, swallowing.

The taste of blood like copper in her mouth, lips pressed tight.

The smallest practice room was free. The best one: the rosewood piano and the soundproofing made it feel warm. There was no one in either of the other two except the student who taught cello. She didn't know his name, just what he did. He never spoke. Just sat in there all the time waiting for pupils, playing or looking out of the window. Anything to avoid catching sight of people. Mr Gregg said he was afraid of the girls and who could blame him haha. She'd never understood the joke too well but it seemed to be right enough. He sometimes didn't even answer the door if you knocked or made out he couldn't see you when you went by you on the stairs. It was possible to count yourself alone, then, if he was the only one here. It was possible to relax. She sat on the piano stool, hunched over her stomach, rocking. C major triad. This piano had a nice tone, brittle and light. The other two made a fatter, fuzzier noise altogether. This one was leaner, right for the Mozart anyway. Descending chromatic scale with the right hand. The left moved in the blazer pocket, ready to surface, tipping something soft. Crushed tissue, something hard in the middle. The tooth. She had almost forgotten about the tooth. Her back straightened to bring it out, unfold the bits of tissue to hold it up to the light. It had a ridge about a third of the way down, where the glaze of enamel stopped. Below it, the roots were huge, matte like suede. The twist was huge, still bloody where they crossed. Whatever it was they had pulled out with them, the piece of skin, had disappeared. Hard to accept her body had grown this thing. Ivory. She smiled and laid it aside on the wood slat at the top of the keyboard, like a misplaced piece of inlay. It didn't match. The keys were whiter.

Just past the hour already. In four minutes the bell would go and the noise would start: people coming in to stake claims on the rooms, staring in through the glass panels on the door. Arpeggios bounced from next door. The student would be warming up for somebody's lesson, waiting. She turned back to the keys, sighing. Her mouth was filling up again, her head thumping. Fingers looking yellow when she stretched them out, reaching for chords. Her stomach contracted. But if she could just concentrate, forget her body and let the notes come, it wouldn't matter. You could get past things that way, pretend they weren't there. She leaned towards the keyboard, trying to be something else: a piece of music. Mozart, the recent practice. Feeling for the clear, clean lines. Listening. She ignored the pain in her stomach, the scratch of paper towels at her thighs, and watched the keys, the pressure of her fingers that buried or released them. And watching, listening to Mozart, she let the music get louder, and the door opened, the abrupt tearing sound of the doorseals seizing her stomach like a fist. The student was suddenly there and smiling to cover the knot on his forehead where the fear showed, smiling fit to bust, saying, Don't stop, it's lovely; Haydn isn't it? and she opened her mouth not able to stop, opened her mouth to say Mozart. It's Mozart – before she remembered.

Welling up behind the lower teeth, across her lips as she tilted forwards to keep it off her clothes. Spilling over the white keys and dripping onto the clean tile floor. She saw his face change, the glance flick to the claw roots in the tissue before he shut the door hard, not knowing what else to do. And the bell rang, the steady howl of it as the outer doors gave, footfalls in the corridor gathering like an avalanche. They would be here before she could do any-thing, sitting dumb on the piano stool, not able to move, not able to breathe, and this blood streaking over the keys, silting the action. The howl of the bell. This unstoppable redness seeping through the fingers at her open mouth.

Scenes from the Life No. 23: Paternal Advice

It is a small room but quite cheery. There is an old-style armchair off to the left with floral stretch-covers and a shiny flap of mismatching material for a cushion. Behind that, a dark fold-down table, folded down. On the left, a low table surmounted by a glass bowl cut in jaggy shapes, containing keys, fuses, one green apple and some buttons. Between these two is an orange rug and the fireplace. The fireplace is the focal point of the room. It has a wide surround of sand-coloured tiles and a prominent mantelpiece on which are displayed a china figurine, a small stag's head in brass, a football trophy and a very ornate, heavy wrought-iron clock. On the lower part of the surround are a poker and a tongs with thistle tops and a matchbox. Right at the edge, a folded copy of the *Sunday Post* with the Broons visible on top. Behind the fireguard, the coals smoke with dross. The whole has the effect of calm and thoughtfulness. It is getting dark.

Place within this, the man SAMMY. He is perched on the edge of the armchair with his knees spread apart and his weight forward, one elbow on each knee for balance. He sits for some time, fists pressing at his mouth as he rocks gently back and forth, back and forth. We can only just hear the sound of a radio from next door, and the odd muffled thump on the wall. More noticeable than either of these is the heavy tick of the clock.

SAMMY exhales noisily. He appears to be mulling over some tricky problem. He is. But we are growing restless in the silence. Suddenly, too close, a noise like a radio tuning and we are in the thick of it.

put it off long enough and it wasnt doing the boy any favours   just kidology to make out it was   just putting it off for himself more like   no   time to face it and get on with it   right   it was for the best after all and a father had to do his best by his boy even if it was hard even if he didnt want to   bad father that shirked his responsibilities no bloody use to anybody   the boy had to be learned right and learned right right from the word go   right   spare the rod   cruel to be nobodys fool that sort of thing right christ tell us something we dont know

The man stands up abruptly, scowling.

no argument it needed doing   just playing myself here its HOW thats the thing thats the whole bloody thing is HOW   needed to be sure about these things tricky things needed to be clear in your mind before you opened your mouth else just make an arse of the whole jingbang just fuck it up totally TOTALLY aye got to be careful only one go at it right had to get it across in a oner and he had to learn it get the message right first time right had to know what you were at every word every move or else

SAMMY walks briskly to the window in obvious emotional agitation, bringing a dout from his right trouser pocket, then a box of matches. He inserts the dout off-centre between his lips, takes a match from the box, feels for the rough side and sparks the match blind. The cigarette stump lights in three very quick, short puffs and still his eyes are focused on something we cannot see, outside the window in the middle distance. Up on tiptoes next, peering. Violent puffing. He shouts. BASTARDS! SPIKY-HEIDED BASTARDS. AD GIE THEM PUNK. WHAT DO THEY THINK THEY LOOK LIKE EH? JUST WHAT DO THEY THINK THEYRE AT EH? and he is stubbing the cigarette butt out on the sill, turning sharply, going back to the easy chair to resume his perch. He runs one hand grease-quick through his hair from forehead to the nape of his neck and taps his foot nervously.

christs sake get a grip eh remember what youre supposed to be doing eh   one think at a time   TIME the time must be getting on. Get on with it. Hardly see the time now dark already. Right. Thats it then. That does it. Wee Sammy will be wondering what the hell is going on what his daddy is doing all this time.

SAMMY's eyes mist with sudden tears as the object of his sentimental contemplation appears in an oval clearing above the mans head. A thinks balloon. Inside, a small boy of about five or six years. He has ash-brown hair, needing cut, a thick fringe hanging into watery eyes that are rimmed pink as though from lack of sleep. It is WEE SAMMY. The balloon expands. WEE SAMMY in a smutty school shirt, open one button at the neck for better fit, and showing a tidemark ingrained on the inside. One cuff is frayed. The trousers are too big and are held up by a plastic snakebelt; badly hemmed over his sandshoes and saggy at the arse. He is slumped against the wall of what we presume to be the lobby. It is understandable his father is upset to think of him: he looks hellish. God knows how long the boy has been waiting there. The eyes, indeed the whole cast of the body suggest it may have been days. And still he waits as we watch.

SAMMY clenches his eyes and the balloon vision pops. POP. Little lines radiate into the air to demonstrate with the word GONE in the middle, hazily. Then it melts too. The man makes a fist in his pocket but he speaks evenly. RIGHT. MAKE YOUR BLOODY MIND UP TIME. RIGHT. Then springs to the door where he steadies himself, smooths his hair back with the palm of his hand and turns the doorknob gently. A barless A of light noses in from the lobby with an elongated shadow of the boy inside. The mans face is taut, struggling to remember a smile shape. One hand still rests on the doorknob, the other that brushed back his hair reached forward, an upturned cup, to the child outside. A gesture of encouragement.

SAMMY: Come away in son.

The shadow shortens and the child enters, refocusing in the dim interior. The door clicks as his father closes it behind and the boy looks quickly over his shoulder. The man smiles more naturally now as if relaxing, and settles one hand awkwardly on the boy as they walk to the fireplace. Here, the man bobs down on his hunkers so his eyes are more at a level with his son's. WEE SAMMY's eyes are bland. He suspects nothing. The man has seen this too, and throughout the exchange to come is careful: his manner is craftedly diffident, suffused with stifled anguish and an edge of genuine affection.

(pause)

SAMMY: Well. Youre getting to be the big man now eh?
Did your mammy say anything to you about me
wanting to see you? About what it was about?

WEE SAMMY: Silence.

SAMMY: Naw. Did she no, son? Eh. Well. Its to do with
you getting so big now, starting at the school
and that. You like the school?

WEE SAMMY: Silence.

SAMMY: Daft question eh? I didnt like it much either son.
Bit of a waster, your da. Sorry now, all right.
They said to me at the time I would be, telled me
for my own good and I didnt listen. Youll see
they said. Thought they were talkin rubbish.
What did I know eh? Nothin. Sum total, nothin.
Too late though! Ach, we're all the same.
Anyway, whats this your das tryin to say, youll
be thinkin. Eh. Whats he sayin to me. Am I
right?

WEE SAMMY: Silence.

SAMMY: Why doesnt he get on with it, is that what youre
thinkin eh? Well this is me gettin on with it as
fast as I can son. Its somethin I have to explain
to you. Because I'm your daddy and because
youre at the school and everythin. Makin your
own way with new people. Fightin your own
battles. I'm tryin to make sure I do it right son.
Its like I was sayin about the school as well,

about tellin you somethin for your own good. But I'm hopin youll no be like me, that youll listen right. And thats why I'm tellin you now. Now youre the big man but no too big to tell your daddy he's daft. Eh wee man?

SAMMY *rumples his son's hair proudly.* WEE SAMMY *smiles. This response has an instantly calming effect on the man and he raises himself up to his full height again. His voice needs to expand now to reach down to the boy. His demeanour is altogether more assured and confident.*

SAMMY: OK. Thats the boy. Ready? One two three go.

WEE SAMMY *remains silent but nods up smiling at his father as* SAMMY *pushes his hands under the boy's oxters and lifts him up to near eye-level with himself.*

SAMMY: Up you come. Hooa! Nearly too heavy for me now. Youre the big fella right enough! Now. Here's a seat for you. No be a minute, then up on your feet.

He places his son on the mantelpiece between the brass ornament and the clock. He shifts the clock away to the low table, pats some stouriness off the shelf with the flat of his hand, then lifts the boy high, arms at full stretch, to reposition him in the centre of the mantelpiece in place of the clock. The boy is fully upright on the mantelpiece.

SAMMY: Upsadaisy! Up we go!

WEE SAMMY: Dad!

SAMMY: What? What is it son? Not to take my hands

away? Och silly! Youre fine. On you come,
stand up right, straighten your legs. Would I let
you fall? Eh? Thats my wee man, thats it. See?
Higher than me now, nearly up to the ceiling.
OK? Now, are you listening to me? Listen hard.
I want you to do somethin for me. Will you do
somethin for me? Will ye son? Show me youre
no feart to jump eh? Jump. Jump down and I'll
catch you.

*There is a long pause. The man is staring intently into the
child's eyes and the child's eyes search back. He is still tall
on the mantelpiece among the china and brass ornaments,
back and hand flat against the wallpaper flora. The man's
eyes shine.*

SAMMY: Show your daddy youre no feart son. I'll catch
you. Dont be feart, this is your da talkin to you.
Come on. For me. Jump and I'll catch you. Dont
be scared. Sammy, son, I'm waiting. I'm ready.

*A few more seconds of tense silence click out of the clock.
WEE SAMMY blinks. His hands lift from the wall and he
decides: one breath and he throws himself from the
screaming height of the sill. In the same second, SAMMY
skirts to the side. The boy crashes lumpily into the tiles of
the fire surround. His father sighs and averts his eyes,
choking back a sob.*

SAMMY: Let that be a lesson to you son. Trust nae cunt.

Love in
a changing
environment

The bakery was how we found it. They gave us the address
and the bakery was right underneath the window, under
where we were moving in. Neither of us had much to bring.
We ferried clothes and a radio, two big cushions, cooking
things and our bed linen along a tunnel of lukewarm pie,
gingerbread hearts, the sweet fat reek of doughnuts. The
bed last, mattress jamming up in the close-mouth, shutting
him in the dark and me on the other side, trapped in the
light and the crusty smell of split rolls. Lunchtime. Tuna
wholemeal and his laughter on the other side of the foam,
the mattress wresting from his unseen grip.

We had only one room and no clock. Hours shifted on
white toasters and morning rye to mid-morning eccles cakes
and iced chelsea rounds. Crumpets, and fruit scones, the
crackling echo of cellophane, the sulphur stink of egg
mayonnaise led us through lunchtime and an hour with
coffee at three was signalled by the moist, animal vapour of
cream meringues. Our teatime table wafted with coffee
kisses or cold potato scones, the odd coconut castle: not our
favourite time of day. But with rising early, we seldom
waited up long after they closed. A few hours with warm

milk by the window, his watering the solitary fern, the fur-leaved African violet. Perhaps, he whispered, there would be flowers. We slept well, waiting for the early-morning drift of wholemeal.

Making love happened most often in the mornings, our bodies joining in a warm cloud of new-baked viennas and granary cobs from the shop beneath, the window hazy with hot chocolate croissants and our twin breaths. The scent of bread rising increased his thrust. Often he would tilt over my shoulder moaning as the oven doors opened in the kitchens beneath, his ejaculation impossible to hold back from the lure of working yeast. His semen usually parted company with me by the time they were shaping danish pastries. The surrounding air was everything and sweet.

The afternoon there was hammering non-stop from eleven till three, we had a mild disagreement. I said something unkind and went downstairs for two cheese rolls and an apple pie for later – we seldom cooked. It wasn't till the door refused I saw the sign. The bakery were selling up. We had toastless beans and cheddar at teatime and I blamed myself. Now I look back, there had been something different the whole morning. I looked up but he said nothing. He didn't think it his place to talk about relationships. An iced finger ran the length of my spine but I pushed it away. Without the companionship of the ovens downstairs, we felt disoriented and went to bed earlier than usual. He put out the light.

Next morning he took ages to come then went for a shower. I made porridge. He had a long walk before arriving home with milk. I found a baked potato place and started bringing back tea in polystyrene cartons, the food chilling over. He quibbled with my choice of fillings and took things

out on the African violet's stubborn refusal to bloom,
denying it water. I tended it alone.

The new owners arrived almost a month later. We lay in
bed, wondering what the noise was, that dull slapping, the
flaccid thud of something thick splaying out against wood.
Then their smell, leaking into the room like gas. A butcher's
van sat below the window. The steady stench of gristle and
turning fat, dead tissue congested with blood became suddenly obvious. Our arms touched as we both turned away,
not sure what to say. I think we were afraid.

Over the week, sudden thuds and hacks began to punctuate
the hours, digging into soft wood. Time ticked on the cold
blue rend of joint and socket, the cracking of bone, the drill
and the saw. Silences afterwards were worse, imagination
tensing for the soft sound of the scalpel, the suck of raw
muscle flenching from the blade, the lick of layer against
moist layer. Relaxation was difficult, sex worse. Mild
putrefaction hung like cigarette smoke under our ceiling
and clogged the close, attracting strays who bayed through
the still night, snuffling through the stained sawdust beneath our window. Sometimes he went out without saying
where he was going, coming home with crumbs on his lapel.
We lost sleep and seldom touched, suspicious of the scent of
each other's skin. Each morning when the meat van arrived,
we fought over the shower, each eager for the sweet soap,
the gush of cleansing water. The day they unloaded the
bone grinder, I packed my bags.

Four streets distant, I moved into a new flat on the ground
floor smelling only of damp. Thinner and wiser, I eat no
meat and avoid cakes. The very sight of them makes me
sick.

Frostbite

Christ it was cold.

And only one glove as usual. The bare hand in the pocket, sweaty against the change counted out for the fare; the other inside the remaining glove, cramped stiff round the handle of the fiddle case. Freezing. Her feet were solid too; just a oneness of dead cold inside her boots in place of anything five-toed or familiar. She stamped them hard for spite, waiting and watching for the fingers of light smudging through the dark, the bus feeling its way up the other side of the hill. The last two had been full and driven straight on. No point getting angry. That was just the way of it.

Nothing yet.

Cloud came out of her mouth and she looked up. There on the other side of the road was the spire. Frame of royal blue, frazzled through with sodium orange, and the spire in the middle, lit from beneath by a dozen calendar windows: people working late. There was a hollow triangle of light above the tip; a clear opening in the sky where she could see the snow flurry and settle on the stone like white ivy. The University.

This was the best of the place now – the look of it. Still able to catch her out. As for the rest, it had not been what she had hoped. Her own fault, of course, expecting too much as usual. They said as much beforehand, over and over: it's no a job though, music willny keep you, it's no for the likes of you – cursing the teacher who had put the daft idea into her head in the first place. Still, she went, and she found they were right and they were not right. It wasn't her *likes* that bothered them, not that at all. Something much simpler. It was her excitement; all that gauche intensity about the thing. Total strangers wondered loudly who she was trying to impress. There was more than the music to learn: a whole series of bitter little lessons she never expected. It was hard. She learned to keep her ideas in check and her mouth shut, to carry her stifled love without whining much. But on nights like this, after compulsory practice that was all promise and no joy, cold and tired and waiting for a hypothetical bus, it was heavy and hard to bear. Even with her face to the sentimental spire, she wondered who it was she was trying to fool.

Low-geared growling turned her to the hill again. This time the effort paid off. Not one but two – jesus wasn't it always the way – sets of headlamps were dipping over the brow, coming on through the fuzzy evening smirr. She bounced the coins in her ungloved hand and watched as they nosed cautiously down through the slush. Then there was something else. A shape. A man lumping up and over the top of the hill, flapping after the buses. One was away already, had overtaken and gone ahead to let the other make the pick-up. She stood while it braked and sat shivering at the stop, one foot on the platform to keep the driver and let the wee man catch up. The windows were yellow behind the steam. She looked to see if he was nearer and he stumbled, slittered to the gutter, fell. The driver revved the engine. The man lay on, not moving in the gutter like an old newspaper. The driver drew her a look. She shrugged, embarrassed. The bus began sliding out from under her foot. Too late already. There was nothing else for it. She settled the case in a drift at the side of the pole and turned and made a start, picking carefully up the hill towards the ragged shape still lying near the gutter. An arm flicked out. She came nearer as he struggled onto his hands and knees, trying to stand. Then he crashed down again on the thin projections of his backside and groaned, knees angled up, fingers clutching at his brow in a pantomime of despair. By the time she reached him he was bawling like a wean. She could see blood congealed, red jam squeezing between the fingers. The line of his jaw was grey.

OK?
The man said nothing. Just kept sobbing away. He was a fair age too.
OK eh? What happened to you grandad?

She had never called anybody grandad in her life. And that voice. Like a primary teacher or something. She started to blush. Maybe she should get him onto his feet instead. Touch would calm him down and he might stop greeting to concentrate. She looked about first to check if there was another witness, hoping for a man. A man who would be shamed by her struggling on her own and come and do the thing for her, leave her clucking on the sidelines while he took over. But there was no one and she knew she had called the thing upon herself any way. Fools rushed in right enough.

An acrid smell of drink, wool and clogged skin rose as she bent towards him, and she saw the knuckles scraped raw, the silted nails. Closing her eyes, she linked his arm and started pulling, hoping for the best. They must look ridiculous.

C'mon then, lets get you up. Need to get up. Catch your death sitting in the wet like this. Come on, up.

He acquiesced, child-like, letting himself be hauled inelegantly straight before he finished the rest for himself. He backed onto a low wall and waited while he caught his breath. O thanks hen, between wheezes, words vapourising in the cold. Am that ashamed, all no be a minute but am that ashamed. All be fine in a minute. Am OK hen.

He didn't look OK. He looked lilac and the sodium glare didn't do him any favours. He puffed on about being fine and ashamed while she foraged in her pocket for a paper hanky to pat at the bloody jelly on his temple, the sticky threads stringing across to his nose. She thought better of it and gave it to him instead – something to do, shut him up for a minute, maybe. But neither the idea nor the mopping up worked too well. His hand stopped at his brow only as long as she held it there. When he saw what it produced the whine started again, O my god hen, o hen   see   o look at that, as he dabbed and looked, dabbed and looked.

You're fine, fine. Just a wee bit surprised, thats all. Take your time and just relax OK? Relax. Where is it you're going anyway?
He kept patting and looked at her. Very pale eyes, coated like a crocodiles, the sockets over-big.

O he'll be that angry hen. He will and am that ashamed. Am a stupit old fool a am. Nothing but a stupit old man. The pale eyes threatened to leak. Who? Who'll be angry?

The trick was to keep him talking and standing up. Every time he stumbled, he repeated what he'd just said. Between repetitions, she found he had been due at his son's house, due at a particular time and he was late. They were supposed to be going somewhere. It sounded like a pub. They were to set off from the son's house and he was chasing the bus because he was already late did she see? She tried to.

Och he'll not be mad. Just tell him you were running for the bus and you fell. How will that get him angry? You'll be fine.

He wasn't content yet. The specs but. A broke the specs hen.

There was a lull. She looked about the tarmac and the pavement. There weren't any specs. Then his hand was into his pocket, fumbling out three pieces of plastic and glass: See? She broke ma specs.

She. He said *she; she* broke the specs. Right enough, that couldn't have happened just now. There had to be more to it, and she knew already she didn't want to hear it. All she had wanted was to make sure he was all right, get him on his feet and back on his way. But this was what she was getting and it was difficult to get out of now. It was her that had started it, her choice to come up that hill. This was part of it now.

Who broke your specs?

She knew it had to happen and it did. He started to cry. He howled for a good minute or so while she cursed silently and patted clumsily at his sleeve, shooshing. He caught enough breath to hiccup out some more: It's ma own fault hen. It was a bad woman, a bad woman. She hit me hen, o she killed me. She had to smile. The exaggeration wasn't just daft, it was reassuring too. He couldn't see her anyway.

Still, even as she told him he was fine, fine, she knew there was more coming she wasn't going to like. The story. A man's story about what he would call a *bad woman,* and he would tell it as though she wasn't a woman herself, as if she shared his terms. As though his were the only terms. And she wouldn't be expected to argue – just stand and listen. The smiling didn't last long. He told her about a pub, having a drink, then a bad woman, something about a bad woman but he hadn't known it at the time, and as they were leaving the pub together, going out the door, she hit him. Knocked him down in the street, hard, so it broke his specs. When he reached that part he gazed down at the bits he held in his hand, taking in the fact with a deep sigh that exhaled as cursing and swearing. He whooered and bitched till he was unsteady on his legs again then started whining. He was a stupit old fool and a silly old man, should never have had anything to do with the bad woman. Bad bad bitchahell. Then there were more tears.

She hadn't reacted once. And maybe it was worth it. He seemed steadier ready to make off again for the stop. She let him walk, moving slowly alongside to keep him straight while he muttered and sobbed about himself. She knew better than to ask but she wondered, step by step, steering him downhill. She wanted to know about the woman. What had he said to make her do that? Was that when he had been cut – where the blood had come from? It must have happened right enough: he would hardly make a thing like that up. But it was hard to imagine this sorry, snivelling wee man provoking it, being pushy or lewd-mouthed. It was in another place though, with another woman altogether. He could have been different. And he must have done something. Unless of course there really were such bad women that went about hitting old men for nothing. What the hell was a *bad woman* anyhow – was it a prostitute he meant? The corner of her eye caught his face, the mottled purple skin under grey veins and a big dreep at the end of his nose. The very idea turned her stomach. Yet she couldn't stop her chest being sore for the stranger: he seemed so beaten, so genuinely surprised by what had hit him not just once but twice that day. He was still muttering when they reached the stop: broke ma specs, cow. She felt her jaw sore with remembering to be quiet. Shhh.

Shh, forget about her eh? She's away now, forget about it. Let's just get you to your boy's place. Get you on the bus. What else could she do?

Canny be up to them hen. She realised this was a confidence. Advice. Canny be up to them. A bad lot.

Aye, a lot of it about. What bus is it you get?

Aye, don't you worry. Get the bus. All be fine in a minute, get the bus.

There was no point in keeping asking, best just to wait with him. The right bus would come and he would recognise it instinctively. Fair enough. Holding some of the weight, she kept her arm under his: the wet frosting on his sleeve burned the fingers of her gloveless hand. He was looking down at something, staring as though to work out what it was.

Violin hen. Eh – violin? Nice, a violin. A like that stuff, classical music and that.

She shook her head thinking about it. Victorian melodrama as they chittered in the twilight under the university spire – Hearts and Flowers. But she said nothing. Knew enough by this time not to respond to remarks, even harmless ones, about being *on the fiddle* or *doing requests,* or any of the other fatuous to obscene things some men assumed a lassie carrying a violin case was asking for. Anyway, the bus was coming now: she could hear it. Good timing. She turned for the pleasure of watching it approach: twin haloes of deliverance.

This one do you? A 59?
She couldn't hear his answer for the searing of brakes. He seemed ready enough to get on, though; his hands stretching out full, paddling towards the pole to prepare for the assault on the platform. She shunted the case to one side with her foot and moved with him. The conductress hauled while she pushed till he was inside, clutching the pole. Then he swivelled suddenly to face her.
Cheerio hen and A have ti thank you very much, very much indeed. Yiv been kind ti me yi have that. He was leaning out dangerously and shaking her hand uncomfortably tightly in both of his, the pole propping his chest. She nodded in what she hoped was a reassuring way, weary. She hadn't the heart left to explain she had meant to get on too, this was her bus as well. She just kept patting and shaking at his hand; giving up to it. He felt daft enough already and it would take forever to pantomime through. She wasn't in any hurry, could easily wait for the next one. Parting shot then. What's the name? What do they call you eh?
The conductress and driver looked but the engine continued to purr neutrally. Her smile was as much for them: indulge it a wee bit longer?
Me? He was pleased. Pat, am Pat Gallagher hen. Pat.
Cheerio then Pat. See and look after yourself a wee bit better in future eh?
His face changed then, remembering. He hesitated for a second, baring his teeth, then he spat, suddenly vicious.
Aye. Keep away from bastart women, thats what yi do. Filth. Dirty whooers and filth the lot a them, the whole

bloody lot. Get away fi me bitchahell – and he lunged a fist. It wasn't well-aimed and she had enough of a glimpse to see it come. It didn't connect: just made her totter back a few steps; enough for the driver to seize this as his moment and drive off, chasing an already sliding schedule.

She stood on the pavement and watched till it went round the corner, then stood on watching the space where it had been. After a moment, she shut her mouth again and pulled up her coat collar. Warm enough now: just as well there was no one about, though she looked round to check and shrugged to be casual just in case. The spire was still there across the road; still beautiful, still peaceful. Snow feathered about and nothing moved behind the gates. No difference. Thankful, she leaned back against the stop: it would be a while yet. Then she remembered the case and stooped to lift it out of the snow, leaving a free-standing drift where it had been. Didn't want it to get too cold, go out of tune. Not as though it was her own. Then, unexpectedly, she felt angry; violently, bitterly angry. The money in her pocket cut into her hand. Who did he think he was, lashing out at people like that? And what sort of bloody fool was she, letting him? What right had he? What right had any of them? She'd show him. She'd show the whole bloody lot of them. Shaking, she snatched up the fiddle case and glared at the hill. To hell with this waiting. There were other ways, other things to do. Take the underground; walk, dammit. Walk.

She crossed the road, defying the slush underfoot, making a start up the other side of the hill.

Scenes from the
Life No. 29:
Dianne

From a first-floor window, a woman with a baby looks down over the street being dug up, full of pits and craters. Two different men, just outside the bus stop, just able to be seen, are talking. You wait in the shelter of the bus stop watching them let buses past, noticing they talk too loud, giggling low in the throat in unpredictable places, making wide sudden gestures with their hands.

so he's two days aff the rigs right, two days aff wi this 200 quid fuckin 200 NOTES christ NOTES fuckin FISTload right he says are yous comin he says so we goes aye and he gets these TAXIS right these TAXIS ti the pub christ pub ti pub right wan efter the fuckin next yin and theres EVERYTHIN right this lagers an brandies an christnoze ken how he canny HANDLE the drink right canny HANDLE it well he's drinking these brandies an lagers an fuckin chamPAGNE chamPAGNE christ teQUILA for fuckssake teQUILA techrist and he COULD haud it man thats the funny thing right and he COULD fuckin haud it, the money, the life then it's

Neither of the men is older than twenty-five. One of them
could easily be eighteen. Their hair is gelled and styled, the
cuts neat, shaped at the napes of their white necks, their
chins rough with bristle. Stroking would leave scores. You
try not to think about that, watching the road. The road is
full of pits and craters.

   dancin boys DANcin so we jist looks right then he's
   ach moan up the DANcin an fuckin away so we
   FOLLOWS him right we FOLLOWS him aff the bus
   up the STAIRS man these STAIRS fuckin STAIRS to
   the hoose fourth fuckin flair christ and in the lobby
   right and he STARTS right he STARTS wi this WEAN
   fuckin wean in the livin room sittin this lassie christ
   pickin her up fuckin PICKIN her up and she's greetin
   right squealin he's throwin her up then the bastard's
   away jist WOOF right WOOF wan minute he's there
   then AWAY FOR A SHOWER BOYS fuck an we're
   left wi the wee fuckin lassie left wi the wean christ the
   NEXT THING he's

The shelter smells of melting plastic, dogs in the rain.
Trying not to look aware, not to look conscious. Across the
road, different men drill a deep trench, filling the whole
street with noise, a heavy underground bore that comes and
finds you even here, buzzing through the soles of your
shoes. One smiles across at the talkers who see nothing but
each other. There is no bus in the distance.

   comes back wi this TEE-SHIRT this short fuckin wet
   fae the shower this TEE-SHIRT, the wyes it's the
   WEIGHT TRAININ boys he says LOOK so we looks
   while he's flexin the muscles this TEE fuckin shirt oot
   the FEEL IT he says and the wee lassie feart wi the
   noise he says FEEL IT ti christ so we're touchin the

muscles jist touchin he turns an he's oot wi this stick
christ big fuckin cue right WOOF roon his heid like a
WOOF fuckin caber or somethin nearly RIGHT IN
THE EYE i says WOOF fuckin COOL IT jist WOOF
lassie screamin he's taken his tee-shirt this TAP fuckin
tap aff this sweat like an hoor an this TAP aff an christ
he says LOOK fuckin shouts and this build some build
tatTOO oan his chest fucking HEART through the
core an DI
ANNE it says jeez fuck DI
ANNE

And the woman with the baby goes on looking down. But
only at you. Only at you.

it was

It was toward evening and the colour was seeping from the grass verge under her feet. Two-storey council terraces with frames of paint borders round the windows, flaking like late-in-the-day eye-liner, lined the opposite side of the road; behind her, a straggling T-junction split the erratic paths of children and women following the ground home with headscarves and late shopping. Both sides of the road had verges with lamp-posts, furred in their own bleachy light, and small close-stacked houses. None of the buildings was new.

Older couples would be sitting on the scratchy roses of their ancient settees inside watching slot telly – its blue-flickering familiarity was throbbing against dark sideboards: flame buds would be growing on coals still smoking with newness in the grates. She could hear Eamonn Andrews telling them that *This Was Their Life*. Seven o'clock?

She wasn't sure if she knew this place or not. Something was homely about it, something that though not kent was not strange. With effort, she turned her gaze down to her feet and the sepia grass; her verge neighboured the dull

macadam of the road to the edge of her vision at what must
be the crest of a hill. Then, it would roll down out of sight
and tumble on till it reached the sea. Overwhelmed, she
knelt to feel the cling of the cool blades wrap the bare skin
of her knees, exposed between long socks and dark grey
skirt. Her eyes closed, near to weeping with the pleasure of
it. Suddenly she was afraid, in panic at the foolishness of her
joy and that someone might witness it. Surely she was too
old for this kind of thing (her eyes felt wrinkled with strain)
she opened them quickly

                                        and found herself standing
at the now-grey privet hedge of one of the smarter pebble-
dashes on the corner, her hands resting on the stubby
hardness of cropped branches. It smelled of twilight and
being outside. Scented stock wafted up sickly from underneath it. Gradually aware of their dull ache, she lifted her
palms, pitted from the striving of the blunt-edged bush, and
slid them into jacket pockets. Inside, her nails trapped
crumbs, vying with them for the corners, for it was now
blue-dark and getting noticeably chillier.

then the glitter of it caught her eye

then the glitter of it caught her eye

There was
something shiny in the earth at the foot of the wall, just
under the drainpipe and less than half-hidden. It was at the
foot of the facing roughcast, across the patch of stock. The
hedge pushed at her blazer. Her hand was on the drainpipe,
a clod of thick rust tapped her shoe: to stoop to look she
knelt

she knelt to pick it up

it was

Dusty, trailing crumbs from her pockets, her fingers – now quite dull with warmth – found its edges and curled under. The smell of the earth lifted as it parted to free one corner.

She knelt to pick it up
It was a face. A little crusted and with eyes shut tight against encroaching dirt: a little flattened from having lain there its indeterminate time and being pressed against the concrete slabs. Her body and her breathing were smooth and calm though her eyes ticked seconds round the rim of it.

Pushing her lips apart and outward, she puffed feeble breath at the closed lids. Then more boldly she began to pick at the half-hard veil of mud with the unclean nail of her right index finger, clasping the whole face in her left hand with its cheek nestled in the flesh cup of her palm. As the flakes fell away, the skin showed pink and surprisingly clean beneath and she became more intent on the task. Most concentration and skill would be needed where the dirt crowded thickest in ridges at the creases of its eyes. She had to change tactic, retracting the nail and brushing with a plump pad of fingertip instead. This seemed better: the silt crumbled and parted fairly dryly to slide out of the cracks it had claimed. She blew gently again to help its progress. There was a sucking sound and an intake of air. Her eyes snapped wide and lips drew back their kiss. It was

The little man smiled as he took her elbow. There was no need to acknowledge anything unusual in the situation for nothing was.

Come on and we'll go for a cup of tea

Immediate bittersweet stab of recognition at a voice forgotten – how long? Her whole heart seemed to move with
pity for the wee figure already making off toward a kettle.
The still lamplight outlined his bald head and traced the
grey nightcolour of his cheek where it moved to prepare
another sentence of encouragement for her to come. It was
a rough cheek, hairily whitened with stubble that had
alternately fascinated and horrified her as a child; she felt its
jaggy trail scratch a skirl of wild shrieking from an infant
mouth, her eyes stretched golly-wide in excitement. *Too
much excitement for the wean.*

Uncle George.
Uncle George.

he was
He was walking ahead.
It's freezing. Come on and we'll get a heat.

She wanted to do something kind and wonderful for this,
the swell of her heart now intolerable, but she couldn't
think what. Not quickly enough, anyway. What was clear,
though, was that it was now her due to be as gentle as she
could for him. He had no awareness that he was dead and
she would not let him know. So he should not suspect or
have to hesitate for her, she spurred to movement then – a
rush to reaffirm his short, bulky presence. They went
jauntily and quietly, lured by the steamy warmth of the
promised tea and its milky sweetness. She knew he wouldn't
live far away.

David

I hated the miss thing and anyway I never taught any of them, not in class; just jokes with Colin and Marie, the couple, Sam like a big farmer's boy and David, sullen behind the blond fringe needing cut. You never knew what he was thinking. There was an afternoon once he came to the classroom door, his face blotted out with the sun at his back only the blue eyes there like something unnatural, unnatural blue. He made me break sweat.

It was last day. They were meeting at Sam's house: cheaper than the pub and his parents were out for the night so he felt free. Funny thinking about parents and being accountable: it reminded you they were just kids really, just kids at the school, the boys hardly needing to shave. So we went there, me and Carol the only teachers into uncharted territory, Sam's parents being away. We handed over the two bottles of cider and he said Kid's drink, cider: too juvenile. They were drinking already out of these little glasses, no more than pub measures; whisky and sherry like after-dinner guests. Sam took the cider to the kitchen, these bottles of cider that were such a joke. David wasn't there so we sat together with Colin and Marie, the couple, making

conversation in fits and starts. Then the doorbell rang and
I knew I was waiting for it: the voice in the hall, clinking of
bottles. I knew it was him because my hands were sweating.
The back of my neck and upper lip. I went to the stereo and
turned it up louder leaving Carol with the talking. I'm not
good with small-talk anyway. Then the boys came through.
We were all drinking out these tiny glasses and getting over
not being used to each other. It was better when I took off
my jacket and sat on the floor with a can that tasted bad but
made me relaxed. I changed the music every so often,
consciously joining in. I hate parties. But it was a quiet kind
of good time we were having, very domestic. Sam had even
made sandwiches jesuschrist as if we were proper grown-
ups I said, and passed them round. It got noisier, turning the
music up when we drank some more. I hadn't eaten so I
suppose it was going straight into the bloodstream because
I was dizzy when I stood up. I sat next to Carol with Colin
and Marie, the couple: Sam and David arguing about
something pointless in the armchairs. Cosy. It was nice to
be included, their just tipping seventeen. Also I might never
see them again. That was what this was about. I must have
been rubbing my collar at the breastbone like a nervous tic:
crossing and uncrossing my legs. I must have been doing
something because the next thing Sam was having to change
the record. And David was looking at me. He was looking
me right in the eye from the chair, leaning forward and
braceleting the glass with one hand, the silver watch-band
clicking on the rim. Sam was telling a joke, Colin and Marie
laughing. But he was looking with his eyes level. I could feel
his watching even with my head turned away. My hand
must have lost the grip on the can. Lager was seeping on my
blouse, the lace edge of the bra starting to show through
and the shock of cold getting warmer. I wondered afterwards if I did it on purpose. But there was this spreading
wetness and the cushion under my skirt burning. I had to

stand up and Sam said he would show me where I could sponge the mark at the sink upstairs. I'll find it, I said, I'll find it, shaky when I walked because I knew what was going to happen. I heard David saying I'll go. I heard him saying it: it's all right. I'll go.

The hall was cooler. I stopped to let him catch up, waiting part way up the stairs. He slid past so our hips touched as he went ahead. Oops he said like a little boy. Oops. Seven more steps and he stopped in front of me, waiting at the bathroom door. My stomach went tight as I turned but smiled saying it was all right for something to say while he put his hand out, pushing the door for me to go on inside. We stopped. Just stood not going forward or back, waiting, my stomach knotting like a fist. The lace moved under the stained blouse. The ripple of my own breast.

His palm was clammy. I touched once. Then he laced his fingers into mine till they were tight. The wood at the side of the door biting my spine. He came closer so slow I wasn't sure if he would or

Our teeth touched, mouths open. I felt him swallow, the skin on my lip stretch till it split, a sudden give from the tightness and I was sliding my hands, tugging on the thin shirt: ridges of warm rib beneath my fingers rubbing my palms on the warm sides of his jeans, the length of seam. He pulled his head back and looked, the blue eyes and smooth temples. Flecks of blond on the backs of his hands, his nails trailed over the blouse, the nipple stiffening where he let his hand wait and I said something I don't remember. I don't remember. Then there was my mouth on his neck, salt nipping the torn skin of my lip. And we weren't kissing any more, just falling back, the pile of the carpet reaching then pushing through the thin stuff of my blouse and I was

arching like a bridge, searching for the zip through the stiff
denim, feeling the weight of him fall closer and the blouse
sliding to my neck as he pushed under the cloth for one
breast. His hardness, stiff, hard smoothness in my hand.
Our mouths separate now, a nudging between my legs with
one knee and his shift into place as my hand opened, the
warm tip wet on my thigh. The slip of a single vertebra.
And he entered sudden and hard not like a man but
guileless, his hair falling into my eyes till by the time I was
sure what we had done he shivered and cut like an engine,
the other heart thumping on my chest and not being able to
think or stop my eyes, not being able. And there was
Sam's voice calling from downstairs if we were all right,
was I all right? Calling his name, not being able to catch
my breath while I wondered, eyes splintering, wondering
what else to say
what else to say

two fragments

I remember two things in particular about my father. He had ginger hair and two half fingers on one hand. The ring finger and the middle one fastened off prematurely at the knuckle, like the stumpy tops of two pink pork links, but smoother. They were blown off during the war. This was a dull sort of thing, though; my mother had another story that suited my child-need far better.

It started with the usual, your daddy in the pub. I could've had a mint of money today if he hadn't been a drinker by the way. Anyway he'd been in there all night and he came out the pub for the last bus up the road, but by the time he staggered to the stop he was just in time to see it going away without him. He chased it but it wasn't for stopping. He'd missed it. There was nothing for it but to start walking. He had to go along past Piacentinis on the corner and that was where he smelt the chips. It wasn't all that late yet and they were still open. The smell of the chips was a great thing on a cold night and with all the road still to go up and he just stood there for a wee while snoaking up the warm chips smell. It made him that hungry he thought he had to go in and get some, so he counted all the loose change in his pockets and with still having the bus fare he just had enough. He was that drunk though he dropped all the money and he had to crawl about all over the road to get it all back because he needed every penny to get the chips. That took him a wee while. And by the time he finally got in, Mrs Piacentini was just changing the fat and so he had to wait. That was all right but the smell of the chips was making him hungry by this time. Just when he was about to get served, a big polisman came in and asked for his usual four bags and because he was in a hurry and he was a regular he got served the chips that were for your daddy. So by the time he was watching the salt and vinegar going on to his bag, his mouth was going like a watering can. He was starving. The minute he got out into the street with them, he tore open the bag and started eating them with his fingers, stuffing them into his mouth umpteen at a time and swallowing them too fast. He thought they were the best chips he had ever tasted. He was that carried away eating them that it wasn't till he went to crumple up the empty bag and fling it away he saw the blood. When he looked over his shoulder there was a trail of it all the way up the road from Piacentinis. He was that hungry he'd eaten two of his fingers for chips with salt and vinegar.

My granny had a glass eye. She was a fierce woman. A face like a white gingernut biscuit and long, long grey hair. She smoked a clay pipe. And she had this glass eye.

My grandfather was a miner, and the miners got to take the bad coal, the stuff with the impurities the coal board weren't allowed to sell. She built up the fire one day and was bashing a big lump of this impure coal with the poker when it exploded and took her eye out. So there was another story about that. Again, it was my mothers: I was much too feart for my granny to ask her anything.

Your granny could be awful cruel sometimes. She drowned cats. She drowned the kittens and if the cats got too much she drowned them as well. There was one big tom in particular used to come up the stairs and leave messes in the close. Gad. Right outside your door and everything. Stinking the place out. I don't like tom cats and neither did your granny. She got so fed up with the rotten smell and its messes that one day she decided she was going to get rid of it. So she laid out food and when it came to eat the food she was going to sneak up on it with a big bag. It was that suspicious, watching her the whole time while it was eating: your granny staring at the cat and the cat staring back. It was eating the food in the one corner and your granny was hovering with the bag in the other. High Noon. Anyway, she waited for her minute and she managed to get it. Not right away, though. It saw her and jumped, but it went the wrong way and got itself in a corner and she finally managed to get the bag over it. By the time she got into the kitchen, with the cat struggling in the bag, she was a mass of scratches. The cat was growling through the bag and trying to get its claws through at her again, so she held up the bag and shook it to show it who was the boss. Then she didn't know what to do next, till she clapped eyes on the boiler. A wee, old-fashioned boiler like a cylinder thing on wee legs with a lid at the top. She got a string and tied up the top of the bag and then she dropped the cat right into the boiler drum. It was empty, of course. She was going to keep it in there till the boys came back (that's your uncle Sammy and uncle Alec) and get one of them to take it to the tip and choke it or something. She was fed up with it after all that wrestling about. She got on with her work in the kitchen, and as she was working about she could hear the

cat banging about in the boiler the whole time, trying to get
out, while she was getting on with the dinner and boiling up
kettles of water for the boys coming home for their wash.
When they got in from their work, the first thing they did
was get a wash: there was no baths in the pit and they never
sat down to their tea dirty. Your granny wouldn't let them.
So they came right into the kitchen when they got home and
the first thing they noticed was this thumping coming out
the boiler. Alec says to her what the hell's that mother and
she tells them about the tom cat. Just at that the thing starts
growling as if it's heard them and our Sammy says I hope
you don't think I'm touching that bloody thing, listen to it.
And he starts washing at the sink and laughing like it was
nothing to do with him. Even our Alec wouldn't go and lift
the lid. So she got quite annoyed and rolled her sleeves up
to show them the scratches to tell them she wasn't feart for
it and she would do it herself. So after she'd gave them their
tea, she got them out the kitchen so she could get on with
it.

She had thought what she was going to do. First, she got
two big stones from the coalhouse and the big coal bucket
from the top of the stair. She put the bricks at the boiler side
and filled the big bucket with cold water at the sink. The cat
had stopped making so much noise by this time so it was
probably tired. This would be a good time. She got the
washing tongs, the big wooden things for lifting out the hot
sheets after they'd been boiled, and went over to the boiler,
listening. Then she flung back the lid, reached in quick with
the tongs and pulled the bag out before the cat knew what
was happening. The minute it was out the drum, though, it
starts thrashing about again and your granny drops the bag
and runs over to the sink for the pail, heaves it over to the
boiler and pours the whole lot in. She filled it right up
nearly to the top. The bag was scuffling about the floor so

she waited till it went still again. Then when it had stopped moving, she gets hold of it with the tongs quick and plonks it straight into the water, banging the lid down shut and the bricks on top.

She went straight into the living room to build up the fire and tell the boys she'd managed fine without them, quite pleased with herself. She would just leave the cat in the boiler till the next morning to be sure it was drowned and get the bucket men to take it away. Sammy was a bit offended. He said she was a terrible woman but they didn't do anything about the poor bloody cat so they were just as bad. There was no noise in the kitchen when they went for a wash before they went to their bed. It was a shame.

Well it was still the same thing the next morning when your granny went in to light the kettle. Nothing coming out the boiler. That was fine. She got me and Tommy away to the school and your uncle Alec and Sammy were away to the pit and our Lizzie was out as well. So that was her by herself and she started getting the place ready for the disposal of the body. She put big sheets of newspaper all round the floor and got the tongs ready. It would be heavy. She shifted one of the bricks off the boiler lid and listened to make sure. Nothing. She shifted the other one off and lifted up the lid. There was a hellish swoosh and the cat burst out the boiler, soaking to the bone, its eyes sticking right out its head. It must've fought its way out the bag and been swimming in there all night, paddling and keeping just its nose above the water, and the minute it saw the light when your granny lifted the lid, it just threw itself up. It shot out straight at her face and took her eye out just like that. Your granny in one corner of the kitchen, with the eye in another and the tom cat away like buggery down the stairs.

Fingers for the army.
An eye for the coal board.
A song and a dance for the wean.

Scenes from the Life No. 26: The Community and the Senior Citizen

A sudden flash, some half-hearted flickering. A three-sided box. It is a compact living room and the chief impression is one of brightness. Yes, a lot of afternoon sunlight is forcing in from somewhere off to the left. It spreads on the pale wallpaper like transparent butter and creates a long rhombus of itself on the carpet; a contained shape from the toomuchness of outside. Much of the floral tracery of the carpet is lost inside it and the pink design is clear only at the fitted extremities. There are no shadows in the corners, only a neat standard lamp with a plain shade, a green wicker chair.

Two very white doors complete the harmony of the composition. They hang as balances on the centre of the facing wall, radiating a high, professional gloss, the more noticeable for their being so close together. On the strip between, some five feet from the white skirting, a square frame reflects fiercely. The picture or photograph behind the glass is almost entirely glared out by bars of light on the surface; but something dark seems to be whispering up through the sheen as of a black-and-white still. We may assume a wedding photograph rather than linger.

On the right, another door, fractionally ajar, and a low
table with an empty glass bowl: opposite, near the light
source and pale grey curtains, an empty display cabinet.
Details obtained by absorption, for our eyes have become
used to the decibel level of light and are veering naturally to
the main interest in the middle of the room.

Centred squarely toward us is a large, dove-grey settee. A
fine stripe shaved into its plain velvet pile makes three
sections of the whole and these, in turn, are bisected by the
lightshape from the window, washing the left of the settee
paler than the right. Just within the shaded part, a solid
figure bulks down the cushions, spoiling the symmetry.
Swathed in navy blue, it is the only dark thing in the room.
The lower buttons of the coat are undone, revealing a
wedge of blue skirt and plump orange legs stretching down
to flat black shoes. There is a scant navy hat on her short
auburn hair, a black shoulder bag resting at one hip. Ah. It
is the HEALTH VISITOR. A young woman, her face is full
and smooth, her lips ripe and dark from recent applications
of warm porcelain; she has been drinking tea. The cup
relaxes in one pink palm — the left. The other hand sports a
fragment of gingernut biscuit (a pleasing colour halfway
between that of her hair and legs) which she waves as she
talks. For though we cannot hear, she is talking: her head
nods and her mouth moves. The angle of her gaze and that
moving mouth prompt a glance in their direction. Yes, there
is someone in the companion chair now we look. Feel free;
she cannot know we are watching.

It is an OLD WOMAN. Three-quarters in profile, her body
conveys an uncomfortable blend of rigidity and exhaustion.
Feet and knees brace tightly together, swollen ankles
jowling over the lip of her slippers, yet her torso slumps and
her neck droops over quite hypothetical breasts.

Certainly, she is thin; tortuously thin: limbs emerge as skinbound sinew from the hems of her clothes. The clothes themselves, a knitted skirt and top in neutral tones, are dull and undistinguished – flesh-colour – though nothing like her own. Her skin is uniformly pale, a waxy cream-yellow without blemish. The hands that for the moment spread from cuff-ends to over the dove-grey armrests seem painted over, or squeezed into surgical gloves. They seem not to possess fingernails. Her hair is no more reassuring: a frazzle of neglected vanity with pale roots and raggedy red-grey ends sticking up untidily like half-rinsed paintbrushes. Beneath hangs her face, and, more obviously, her mouth. It gapes. And there are silver trails at its corner. Occasionally, she makes a tentative dab at the runnel of saliva, but the sheen seems to vanish only long enough for another thread to form and ooze back along the same path to her chin. The eyes, too, shift continually from side to side, suggesting a nervous or ingrained habit. She has certainly let herself go.

Between the two of them is a low table strewn with tea-things – an empty cup and saucer, a second saucer and teaspoon, an opened carton of milk and a blue plate with one remaining gingernut. It seems they have been sitting for some time.

The HEALTH VISITOR stirs. The scent of the room rises – a faint cloy of earth and cold meat we had not noticed before. Now there is a soft scuffling as the HEALTH VISITOR uncrosses her plump legs, the creak of the settee, then the dry click of the cup against the saucer as she sets it down. Someone increases the volume further.

HEALTH VISITOR: No other visitors tonight then? Just yourself?

OLD WOMAN: *Silence. Shakes her head and dabs at her mouth.*

HEALTH VISITOR: But everything's fine just the same? Keeping well eh? I say you're keeping well.

OLD WOMAN: *Silence.*

HEALTH VISITOR: That's good. All the messages in for the weekend – nothing I can get you?

OLD WOMAN: *Silence. Nods her head and moves her lips.*

HEALTH VISITOR: It's good to see you're keeping yourself busy anyway. Keeping busy eh?

Throughout this exchange, the OLD WOMAN has been struggling with her face and now manages to make a slack oblong of her mouth with lips parted and some teeth showing in the divide. Once attained, its maintenance is no easy matter. The grimace is tight, cutting creases into her cheeks and her dribbling is markedly worse. But she holds it there, and through its effortful set dredges up her voice and an answer.

OLD WOMAN: Try to.

HEALTH VISITOR: Good for you. Good for you, Mrs Maule. Pity there aren't more like you. Well, we know don't we. It's up to yourself in the last analysis, isn't it?

The HEALTH VISITOR has begun to wrestle up from the settee, clutching her bag then standing to smooth down the creases and crumbs from the navy coat, restoring her authority. It is a signal. The OLD WOMAN takes it to begin her own procedure for rising, grasping the armrests with whitening knuckles, bracing her feet and pushing, pushing till finally she is erect. And all the while she has managed to support the grim rictus we now know for a smile; holds it and strengthens it in triumph though her eyes droop and the muscles quiver. When she stands she is grinning still. The HEALTH VISITOR reddens with relief and satisfaction at her own restraint whilst staging an unconcerned fastening of the lower buttons of her coat. They pause together for a moment, their backs to us, then move slowly around the settee and towards the doors.

HEALTH VISITOR: Another nice cup of tea, Mrs Maule. Always appreciated.

OLD WOMAN: *Nods.   A   low   hum   of acknowledgement.*

HEALTH VISITOR: Anything you've forgotten to say to me? Or we haven't talked about yet?

OLD WOMAN: *Silence.*

HEALTH VISITOR: And I suppose you won't let me help with the cups this time either? Eh?

OLD WOMAN: No no. Fine.

This concludes just as they reach the doors and we begin to appreciate the artistry of the HEALTH VISITOR in this professional and crafted leavetaking. It has been tailored for no awkward silences, smoothing her exit for them both. Now she selects the right-hand door of the pair, turns the handle and pushes to reveal a porch beyond. She steps into this bridge between the inner and outer spaces, reaching. The exterior door opens to an immediate balloon of traffic sound, alarmingly loud, and softer, unidentified scuttling. We can see a flap of sky, too – a thick triangle of afternoon blue. The HEALTH VISITOR stops, acclimatising, then turns for her farewells, filling the box of porchway and blocking out the slices of external things. The OLD WOMAN stays safe at her end of the runway.

It is time to speak again.

HEALTH VISITOR: I'm away then. Cheerio, Mrs Maule. See you next week. Cheerio then. See and look after yourself now.

If the OLD WOMAN speaks, we cannot hear. With a click and a shudder, the noise cuts and the HEALTH VISITOR is gone, leaving a last cheerio trapped in the silence. The OLD WOMAN closes her interior door and stands motionless. A car horn sounds cheerily outside. The OLD WOMAN continues to face the white door. Her shoulders expand and drop. That is all. When she turns we see the harsh stretch has erased from her mouth and her eyelids are shut. She waits, breathing deeply till the tautness in the room breaks down and settles around her feet; she waits till we feel something has been accomplished. Now we advance.

She begins by clearing the tea-things and carrying them off to the room on the right. She nudges the door open enough for us to see inside to a sink, draining-board, racks of cleaning materials in bottles. She settles the tray on the stainless drainer, then, with a jerky delicacy that suggests distaste, rinses the cups, saucers and single spoon at the cold tap. As each emerges from the water, she drops it into a red plastic bin at her foot. The washing-cloth follows, then, unrinsed, the blue plate and its remaining biscuit. The bin swallows them whole, snaps shut. She wipes her hands against her skirt, reaches and opens the white kitchen unit above the sink. It is scrupulously empty, save in one blushing corner where a red packet flops untidily. The bin accepts this too and the cupboard is clean.

The milk carton is waiting. She takes it from the tray and tips the last of it down the sink, erasing white stains with swirling water. But the determined vigour of her performance begins to tell, for her breathing is audible and she is bracing her arms straight, supporting herself at the edge of the sink. She increases the flow of the tap, masking the sound of her working lungs, but the beating rise and fall of her frail chest seems to worsen. Her head droops, eyes stare: something worming in her throat forces her mouth wide in a retch. The coursing of the water exaggerates deafeningly: we feel the cold scent of steel and the pulsing at her temples – reaching to know what is wrong. Some of us go further. For now the flickering comes again and – single frames of something. Flashing too quickly, a confused mesh of images, unkent things, disconnected pieces.

There is the OLD WOMAN *standing at a full-length mirror in a too-thin nightdress, feeling at her hips through the cloth: now her face at a magnifying mirror, bloated and salivating: a white lavatory bowl darkening with regurgitated matter: a still glass of clear fluid and a clock: a jumble of bones weeping on a bedspread: vomiting.*

But this is revolting. Our empathy snaps back. A thick whiff of nausea, a blink or two, and we are relieved to find the shock has jolted us out of the kitchen and back to our vantage point in the living room. There, reassuringly on the right again, is the OLD WOMAN buttressed at the sink. She recovers in her own time, turns off the tap, straightens her face to the slack-jawed norm. She is coming out – perhaps we should go.

But one door still retains its secret. It radiates whitely from the back of the room. Curiosity makes us stay as she crosses the floor and enters through it, though she closes the blank panel on us almost immediately. A little aural concentration will do: whistling taps, pounding water obligingly reveal an off-stage bath. Soon, the sounds of its filling accede to the shuffle of resettling liquid and some coy splashes. Still, it does not do to be too interested; we have learned that from experience. We deflect attention to an idle re-examination of the living room, its pale colours and lightweight furnishings. The diminished rhombus of sunlight on the settee and the carpet shows some time has elapsed. The shifting music of bathing plays from behind the closed door, and, with the monotony of the surroundings, does much to restore serenity. Perhaps we begin to doze. For it is not till the draining gurgle from the bathroom and damp scuffling of the OLD WOMAN'S towel that we notice the box, halfway up the wall next to the lamp. At first glance, it passed for a telephone, but now shows a something smaller. There is no receiver. It takes some narrowing of the eyes before we see the switch and the muzzle of an intercom. The box and the surroundings click. This is a sheltered house. Behind this box, in some other place, another living room, is a listener: a caretaker elsewhere, yet securely here in representational plastic. Ah. A little weight drops from our necks.

It is all more containable now, and we can afford a little

sentimental soft-focus as she appears at the bathroom door, through a spill of mist in a white dressing-gown: an angel in an aura of condensation. Her hair has frizzed out fetchingly with steam and combing, to a frail red and white netting about her skull. Her face is pink, fuller; pretty with rubbing and the heat. And now she moves, her co-ordination seems easier, as though the invisible bath has oiled the joints to suppleness. More marvellous still are her eyes. Something in the hot-water clouds has freed their colour. They are larger, wider: an unnaturally lucid azure. It flashes from under the lids as she turns her head left to right, right to left 180° and back; electric blue pulses from a cardiograph. Satisfied, she crosses the room to the window. She draws the blind, cutting the lifeline of the light shape on the floor and the room relaxes into matching shades of grey. The glare on the wall-mounted photograph, too, drops with a blink, attracting attention. She approaches, looks, touches once. When she turns, we see her rest one fingertip vertically against the flat lines of her lips: *does not equal*. Then, soundlessly, she stretches her hands to the ceiling, fingers in fans, and arms at full reach. They pull away from her till the striving burns: a whimper of pain breaks her concentration. Enough.

Something begins. Some timetable sets in motion with her firm, fluid movements. Her meticulousness suggests planning; preparations made for a specific moment, and, despite our intrusion, the moment is come. She has no need to seize – her grasp is assured. We are too far and at the wrong angle to read her expression with any degree of accuracy, but the set of body, calm manner and miraculously closed mouth show eagerness, excitement. It seems inappropriate now to cast her as the OLD WOMAN – we must search for another name. Was it . . . yes – it is MRS MAULE. This is MRS MAULE setting her home to rights.

Already, she has moved the armchair away, off to the right. As she rolls aside the settee, a flat, brown packet appears on the carpet in the space it vacates. The centre of the room is a newly-cleared stage with this single prop. She plumps the settee cushions, erasing the cooled hollow that held her recent guest (now visiting health upon others, elsewhere, with different cup warming her hand) before collecting the rest. First the coffee table, lifted and centred in the thicket of woven flowers, the surface dusted with one cuff. Now, the packet, laid accurately straight along one edge of the table-top. It is an unremarkable packet, just brown paper with a serrated lip.

To the bathroom next, leaving the door wide. She lifts an orderly pile of fleshy things – the discarded clothes – and drops them into a wicker basket; straightens the bathmat and the towels. There is a small white cabinet above the sink, and two shelves inside ranged with bright bottles, boxes and tins. She pushes her hand among the colours to select a tiny brown jar, then closes the cabinet and the room. They have served their purpose.

Only the kitchen door remains. She wades patiently across and enters, alone. The rattle of a blind, whine of the tap, then she surfaces with a tall glass and a bottle of lemonade. A little awkwardly, she manages to fasten this door too, sealing the interior. The set is ready.

MRS MAULE reaches the coffee-table to settle the bottle, glass and pill jar in a neat row along the edge of the bag. She opens the lemonade bottle, then kneels upright behind the table and the row of instruments to fill the glass with sizzling liquid. A pearl-string of bubbles, shiny in the half-light, marks a level a few inches from the rim. The rejected bottle sits open on the floor. For a moment or two, she stares intently at the brown bag before picking it up, gently, with both hands to spill its filling over the table-top. A scatter of paper – several sheets in fresh to faded shades of white. One after the other, she lifts and presses these flat, building a tidy pile. Each surface spreads in turn under her fingers, some showing heavily-typed faces, some showing nothing. It takes a little time. MRS MAULE glares hard at her work, her hands resting on the edges of the sheets. It is difficult to discern where paper stops and flesh begins, for the light is very dim now and the blood that quickened in the bath is slowing, drawing colour as it cools. Her face is settling as she sits, creases returning where warmth leaves. It deepens as we watch: she is making us wait. Second after second – almost five minutes. It would be easy to let attention wander, cast around the room, but what is there to see? It is neat, drab, orderly. All that moves are the silver beads in the lemonade, shushing a silence from the top of the glass.

It concludes at last. She gathers animation slowly, first opening the pill jar to pour the contents, a straggle of yellow tablets, across her papers. She discards the bottle and turns to the glass, raising it in her left hand. The rest is brisk and decisive. It is a routine. It works like this:

1. A couple of tablets in the right hand;
2. Sip;
3. Insert the pills between the lips;
4. Snap down;
5. Sip;
6. Swallow.

Each cycle ends with a pause, sometimes a curling of the lip – then begins again. And with greater or lesser pauses, greater or lesser doses of the yellow tablets, she absorbs the whole cache. It takes about four minutes in all, not a long performance, and manages to retain interest throughout. At the end, at least half the lemonade remains in the glass, but the waste is immaterial and she pushes it to one side of the table. Her small weight shifts to one hip, freeing her legs to stretch out in stages. Then, manoeuvring lumpily on her elbows, she lowers her back, lying flat on the carpet. She is staring at the ceiling. One hand is restless at her side. It twitches until she accedes to its need. Her gaze does not flinch as she lets it become a thing apart; rising to pluck at the candlewick belt, slipping inside the border of her gown. It fumbles there under the cloth, stroking at one hidden breast. A caress. Soon, she is still again. We notice the crook of her elbow is dry and bulbous: the bath-plumped tissue deflated, unattractively aged once more. Within the waxy face, her eyes keep searching the ceiling. Let her wait on. We have other things to do.

Into the Roots

It was raining and her hair was getting wet. Not a true rain, but a drizzle, layering a blur on individual strands, thickening into fat drops and sliding down to the scalp. She could feel it there already, spreading with the feel of insect feet. Her hair was flattening with the weight, darkening under a dark sky from russet to the vague amberblack of wood resin.

Alice's hair had always been excessive. Even the earliest of her baby-photos showed it, wee face struggling out from under heavy cloud. It had been white. She had been told as much and could see in the pictures it was true; hair matching the colour of the starched frills under the dazzle of the studio lights. What was not part of a coxcomb strayed out fuzzily as though the child had been plugged into an electric socket or struck by lightning, accounting for the expression of boggle-eyed terror. No matter how hard she looked, it was impossible to detect eyebrows. She supposed they had been white too.

Ash, strawberry, ginger red.
It got darker and it got longer. Through primary school, she

carried the weight of its spine-length tangle, brushed, teased and woven into itself by her mother's efforts of will to a tightbound pleat. Still, it slipped the ribbon to blossom out behind as she ran, shrieking, in the playground.

Evenings had been spent with head bent in contrition at the fireplace, clamped between mammy's knees as she tore out the knots and condemned them, spitting, to the flames. The longer it got, the more wayward it became. Enough was enough.

She had her first salon cut at the age of eleven: a new uniform and a new persona for the big school. She had been taken by the hand to Carrino's and given up to the dresser — mammy had other things to do. It crossed Alice's mind she was feart to watch. In the mirror, she saw the familiar coat retreat, open into a square of light, then cut from view as the door clicked across like a shutter. Alice was left gazing at her solitary self and was suddenly, thrillingly aware that this was the last of something. Last snapshot of childhood. She closed her eyes and heard the scissors slice.

Alice had known at the time, had said so, she would never forget the feeling the first incision had induced: as though her head were rising like a cork from the bottom of a sink of water. The dresser gave her the still-writhing pleat to hold: a thick-ended shaving brush petering away to elasticated nothing. She clutched it during the rest of the cutting as someone else emerged in the mirror. A long neck, very white from lack of sun, had grown up in the dark like a silent mushroom. The face was very pale and wee inside a curling auburn crop. They stood her up and dusted off the trimmings then handed her back. Mammy let her keep the pleat and she took it home to put into a shoebox; keeping it to take out every so often and remember who she had been.

Then mammy started calling it *that thing*, brewing a distaste for the precious, matted snake-in-the-box, though when it disappeared, no one admitted having thrown it out. It didn't really matter: it was discovered only years later and by that time, the hair was long again.

That first cut triggered fresh growth. So much that within two years, its mass had taken Carrino's so long to dress she had been late for the school dance. Slipping embarrassed and hair-sprayed stiff into the squeaky gym-hall with its frenetic Grand Old Duke and illicit kisses. She was never a relaxed child but managed to join in. Enjoyed herself, too: looked well in her home-sewn velvet and starched collar, but she went home alone. People couldn't see her eyes through the fringe and were suspicious. Alice liked it that way.

It brought its penalties, too. She remembered those interchangeable small boys who had chased and pulled her pigtail, hoping for a scream that she never gave. Bloodied her lip sometimes, caging in the pain with defiant teeth, determined not to let it show. And there had been a spider trapped in it once, a dark, struggling shape in the red mesh that shook her rigid with fear, numb for what to do. A boy again, this time one with the temerity to approach gently, had come to the rescue. He extricated both the spider and herself into their separate selves again without undue damage to either.

She folded her eyelids into a crease. Was it Charles? She supposed it must have been. Fourth year, so it was more than likely. That was the year she had dyed her hair for fun, two separate occasions and two colours, before letting it go its own way without further chemical intervention.

The stripes of dye were visible if you looked hard enough, and he must have looked hard to get the spider. Long red step-ladders, falling in fudgy bands of auburn from a straight white centre parting to well past her shoulder-blades. They had all looked the same. She kept a sixth-year photo: an avenue of senior girls with equiparted skulls and peaky faces aloof to the camera. She was there, right in the front row, fashionably sullen and mini-skirted; a leggy book-end with the girl closest. That other girl lived some-where else now: two weans and no man. That would have wiped the smile off. As for the rest, Alice knew little or nothing; didn't keep up with old acquaintances. It was her mother had done that and it was an easy thing to take for granted when the woman was alive. Just a necessary part of visits home, those tedious chants of births, marriages, turns-up-for-the-books. Scandals. Till she became one her-self and moved in with the man, *living in sin* in Charles' flat. Strange now she thought of it. She had never called it hers, for all her work and care there. Always *Charles' flat* or *Charles'* where she had swirled fair beard-clippings from the sink, smoothed sheets, sewed neat cushions and learned to cook. She had never noticed at the time and now was too late.

She promised herself a haircut for the week she left – butcher the whole lot short because he had liked it long. But the break had dealt unkindly with her face and the thought of staring it out in a public mirror appalled her. She stayed in instead, putting paper on her own terrifying walls, in a place she would have to learn to call home. She tested smiles in the sheen of a clean bathroom sink, took pleasure from finding single strands of his blond in the weave of her jerseys. Kept finding them too, for a surprising length of time. Though now, sometimes, they weren't real.

Still raining. Misting down now and seeping across her head like melting syrup. Alice was becoming irritable. This was meaningless, merely making it worse. What did she think she was doing out in this weather? Some idea to lift her depression, take a few photographs: the dull metal lump of the camera nuzzled cold into her palm in the folds of her pocket. The others were way on in front. No, it wasn't helping: she was feeling no better and the continual smirr reinforced her suspicion that in walking alone, she was walking with a fool.

The backs of the people on the road ahead grew neither nearer nor further. One minute, she seemed to be gaining and the next they wavered like slipping frames of cine-film and were again inexplicably as far as before. Blurred vision – just another side-effect to make matters cloudier. Bloody pills. She wondered if she should force herself on, fight the cold denim cloy at her legs and catch up, as though she had fallen behind to tie a shoelace, admire the view. But she deflected the impulse easily. Own company was safest when these moods came.

The decision made her feel much better. Immediately, she stopped walking, stopped trying to make up lost ground and stood still in the middle of the road. Relief rubbed into her shoulders, at the base of her neck, warming affection for the disappearing figures ahead. Let them go.

And this was as it was meant to be. Alice stood and watched the familiar backs retreat as in a mirror. She closed her eyes and heard her heel twist in the gravel of the road; opened them. And there was the broken tree; split and blasted to the sky. Blood rushed to her lips as she smiled. It was a greeting. The tree waited. Alice stepped up onto the banking with one hand stretching and moist eyes. The tree glistened in the rain. Rich red and shrouded in grey. Mushrooming fungus spurted from all its orifices but one and that one she made towards. An eyesocket of a hole, with a swollen lip of bark and moss that only made the wound seem more raw. It would hurt, but had to be done. She steeled the muscles of her arm, flexing with the sound of metal swishing in her ears and cupped one hand ready to receive.

Choking back her fear, Alice thrust out and plunged two clawed fingers into the hole. It was full of hair.

Breaking
Through

From the outside you would never have known. People passed in the street and never looked up. All they saw was the boarded-up shop, the empty flat next door, the open close-mouth swallowing in to the dark. But if you went in, feeling through, you saw a square of light high on the end wall, reflecting a shape of itself down on the grey stone steps. The steps had cream edges. They curved and rose to her own front door and opposite, the Sisters' door. The Sisters were very old and indistinct: powdery faces in fur coats, spindly ankles hanging beneath. Their eyes smeared behind thick glasses. They never spoke.

But from outside, there was no hint of the two rooms or their people, perched over the hollow shape that had sold tobacco and sweets, daily news. They were virtually secret.

There was more too.
To reach it, you had to ignore the stone steps and meet the darkness at the flat butt-end of the close. Then you screwed your eyes up tight and there was a brown door with a latch. You lifted the latch and the light spread in a triangle over the paving and you could see, straight in front, the green

hedge like a surprise and the grass. Over your shoulder the car noises, the talk and whistling of people, widening and fading as they passed, and you in the dark with the unsuspected grass and birds and sky. It was better not to wait too long here. Sometimes the wind would come and slam off the blue and green and leave you alone in the deep brown of the close, a stinging hand where the door had been. It was better to slip through and shut the door quickly behind, then turn round and stand in this new place with the garden and the slab path at your feet that took you to Bessie's on the left, the wash-house on the right. Furthest away, the wall that made a boundary of the cemetery. Fingers of obelisks, the tips of tombstones behind the hang of some unidentifiable tree. The two houses, the wall and the hedge made a square and filled it with grass. The brown strips up the sides made Bessie's garden: she had wallflowers. The grass was a drying green and a place for sitting. The Sisters made no claim on it so there was an easy share between Bessie, Janet and her mother. And Blackie. Blackie was Bessie's cat.

Janet visited Bessie at regular times and sometimes other times in between. Most often they sat together in the low front room with a cup of tea each and some biscuits or slices of cake on a plate. Plain cake. Behind their backs, the bedroom that Janet had never seen, at the other side the space with the cupboards and the ring for cooking, the place where you washed cups. The three rooms made a row, like square beads on a string. They were always in the middle of the row, the living room where all the space was filled with big furniture. Bessie would squeeze through with the tea to the chairs at the fire and after that they didn't move. They didn't speak much either. Bessie was not conversational and Janet was shy. Bessie was old with rolled-up hair in a circle round her head and lines on her neck like a tortoise. She was small and thin. Janet was merely six. The attraction in going was not the house or the old woman. The attraction was Blackie. Blackie was lithe and straightforwardly dark till he rolled over. His underside was shock-white. Green eyes, pink ears like a rabbits inside and white whiskers. You could count them. The main thing about Blackie was NOT TO TOUCH. She wanted to touch but didn't. It was good to watch him but better when he rubbed against bare ankles or jumped to make a nest on a carefully stilled lap. That wasn't often. Janet sometimes watched him playing in the garden, and, if Bessie was not there, stroked his warm white underneath as he stretched on the grass. This never eased the wanting though, it was never enough. What Janet wanted was more than that. As though she wanted to feel the essence of the fur, absorb it through the skin till it was wrapped about the bone and part of herself. The want was sore. And the want was always most in Bessie's front room with Blackie on the rug looking into the fire.

Bessie never said much. She was dour her mother said. Terse. This much was a solid, a reassuring nub in their relationship. There had to be something badly wrong then, the day Bessie shouted from the door then rushed up beside her as she played on the grass, arms knitting at nothing, eyes searching for something she couldn't see. Janet knew to follow, fast-moving now the words had stopped, over the grass and brown borders, the weedy slabs to the door and inside, past the cabinet and armchairs.

There was the usual tan-colour of the fire surround, the ornamental brasses on the mantelpiece. Inside, a black-backed roaring fire. And inside that, framed in flames, the upright vase of the black cat, sizzling in a mound of coals. The fur was catching slowly, jets budding along the dark outline as he sat: front legs taut and tail curled over the paws, head high with the ears in points, their pinkness glinting in the reflected light. Sheathed in golden-hearted arrows of flame, Blackie burned. His eyes were full as green moons.

Something shook her arm. It was Bessie, trying to rouse the child's instinct for action, one to which she herself was lost. Falling on her bare knees, Janet fumbled for the poker at the edge of the tile, raised it then faltered. The cat in the fireplace, the child on the rug: their gaze met and steadied. And Janet knew she would do nothing. She had been taught to respect his privacy too well. It was Bessie who lunged at the coals. The pyre split, caught the inrush of air and blazed higher. A heady, throbbing purr curled suddenly about the room as Blackie seethed, scintillated like a roman candle with the fur searing down and in till all his blackness dazzled out in reds and sparking yellow. The last of him was a flash of green eyes slatted black, a stink of scorched meat. Pork.

Bessie dropped beside the child on the rug. The purring sound had gone and the fire licked tamely in the grate while Bessie sobbed on the hearth, rocking over her knees. Janet put out a tentative hand and held it just above the woman's pulsing shoulder. They were not intimate enough to touch but Janet held her hand there, in the curving space above, till the woman raised herself to face the fire. Her cheeks were quite dry. Though her whole frame shook, there were no tears. Janet allowed herself to relax a little but never took her eyes from Bessie's face. You never knew. Seconds ticked from the mantel clock. Eventually, Bessie clenched her fists and spoke to the open box of the grate: It was what he would have wanted after all.

She closed her eyes and sighed, accepting.
It was settled between the three of them.

It was well after teatime the next day when the girl chose again to slip through the brown door and along Bessie's path with her arm raised to knock. It had seemed the best time: late enough for only a short visit but enough to show she remembered. She waited a moment, concentrating, before letting the tight ball of her knuckles strike. There was no answer. This was not all that unusual: Janet's knock was feeble at the best of times and Bessie was going deaf. Today, it was understandable if both gave in to their weaknesses. She moved away from the door and inched to the front-room window, the chap-shaped hand boned in to her mouth. Inside, in the usual chair, the old lady sat staring into the fireplace. It was the dull twilight time of night or day and the fire was new-built. It existed still as a tumulus of coals with the smoke streaming out between black hollows, twisting together in a spit-colour column up the chimney. The underside glittered faintly. Bessie sat deep in her chair, looking.

Janet felt sad and rubbed her fingers lightly on the glass. The old woman didn't see any more than she heard. It would be better to come back later maybe. The girl shuffled over the spongy evening grass, on and across to the wall. There was only the cemetery and a few late birds.

Janet was still looking out counting the tombstones melting against the fog when an echo of her name from a thin mouth reached her shoulder. Bessie was standing at the door, a furrow on the waxy yellow brow, waiting. There was something strange here: not just that Bessie should call out but also that she wasn't properly dressed. She was draped in dark, rose-coloured candlewick, held together at the waist with one fist. Her hesitation meant Bessie had to call again and wave the free hand to encourage. She didn't seem angry, just impatient, stepping aside for the child to go

inside before she came after. The door closed with a dry
squeak of rust.

It was stiflingly hot. The fire had been banked very high and
was fully alight now, flashing seesaws onto the wallpaper.
Janet stood next to her chair while the old woman faced
her. There was something in her hand, held out in an
envelope of fingers. It hovered over the space where Janet
was expected to open, holding out for whatever was inside.
She uncurled her palm and Bessie did the same. A silver-
coloured ball dropped from one to the other: a split sphere
with a bearing inside. A bell. Blackie's bell, cold and whole
through the flames. Janet stared for a moment then raised
her eyes. They watched each other and the fire crackled.
The room was very still, comforting. They touched briefly.
Only once.

Bessie stepped back a pace from the rug to let the rose-
coloured candlewick fall. The child watched her coating of
papery skin, limp about the bones and yellowed in the
firelight as Bessie stepped up, raising one foot onto the tile
surround and nudged the poker aside. Janet kept watching.
The old lady steadied herself and breathed deep then in one
gliding movement, thrust her body forward into the flames.
She managed a half-smile as the child lifted the poker to
help.

Fair Ellen and the Wanderer Returned

It was as she rose from stooping, Ellen saw him coming across the grass. Indistinct, with the sun behind him and the big blue sky with the tips of the spruce jagging in. From the bottom of the hill, a line of villagers stared up after him, looking to see what would happen, but it was the man that filled the centre of her vision. She saw all this in a single moment, drawing breath, and knew at once.

When he was close enough for her to be able to make out his features, he stopped, staring deep. She was fully erect now, holding the bunch of herbs fresh for the stew. He was trying to smile: she could see him trying. Then he came nearer till he was right in front of her with his blue eyes much as they always had been, but bluer; cracks tracing his brown face where there had been none before. He spoke.

Is it you? his eyes searching.
Ellen.
then he fell to his knees, keeling toward her skirt. With both hands he pulled the cloth to his weathered cheek and she felt the weight of it, tugging at her waist as he sank his face into the hemp. She reached slowly to touch his hair, saying

nothing. His hair was thick and greasy under her fingers as he moaned into the dusty cloth.

I have dreamed of this. Dreamed and dreamed of this time, into the rough brown cloth. Her arm that reached to him was spattered with fat from cooking and smelled faintly of garlic. When he stood again, he clasped her elbows in his hands and drew her nearer.

I've come home. As I said I would.
He was breathing heavily and she turned her face a little from the heat of it.
I've come back for you Ellen. We need never be separated again.
and he was full with something, his eyes brimming.

All the time as he spoke, she stared with her eyes round, looking into nothing, and when he dragged her close, burying his face into the skin of her neck, she held still and stiff as an ironing board, staring out past his greasy hair to the tops of the spruce trees. He wept and shook against her while the people swarmed at the foot of the hill, peering up yet coming no closer. Something wet touched her, a warm wet suction on the skin of her neck as the man clutched like a garland of need round her shoulders. A kiss. She had almost forgotten the shocking intimacy of such a thing. A kiss.

He drew back then, looking intently into her face. She could see the lines about his eyes and mouth, a snailpath of scar on his brow. The hair that jutted from the skin was shot with grey.

Speak Ellen
but still she did not.

Speak. I've come back. I will never leave again. We can be
together now together always.

He shook gently at her shoulders, as though she were asleep
and he need only wake her.

Ellen, I've come home.

Yes.
Her first word to him in ten years.
Yes, you've come back. I can see that.

The tears still washing his eyes made them shine like
pebbles in the ebb of a rock pool and his smile was full-
lipped and tender for her while the scent of the garden
herbs, fresh-cut, rose between them.

You have come back as you promised and I'm grateful. But
you have come back too late.

She let him stare. It took time till the dullness began filming
on his face, seeping slow into his features. She let it take
time, then spoke again, knowing he was ready now to hear.

You have come back too late. I am married.

He drew away slowly, still looking as a stiffness moved
through his body firming like a wall against the words.

I am married and it will do no good to pretend anything
else.
Her face was set and he could do nothing against it so he
turned away, sudden and fierce that she should tell him
merely what was true and not what he had come to hear.

How – married? Tell me who. Tell me who.
His voice was loud and skirled away to the foot of the hill
where the people still clustered, watching. A show.
Tell me who.
Ellen waited
who?
till his words were quiet as a whisper of leaves on dry grass.

It does no good to be angry. Anger has no future.
She spoke flatly and her face was very hard from having
seen his rage.

What of your promise to me? He spoke for something to
say.

I made no promise. It was you who left. I have always been
here.

He stopped to think, for it was true enough, but he would
not let it be.

I kept my word. I came back. You did not wait for me. Now
I come back to find it has been for nothing. His voice was
rising faster and louder as he loosed the words.
You did not wait.

Then the air between them grew thick. The blood rose in
her face and her eyes glittered black as coal. For a moment,
he thought she might fall from her trembling, then it
stopped, the blood draining back till she was white as death
and just as still. The herbs fell to the muddy grass and she
tilted her head back to the sky, stretching her neck so a
smear of grease rose like a wound at her throat from the
edge of black wool. Then she laughed. Very soft and with
no cheer to the sound, like ash grinding in the grate.

He shifted from foot to foot, unsure. He had been ready to turn away, balanced on one heel to spin from the denials he was sure would come and now the set of his body was wrong: it was no longer fitting. He did not know what she would do and was afraid. Ellen straightened, stiff as before, and crossed her arms over her breasts. She held him in a long, black look.

I waited.
Her voice was full of splinters.
I waited long enough. One year, then another and another I waited while my father sickened and we took on the work of the farm: me and my mother with the sick man to nurse and the land to work and the house to run and I waited. When he died and we sold the stock, I waited as I dragged the plough, fetching and carrying with my hands callousing, waiting in all weathers while I looked out at the sea from the fields. When my mother sickened too and I thought there must be nothing left for us, he came. I turned him away and still he came: an old man with a wedding ring and a promise – a share of money to live. We had nothing and none to give and I turned him away until he asked me, then it was settled. I married him and was dutiful, living through his drudgery and his kindness both till she was dead too. Now he is weak and ill in his turn, an old man who lies in bed while I fetch and carry and grow withered with the years and the waiting. Perhaps he will die soon, but I do not think so.

Her voice was very low and dark. Now it came lower still and the hill was quiet to listen. A bare whisper, yet every word came clear.

And still I was waiting. Something in my heart was watching every day for the sight of you, so I thought it a ghost when you rose finally on the crest of that hill. And now I wish it had been.

Her eyes were hollow.

For now you are here, even hope is lost.

He stared at her, full of bitterness for she had taken away his right to self-pity. He did not know how to answer.

You should go now. Go and not come back.
Yet he waited on, unwilling to give up his dream. He spoke a last hope.

If he should die –
and she cut through his words like a knife across meat
If he dies I will be free. Look at me. I am grey and cold with waiting. Did you never wonder how it was for me? And do you think now I want to wait again, to fetch and carry for you when your time is come after all these years of nothing? If he dies I will be free for the first time. I have done with waiting.

I loved you. He said it simply and his eyes were dry.

Maybe you did.
Their eyes met and broke.
But it was a long time ago.

He looked at her for a long moment then turned to begin, moving away from this woman in her dowdy hemp and coarse wool. When he reached the rim of the hill, he looked back, blotting the sun.

Youre a hard bitch

he said and walked out of sight, careful of every step. She saw him leave, saw the people scatter as he went down for there had been nothing to see after all.

She stood looking till it grew dark and the shouts of the old man calling for his supper drifted toward her like smoke from the cottage.

Scenes from the Life No. 24: Bikers

The bright interior of a chip shop. There is the counter and, beside it, the clean glass case, waiting for the hot fish. Behind the servery, the wall is a multicolour glitter of sweetie jars, spilling forward in ordered ranks of foil-covered bars: chocolate, toffee and boiled sugars. Everything shines, reflecting itself in the hard, grey flooring and formica.

Set apart are four long tables and eight benches in padded red plastic, blossoming yellow foam at corner cracks. Above, a red clock reads 10.30 unchangingly. There is no queue and not much smell of frying yet.

Someone sits on the table nearest the door, balanced on the linen-effect surface with his legs splayed and the table tip protruding between. It is BIG JIM: a man of about nineteen with a broad build that tends to plump. He wears a recognisable-enough outfit for one who rides or aspires to ride a motorbike: denims faded grainy-white at the knees and crotch, an undistinguished blue tee-shirt and a charcoal leather jacket. The jacket shows cardboard-coloured creases at the joints and its leather is quilted at the elbows and in epaulettes at the shoulders. It is unostentatious, however: no heavy lapels, no collar but a thin mandarin strip with a stud – certainly no badges or mottoes. Fully unzipped, it falls stiffly apart to slide across the front of his body when he moves his free arm. The other is trapped by the fingers in the tight left pocket of his jeans. His shoes are pale beige suede, a smart Italian design and remarkably pristine.

BIG JIM, too, radiates cleanliness. Under neatly-cut waves of black hair, the skin of his forehead is luminous, the face clear and florid as though freshly towelled. His temples are babyishly smooth, lips ripe and swollen as fruit; soft ham pinks against the blue cut of his eyes. The single visible hand is thick-fingered coral with nails brushed pearly as the insides of seashells. He seems to smell at once of warm engine oil and cotton, worn leather and talc.

There are two others, sitting next to JIM at the red bench of his table. The skinny ash-blond is angled awkwardly between table-edge and the padded backrest, twisting in as though to converse more easily with JIM, though their eyes never meet. The words aim at the other's quilted shoulder or the floor: the content of what is spoken does not seem to determine which.

The third of the group is a bushily ginger-haired man, seated squarely about a foot along the settle from his friends. His elbows stretch wide along the table rim, bowing in to grip a pyrex cup, gently, in the thumbs and fingertips of both hands. His lips are parted, eyes vacant as he stares at the wall, ignoring the conversation on his left. Occasionally, he peers into the milk-film of the coffee cup; nothing more.

It is JIM who does most of the talking. The blond may

agree, nod, listen a good deal, but is answering chorus only. It is hard to know where we should break in: they seem so self-sufficient and give so few clues. It may as well be now.

Butterfly valves.

Jammed. Like constant choke eh.

He makes a sucking sound as though drawing on a cigarette.

Gap too wide. Corroded head mibby. Check the spark.

Already it is reassuring. No matter how much of the exchange we have missed we have lost nothing, for this is not narrative. It is a cyclic discussion where any starting point is as good as the last for everything will be repeated sooner or later. Mechanical hypochrondria.

Aye. Butterfly valves right enough.

Insulator OK.

They chant in minimalist verses, machine-shop precise to make patterns of tappets and points and overheated coils; they cite the intimacies of decoking, gumming and greasing and, though their intonation never changes, their eyes shine. A ritual by heart: components of tea-ceremony delicacy for Zen brothers in black leather robes.

But we are getting carried away. BIG JIM seems to have paused for thought while our attention has been elsewhere and the mood has altered. His brow has darkened and when he speaks now it is no longer poetry: it is far too comprehensible.

Told him but. They canny prove it. Canny prove nothing.
Canny make him. Might no even be his. Canny be sure.

JIM and the blond are staring at the same square of lino, as
though something is appearing on its surface through the
floor. JIM's eyebrows rise in disbelief.

Mind that lassie two year ago.
Big Cass would've married her as well. Settled – had it her
own way. No problem. Jumped in front of a lorry. Mill
Road corner.
All over the road eh, all over the road. Still see the skids.

Bloody daft. He was gonny marry her as well.

BIG JIM relaxes his gaze, clouding his eyes to let them settle
more placidly under the lids once more.

Canny touch Jazzer though. Canny prove it. No even his,
but.
Me an Beejay helping him wi the matchless later on. Still in
bits. Off the road a month already.
Terrible.

Neither the blond nor the redhead respond. JIM waits for a
moment before rising from the table, creaking. The blond
calls after as he reaches the door.

Checked the circuits last night. Fine.

JIM turns.

Clogged jets.

A sudden spiteful hiss of hot fat announces the owner,

setting about his day's work scalding the first batch of chips. The place is immediately cheerier. They raise their voices to arrange things. Jazzer, Cass, Beejay, Spazz and Big Jim: they will gather at the Mill Road Corner with their bikes revving for greeting, repeat the day's business and cheer up an old friend. They smile at each other with the promise of their meeting. Later, there will be no digression. Their minds will be clean, prayers for gods that will one day run smooth as silk, purr like kittens, ride like dreams.

Need for
Restraint

suddenly
they were both on the ground clutching up
gouging and hacking with hands pulling at cloth and
snatches of hair wound on fingers the flat of flesh slapping
dull on tile

THERE IS NO REASON FOR THIS

She stood looking while the men made their terrifying
violence inside the muzak of the shopping mall. Runnels of
people practising mass avoidance kept to the other side of
the walkway. A man in a suit skipped over a wrist and kept
going, just kept going. Then there was a click off the paving
and a crunch like bone jesuschrist and dark hair splashing
out, the thud of soft bodies through the soles of these shoes.

THIS IS NOTHING TO DO WITH YOU

But somebody had to do something. She felt her mouth
hang slack. People were stopping. They were looking.
Somebody should do something.

A hand.

She watched as it moved, a hand stretching. Those thin white fingers. Her own hand reaching for one of their shoulders. And she thought she spoke. Somebody will get hurt. It was a thin testing voice she heard. Her mouth felt hardly used and the shoulder in front was melting under her palm as though neither she nor the voice were there. But she was there. An elbow clipped her knee and made it sure. She was. People were looking.

Somebody will get hurt if you don't stop it.
The dark man stopped, his fist raised. He looked round.
Somebody's supposed to get hurt, that's the fuckin idea.

Of course. The obviousness of the thing made her dizzy and hot with her own stupidity. It made her not able to think so the action, when it came, was instinctive. It was beyond her control. Her hand thrust forward, reaching for the stranger's face. She watched her fingers stroke his cheek, the light burr of stubble on the tips. One clean kiss of skin where nothing moved or sounded, and dreadfully out of place. The man's arms flailed towards her, jerking backwards as though she had scalded him, his face twisted. He steadied himself, staring with his eyes narrow and just as she thought he might hit her, looked quickly aside. Alert. The other man was struggling to his knees, preparing. It was going to resume. Then a pair of hands, rough, grainy hands flapped like wings into their tightening space. Not for her. They came to make way for information.

Enough boys.
The men hesitated.
Enough. That's enough. Break it up eh.

Another voice, weaker than the first, backed up the same.
Aye enough boys godsakes.

And it was. There was some grudging dusting down, some
hard looks but no more words, no fighting. They had
known what to do and say, these men. She had not. People
were moving about again, breaking and slipping into the
mass and leaving her standing. She felt clumsy, inept.
Female. Within seconds it would be impossible to tell those
who had seen from those who had not. It wouldn't matter.
None of it would matter. Walk. She should walk.

THIS IS NOTHING TO DO WITH YOU

and the supermarket was just at the end of the mall. Hardly
any distance. She began to walk then, stickily, watching the
neon expand, the letters grow. The sheen on the windows
faded when she got close. Inside was full of people, check-
out queues and girls in loose pinafores stacking boxes. The
face floating between them was herself, a reflection off the
glass wall. She looked down, scowling at her hands. They
were trembling.

BUT THERE WAS NO REASON
this overwhelming nothing of a thought
NO REASON

Her stomach tightened as she looked up. The white glass
face would still be there. It was important not to see it, to
try to remember.
She was WHERE
outside the supermarket. Here with her back to the fountain
in the precinct and she was WHAT WAS IT
waiting for Charles. She was meeting Charles here at the
fountain: Friday ritual of shopping at the end of the week

then take the bags home in Charles's car. That was it. She was meeting Charles. WHEN
at five.

Five.

Christ it was past that now. Her eyes flicked from the watchface and he was there: Charles in the doorway of the chemist opposite. He was looking in, investing crepe bandages and tubes of lubricant with significance to kill the time. Alice felt her shoulders relax. She knew who she was when she saw him there. She was Alice because he was Charles, her man. He was waiting for her. There was no telling from the set of his face that he hadn't been checking his watch, building a grudge at having to wait in this public place. He kept looking in the shopfront, not knowing she was there. The usual relief, the usual anxiety. She was in no mood for blame but she was also late. There wasn't time to work out tactics. Not now. Breathing deep, hoping for the best, Alice crossed to meet him.

Routine found its feet the moment he saw her. There was the usual touchless greeting, smiles no greater or less than they always were. Already they were exchanging nothings about the working day: already the word FINE had been overused satisfactorily. As she was forming it again, Alice knew very clearly this wasn't what she wanted. This wasn't it at all. She wanted something at the corners of her mouth to tug out of shape; wanted him to see and ask what was wrong. She wanted him to notice. The smile was stuck and she let it stay there, getting maskish and ugly, seeing him look and not look. His eyes swerved, deliberately finding the fountain, staring it out. That cold set of his jaw and the sigh. Soon the Smalltalk would get stiff: bitty and challenging. Applying a course of correction while he refused to look her in the eye. He would not ask. She would not ask him to. If she persisted, there would be silences, an uncompanionable coldness as they trailed the supermarket shelves. He would turn that self-sufficient way, keep himself clammed and tight into the evening. It could go on like that for days. She knew all this. She knew it wouldn't make any difference. But she wasn't able to stop. The need to speak was terrible now. Saying, saying anything, might loosen this lump in her chest. This time, she'd keep it light, not whine at least. If they laughed it would be better.

Something funny. Something funny just –
He had focused past her. He was looking into a place behind where she was, making her an obstruction to his clear view.
I don't feel very well.
This was at least true.
Oh, he said.
People were looking. She had to go on, making this messy account in disconnected fragments.
Two men. Two men started fighting. In front of me when I was coming to meet you just now. Just over nothing. No reason for it and nobody did anything, they just stood and –
What did you expect them to do?
He knew though he asked. He asked what had to come.
And I tried to stop them. I said someone will get hurt and one of them, one of them –
She was hot, sweating because she knew she was making it worse and not better and she couldn't seem to stop. She knew she should know better. And he knew too. He could hardly keep his head upright.
Her voice was out of shape
and one of them said that's the fucking –
DON'T SWEAR

A vitriolic stage whisper so expected she wondered if he had spoken at all or if she had made the sound from her own fear.
– and he looked at me as if

But Charles knew exactly how the man had looked at her. The words jammed. They stopped. Something wormed in her throat and her eyes were filling up. Charles shook his head. Between anger and despair, he hissed: christ there are people looking.

There was the dull thump of his fist against glass. Alice knew he had turned his back. Soon, he would walk away into the shopping mass and leave her to go home alone. She had not even said what she wanted to say. Feet clattering at the fringes of her vision hurt, a soreness in the temples as she stared down at the tile. Its red colour was blurring now, melting. Something was playing, uninvited, on the backs of her eyes.

It had been a dark evening through long windows. Thick royal sky and a luminous part of a moon and the street beyond the glass in cast-off bronze from the sodium lights. Grass on the verges grey and orange. Then the shouting: drunken loud-mouthing as the men rounded the corner and the shapes and the noise of them pushing and shoving. Like animations on a screen. Then the change: something quick and one of them rocking forward, calling out. A sheen. It was something shiny. Her mouth flexing, realising a knife and the three men tangling and dissolving in the half-light, the shouting changing to something metallic. Blood. And seeing that, her chest rippling with wakefulness and that terrible need to do something, thinking of the blood. She remembered reaching the door and being full of breath, pushing. But it was not wood or glass beneath her hand: she was pushing at warm cloth. Warm cloth filled with flesh so she looked up and it was Charles. Charles blocking the way with his eyes very blue, the voice calm with his information: it was

NOTHING TO DO WITH YOU
NOTHING TO DO WITH YOU
NOTHING TO DO WITH

buzzing through his chest and into her palms and the screaming rising outside while she pushed again, needing to break free and go. And suddenly his voice changing, hard as the grip on her wrists, repeating while he held her still: it was NOTHING TO DO WITH YOU and she was GOING NOWHERE and NOT INVOLVED; louder and angrier if she struggled.
NOTHING TO DO WITH YOU
NO REASON FOR THIS

And it was then she felt hate boiling like gas through the veins, up and through the skin like branding. There was no reason between them. No reason. The street and the men were just something outside and far away. Everything was here, inside the room with this man and this woman, she in his arms and shaking with rage till he was holding her tight. Holding her. She stopped twisting, looking down and he looked too. He was holding her. Their shapes cut against the black night-glass of the window: a man and a woman embracing in a room. Alice and Charles and this fearful, ringing nothing. He let her go quickly and covered his face with his hands. They stayed apart for the rest of the night, ignoring the street outside and the faint cries rising over distant roofs, the drips of blood on the pavement. They did not mention it again.

A scraping of heels like chalk on slate came too loud. There were the tiles of the precinct, rush-hour shoes. It wasn't right that this be here. She was at fault somehow. To have seen so private a thing before so many strangers, these indifferent shelves, boxes of liniment. But he was still turned away and it was impossible to speak. He flexed, his coat steeling. To speak would only make things worse. Yet if she touched him now, he would go without her. That might be kind. It would be something. Deliberately, she reached, tipped the warm cloth of his coat. He broke free as she knew he would, moving to merge with the crowd.

People were looking. People were looking.

Plastering the Cracks

It was more serious than I at first supposed. Not that I hadn't known the place needed attention. I knew all right: there was a lot to do and I was quite confident I would manage. For the most part, I was right. But when I started in that back room, peeling back that first strip of bedroom paper, the issue became more complex. Plaster clung and came away with the paper, leaving soft craters in the wall, pouring little rivers of silt when I touched them. It was regrettable but obvious I would need help. I tore down the rest of the paper anyway, letting more plaster drop and lie among the cast-off bits. If I had to hire someone, the room was going to look its worst. I wanted my money's worth.

I researched the *Home Handyman Encyclopaedia* that night. There wasn't much in the way of advice but I managed to find some information about structural damage and that made me feel a bit better. I could drop in some background knowledge, sound informed so they wouldn't try and fast-talk me or bump up the cost. The services page in the local paper had plenty of small ads, all different. I scanned each in turn and chose two plain minimalist efforts, ringing them heavily with black biro.

The call-box at the end of the street was working and I got through first try. Arrangements were polite and brief: both could come round to estimate next morning within half-an-hour of each other. The whole business had taken less than five minutes to set up – smooth as silk. I made a few calculations in my head on the way back: a couple of days for the plastering, maybe another fortnight for my work on the rest of the house, then move the furniture in. It could be done no bother. I pencilled the notes into my jotter when I got in and poured myself a whisky. I read the *Home Handyman* till it was too dark.

Next morning, I didn't need the alarm. I was up and shopping for warm rolls and a morning paper before seven. Two jumps ahead. The first man was at the door by eight.

He was thin and dark, belonging to the more detailed of the two ads. His inspection of the bedroom unaided took six minutes. He was chatty but pretty po-faced. I had to understand it was more than just plastering the cracks. The whole room would need to be stripped down and resurfaced, some floor panels replaced and the old fireplace could be knocked away. Did I know there was rising damp too. He could do the lot for a fixed price of two hundred pounds and begin in a fortnight. When I didn't say anything he told me to think it over. Phone in a few days, check the estimate; let him know. He let himself out.

The next one came twenty minutes later. He had a red face, not much breath and an over-tight shirt. His trousers sagged. A woollen bunnet jammed too far down his brow made it hard to see his eyes and I lost concentration on what he was saying till I realised he had stopped. Then I took him through. He went in gingerly, padding at the walls. I was going to leave him to it, then something hooted behind me and I wheeled back. He was facing me directly, too close. The face under the bunnet was rawer in the pale light, his clothes dustier. Another hoot and a rumble, then the fists gesturing near my face. He was explaining something but I couldn't catch it. Just couldn't get the drift at all. It was as though he had a terrible speech defect and no teeth. He kept going through, repeating the same things a few times and miming with his hands. I got the gist it was an estimate. I repeated it: he could do the plasterwork and brick the fireplace for fifty pounds. That wasn't it. I had got it wrong: he held up three fingers, sighed and wrote in pencil on the wall, thirty pounds. He could do the work for *thirty pounds* and start as soon as I liked. I asked him to start next morning, and a smile spread under the hat as I shook his hand, a huge hand with hair all the way down to the nail. My own disappeared inside it. I went with him to the back door and gave him a key in case I was out when he arrived, then waited, waving, till he was out of sight round the corner. That was it. I was pleased with the morning's business. I had thought of everything, hired someone to work for me at knock-down rates: I could handle things. I was nobody's fool. Nobody's mug.

Some time after 11.30 next morning, he arrived. I heard the word LATE as I let him in, but couldn't recall having specified a time and said nothing. In any case, he had already begun shuttling between a blue van outside and the bedroom, filling the place with stuff; floury sacks, plastic bins, canvas bags, big polythene pokes full of grey powder; tins of putties, cans, small foil-covered squares and fattily transparent paper bags. I watched from the corner of an eye. On the fourth or fifth journey, he went into the room and reappeared simultaneously at the back door. The second self had the sun behind it, and was smaller and thinner. When it came down the lobby it was another man altogether. I was a bit shaken anyway, and went back to fitting the carpet. It wasn't long till I started enjoying myself. I liked cutting the hemp, the awkwardnesses and angles of the room. I had a new ruler. As I worked, soft shuffles on the other side of the wall increased my concentration. Grating whispers. Stone, sand, knuckles on board: a cushion of low, male voices. There were two of them now, bridging the space between our separate rooms with muffled somethings. Wool and foam parting roughly under the Stanley knife, human warmth seeping beneath the skirting.

Shortly after one, I went out for a hot pie and a doughnut from the bakery. The cooker wasn't fitted yet and besides, I liked going there for the savoury scent of it and the heat. I was going to spoil myself since I'd finished the carpet. An overturned cardboard box did for a table and the bakery pokes for plates. Even so, the feel of the place still wasn't right. I could hear myself too plainly, moving about, and realised what I was missing was the company. I got out the radio and turned on whatever there was to fill the space. I started to wonder if they were eating, too. Maybe they were eating just as I was, hearing my radio. Maybe they liked the sound of me through the wall as much as I had enjoyed them.

Now there was nothing at all. The last part of the grey meat went cold in my fingers as I listened for them listening. When I noticed, I threw it in with the carpet offcuts and slithered the grease off down the sides of my jeans: I'd have a bath later. I could induce no interest in the doughnut and put it back inside the poke: it would keep. I turned the radio down and slid a fresh blade into the yellow Stanley handle.

KETL

A word and a sound like a tearing sheet made me turn
abruptly.

KETLHEN IH

The fat man crammed the living-room doorway. I had
heard nothing of his approach and here he was right inside
the room, speaking. He sipped self-consciously from an
invisible cup to help me with the words.

KETTLE. ONY TEA.

I got up and backed him down the lobby, gesticulating into
the space behind him as I walked forward. Once we got to
the kitchen, I pointed out the kettle and ran the cold water
too hard to demonstrate his welcome to it. The wool bobble
nodded. Mushrooms of hairy flesh popped between his
shirt buttons as he moved. Under a thick lip of fat, settled
on the waistband, his trouser catch was open. I flicked my
gaze away quickly but he was happy at the taps and hadn't
seen me looking so I slipped back out. Back down the
tunnel of hallway, into the brightness behind the livingroom door. Snug crush of nylon pile under my knees, I was
absorbed for the rest of the afternoon, wiring.

At 4.30, a muffled shout hurled up the lobby and the bobble
hat pushed round the door.

SUZ SUZ THIDAY

He filled his lungs heavily several times while I said nothing.

BACK THIMORRA OKAY

SOAKAY HEN

he insisted as I tried to get up, a good-natured dismissal as
he saw himself out. Irritation at my own cluelessness hung
on through the diminishing sound of feet. I hadn't been able
to hear him right. No, *that wasn't it*. I had heard perfectly
well. It was more that I didn't seem able to get to the bottom

of what he was saying. I couldn't work out a meaning. It reminded me of a habit I got into as a child, something that passed the time on long bus journeys. I would let the engine noise sink me into a kind of hypnosis till the sound lost its significance. Then when people spoke, their words became simply noise, disembodied from sense. Conversation became at once incomprehensibly foreign and deeply soothing; threatless music to block out exteriors. I could switch it on at will. I encouraged it. But when it began to affect me unbidden I was frightened and stopped the practice by sheer effort of will. Now, a shadow of that fear crept into the bare living room and up my neck, till a sudden raucous farting from the street chased me to the window. An ancient exhaust on the carcass of a blue van. I clutched the sill and watched it pass; T. G. BOYD BUILDER and a snatch of bobble hat.

I was painting when they let themselves in, calling their arrival down the hall. The fat man flooded the door-frame. MAKE TEA FIRST EH. It was quite clear, I heard him fine. There was also a promise of self-containment about it that let me off having to make silly smalltalk. Gratefully, I shouted through for him to take some rolls if he liked, and soon after, heard them in gentle manly rifts of appreciation through our wall. I thought of them in there, in my bedroom, eating buttered gifts with hot tea.

By lunchtime I had the makings of a headache. The narrow window-frame needed a great deal of concentration and I had already smeared the glass twice. Maybe I needed my dinner. It would be nice to be out for a wee bit of fresh air too, away from the paint fumes. Only a short walk to the bakery, but it would do.

I selected a sausage-roll and an empire biscuit. The woman

touched my hand giving me change and called me dear. I
was feeling better already. The lobby was thick with dust
when I got back; enough to make the air visible. Dull thuds
from the bedroom confirmed they had started on the
heavier stuff, knocking away the brickwork or something.
While I made my tea, the thumping got worse. There was
no milk. I looked around a bit before realising it was likely
in with them – in the bedroom with their morning tea-
things, but I wasn't going to interrupt their concentration or
my privacy to collect it; it wasn't that important. I settled
for black and walked back through chalky clouds, roaring
like dry ice under the door.

I enjoyed the food. I'm sure I did. After all, I had been
painting all morning and I was hungry. But I was increas-
ingly aware of the headache all the time I was eating. I
thought it was most likely the noise from the back room
that was doing it, or the hangover of turps. I rubbed my
temples as another crash like rockfall billowed through the
wall, followed by muttering and laughter: I clearly heard
the word STARVIN and others less distinct. I picked up my
brush when it stopped.

It was a long afternoon. The window smudged to spite me
and I got fed-up wanting it done nicely in favour of merely
getting the thing finished. My eyes frazzled as the paint
wiggled off the brush-end like white insects. I was still at it
when I heard them packing up to leave. That time already.
I took their tip, waited till they had gone for sure then
wandered up the lobby. Some tea, maybe, and yesterday's
doughnut to keep me ticking over. A wee doughnut would
do me fine.

It wasn't there. I checked all the likely places and a few of
the more bizarre. I knew I hadn't thrown it out and I knew

I hadn't eaten it either. I caught a glimpse of the bag near the sink. Its whiteness hurt as I picked it up and I had to peer to make out some thin pencil scrawl written on the lower edge. It was a message. THANKS FOR THE DOGNUT. T. G.'s writing. He must have assumed it had been part of a lot with the rolls. Then I remembered about the milk; it would still be through there as well. Right. I would collect it now. It was time I checked up on what they had been doing in there anyway. It had been two days after all, and it couldn't be far from finished. Hadn't even expected them to stay this long, not for thirty pounds. Not for thirty pounds for two of them. Christ. I could hear my head fizzing like Alka-Seltzer. What if the estimate had been partial or something? for materials only, and labour was extra? What if I hadn't understood? I rushed down the lobby, then pulled up stiffly at the closed face of the bedroom door. I took two deep breaths. Then I twisted the handle and walked unflinchingly inside.

Inside.

It was light and dark at the same time and the walls were moving. They were sliding and changing colour in huge suppurating spots. In the middle of the textured ceiling there was a glittering ball of mirror chips, rotating and sparking out light that turned on the wall in formless, spreading blobs. For a while, I was too taken in with this to see much else. It was only with much effort I managed some furtive glimpses of the rest of the room. There were long poles in one dim corner, leaning like clothes props, and tool-sacks, pregnant with hidden lumps. Bottles of dark fluids, metal bars, cups of powder. Near the blinded window, a huge sofa, piles of magazines, empty cans. And the remains of my doughnut. Around and under everything, the floorboards were still bare, the walls still meshed with soft cracks. I couldn't see what they had been doing to the fireplace since it was masked with an old-fashioned fire-screen, heavily embroidered with leering birds of paradise and peacocks whose eyes glowed and receded in the coloured rays from the ceiling.

And there was the milk, inches away, near my foot.

Seeing it there restored some of my equilibrium. Just a green and white carton with dark brown lettering and a cartoon drawing of a cow relaxing on a milkstool. I fixed my eye on the smile of the cow, trusting it to keep the rest at bay. For the rest – I knew even as I was watching – the rest was not really there. It was ridiculous. If I ignored it, it would go away. My head pounded as I stooped to pick up the carton and walked backwards out of the room, keeping my breath steady till I got out. Then I pulled the door shut too hard and loosened more plaster. I could hear it scratching against the boards inside. Too bad. I had to stop it spreading to the rest of the house, keep it under control. Then I knew that was daft. My own over-active imagination. I wanted to smile. HA HA I laughed up the hall; HA HA along the tunnel into the dark. Time I had that tea and a bit of a rest. Yes, a nice cup of tea then I would relax for the night. My mind was made up to forget the whole thing till the next morning. Yet I tiptoed to the bathroom and moved the sleeping bag round on the floor before I went to sleep.
Better safe.

Accordion music. Accordion music woke me. I sat up still inside the sleeping bag to listen. There was a rhythmic swishing noise as well, and both were coming from very near. They were coming from the bedroom. I heard a clear single word: HOOCH – and some undistinguished guffawing. I checked the alarm. It was well after ten. I had overslept and they had let themselves in, had started work in the back room. Then I wondered if they had come up the lobby as usual, opened my door, looked in on me when I was asleep. Maybe spoken about me, laughed about me when I couldn't hear. I was irritated, embarrassed and confused. I didn't want to go to the bathroom if they were in the hall either. The easy way out would be to go across the road – wash and breakfast in the bakery coffee bar and give myself time to come to. I would think of something then. Laughter welled up behind me as I slammed the front door.

It worked, though. By the time I returned. I felt much brighter. I made a lot of noise with the front door so they would hear. I had worked out a plan as I sat in the shop and knew exactly what I was doing. It was time I pulled myself together and started moving around my own home as though it was my own home. They would walk all over me if I didn't.

I strode purposefully across the carpet and down the lobby, then stopped at the bedroom door to listen for my moment. They were talking. The words SOON and OKAY came through the accordion tunes, then T.G.'s voice cut clear, making perfect sense NO BE LONG NOO and sighing.

It took the wind out of my sails. If everything was well in hand, there would be no need to get heavy-handed. They seemed to be gathering stuff together. I slipped away into the kitchen. The first thing I saw was the milk carton. A fresh one. They had brought me a new pint.
AYE. NEARLY BY. DO WIYA BATH EH. I kept the voices in my ears and picked up the carton, holding it to my chest. Things were all right. Everything was under control. T.G. began to sing tunelessly in a light baritone.

I didn't need the tea but I made it anyway and went to sit with it in the living room and check the list I had written.

1. SORT OUT BUSINESS – SEE ROOM!
2. HOW MUCH LONGER?
3. Second coat on interior door.

I scored out 1 and 2, ringing 3 with a flourish, then switched on the radio for the shipping forecast. I was almost relaxed.

The door proved easy after yesterday's window frame. Paint rolled off the brush in merging strips while people talked about gardens on the radio. When it got boring, I switched off and went on with the paint. So I didn't notice the silence at first. But it thickened as time passed and I soon checked my watch. After two. That meant no sound at all from next door for well over three hours. They couldn't have gone already because I hadn't paid anything. And the van was still there on the other side of the road: T. G. BROWN murky under the filth. I moved quietly to the bedroom door. Nothing. I tapped at the closed panels, listening hard. Then something bubbled suddenly behind me, the plumbing groaned. Instinctively, I propelled myself forward away from the noise and into the room. I should have known.

There was a deckchair in primary stripes right in the centre of the bare boards. Crushed beer-cans and two billiard cues made a pyre in the corner near a crude newsprint pin-up. Another corner glinted with dustless tools, polished chrome and steel. Breathlessly, I scanned for evidence of their labours. The cracks on the wall nearest me had peeling oblongs of sellotape over their mouths; those higher up seemed completely untouched. An old piece of skirting had been re-attached with orange plasticine, bulges of it oozing between the wood and the wall. Some stone had been chipped off the fireplace and lay in a heap where the surround had been. The grate was full of crumpled bits of the *Daily Record,* strapped in place by a mesh of masking tape. The bubbling noise rose up again, more identifiable this time. The rush and whinny of water. It was coming from the bathroom. Splashing and muted giggling. T.G.'s unmistakable enunciation: SOAP. Then I saw: pencilled on the grubby plaster round the lightswitch, a scribble of naughts and crosses and some words. APRIL FOOL. Water rushed in the bathroom. The bastards were having a bath.

Furious, I lunged for the living room and hunted out some paper. I forked the pen out from under the tool-box then sat to write.

OUR CONTRACT IS TERMINATED FORTHWITH. PLEASE COLLECT YOUR STUFF AND LEAVE.

Then I fished out the three ten-pound notes I had kept in my purse from their first day, waiting for them. Too bad if I had got it wrong: it was all they were getting. I put them with the letter into a manilla envelope, sealed it, stormed down the hall and unhesitatingly stuffed the lot under the bathroom door. The sound of towelling stopped abruptly. There was a dry click of paper as a fat hand found the envelope. That was enough. Blazing with trepidation and triumph, I left the house and walked as fast as I could to the bus stop.

All the streetlights were burning when I got back. The van was gone: I had seen that much as I walked up the street. I called out at the back door to make sure: COOEEE. But nothing answered. The kitchen was very dark inside, darker

even than the road, but I waited till I got used to it and
found I could see pretty well without putting the light on. I
preferred it that way. I would have a wee look in, then plan
for tomorrow; check out what had to be done in there and
work out how to do it myself.

Fresh start. I had my *Home Handyman,* my notebook. I
would manage.

The doors gaped in a Russian doll series behind me as I
made through to the bedroom. It was open, and the blind
for once was up. I looked.

The walls were smooth, the fireplace bricked and flat. The
drying plaster had been sanded and a heap of plaster dust
smoked in the corner near my kitchen brush. On the white
window-sill, outlined in moonlight, were some bits of paper
and something silver. The spare key, a dull, crushed oncer
and a note from T.G.

CHANGE.

later he would
open his eyes in a
strange place,
wondering where
she

They'd planned it for his sixty-fourth birthday, her having been retired a few years now and his redundancy money spent. Thursday: the day the mobile library came round. She had handed him the book with the bit underlined, in pencil so she could rub it out before she took it back: just the bit that mattered. He thought at first it was something to do with her amateur theatricals that she'd done for years up till the bad hip meant she couldn't get out and about as much, but it wasn't that. It was something different altogether. Maybe if she hadn't liked biography. Koestler. She remembered it because she didn't know how you said it, how the sound of the word went. Even if she'd gone to another shelf. It was his ticket that got the book out, him not being a reader. She pointed that out. He looked at it eating toast and didn't say yes or no just nodded: he had heartburn. But two nights later he put the book on the mantelpiece while she was looking at the TV. It was closed but she looked up anyway, knowing, with the look on his face saying he'd been thinking. And he knew from her looking up, watching his face like that, it would be his responsibility. They said nothing else. She went back to watching the chat-show host talking to people she'd never

heard of, listening to the creak of the stairs under his
weight, quieter with every footfall.

It was probably the night she said she'd a notion of ice-
cream, eaten nothing all day but had a notion of ice-cream
and nearly 11 o'clock with the cafes and everything shut it
took shape. He had taken the car rather than walk to find
somewhere because you never knew in those precincts late
at night, the screaming and so on. With them not going for
the Sunday drives any more it would be something for the
car to do, open the engine up. It gave him a fancy for a
drive, just round the ring-road and back, past the digging.
There were always cones these days, right along the edge of
the road or making islands in the middle. They were
building a wall. He slowed down a bit to look at it, nearly
finished. End to end as long as the fencing that had been
round where the steelworks used to be. Just bricks. Maybe
they would plaster it over to make it look better later on,
put one of those murals on it. A mural of the steelworks.
His hands felt dry, coated with dust, feeling for the absent
plaster.

The only place this far out was the Little Chef. It was
bright anyway. He had a cup of coffee, sitting in with four
men eating and a pair of girls with black hair and white
faces, even their lips powdered over and black rings round
their eyes like bruises. The place was full of some music
you couldn't quite identify or hear properly. He sat with
the coffee, trying not to watch the other people too
much and listening to this terrible distant music till a girl
with a mob cap came and tried to refill his cup that
wasn't empty. You couldn't finish the coffee in these
places. Halfway out the door he remembered about the
ice-cream, about the whole point. She would be
wondering where he was and Pieroni's would be shut.

He had to go back inside, letting the door swing hard behind him.

There was ice-cream in the chest freezer next to the computer game machines. He'd have to take something with being away ages. No vanilla, only chocolate cone things and blocks of stuff with flavours. Maple and pecan nut. She had a sweet tooth. He paid the money and left with the ice-cream burning his hand through the paper bag. On the way back, he noticed the petrol light, orange dot on the dashboard as he was approaching the wall and the flat stretch at the old steelworks but he kept his foot down. He didn't want to double back now. Then, for no reason he could think of, he remembered the book. The book. He watched the wall in the rearview mirror, big wrapper of it round the derelict space getting smaller. She was fine about the ice-cream when he got back. He made her a cup of tea to take up and sat on downstairs thinking. He thought all night. It was a change to have something to think about. Neither of them slept much these days anyway.

Not the next morning but a couple of days or so after he said. Waiting for her to bring the breakfast. She didn't even look up, just tipped the egg on his plate: always a whole egg though he only ate half these days what with not being able to taste much and the texture sometimes making him feel sick. Then she stood, waiting for the plate as usual, the half white and yolk oozing over the hairline crack on the blue painted lip. There was nothing ostensible. But when she was pouring the tea, he felt a stiffness between her arm and his shoulder, something different in the space over his head. When she sat down he saw her eyes had filled up so he knew she had heard. She didn't always hear. Next morning he could tell she'd been thinking about it too. She suggested the paraffin. A refinement.

Preparation was minimal. She looked out the marriage lines and the two policies while he went to the filling station. He came back with a full tank and a bar of chocolate, the kind she liked, out of habit but she didn't smile. She was worried about the house.

I know but I can't help it.

He couldn't think of anything to say, just waited, clinking keys, watching her manage the sleeves of the pink tweed coat she bought cut-price and never liked, folding the paisley scarf. She had to push the plastic flowers in front of the cracked bit of mirror to put on lipstick. He wondered about getting his hat then didn't because she was turning towards him, looking anxious, pressing the stud at the coat collar. It wouldn't shut. She gave up and looked round.

Nothing else?

The plastic bottle with the paraffin was already in the car from the morning. There was nothing else. But neither moved to the door. There was a tug of something there, something between them like an invisible mesh of threads, the possibility of embrace. When she looked away, it broke. They left the chocolate on the sideboard, unopened. The car started first turn, without shuddering.

Life in the old girl yet, he said. The smell of petrol from the leaky tank was overpowering.

Now there would be the drive across the bridge and into the wasteland by the steelworks wall, the wait in the sickly upholstery smell with the handbrake on hard, the car ticking over like a child's cough. Ticking over and lurching as though it might stall, the way it did these days, so you could never wait too long, the car not suited to idling. They would avoid the other's touch as they turned in the tight space, when she reached into the back to find the plastic bottle, moving to pour the paraffin, keeping dowsing till it was all gone and the fumes making her turn to roll down the window before she remembered not to. The windows would need to be shut. Almost a joke. Then the engine revving back from the brink of a cough, his hand jerking and relaxing on the lever, the car beginning to roll. And he would tilt the tyres over the crest of the mud hill, set the wall in his sights and drive, accelerating till the engine whines and the bodywork trembles, her hands blue-veined on the dashboard, holding the ledge tight.

Life in the old girl yet.

The realisation he is speaking for something to say before he shuts his eyes and presses his foot harder, determined not to swerve.

The meat

The carcass hung in the shop for nine days till the edges congested and turned brown in the air.

People came and went. They bought wafers of beef, pale veal, ham from the slicer, joints, fillets, mutton chops. They took tomatoes and brown eggs, tins of fruit cocktail, cherries, handfuls of green parsley, bones. But no one wanted the meat. It dropped overhead from a claw hook, flayed and split down the spinal column: familiar enough in its way. It was cheap. But they asked for shin and oxtail, potted head, trotters. The meat refused to sell. Folk seemed embarrassed even to be caught keeking in its direction. One or two made tentative enquiries about a plate of sausages coiled to the left of the dangling shadow while the yellowing hulk hung restless, twisting on its spike. These were never followed through. The sausages sat on, pink and greasy, never shrinking by so much as a link. He moved the sausages to another part of the shop where they sold within the hour. Something about the meat was infecting.

By the tenth day, the fat on its surface turned leathery and translucent like the rind of an old cheese. Flies landed in the curves of the neck and he did not brush them away. The deep-set ball of bone sunk in the shoulder turned pale blue. There was no denying the fact: it had to be moved. The ribs were sticky and the smell had begun to repulse him, clogging the air in the already clammy interior of the shop, and he could detect its unmistakeable seep under the door to his living room when he was alone in the evening. So he fetched a stool and reached out to the lard hook, seized the meat and with one accurate slice of the cleaver, cut it down. It languished on the sawdust floor till nightfall when he threw it into the back close parallel to the street. As he closed the shutter on the back door, he could hear the scuffling of small animals and strays.

In the morning, all that remained was the hair and a strip of tartan ribbon. These he salvaged and sealed in a plain wooden box beneath the marital bed. A wee minding.

Fearless

There would be days when you didn't see him and then days when you did. He just appeared suddenly, shouting threats up the main street, then went away again. You didn't question it. Nobody said anything to Fearless. You just averted your eyes when he was there and laughed about him when he wasn't. Behind his back. It was what you did.

Fearless was a very wee man in a greasy gaberdine coat meant for a much bigger specimen altogether. Grey-green sleeves dripped over permanent fists so just a row of yellow knuckles, like stained teeth, showed below the cuffs. One of these fisted hands carried a black, waxed canvas bag with an inept burst up one seam. He had a gammy leg as well, so every second step the bag clinked, a noise like a rusty tap, regular as a heartbeat. He wore a deceptively cheery bunnet like Paw Broon's over an escape of raw, red neck that hinted a crewcut underneath; but that would've meant he went to the barber's on a regular basis, keeping his hair so short, and sat in like everybody else waiting his turn, so it was hard to credit, and since you never saw him without the bunnet you never knew for sure. And he had these terrible specs. Thick as the bottoms of milk bottles, one lens patched with elastoplast. Sometimes his eyes looked crossed through these terrible specs but it was hard to be sure because you didn't get to look long enough to see. Fearless wouldn't let you.

There was a general assumption he was a tramp. A lot of people called him a tramp because he always wore the same clothes and he was filthy but he wasn't a tramp. He had his own house down the shorefront scheme; big black finger-stains round the keyhole and the curtains always shut. You could see him sometimes, scrabbling at the door to get in, looking suspiciously over his shoulder while he was forcing the key to fit. There were usually dirty plates on the doorstep too. The old woman next door cooked his meals and laid them on the step because he wouldn't answer the door. He sometimes took them and he sometimes didn't. Depended on his mood. Either way, there were usually dirty plates. The council cut his grass, he had daffodils for christsake – he wasn't a tramp. He was the kind that got tramps a bad name: dirty, foul-mouthed, violent and drunk. He was an alkie all right, but not a tramp: the two don't necessarily follow.

The thing about Fearless was that he lived in a state of permanent anger. And the thing he was angriest about was being looked at. Sometimes he called it MAKING A FOOL OF and nobody was allowed to get away with it. It was a rule and he had to spend a lot of time making sure everybody knew it. He would storm up and down the main street, threatening, checking every face just in case they were looking then if he thought he'd caught you he would stop, stiffen and shout WHO ARE YOU TRYING TO MAKE A FOOL OF and attack. Sometimes he just attacked: depended on his mood. Your part was to work out what sort of mood it was and try and adjust to it, make the allowance. It was what you were supposed to do. Most folk obliged, too – went out of their way to avoid his maybe-squinty eyes or pointedly NOT LOOK when they heard the clink and drag, clink and drag, like Marley's ghost, coming up the street. Then the air would fall ominously silent while he stopped, checking out a suspicious back, reinforcing his law. On a bad day, he would just attack anyway to be on the safe side. Just in case. You couldn't afford to get too secure. There was even a story about a mongrel stray he'd wound into a half-nelson because it didn't drop its gaze quick enough, but that was probably just a story. Funnier than the catalogue of petty scraps, blows that sometimes connected and sometimes didn't that made up the truth. It might have been true right enough but that wasn't the point. The point was you were supposed to laugh. You were meant to think he was funny. Fearless: the very name raised smiles and humorous expectations. Women shouted their weans in at night with HERE'S FEARLESS COMING, or squashed tantrums with the warning YOU'LL END UP LIKE FEARLESS. Weans made caricatures with hunchback shoulders, cross-eyes and a limp. Like Richard the Third. A bogeyman. And men? I have to be careful here. I belonged to the world of women and children on two counts, so I never had access to their private thoughts voiced in private places: the bookie's, the barber's, the pub. Maybe they said things in there I can have no conception of. Some may have thought he was a poor old soul who had gone to the bad after his wife left him. Romantics. I suppose there were some who could afford to be. Or maybe they saw him as an embarrassment, a misfit, a joke. I don't know. What I do know is that I never saw any of them shut him up when the anger started or try and calm it down. I remember what women did: leaving food on the doorstep and bottles for him to get money on; I remember women shaking their heads as he went past and keeping their eyes and their children low. But I don't remember any men doing anything much at all. He didn't seem to touch their lives in the same way. They let him get on with what he did as his business. There was a kind of respect for what he was, almost as though he had a right to hurl his fists, spit, eff and blind – christ, some people seemed to admire this drunken wee tragedy as a local hero. They called him *a character*. *Fearless is a character right enough* they would say and smile, a smile that accounted for boys being boys or something like that. Even polismen did it. And women who wanted to be thought above the herd – one of the boys. After all, you had to remember his wife left him. It was our fault really. So we had to put up with it the way we put up with everything else that didn't make sense or wasn't fair; the hard, volatile maleness of the whole West Coast Legend. You felt it would have been shameful, disloyal even, to admit you hated and feared it. So you kept quiet and turned your eyes away.

It's hard to find the words for this even now. I certainly had none then, when I was wee and Fearless was still alive and rampaging. I would keek out at him from behind my mother's coat, watching him limp and clink up the main street and not understand. He made me sick with fear and anger. I didn't understand why he was let fill the street with himself and his swearing. I didn't understand why people ignored him. Till one day the back he chose to stop and stare at was my mother's.

We were standing facing a shop window, her hand in mine, thick through two layers of winter gloves. The shop window was full of fireplaces. And Fearless was coming up the street. I could see him from the other end of the street, closer and closer, clinking the black bag and wheeling at irregular intervals seeing if he could catch somebody looking. The shouting was getting louder while we stood, looking in at these fireplaces. It's unlikely she was actually interested in fireplaces: she was just doing what she was supposed to do in the hope he'd leave us alone – and teaching me to do the same. Fearless got closer. Then I saw his reflection in the glass: three days' growth, the bunnet, the taped-up specs. He had jerked round, right behind where we were standing and stopped. He looked at our backs for a long time, face contorted with indecision. What on earth did he think we were plotting, a woman and a wean in a pixie hat? What was it that threatened? But something did and he stared and stared, making us bide his time. I was hot and cold at once, suddenly sick because I knew it was our turn, our day for Fearless. I closed my eyes. And it started. A lot of loud, jaggy words came out the black hole of his mouth. I didn't know the meanings but I felt their pressure. I knew they were bad. And I knew they were aimed at my mother. I turned slowly and looked: a reflex of outrage beyond my control. I was staring at him with my face blazing and I couldn't stop. Then I saw he was staring back with these pebble-glass eyes. The words had stopped. And I realised I was looking at Fearless.

There was a long second of panic, then something else did the thinking for me. All I saw was a flash of white sock with my foot attached, swinging out and battering into his shin. It must have hurt me more than it hurt him but I'm not all that clear on the details. The whole thing did not finish as heroically as I'd have liked. I remember Fearless limping away, clutching the ankle with his free hand and shouting about a liberty, and my mother shaking the living daylights out of me, a furious telling off, and a warning I'd be found dead strangled up a close one day and never to do anything like that again.

It was all a long time ago. My mother is dead, and so, surely, is Fearless. But I still hear something like him; the chink and drag from the close-mouth in the dark, coming across open, derelict spaces at night, blustering at bus stops where I have to wait alone. With every other woman, though we're still slow to admit it, I hear it, still trying to lay down the rules. It's more insistent now because we're less ready to comply, look away and know our place. And I still see men smiling and ignoring it because they don't give a damn. They don't need to. It's not their battle. But it was ours and it still is. I hear my mother too and the warning is never far away. But I never could take a telling.

The outrage is still strong, and I kick like a mule.

Scenes from the
Life No. 27:
Living In

A spacious room. One side is dominated by a wall-shelving unit with a stereo, video, recording units, speakers and amps, some books and a HUGE TV. There are also some bottles and cans of lager as a 'cocktail' section. A modern armchair sits squarely in front of this unit, facing the glowing green lights of the sound system. A few open books on the carpet, an overturned (empty) wineglass, a Rubik's cube or some such 'adult' toy. Opposite these, a desk, a drawing-board. Lots of crumpled paper and writing things on the desk. There is a large mirror and a cork pinboard above it. Some plants.

Between, deeper into the room, a sleeping area with a large bed, wardrobe with set-in mirror, bedside table and a canvas chair. On the bed, a thick dishevelled duvet. The fitted carpet is strewn with cast-off clothes, a pair of trousers hang over the chair arm.

Furnishings throughout are tasteful but pedestrian: everything self-coloured in subdued shades. Nothing is patterned; none of the plants are flowering or exotic. No cushions; no ornaments on the shelves.

To one side, in a corner, is a sectioned-off bathroom with a permanently opened door: it should not seem too separate from the rest of the room. The sink and toilet bowl are clearly visible. There are lots of jars, bottles and tubes ranged along the back of the sink and on shelves. Behind the sink, an enormous mirror. The toilet seat is UP. There is a towel crumpled on the floor, and another draped untidily over the bath rim.

Light enters from a sloping skylight above the bed, angled to make visible a diamond of greyish sky. Light level should suggest an extremely overcast day, twilight – something of that sort. The same level obtains for almost the entire play.

Articles on the floor interjoin the different areas of the room. There is also a telephone, coffee table, poster on one wall.
THERE IS NO KITCHEN APPARENT.
Other minor properties will be indicated in the text.

Note for the ACTOR.
TONY *is entirely suggested through improvised movement.* NEVER SPEAK. TONY *is at all times a presentable and pleasing figure, trim and tall (though not excessively so) fashionably good-looking. His clothes and hairstyle are neat and businesslike, but he wears them with a casual stylishness (or vice versa). Maintain his neat appearance by occasionally checking that cuffs, trouser-crease etc. are as they should be, smooth down hair, check shoulders . . . but keep this unobtrusive.* TONY's *movements are graceful and masculine: even at his most relaxed he has dignity. He is smooth and unhurried, never coarse or clumsy. His movements and any noise he makes (humming or sighing, spitting out water, etc.) is retrained, almost self-conscious.* NEVER ALTER HIS EXPRESSION. *The steady but eager blankness of* TONY's *face throughout is essential to a*

correct interpretation of the character. Never slip from
character or acknowledge the audience in any way.

Act 1

Half-light. A fairly lengthy stasis before a digital watch
alarm begins to play 'Clementine' thinly. The lumpy duvet
twitches and moves. Slowly, the head and hands of a man
appear from the top. It is TONY: his eyes still closed. The
watch continues to sing through his waking ritual. His feet
find the carpet first, then his torso rises to let him sit with
his head hanging forward over his knees, the corner of the
duvet still hiding his crotch. He reaches for the watch,
silences the music, straps it to his wrist. In slow stages, he
rises, stretching a muscular body. He has been wearing blue
cotton briefs in bed. Only now does he open his eyes. (He
does not contort his face to wakefulness – even newly
emerged from sleep, he is a handsome man.) He blinks a
good deal on the way to the bathroom where he picks up
the fallen towel at his feet and drops it over the edge of the
bath before standing poised at the toilet bowl. With his
back to the audience, he empties his bladder, soundlessly,
and without undue disturbance to the blue briefs. Now he
takes a few squares of white toilet paper to carefully wrap
his penis and nestle it gently back inside the briefs. (Allow,
time and precision for these manoeuvres which are to be
executed with utmost discretion; it should not be possible
for even the most prudish member of the audience to take
offence here.)

Once this routine is accomplished, he carries on with the
rest of his preparations: running the taps at full power to
wash his face and drying it vigorously with the towel,
sponging under his arms and across his chest then brushing
his teeth thoroughly. (NB: a bearded actor will be able to

take much longer over this part by spending time trimming the beard and moustache into the sink.) Once he has finished, the damp towel is once more relegated to the floor. TONY turns his attentions to the lotions and unguents on the shelves: he carries this out routinely. First, he applies roll-on deodorant to his armpits, then sprinkles some talc on his chest, rubbing it into the skin with firm, long strokes. Next, he selects a bottle of aftershave to dash some into his hands and slap into his face and neck (neck only if bearded). He may also add a discreet touch to his pubic hair as an afterthought – gingerly. He examines his face for some time in the large bathroom mirror, flicking away a fallen eyelash, checking a dubious patch of skin, inspecting his teeth, etc. THE EXPRESSION OF HIS FACE NEVER ALTERS. After this, he turns back to the bottles and tubes, sprays something under his arms from an acrosol, adds a touch more aftershave, brushes his teeth again and strokes his neck.

Fully awake now, he moves purposefully and decisively back into the main part of the room and begins an assualt on dressing. He begins with the trousers over the edge of the canvas chair, putting them on as he stands, then adds the items strewn on the floor in turn: a white shirt, a dark tie, pair of dark socks. Last are the dark shoes at the side of the bed. Checks himself over in the wardrobe mirror: he looks GOOD. Now he rakes his hair with his fingers, combs it through into place (replacing the comb in his trouser pocket) and shakes his head to naturalise the effect to his satisfaction. A jacket from the wardrobe completes the outfit: he drapes it cavalierly over one shoulder. Expressionlessly triumphant, he gazes at his neat reflection (he does not smile).

Eyes still on his mirror self, he checks for wallet, keys and cash by patting at various appropriate pockets. He is ready.

Erect, he marches out and off through the audience. He looks fine, assured, masculine. Fathomless.

Act 2

The room as it was left. Nothing is different. Street noise begins to filter through the skylight, making the room seem all the more still and quiet within. Then a series of distinct and discrete sounds, building in volume so the last in the series is very loud indeed.

1. General traffic noise, cars ticking over, etc.
2. A motorbike running, then revving repeatedly.
3. A car taking a corner too fast.
4. Drunken singing and cursing, indistinct obscenities.
5. A clicking of shoes on a pavement, then jeering: the banter of men catcalling. It becomes progressively more blatant and aggressive then stops. A burst of wolf-whistling.
6. Chanting (football slogans?) and a breaking bottle.
7. Some grunting and scuffling; the sound of running and angry obscenities.
8. Silence. An ear-splitting wolf-whistle.

The diamond of sky in the skylight glows and changes to a very bright blue then dims to its usual wash.

Act 3

TONY walks through the audience and back on-stage. His jacket slewed over his shoulder and his collar loosened suggest a hard day. He throws down the car keys onto the coffee table and drops the jacket on the floor before turning on the radio. It plays soft music interspersed with long sentences – not particularly audible. He selects a can from

the shelves then sits to peel it open and spread comfortably
in the chair, the can in one hand, sipping every so often with
his eyes closed. The radio plays and he eases into relaxation.
The man, the can and the radio make a soothing triangle for
at least ten minutes. Then he opens his eyes to press the
button which activates the HUGE TV. He sits up to look
into the screen briefly and finish the remains of the can. It
shows discontinuous bits of old films – Westerns, adventure
stories, gangster movies, etc. – bits of detective serials, car
chases and adverts, sometimes cartoon figures and
newsreel. The volume is very low. Rising, TONY begins to
wander about the room, picking up the odd book, riffling
through his record collection, etc. Soon, he takes another
can with a long glance at the part-nude figure on the back
before tearing off the ring-pull. He drinks from this through
his tour, making inspections, mental digressions. He is at
peace, relaxed in his ownership of the place: he is a man in
his own home. At some stage, he may put a record on the
stereo; again very softly. The combined volume of the radio,
TV and disc are never too obtrusive or harsh. Eventually, he
looks at his watch and settles into the easy chair, selecting
his favoured channel. It shows the same as the other one.
He falls asleep facing the TV and the green indicator lights
of the stereo deck. By turns, the noises of the machines fall
away, till there is only a soft crackle sifting from the TV. It
is then that TONY wakes, dropping the empty can on the
carpet. He looks round, rises, rubbing his neck, and goes to
the bathroom.

His evening ablutions are much less mannered and shorter
than those of the morning: he washes and dries his face and
brushes his teeth. Even the water runs less forcefully. He
slackens his trousers and pees noisily into the toilet bowl,
shakes his penis and discards the tissue from his briefs into
the bowl before flushing. His flies undone, he comes

through to sit on the bed where he undresses. Trousers return to the canvas chair, the shoes and socks, shirt and tie lie where they are dropped. Without rising, he swings his legs up to slot under the still-dishevelled duvet, removes and sets his watch, then places it on the bedside table. He has finished with the day: he sinks well under the warmth of the duvet and rolls away from the audience to sleep.

Everything is still for a long time.

Next to the recumbent figure, the lumps in the duvet move. Minutely at first, then more noticeably they move toward TONY then undulate in small rhythmic patterns above his body. TONY inhales loudly: the movements stop: he rolls abruptly away, back out to the audience. There is silence and stillness and TONY's eyes shut very tightly. Nothing happens for a few minutes. Another mild movement behind him. He sighs deeply, sets his mouth hard and rolls onto his face. Another period of immobility and stillness. TONY's form relaxes slowly, completely. He has fallen asleep.

Stars appear in the strip of sky above the bed. They glow very brightly as the set darkens till the shape of TONY in the bed has a silver outline. The bed pulses again: there is something under the lumps in the duvet – something *is* the lumps in the duvet. It moves again, then emerges in one sweep to stand at the end of the bed. It is a naked woman. Soundlessly she moves round to look down at the sleeping man, stroking the place above his head with one hand, taking great care not to touch. Then she moves more centrally to face the enormous mirror at the wardrobe. She stares and stands steadfastly, unblinking so her eyeballs shine in the dark and through the gloom, her skin looks very pale and downy, starlit. Gently, liquidly, with spread fingers, she traces her hands lightly over her body: lingering on her shoulders, over each breast caressingly in turn, stroking across her ribs and down, over her stomach, firmly and repeatedly across her thighs and hips: soothing strokes. This takes some time and can not be rushed if the right effect is to be achieved. Her deep concentration, intensity and absorption in the task, the feel of skin under the fingertips are paramount. Then, nearing completion, one hand glides upward to clasp a shoulder and shield her breasts as the fingers of the other fan deep into her pubic hair. Head erect, she looks into the mirror, into the white contours of her body curving out of the darkness.

TONY sleeps.

Addendum

Note to the ACTRESS.
Extreme stillness is demanded for the part. NO ONE is to know she is there until the moment comes. The audience must never be sure whether she is substantial or not.

Nightdriving

1.

and he was missing the kids and couldn't sleep so we drove
down to the shore, right past the barriers and warning signs
to the edge of the cob, the headlights swinging out across
the drop to the sand. It was so dark I couldn't see anything
over the water from the other side and the sea was just a
noise like nervous cellophane, like cellophane crushing in
someone's hands. He got out, walking with his back
melting in the dark till he was just a blur at the end of the
breakwater, a milky stain coming and going in the pitch-
black middle of the noise of the sea and the wind outside.
And I sat on in the car, twisting to see past where the
headlamps cut a wedge across the sand. The rushes showed
white needles in the dips of the dunes; dunes and flakes of
litter in the ash-colour sand. And I was frightened. I opened
the door shouting I'M COMING TOO, I'M COMING
WITH YOU but the wind blotted up in my mouth and I
knew there would be no answer. There would be no answer
because I couldn't be heard. Then I started to walk to the
edge of the cob, stumbling over shale, afraid I'd fall and tear
my hands on the edges of broken shells. So I stopped.

I stopped because there was no help for it and stood peering out at the visible sand, searching for what I couldn't see. It was too dark. Yet I didn't want to show how scared I was, keeping looking for movements through the dunes in case anyone was there, in case something was coming. Only a crazy person would be out there in the middle of the night in this howling wind but I kept looking out, into the hard echo of the waves I couldn't see, over the strip of grey sand thinking *There is something more I can't make sense of, something more to come* and getting colder and colder. He was still out there at the end of the breakwater and there was still no answer. The rushes on the dunes were rippling like hair, the battered ends of the waves falling beaten on the shore. The waves kept coming inshore.

2.

since visiting was very free but I was never sure if he would come. The floor was soft so it was sometimes sudden when he did appear, walking silently down the tunnel of strip-light: his steady walk to where he knew I would wait. And we went out across the soft tiles to the fresh night air and the borders of the car park outside, slipping our hips between the cold metal curves of people's motors. He strapped the seatbelt tight across my chest to hold me down then he'd cough the ignition and the tyres cracked over gravel towards the motorway and we'd go speeding down the motorway in pure white lines. He would press the accelerator hard so I sank back into the leather, the seatbelt gripping my chest and clothes spreading black against the green leather skins. He would wear blue. Then we'd snake out onto the open lanes and uphill, the whole frame lifting while he reached to turn the music loud with one hand on the wheel. And the rising and the music would fill up inside the car; pressing my spine, bowling me back against the falling leather so I could hardly bear it. Sometimes he would smile from the corner of his mouth, feeling for overdrive with one hand on the wheel and we were tearing down the white lanes, their patterns in the mirror streaming behind like ribbons on the wind. And all I could see on my back were the overcrowding stars of the streetlights, the yellow v-strip dazzling through the music swelling up like bursting glass on the curved road back to the ward.

3.

It's not my car but someone lets me use it if I promise to be careful coming home late. The road I have to travel is treacherous and twists through countryside so there are no lights to mark the edges, just the solid dark that rises with the hills on either side. There are never many cars. You see headlamps float over dips in the darkness and know there must be a road beneath: an unseen path below the rise and fall of the beams in the blackness on either side. And sometimes you see nothing. Not until they slew from nowhere, too close from a corner that didn't exist before, a hidden side-road or farmhouse track. Light veers under your fingernails and there is a second of sudden wakefulness, too much brightness in the car from the other presence outside. You see your own grey hands wrapping the wheel, the swirl of grass like water in the gutters. Then somehow it's over. Only the red smears of tail-lights dwindling in the mirror show it was ever there and you are driving on. The steering leather under your fists, its turning. The road looks new. It looks like nowhere you have been before.

And you remember.
You keep driving and remember.

The city road is a narrow stretch with hills that rise on either side, steep like the sides of a coffin: a lining of grass like green silk and the lid open to the sky but it is a coffin all the same. The verges hang with ripped-back cars from the breaker's yard, splitting the earth on either side, but you keep on going, over the dips and bends between the rust and heather till the last blind bend and it appears. Between the green and brown, the husks of broken cars: a v-shaped glimpse of somewhere else so far away it seems to float. It's distant and beautiful and no part of the rest: no part of the road I am travelling through, not Ayrshire, not Glasgow. It comes and goes behind a screen as I drive towards it, a piece of city waiting in the v-shaped sky if this is my day to make a split-second mistake. It's always there. And I know too it's simply the way home. I accelerate because it is not today. I am still here.
Driving.

things he said

Awkward, the two of us virtual strangers going to a concert and shy. I wanted to know what he thought of the music, friend of a friend, someone who looked as though he was on the verge of saying something all the time.

London is lonely he said; easy enough on the phone, the things he said in those odd inflections, just the voice and that detached, since I hardly knew the set of his face. That closeness, a scandalous thing between virtual strangers, letting the unfamiliar voice coil into an ear but allowable so it didn't feel out of place offering: he could stay over, his going to London the next morning and the train easier from where I lived. The mouthpiece breathing after he said yes and I thought we could talk.

The concert was something agreed, neither of us able to look the other in the eye yet, a place to be that was not personal. The things he said were particular. We thought the same things about the music and that made it better, made us relax. It was raining when we went out, running to be clear of it. The two grey flight-bags, one with a bottle bulky in the pocket, made red marks on his hands.

Going up the stairs, neither of us spoke. He left the bags in the hall, fished out the wine. On separate seats, awkward, the two of us virtual strangers alone in the same room for the first time but determined, we tried to feel at home. The things he said. That kisses were a threat, not able to be direct. Sexuality became a byword, leaning forward on the chair and flexing his hands, my fingers on the neck of a glass. Kisses were a threat, a resonance at the back of his throat before he looked me in the eye. If you get the men and women thing right, everything else follows. The angle of his arm, his eyes huge. I said maybe you'd like to lie down now but there was something else to drink, something else to drink. Finding more to say, lighting cigarettes and holding the bottle by the neck, never letting his eyes shift. The things he said, not ready himself for how much. And when he stopped, knowing I was there, that the things he said put me past sleep, he stood up. Smoke trailing over his lip like gauze, the rims of his eyes grey.

Cold in the kitchen at five thirty, his arms opened without thought.

The things he did.

A Week with
Uncle Felix

'Clementine.'
The buzzing came clearer by degrees.

Duncan humming through the engine noise, the same bit
over and over. Grace was muttering at the same time, paper
crackling under her thumbs. She could hear clearly now,
head pressed into the car window, that comforting rattle of
the skull that made you want to hold onto the moments of
being not awake. Not yet. The shuffle and the cough: you
could feel her turning, drawing breath.
    Here. Sleepy.
Grace's voice closer than she'd expected. Then a bump and
grind of gravel shuddering up through the tyres as the car
tilted under some ragged shade. The engine shudder
bounced the damp glass under her cheek then cut to
nothing.
    Here, Teeny. Teeny Leek.
Grace knew fine she would only be pretending now, but
she wasn't bothering, just zipping up the bag ready to get
out.
    Rise and shine.
The front doors opened and shut again, leaving her to it.

The girl opened her eyes. Squeals starting up already. Cards slithered on the blanket as she turned to see. People were outside, through that fog on the window, merging and separating on the silent grey grass. Duncan looked even shorter when he stood next to her like that. Like Olive Oyl and Popeye and smiling too much. The other one was even taller than Grace. There was a movement like dancing before they fuzzed over completely. Lifting the sleeve made more cards fall. She was reaching for them when something moved outside, rustling the branches, veering close to the glass. Then the catch clicked, a swirl of night air retracting her legs under the tartan. Leopard-skin with shadow, the man crouched in the open door-frame. Uncle Felix.

Out you come Sweetheart.
One shiny eye free of the patches of dark. It took a moment to realise who the Sweetheart was. Then whether it was a joke. He was holding out his hand.
Out you come.

Things spilling as she inched forward, unpeeling her thighs from the vinyl, crumpled sweetie papers rolling at her feet like coloured beads. Making a mess as usual. She was stooping to pick them up when the hand fell on her shoulder. It wrapped the whole bone.
Never mind that, love. It'll keep.
His eyes were the colour of old paper.
You don't remember.
The English accent, the lips disappearing when he smiled.
Long time ago, love. Uncle Felix, your dad's brother.
Hello pet.
Grace's face pushed into the space between them, creasy and moon-coloured in the dark.
Just like your daddy, that's what we always say isn't it

right? Just like our Jock. Do you remember Uncle eh? She
likely won't remember.
Her teeth slipped and she bit down to make them lock
back.

Let's away into the warm. We can do all this in the house
eh?
Duncan clicked his tongue. It meant he was hungry.

I'll do this and youse get on in.
He threw the keys up and bounced them off his shoe into
his hand: a party trick to make them laugh. They all did.
The man moved first, turning on his heel and roping an arm
round his sister.

I get the best bit as usual.
They had the same kind of mouth. Duncan was already
picking things up, grunting to get by his stomach.

That's right enough. Like as two peas. Two peeolas.
Grace's voice fading, red gravel frying under her shoes.

The path was outlined in light from the door, dented net
curtain in the window: he would have been looking out to
see if they were coming. A smell of night-stock got heavier
as she walked. No roses though. Her mother had said there
would be roses. The man went on inside while Grace stayed
behind on the porch, making a performance of wiping her
shoes. They didn't need it but it was manners, it was what
you did. The girl stopped and did the same, looking in past
the door. Black beams lined the hall ceiling till they
disappeared through the wall at the far end. Beams for
heaven's sake. Scrolls on the green hall carpet. And these
horrible school slip-ons. Grace was watching her, that smile
she did when she thought you didn't know she was doing it,
lumpy veins right down to the backs of the flat shoes.
They'd stopped marching now.

Age before beauty eh? That right?
The woman went first.

Felix was in the kitchen, finishing at the gas and sitting the kettle on the bloom of flames. Through the acrid match smell, she caught a thickness of sauce and spice: man smells. Grace didn't seem to notice. She was into a cupboard and rummaging for something without being asked. The girl sat on the corner of cold marble table as the man swirled water from a rubber-nosed tap into a brown teapot then turned to look at her, folding his arms and leaning back against the sink.

Quiet one, aren't you? What are you thinking pet?

With nothing to say, the girl smiled and looked at her feet. The toes were scuffed as well. Grace rattled about with tea stuff, oblivious. It would have been good if she'd said something but then Grace didn't always hear what folk were saying. The man kept staring. Sooner or later he would say something about looking like her father. That was usually what folk said, sometimes with the jings crivvens stuff about her age: Only eleven, they grow up that quick these days and so on. People always said something and it was usually just for something to say. She could feel the stare from here. It would have been good to go over to the window and look out, pretend to be interested but there was nothing to see, just bits of kitchen reflecting on the black. She yawned. The man thought it was funny.

Straight to bed, I should think. You've had a long day.

Eight hours on the road and she's been good as gold. Grace flourished the teapot. She was putting on that cute voice she did, like a cartoon mouse.

Can amuse herself that one, no trouble to anybody. Am I right?

That's what I remember, he said. Never a cheep out of you last time either.

Don't remember, do you? said Grace. She doesn't, eh? She doesn't remember.

The voice was starting to get on her nerves. It was embarrassing and it was also wrong because she did remember. She remembered lying in the big room listening and the door opening, the big shape of a man coming in from the outside to pick her up, the cold off the buttons on his coat. The smell of tobacco. He had carried her, just carried her about till she went back to sleep or something. Another time, somebody that was probably her mother repeating the same words: Say thank-you, say thank-you for the nice present. And she had run away. She couldn't remember what the present was but she remembered him being there all right. Remembering hadn't anything to do with it though. She wasn't really being asked at all.

You don't remember, eh? Dozy? Dozy Dora?

Grace was just showing off. The girl looked back at the floor and Felix laughed.

Right then! I'll take you up. It's all ready: changed sheets, the lot. Waiting since yesterday.

The hand held out to show the way to the hall.

Ladies first.

There was a row of photographs up the stair wall, shiny behind frames. He stopped halfway up, pointing one out; black-and-white going brown. It had twelve-blurry young men in matching outfits and hats, all laughing and waving at the camera. His nail tapped at one of the uniforms in the back row.

Me. RAF Bisley 1944. Good looking eh?

She smiled a bit and peered to please him but it didn't look like anybody, just an arrangement of grey under a hat brim.

Good times with the bad, love.

The top stairs creaked and there was more of the green carpet on the landing. He showed her three doors that were the bedrooms and bathroom, then another piece of staircase past the window where you could hardly see it. He put on a switch, lighting up the door at the top in fits and starts. The bulb was faulty.

And up here, all yours.

His back flashed off and on as they walked.

Upstairs, the room was stuffy with stale sunlight as though the window had been closed a long time. He was already pulling curtains when she went in, hanging the black space with flowers and leaves. There were rosebuds on the quilt, matching stuff. Single bed; they shared the double at home.

This all right, madam? He rubbed dust off the bedside shade. Nobody uses it much these days.

The last word stamped out by feet, thumping up from the landing.

Lovely, she said but he couldn't hear her right. She was shouting it again as Duncan breenged in out of breath, pushing past to drop the case on the mattress. The whole bed shook.

Straight to bed she says. Up the stairs she says.

He mopped his brow, pretending the case was heavy and looked at the other man.

Just this minute here and tired already eh?

They smiled at each other: a tall thin man and a wee fat man sharing her from opposite ends of the rug. They were all looking at the case. It was burst up one side. They kept old sheets in it at home, stuffed at the back of a cupboard.

Well then.

More looks and nods.

Goodnight love.

The words hung on in the space as the door closed; fainter creaking on the stairs, muttering and laughter. The case was still rocking on the bed springs.

Morning showed a wicker chair, dresser, bookcase with no books. Wallpaper with roses. She could see without having to open the curtains. And no need to he dead still for ages; nobody to moan you'd been kicking in your sleep or you'd taken all the blankets. She stretched to use up all the space deliberately. Her mother could be doing the same thing, this same minute. On you go, take her. Do me good to get rid of her for a week. Sometimes she laughed when she said things like that and sometimes not. This time not. Grace said Och Greta then pretended she thought it was a joke. But it didn't matter now. It was good to be here: your own bed, your own room. First thing in the morning, whole holiday to go and England outside. You could do anything you liked.

Up and rummaging through the case, she remembered. There would be problems with the bathroom downstairs. The bathroom downstairs and there being men about the place. She couldn't go down the way she would have at home, straight out of bed in the white knickers and bra. They'd see you. Not just men: Uncle Felix. He used to be in the RAF for heaven's sake, the photo they had of him in the chocolate box where he looked like Clark Gable with the wee moustache and Brylcreem. They had lots of that photo: her mother liked it. The Best of a Bad Shower. Not like the other four he'd come off with their po-faces and dirty nails. Not like Your Bloody Father. Fancy manners and the English accent, even his name something different. You didn't walk around in front of a man like that in day-old underwear, things you had slept in. Dressing gowns made sense after all. Proper people had dressing gowns. There wasn't anything like one either. It would have to be the fresh tee-shirt and yesterday's jeans. And being quick. She'd have to be quick.

Grace was there at the foot of the landing, looking pink.

There you are. Your Uncle Felix isn't in there. She meant the bathroom.

On you go and hurry up, then we can go down together. I'll wait.

She stood right outside, shouting at the door. It got fainter when the girl turned on the tap, like a chicken up a tunnel: harmless but not quite human. But it didn't go away. Her own name too many times: Senga. Senga, Senga, Senga. She ran the tap harder and sank her face into the water.

The smell of fish and coffee came halfway up the stairs. The kitchen was misty with it. Felix stood with his back to the sink, eating the substance of the fish smell from a blue plate.

Well, Grace said, rolling her eyes. Well.

There were four poached eggs in a soup plate in the middle of the table beside a box of unidentifiable cereal, toast, butter and different jars. Grace stood for a minute looking. They were being spoilt she said. She couldn't think, just could not and she'd never recover from the spoiling. There wasn't anything to serve with so she had to get up again as soon as she sat down. There weren't any bowls either. The girl took toast. Felix smiled through hairy bones, dislodging something from between his back teeth.

How about town this morning? Plans in the offing?

Grace served herself an egg. He stretched and walked across to the girl's chair.

Shops, miniature village maybe.

The chair dipped as he leaned his weight against it, rumbling the last word along the spars into her back. There was a faint tang of fish from his breath.

I'm going that way anyway. Take you in if you like.

You'll like that.

Grace chewed a piece of crust, drizzling milk into the girl's tea.

Likes history you know. History and all that kind of thing. Good at the school.

Black bits on the sides of her mouth and her teeth were silted.

No need to rush: take your time, ladies, take your time. We've all day. All week if we want. The chair creaked as he released his grip and walked to the window. All week.

He lit a cigarette with the match inside his hand, first draw.

Trying not to walk on the cracks. The wee boy tottered, his hand reaching for the steeple. He deliberately didn't grab at the last minute and fell, the hand thumping into the cemetery wall before his mother came and picked him up, howling. They stood back from the model church to let them past, the boy with blood on his knees, to the toilet on the other side of the entrance queue. Grace had got a fright but at least he hadn't knocked anything over.

Need to be more careful. Specially when it's busy. It was worse than busy but they stuck to the path with the other tourists, squeezing by the edges of the miniature houses to see the details. It was what they'd come to do. Window displays in the tiny shops, real flowers in the park and the graveyard. It was probably better than the real thing because they'd missed out the public toilets and the housing scheme, things like that. Grace said you had to admit it was nice. She admitted it herself umpteen times. If you looked closely though you could see staples holding the thatch onto the real thatched cottage but it didn't seem right to say. You probably weren't meant to look that close and it would just be twisted. It would put Grace in the huff as well. Anyway, it *was* nice. Nice enough. Felix hadn't come: just let them

out at the corner then drove off somewhere else, leaving the
two of them on their own. There was no real reason to be
annoyed by it. She was probably just too hot. They did
another lap then bought tea and hot dogs from a van just
inside the park gate. Grace paid, handing over the paper
cup and screwing her eyes up because of the sun. They were
having a good time to themselves, just the two of them.
Maybe they'd try the shops next. All the bins at the exit
were full. They left their cups rolling at the side of the wire
mesh, dribbling the dregs of tea.

Postcards were easy: nearly everywhere sold them. Other
things took longer. There wasn't a supermarket: four
antique shops, a cheese shop and an Edinburgh Woollen
Mill but no supermarket. They only needed messages for
the week. A couple of streets away, they found stalls and
single shops that would do. A butcher in a daft straw hat
wasn't pleased about the Scots fiver and snapped it open
towards the light, peering while Grace said she was sorry.
He took it eventually when she said there wasn't anything
else and said how bonnie he thought the wee Scots lassies
were to show there were no hard feelings. They didn't buy
anything else till they went to the bank. They walked back
and found a note behind the taps to say Duncan and Felix
wouldn't be back till teatime.

Well that's fine, she said. Gets them out the road. We'll
can do what we like as well then.
She lifted a lump wrapped in tracing paper. It started
changing colour while she held it up in her hand. They'd
have a cup of something and a rest. A rest more than
anything else. A nice rest. Then she saw the blood oozing
down her arm in a twisted line and shouted. The meat was
dripping on the lino as well. Senga went upstairs without
waiting for the tea.

The attic was quiet, curtains were still closed from the
morning, the bed still unmade. She'd forgotten about that.
She didn't make beds often; even when she made the effort
they weren't done right anyway. The case was open at the
side, things jumbled on the top. They would crease. Only
here a day and all this to tidy up. Not yet though, not now.
Maybe Grace was right: a wee rest would be good. She was
maybe still tired from yesterday; travelling made you tired.
Grace would probably go for a lie down as well. She sat on
the edge of the fankled sheets and tilted back onto the
pillows. Then she saw the photograph: a plain frame behind
the lamp on the bedside, obvious enough though she hadn't
seen it last night. It was the one of her waiting in front of a
brick wall in a white net dirndl skirt, staring up at the sun
under that daft hat. A handbag as well. Sunday School Trip.
When you looked hard something about the eyes was the
same but not much. It wasn't really her at all, just a six-
year-old wean waiting for a bus. There was something
written along the bottom. *Senga, Jock's girl, Saltcoats.* Neat
handwriting like a woman's. There was another photo as
well, flat and dusty on the bottom of the cabinet shelf: pale
cream and brown profile of her father now she brought it
out to see. He never smiled in photos. Dour, her mother
said. Twisted. It was the same mouth that Grace had,
Felix as well. She looked back at the picture of herself. She
wasn't smiling either. Both pictures slotted back into the
same dust marks before she pulled the covers over her head
for shade.

A face inflated over the rim of sheets when she opened her
eyes. It was Duncan, smirking. Everybody was wondering
where she had got to, he said, eyes huge behind the specs.

A terrible lassie. Always tired. Ha ha. He ran his hand over the top of her head and said to be quick.

The tea wasn't ready at all. There was just a clutter of cutlery on the table and place mats. Offering to set places would never have occurred: they ate off their knees at home, in front of the TV. But there was this table here, a bit of the house for eating and nothing else in the corner of the living room. The men were watching TV somewhere else. She could hear the news reading itself as she struggled with lefts and rights, forks and spoons. It was good: the men at their business while she set the table. It was what you did, what proper people did off the leash of know-nothing, couthy Ayrshire and a house with no men. That thing with the salt and pepper shakers would be a mustard pot, a spoon sticking out the side. Like yellow oil paint. Even the smell.

Cooee.

Grace's face poked through a hole in the wall. Then her hands pushing out plates and disappearing again when the girl took them, back to the noise of pots. The men appeared, knowing without being told and started pulling out chairs, talking loud about football then Grace came through with the other plates, smaller ones. Senga gave her two to the men. Duncan said he was starving. He always said it. Felix cleared his throat.

Ladies and Gentleman, tonight we do things in style.

He brought a bottle out from under the table. Grace squawked and clapped.

Only one though – don't want to overdo it.

The glasses were out along the bureau. Grace and Duncan exchanged a look as he poured four and Senga tried to look as though she knew she was being spoiled and appreciated it. They held the glasses out into the middle of the table when Felix did it.

Blood ties, he said. To us.

They clinked raggedly, all smiles. It tasted like thick metal in the mouth, the smell of warm pennies. Grace said Well! and pretended to be dizzy as he poured her some more. She was in a better mood and everything was going to be fine. At the other side of the table, Duncan sunk his knife into the chicken breast and asked for salt.

White.

The curtains split in one tug to leave her standing like a crucifix inside the drench of light. Just brightness at first. Then isolated islands of green as she uncreased her eyes, joining to a lawn and two rows of trees, eight or so, close enough for their branches to meet over the channel of grass. An elbow of branch was leaning on the sill outside, spreading leaves against the window. And something else now she looked, flat, purple smears like lipstick mouths. She moved her hand to see better. Plums. Attached to the ends of thin sticks where they were growing. Living things. There were more in the garden, dark shapes among the green when you looked. Beyond that, the high fencing where the wall of sky attached and went straight up without stopping. A string of pale butterflies knotted to the fencing with green thread. Sweetpeas. There were no hills behind the tops of the trees and no sea in the distance. Second day here and this was the first she'd seen the view. First she'd opened the curtains, that's why. Lazy bitch. Imagining her mother saying it made her laugh out loud. Plums right outside for heaven's sake. She rapped the glass with her knuckles and watched them shiver.

Downstairs, Grace was at the sink, pasty in a print dress and open sandals, bare toes poking out.

Hello, stranger.

She went on rinsing cups and didn't turn round. The coffee smell meant that Felix had been and gone: it wouldn't have been made for anybody else. Grace stood to one side to let her by with the kettle.

You could make some for Uncle Duncan, she said. He's out with the motor.

She had on her headache face, rinsing the same cup for ages.

Never done with his motor.

The girl put tea straight into the mugs. Never mind about the bits. Safer than rooting about near the sink for the pot. It would also be good to get out. You couldn't ask what was the matter because she'd make out it was nothing and maybe take the huff because you'd suggested it. Worse, she would make out she hadn't taken the huff either. At least the milk and stuff was out on the table so there was no need to ask for anything and risk it. The teaspoon as well. Duncan took six sugars. She managed to stir them in silently. The spoon didn't even whisper.

Aye aye.

Duncan levered slowly out from under the bonnet, sighing. Cheers, he said. The mug had a grease stripe already: his hands were black. For a moment she wondered if she should ask if Grace was all right then knew she wouldn't. He likely wouldn't say either. Some things he just blanked out. Like the time they hit a dog coming back along the Dairy road at night in the car. He got out a minute, came back in, turned the ignition and just kept driving with his eyes set on the road. She'd been just about hysterical but knew not to speak. The one time she got near it, he started whistling. He drove her straight home and said what a nice run they'd had. A nice run. Neither of them had ever mentioned it again. He looked at her over the the white rim, closing his throat.

How's the girl the day then?
Fine, she said.
Questions like that weren't really questions at all. It was embarrassing. Neither said anything for a while. Duncan took another mouthful of tea.
Nice place eh? Front green and everything.
I saw the garden out the back this morning, she said. Sweetpeas. You can see them from the window.
You know who was the sweetpea man? Your dad liked the sweetpeas. He was the boy for the flowers all right. Green fingers.
He blinked and shook his head.
Sweetpeas and roses: that was your daddy. That was Jock all right.

There were no flowers at home, unless you counted the poppies that came up between the potatoes. They had potatoes and rhubarb, occasionally cabbage. Things you could eat. Duncan rifted and sighed.
Your Aunty June's garden that one.
He was wanting to tell a story.
Never met June, sure you didn't.
The story was ok. There was a long bit about the RAF and planting things, getting the garden nice for Felix retiring. Then when it happened it wasn't like anybody expected. He was out of the RAF only four weeks. June was pruning currant bushes and got tired, went for a lie down. Duncan looked into the bottom of the mug, tapped his nail on the rim. The Scottish side weren't asked to the funeral, of course. Too far away and too little notice. Still you'd have liked to have been asked. She waited for a moment then realised it was finished and didn't know what to say. It was

like when he sang those terrible songs about Lonesome
Cowboys or Old Shep; he liked you to look sad when he
sang them. Grace did it as well. The worst was the time they
went to the sad film about three animals that got lost and
Grace kept greeting and Senga had had to hold it in, eyes all
filling up but the sound of Grace greeting like that made it
impossible. Then on the road home, they'd asked if she
hadn't liked the film, just because she hadn't been greeting
as well. As though she was faulty or something. It just froze
her up so she never knew what she really felt about things
at all. This story about the garden wasn't even all that sad.
Felix didn't look the gardening type, thin fingers like a
doctor. If you really thought about it, you could see how the
garden would quite annoy him, having to be looked after
when it wasn't his really. Thinking about it that way made
it easier. Duncan was still waiting with the empty cup.

I'll take these in, she said. Maybe I'll go and see.
Duncan smiled. He probably thought she wanted to go and
moon about on her own now, thinking about the daft story.
It was impossible to shake him off.

That's the girl.
She felt him watch her all the way up the path, grinning
before he stuffed himself back into the waiting gullet of the
car.

The trees had looked small from the window. Underneath,
even the lowest bits made you reach, leaves bunched
together where the fruit was thickest: green, red, purple and
black-colour all on the same branch. Loads of things. It
made her dizzy leaning back to look up but she didn't want
to lean against the tree itself. There was no telling what was
living in it, under the bark. She staggered backwards as her
foot slipped on something soft, more of them on the ground
between the bits of fallen bark.

Windfalls: that thick sweet smell like metal. It was fermenting. That was what happened to rotten fruit. It lay and rotted and the sugars came out and something else, she forgot what. Wanting to look closer, she dropped to her hunkers and reached for the nearest. Dark red, the skin loose and warm. It slipped when you touched, the flesh separate and firmer underneath. Her finger left a dark shape of itself where it melted off the bloom. She opened her hand and picked up the whole fruit; thumb and first fingertip, end to end, lifting it nearer. Then it became something else. Grey blue fungus furred one side of a gash underneath, a running sore oozing brown pulp and something else. Something moving. Thin black feelers twitching towards her hand. Dropping it was immediate. Even then it wasn't far enough away and she drew back from under the shade of the trees, staring, wiping her hands against the jean seams to get rid of the feel from her fingers. Black movements flickered at the corners of her eyes, everywhere now she looked. Ants. It was just ants. Ants couldn't do you any harm. The grass kept moving, wriggling under her feet. Shivering, she went inside for a cardigan.

Lunch.
At home you call it dinnertime but it is really lunch.
Cold meat and pickles, halved tomatoes, bread and butter for three. Felix was still out. Grace took a notion to sit out afterwards but nobody else wanted to. Senga watched from the window as she appeared outside alone with a candy-stripe chair and a magazine. The magazine flapped too much when she tried to read it so she had to give up and just sit, staring into space. From inside, the windowframe made a border, like a painting. Whistler's mother. It waved at the girl looking out, pretending to be comfortable.

The girl spread her cards on the tablecover. Three. You had to send postcards but they were always difficult, especially when you hadn't done anything. The things on the fronts of the cards didn't help either: pictures of the model village about twenty years out of date. The wee boys in the background were wearing shorts and school caps. School caps for heaven's sake. Another one had no people: just the models pretending to be the real thing but you could tell if you looked hard: the smoothness of the road gave it away. She flipped one over.

Dear Mum, the house is lovely and the weather is nice and warm. This is the model village, we went there yesterday and it is lovely. We had our dinner out in the garden. We are having a great time. Don't miss me too much haha. Uncle Felix is asking for you.

Grace seemed to have fallen asleep. The girl watched the bird-flap of the fallen magazine, sun through the window falling hot on her neck. Twice, the slide of her elbows jerked her awake.

The third time it was the clink of bottles.

Then two voices. A man and a woman. The garden chair was empty. It was Grace in the kitchen speaking to someone. Felix. It wasn't possible to hear the words properly but you could tell who it was all right. She pushed her feet against a table spar and stretched, listening. There weren't any men at home. Duncan didn't count. It was good to listen just to the depth of it, the low echo coming through the wall, rocking on two legs of the chair with her eyes closed. It could only have been moments. Then a snap that meant someone had gotten off one of the kitchen chairs. Before the girl had time to open her eyes, Grace's voice

came again, clear as though she had spoken in the same
room.

She's bound to be funny, a bit withdrawn. You know
what I mean. Not like a normal lassie.

There was a sound that could have been a cupboard
opening.

I wouldny say anything against Greta but she's still thon
bitter way. She says things, twisted things. Have the wean
twisted as well before she's finished.

The voice dipped further.

See it already.

Her footing slid on the table rung as the chair tipped
foursquare on the carpet. They could have heard it. The girl
looked round to the kitchen door. They would think she
was here on purpose, listening deliberately to people who
thought they were private. It was too late just to appear
round the door and say: they would wonder why she had
been waiting so long before coming through. It would look
worse. But they were bound to come through eventually
and it wouldn't be good to be here, in this place. Silently,
she gathered up the cards and slid the chair under the table
where it belonged. The carpet shuffled again when she
moved, when she tried to inch the door back. It was nearly
wide enough.

There you are.

Felix watched her from the kitchen hatch.

What are you being so quiet about then eh? He was
smiling and trying not to, amused by her. Her mouth stayed
shut.

Anyway, just the girl I'm looking for. Duncan says you're
asking about the garden, about the trees and things. The girl
couldn't remember. Her neck was hot.

I went for a look. Just a wee look at them. Just to see.

Maybe she had done something wrong and should apologise. Maybe he didn't like her going into the garden. June's garden. Maybe because she hadn't asked first.

It's lovely, she said. The flowers and everything.

Sometimes compliments made things better. He was scratching behind his ear, not really listening.

Said he thought you wanted to pick some fruit or something, yes?

She couldn't remember saying anything like that. Not out loud and not to Duncan because he repeated things you'd said. He anticipated: interceded without being asked. And he got things all wrong. It would be Duncan right enough then: something she'd said and he'd mixed it up as usual. Her own fault for saying anything in the first place. She nodded to accept her part of the blame. He wasn't even looking.

Why not eh? Doing me a favour, pet, tidying the place up a bit. I'm afraid it doesn't get the attention these days. Be my guest. Unless –

He shrugged. She was trying not to think about ants and adjusted her face to look happier. It wasn't a row after all.

No, I'd like to. I would. I can even go now if you like. I can get them for teatime, put them on the table mibby. I would like to.

It came out too quick and stuttery but he looked pleased.

Whatever you like, sweetheart. Yes. Now if you want.

He squeezed her backside as she went through to the kitchen, then shouted after as she sprinted out over the grass.

Watch out for the wasps.

The thin face in one oblong of the window lattice. She kept her back to it and tilted up, ignoring the movement in the leaves, reaching with her eyes tight shut.

Duncan said they gave him heartburn and the skins got
beneath his plate. But they looked nice. Everybody said they
looked nice, washed and buffed in a glass dish on the table.
They all ate spongecake instead.

Always tell home-made.

Grace had icing sugar on her chin.

Get a nice one at the WI on a Tuesday. Felix sucked his
fingertips and picked up crumbs. Answer to a bachelor's
prayer.

Duncan didn't say anything, just rifted. He always did it at
the end of a meal when there was nothing else to come.
Grace usually said You're welcome I'm sure but didn't
tonight. It was because she hadn't made the cake. They left
the plums and went to the sofa, then Felix brought out a
bottle of whisky.

Bugger the washing up, he said.

They all laughed and he said it again.

Bugger it. Let's be wicked for once.

After a while he put a record on as well. They can't take that
away from me. Frank Sinatra. They sang bits of the lines
and all joined in on the last one. Duncan poured more drink
and put on Harry Belafonte. They weren't really listening
any more anyway. Grace was doing the story about the time
they got chased by somebody when they were teenagers and
other stuff would follow that, things about before Senga
was born. They were all meant to be funny. Grace hooted
at her back while the girl watched the needle, the seasick
bounce over and over because the record was finished. They
said nothing about her father. Maybe there weren't any
funny stories about him. The turntable started buzzing. A
chink of glasses.

Someone carried her to bed.

Shot.

A crack and patter of applause. A man in white glared as he followed the line, shadows chasing the soles of canvas shoes. Slingbacks weren't allowed on the grass.

Heavy.

Groans and hands up to chins. No cloud overhead. The square of crewcut green was open to the sky. Borders behind the three benches had rose bushes pruned back to stumps, acid fists that would be dahlias in a couple of weeks but were nothing yet. A few everlasting daisies stared dry-eyed up at the sun. The other two benches were empty.

Wide.

The girl stretched, pulled at the neck of her shirt as Grace came back near the trench, kicking the bowls with the sides of her shoe.

Aunty Grace.

Aunty. Wee girl voice.

Can I go for a walk. A wee walk. Just the shops. Grace's eyes were blanked out with the light on her specs.

Just a look at the shops.

Grace kept looking, her mouth slack. The girl pursed her lips. It was hard not to get fed-up with it, knowing what was most likely coming anyway: all the daft questions before you got to do anything on your own. No you wouldn't get lost and yes you knew what the address was, you knew where the bus stop was and to ask if you got lost, etc. As if you were going to get lost on purpose. It would have been quicker at home. But Grace wasn't her mother. She was just being careful in case she got landed with the blame for not looking after you right. Her toes were sore, crushed into the pointy tips of these shoes. She couldn't think why she'd worn them.

Someone shouted: it was nearly Grace's turn. She came up to the side of the ditch, raking in the big cardigan pockets, the end of her tongue poking between the teeth. She found what she was looking for and reached, unsmiling, to push it into the girl's hand.

Back for your tea, mind. Don't get lost.

A key and money: a pound note wrapped round loose change. She was halfway up the green when the girl looked up, past where Felix was stooping, peering under his hat for the jack. Duncan waved.

Boots the chemist: blue and white, reliably the same. It flipped the street into something more familiar through the arcade of antiques and gothic lettering. Antiques for heaven's sake, six in the one stretch of road. She bought nail-varnish. Sugar Plum: private joke. Then a cup of coffee in the tearoom with Grace's money. Outside, there wasn't much else worth seeing. It was when she crossed the road to check times from the bus stop she saw the sign to the museum. It pointed behind the place they'd bought the postcards the other day, in a square of ground with what looked like gravestones outside. There was no one on the door and inside, just a big room like a drill hall ranged with cases, a sentence dying into echo as two people at the far end turned to look. She walked to the first cases, as they turned away, keeping her shoes quiet on the wooden floorboards. Bits of flint tricking the light as fossil remains, old coins and nails. The open display of farming things was better: thatching tools and a cider press with a carved wooden bore like a giant thumbscrew. At least they looked local. Threshing things, flails, rakes with rows of blunt teeth, a scythe. At the far end of the hall, stocks, manacles and a round cage affair hung on the wall. A scold's bridle. The metal hoop had bands of rusty iron on either side and a hinged piece that forced a flat iron spike inside the mouth when it closed. Some had points to prevent the mouth from closing, others, leather tongues to soak up saliva. For wives who scolded or told lies. The card used exclamation marks

to show it was a kind of joke. War memorabilia took up all
the rest: child's gas-mask, a ration book with unused
coupons, a parish register with brown writing, pinned like
butterflies on green baize. The last was a free-standing
glass box under the exit sign, with an old shop dummy
in RAF blue and some other bits and pieces.
HEMMINGFORD UNDER FIRE. The uniform was too
big so the dummy's limbs looked wasted, the painted hair
and the eyes had peeled down to the plaster. Sellotaped at
eye-level, a smeary photograph of a man in an open field.
He was holding a chunk of metal and smiling fit to bust.
ENEMY AIRCRAFT SHOT DOWN OVER LOCAL
FIELD 1944.

It was over the man's shoulder now she looked again, like a
dinosaur carcass. The fuzziness in the distance could have
been smoke. The chunk of metal in his hands was identifiable at the bottom of the case. It looked blacker in the
photo but then they'd have polished it. The bits were still
stained when you looked hard, blotched with yellow and
brown where they sat on that shiny cloth. If she tilted her
head she could see a card between folds. Parachute silk,
unused. Her eyes flicked back to the photo. Cows near the
back of the field and a washing line in the distance, trees
and smoke: the burned-out shell dripping wreckage like
rotten meat. In the spaces between, unimaginable things.
The card at the dummy's feet said the parachute had never
been used. Inside the sellotape rim, the farmer grinning out
at the camera like he was on his holidays. He had terrible
teeth.

Someone coughed. A man near the fire extinguisher, clinking keys. The couple had left already. Closing time was five-
thirty. It would be after that now. The girl uncurled her
hand from the coins in her pocket, the palm scored and

smelling of stale metal. She didn't even know what the fare was, when the buses came. After promising as well. After promising.

Grace was setting the table herself when she got back, breathless to show she'd been running. There was no row. Grace was in a good mood, singing when she brought through the plates. Tongue salad. Nobody else said anything about being late either. In the end, it turned out she wasn't: they were having tea earlier because they were going out, just the pub at the other side of the village with some people Felix knew.

You wouldny be wanting to come really eh?
Grace spoke through the last mouthful of something. Half a scone sat among the chip smears and leftover salt on her plate.

Would you eh? You could come but it's a pub. You don't like that kind of thing eh? All old folk as well.

Oldies right enough.
Duncan tapped the heel of his knife on the table, eyes on the butter.

It's an old folks' outing haha.

You can come if you want, love. Felix lifted his cup. Let her come if she wants.

It's no interesting for a lassie her age though. Bowling club talk. It's no interesting is it? You wouldny find it interesting. Do you think you would? Sure you wouldny? It was the cartoon voice again. The girl shook her head, watching with her hand over her mouth.

See?
Felix kept his face straight. He looked like the photo of her father. Senga shook her head.

Honest. I'm not bothered.

Grace was pleased, pouring tea the girl didn't want, adding milk and sugar without asking.

Likes to read, she said. Probably quite pleased we're away, eh?

They gave her Dairy Box in a cellophane wrapper and a reminder she could come if she liked. The car dipped out of the drive with hands in every visible window, waving as though they were away for years.

The talking head on TV was still reading news, Duncan's programme. She tried all the buttons then switched it off. The records were no use and there wasn't even anything worth reading: a pile of ancient *Readers' Digests* full of American things and jokes that weren't funny, drawings that didn't look like real people's insides. Half the time they did them blue or green for heaven's sake. She stacked them back into the bookcase in the right order, the newest looking one on top. A jigsaw or something would have been good but she didn't know if he had one, where he'd keep such a thing if he did. It was still someone else's house, someone else's things. Different rules about what was what, being feart to do things in case they got on somebody's nerves. Without him here it was just the same. There was dust all over her fingers. Nobody could have touched those magazines for years. The photos on the walls were all ancient, all men and aeroplanes. There was nothing to do down here. She looked up at the ceiling then walked out into the hall. It was getting dark already. Those coats behind the door like hunched shoulders over big wooden pegs. It got to that in-between time of night quicker here, when it was too dark with the light not on but that horrible yellow colour when it was. She put the light on anyway, showing up the stouriness of everything, ridges of it along the banister rim. It was even darker upstairs. Looking at it made her stomach feel cold. But all you had to do was refuse to look scared then nothing could touch you. And there was the switch down here as well. Stupid. Her neck prickled as she reached and put on the second switch, watching the light bleed out over the steps. Being feart like this was stupid.

A glow of streetlights filled the landing window when she got to the top, somebody whistling outside. Knowing there were people outside was a good thing, even if you couldn't see who. The nearest bedroom door was off the catch, a pair of Duncan's green socks just inside on the floor. They made this whole end of the landing smell salty. The door opposite was shut. Properly shut. It wasn't near enough the window to see much from here: a reflected row of other bedroom windows, curtains and lampshades. The whistling was fainter. The shut door seemed closer.

Hardly had to touch the handle at all.

A dark smell like ham spice curled out, thickening the air like dust. Uncle Felix' room. It would be beneath her own, the square of visible window showing the same leaves. Their shadows twitched along the facing wall to make patterns on the dresser. Even in this half-light, you could see the top had just a hairbrush and a comb, a few china figurines. None of the clutter of bottles and lotions that covered everything at home: female things. The dresser mirror filled completely with red candlewick reflection from the double bed and there was a backwards photo over the headboard. She cut free from the door one finger at a time and stepped beyond the threshold, slowly in case the boards creaked. It was a wedding photo, the woman in a wedding dress, yards of net from the head-dress drifting across the man's dark suit, the lipstick black inside the white face. There were more people behind them. The extra step nearer to see was too close, dunting heavily into the bedside table. The lamp rocked but stayed upright. She'd have to be more careful, reaching to straighten the shade, smooth over the cloth on the surface. It had two cigarette burns along one edge. Then beneath, inside the shelf, she saw the magazine. Huge breasts and painted nails on the cover. She held her breath, staring, then reached and picked it up. The pages were thick and dry, wavy as though it had been dropped in the bath. The woman came closer, pushing her own breasts together with those long-fingered hands. The next page was much the same, this time with the woman looking right at you, that terrible old-fashioned make-up round her eyes. Just staring, sticking out her tongue. The girl swallowed and lifted another page. This time the paper tugged back, just once before it gave, unpeeling with a light rip. The girl's stomach dipped as she opened it out to see. Tear marks: two women's faces seamed with white where the paper had separated. She shut the magazine then opened and shut it again. She turned the right page to the top before she put it back in place and walked backwards out of the room, closing the door quietly, listening. There was nothing to hear except the buzz of the overhead bulb; her own heartbeat as she stood at the top of the stairs, holding her breath. That prickling feeling along the back of the neck that let you know you were being watched. Sweating now, the girl turned, clutching and unclutching her palms. A sheen of eyeless smiles, the watchers looked back. Just photographs, barrack-boy grins from the frames on the landing, their thread of soundless laughter spinning a web into the thick air, the space between herself and the way down. She shut her eyes and kept walking.

The garden was just blackness falling from a ragged line of royal blue, a super-imposed ghost of herself floating in the way. There was no telling how much longer it would be. But she wouldn't go up to bed. Not till they were back. Her stomach flexed as she poured cold tea down the sink and made a fresh cup, wandered back along the hall carrying it close to her chest. No more noises. That creaking upstairs was just beams, wood settling. That was what wood did, it settled. Creaked and groaned in the joists. She fumbled a hand round the corner into the living room to switch on the light, then walked across to the window. Nothing. The TV was still terrible. It would be good to be able to stop thinking about the magazine, about going into the upstairs room. But it wasn't possible to forget. Not possible. Not possible to say to anyone either because. Just because. She didn't want this tea either.

Halfway to the kitchen she stopped and looked to the top of the stairs again, listening, in case. The door opened too suddenly then, thudding hard against the inside wall as Felix stumbled in over the step then the cup was falling from her hands, spattering tea and broken china as Grace appeared too, stopping talking in mid-flow. The beer haze thickened as they stood, looking at her clueless in the middle of what she'd done. Outside, 'Clementine' whistled on oblivious through the shutting of car doors. Felix moved first.

Oops.

The voice was too loud.

Oops. That was silly.

It slurred. Grace was away to the kitchen for a cloth already as he came forward, touching the girl's shoulder. She couldn't look up, couldn't lift her eyes from the mess seeping through the carpet pile and turning it black. Duncan's voice saying What's up? at the door and Felix asking if she was all right, nudging the shoulder under his hand.

You're shaking, pet. It's all right. No harm done.

She could scent drink, the slurriness in the voice. He turned away and spoke at Duncan's face as Grace pushed through, scrubbing with the cloth at the wet carpet.

No need to be upset eh, he said.

Grace snorted, still scouring, then cut her finger on a chip of cup handle and said Bugger it. Bugger it. Grace hardly ever swore. Yet the girl's mouth wouldn't open, that knot in her throat like sickness rising till it hurt while Felix watched. Duncan kidding on he was invisible at the door. This fuss over nothing. Grace sucked her finger.

Silly lassie.

Struggling not to be angry. It was worse than shouting. It was terrible, so embarrassing you wanted to faint just to escape from it, you wanted to die. The girl's throat constricted sharply. Bad to worse, that horrible greeting noise in the middle of no noise at all and she was making it, not able to stop. A sigh. Grace would be shaking her head.

What's the matter now eh? You tell me.

She's all right. Shhh. Just leave it be. Leave it just now. They were supposed to be whispering. The dishcloth shifted in Grace's hands. She was angry.

Shh. You're all right, love. Aren't you? All right, eh? No harm done. That big hand wrapping her shoulder again.

I'll take her up maybe. Just tired. Tired eh? She's all right now though. She's all right.

It felt terrible smiling, knowing her face would be swollen but it was what he wanted her to do. He waited till she'd done it. Even remembering about the magazine, she creased her swollen lids and smiled.

Grace was already at the sink, polishing knives.

You're early, she said.

Nothing else. She went on dropping things into the drawer. The table was already set. The girl crossed to the window and looked out to avoid conversation. The noise of cutlery stopped, exchanged itself for the rustle of bread. Paint runs over the lip of the sill came into focus, sharp white against the haze of leaves and sky outside as Grace started singing, rattling the grill. She was being polite on purpose but that didn't mean she didn't remember. The smell of fat and burning crumbs. The idea of food made her feel sick. She wasn't wanting any breakfast. Wasn't wanting to be here, the kitchen too full of smoke and not talking, the feeling you weren't able to get away. Outside in the garden would do, up at that fence and looking out over the road, watching the cars going past. No hills, no sea; but at least the cars going somewhere. If she could just open her mouth, open it and ask. She sighed instead, hearing Duncan's shuffling along the hall in his socks.

Aye aye.

Grace pouring water for tea and the creak of floorboards. There was no point in being at the window any more. It was misted over with steam.

Aye aye.

He had on those green socks, the ones off the bedroom floor the other night. Her back straightened as she inhaled, mouth searching for a smile. Duncan came across with the pot, a handful of spoons, grinning. She watched her hands, turning cups upright in their saucers, without focusing her eyes. That way, she managed when Felix came through. She managed all the way through breakfast.

Don't run away and hide. Little piece of information.
He called her back as she left the table. He was waving a cigarette when she turned, digging the fingers of his other hand into the matchbox.

Outing. Leave about twelve or say. Time to put on a frock if you like eh? And a smile.

He looked up as the match sparked.

Pretty girl when you smile.

The glass was too full, spilling when she walked. It got worse when you concentrated, the sides getting slippy so it was getting hard to hold, the plate in the other hand not able to be put down. And so many people. The 'Fox and Grapes' was full of horse brasses and pictures of dogs, little lamps with leatherette shades. The tables were packed close and too wee, but they crammed tight, a circle of the glasses in the middle and the plates on their knees. Pork pies and cider: Felix said they had to. They just started when two other men came and Felix rolled his eyes. His mouth was full of pie. He swallowed and said everybody's names. The men said Ock Eye the Noo and Hoots Mon then pretended they thought Senga and Grace were sisters before they went away again, kissing hands. Duncan thought they were well on. Every so often, they waved.

The pie was fatty. Senga left most of it and ate the bits of salad while the place got noisier. Felix winked at her drinking the cider and they went back in a good mood, the two men still in there at the bar, shouting Cheerio. But it was hot on the walk home and the headache the girl had been trying to ignore in the pub got worse. By the time they got back it was making her eyes hurt. When she asked to lie down, Duncan laughed. He said it was the cider. It might have been true: the stairs were making her feel worse. She ignored the clothes over the floor, the bed left unmade from the hurry this morning and crossed to the window, pressing her forehead at the cool, flat glass. It was

good momentarily but heated up too fast and left marks
when she pulled away. Outside, wet leaves splayed flat
between drips of condensation. Fresh. They made you
want to reach out, reach your whole self in amongst them
with your eyes shut, touching till your clothes stuck to the
skin. The idea of cool leaves on your eyelids, the soreness
inside the head. Closing her eyes made her dizzy and she
opened them again. At least she could open the window. It
looked as if it hadn't been opened for years, paint along the
inside of the catch. It was stiff even when she pushed with
both hands. On the next push it gave, cracking as the frame
breathed out. It didn't open far because the hinge was
painted too, but already bits of twig poked into the space
she made, widening the air inside the room with nervous
momentum, the smell of green. It opened out inside your
lungs when you breathed. She flexed her fingers and slid
her arm outside. Touching one leaf made the rest dip,
balancing drops of water, drumming when they fell. Lower
down, the plums made soft thuds against the glass. She
could reach from here, if she stretched, stood on her toes.
It was easier if she turned her head to the side, then she
could feel them just within and out of reach, tipping the
backs of her fingernails. She relaxed her shoulder then held
her breath to stretch again, pressing her side against the
window. Something touched back this time: a sizzle on the
skin that made her draw back suddenly, scattering water as
far as the quilt.

It didn't hurt immediately.
The incision, though certainly felt, was not pain. More like
burning: the root of her index and middle fingers with
these tiny pinholes when she looked. Stings. That was what
it had to be though she had never been stung before. It was
different to what you thought: not sore to start with. But
hoping it would go away wasn't going to work. She could

feel it already as she tried to close the window again, pushing out stray ends of tree. When she looked again it was swollen, filling out with heat. It even looked different, curled like a claw on the end of her wrist. Her own fault: she shouldn't have been opening the window in the first place and now she'd have to go down and tell them, make another fuss after last night. But she'd have to: this searing getting worse. As long as there wasn't any more of that crying, not this time. The important thing was not to cry.

White as a sheet, love.
She wished it hadn't been Felix but it was. Felix who was there at the foot of the stairs, who took her along the hall to a cupboard under the stairs smelling of must and turps, reached under the sink for a plain bottle, then slackened the top with one hand with the other tightening on the wrist as though he were trying to cut through to the bone. It hurt. Everything had hurt, like when he pushed her hand into the brown puddle at the bottom of the sink and held it there but she hadn't given anything away. His grip slackened as the throbbing died down. Now it was almost soothing, just a pulse under the skin. There was sweat through the smell of vinegar and she noticed how close they were.

White as a sheet.
The sink made a noise as it drained. The man stood back, reaching for a crumpled tube on the surround.

Nasty. How'd you manage that one?

Looking out the window, she said. They must have been on the ledge, something like that.
The words were shaky and not easy to control. She knew she was going to lie.

It was when I was tidying, putting things away.
She didn't know why she was saying these things. Her

mother said she couldn't tell the truth about anything, never admitted to anything.

I just didn't see them.

The stink of vinegar and the heat in the tight space was making her dizzy. He patted her hair and drew her nearer his chest, tipping her forehead with his lips.

There, pet. Too easily upset, you know. It doesn't matter.

She was blushing now, knowing he was thinking about last night. Her stomach dipped. Maybe he had found the magazine.

Spilt milk and all that. Life isn't as serious as you think. His heartbeat, the ridge of his vest under her cheek, the smell of hothouse. Nothing else. She pulled away and smiled because it was what he wanted. That way he might leave her alone.

That's my girl, that's more like it.

She nodded to let him know that's just what she was. Just his girl.

They sat her outside all afternoon, dosing her with cups of sickly tea and Grace's magazines. Felix was drying dishes when she came back in. He heard her coming and wiped his hands. They'd eaten, he said: thought she'd fallen asleep and hadn't wanted to wake her up after all that excitement. There were sandwiches left on the table, covered; a slice of cake. Duncan and Grace were out. The girl pushed her plate to the edge of the table, her back to him.

Aren't you going as well?

She was lifting and laying the knife, studying the blunt edge.

I mean how come you're not going out too?

The whisper of drying cloth stopped.

You don't have to. You don't need to if it's because, it's just me. I'm all right.

He started the drying again.

I know.

There was a dry click as he sat something on the surface.

Now, will I put on tea or not?

She nodded and lifted one of the sandwiches. Triangles.

How's the hand?

A shout through the noise of filling kettle.

She looked down, gripped her fingers with her mouth full of fish paste. Now he asked, it was stiff. And reeking of vinegar.

They spent the evening watching the end of a film, the news, then a serial that meant it was Thursday, making jokey remarks about the programmes: silences between. Her mother didn't like talking with the TV on. Shhhhh all the time. Shhh to hear the words. It occurred to the girl she was happy. He liked her being there. Maybe she would be able to get round to the subject of her father. Dad. The word never felt right. What she could remember wasn't good: cigarette burns, the stink of drink and being woken up in the dark, shouting. Crying and hysterics. A man propped up against hospital pillows not sure who she was. She sang to him and he cried before Grace took her away. She didn't even know what it was he'd died of. Maybe that would make a difference. But this wasn't the right time: it would spoil things. They ate the last of the chocolates, cherry cup and orange cream. They tasted of vineger. Felix said he could smell her from here and ran her a bath, shouting up the stairs while she undressed. Maybe he even liked her. But he hadn't found the magazine. Not yet.

A single-bar heater was burning in the attic when she came back from the bath, the curtains drawn. And a dressing gown behind the door, pink with shiny cuffs and shoulders. Grace was right enough: he spoiled folk. The dressing gown was too nice to put on, that cold feel from the satin, a scent of stale powder. She put it back on the hook and dropped the towel, walking towards the fire. She could see herself in the mirror now, skin scarlet from the orange glow, red buttons on her chest, a heart-shape of hair where the legs stopped. The face wasted it. She turned away from the mirror and stooped for the switch on the side of the fire. The wrong hand. She pulled it back too late: heat had already drawn the stings to a pulse again. It kept her restless all night.

Here's Sleeping Beauty, here she is.
Grace snapped the girl's bra-strap as she went past.
Dozy Dora. Rascal.
Duncan was much the same.
Did you forget eh? Last day of the holidays and you forget? I don't know. What'll we do with ye?

The smell of fish and coffee hung over the kitchen. Felix brought a bottle of milk and examined her hand before he went back to the window, not joining in. He sometimes ate standing there as well. Grace sat toast on the girl's plate and nudged the butter across. They'd had a good night out, folk they hadn't seen for ages. Now it was her turn. They could go into town for a look at the market stalls if she liked.
Wee look round, said Grace. Souvenirs. You like that kind of thing.
Duncan scratched his nose with the end of the buttery knife.
And photos. Canny go home without the photos. Sure ye can't? Show your mum the good time you've been having.

Felix poured what was left of his tea down the sink.

Well then. Five minutes girls.

The toast was cold. Even with butter on, it wouldn't be nice. The girl settled for tea as Duncan got up to take Felix' place at the window, looking out. The sky was thick blue. Aye Aye he said and sighed. Grace started stacking plates.

Yoohoo.

Duncan took a picture of Felix looking up. Grace wasn't pleased. That wouldn't look like anything, he wasn't doing the thing right at all. She stood beside the car, coat over her arm, waiting till they lined up. He took two beside the car before she shifted them again. Two next to the flower border before Duncan took over. They moved round the side of the house, in front of the trees, into the back porch, near the ivy up the side wall then back again for some in the drive. There were some under the window from a distance to show the thatch and the grass before Grace took a crabbit turn and refused to stand in the sun any more. Felix posed at his front door alone, then for another with his arm round Senga. He took the camera himself for the last one, of Duncan, standing to attention at the car. The plastic seats were sticky and too hot when they got in.

That's what you get for bringing it out of the shade, Grace said.

Her lipstick was starting to melt.

She blamed the crowds on Duncan as well.

Supposed to get here early and avoid this. Photos.

He wasn't bothered, just went off on his own to a stall with car sponges and windscreen wipers. Grace said he would probably stand there all day. The others stayed together and looked at tea-towels, butter dishes, key-rings. Lunch was bacon-and-egg pie from a stall with coffee in waxy cups. They decided to walk back for the fresh air so they didn't

have to get in the car: it had been parked out of the shade
again. Duncan would need to drive it back himself. He
finally took the huff.

It'll not be this tomorrow, he said. Not be much walking
back home. I bet it's raining in Saltcoats.

Och Duncan, said Grace with her mouth twisted. Last
day for goodness' sake. Sicken your happiness. Just be quiet
if you canny say something nice. Just give us all peace.
She kept going even after he'd left, silent and with his jaw
tight.

Ye can't have everything. After all we've got the scenery.
The mountains and the scenery.
There was a pause as if she had forgotten the next sentence
before she repeated herself.

The mountains and the scenery after all.

The mountains. There weren't any mountains in Saltcoats.
Just the shore and the smell of rotten seaweed. The mountains were in the Highlands and they had never been there.
But Duncan shouldn't have upset her like that. It was too
soon to think about tomorrow but now he had forced it on
them. The journey North, stuck in the car for hours at a
strict fifty while other cars overtook: sandwiches and tea
from a flask, stuffiness and stops at petrol stations for toilets
with queues and no paper. Last day as well. He shouldn't
have. But he had now. Grace was upset. It kept up through
the afternoon, the ferrying back and forth to the bedroom,
packing and changing her mind about things, muttering.
The best thing to do was keep out of her road, out of
Duncan's road too while he footered with the engine, the
same as usual, staring under the bonnet and polishing things
that were already clean. At the back of the house there was
only flat distance beyond the trees, quiet. Felix was standing
looking out over the fence. It just reached the level of his
eyes. He knew she was there without turning round.

Just thinking the place needs attention eh? I never seem to have time. Anyway. He clapped his hands and rubbed them together. All packed up for the off?

They looked at each other and his smile got wider.

Been a quick week. You can get too used to your own company.

A wasp hovered silently near his shoulder, then shifted towards the fence slats. He caught the line of her eye and turned to see.

Past their best.

She couldn't think.

Keep meaning to thin them. Know who liked those?

The sweetpeas; he thought she was looking at the sweetpeas.

Your dad, love. He liked all the colours.

He put his hands in his pockets and straightened.

Just a tiny little thing the last time I saw you, just so high. He estimated off the ground with one hand. And look at you. Make-up and nylons. You wonder where the time goes. You remember your dad? He cleared his throat.

You can ask about him if you like.

They looked at the grass, the tip of his shoe pawing a channel. The girl's chest felt tight and she didn't know what to say. Photos weren't it: they had photos at home. And that wasn't really like knowing anybody. But this stuff about what flowers he liked or the colour of his hair wasn't it either. You couldn't ask what was he like: that was the kind of question you never got much of an answer for. Or it got turned into something else: drunk and violent, a good thing he died when he did, wasted his life and tried to waste everybody else's etc., etc. Her mother did all that stuff without asking and it still told you nothing. So what was it? She looked at the man's shoelaces while he waited, not knowing. If she didn't speak soon,

he'd get fed-up or talk about something else, walk back to
the house and that would be it finished. She'd never get the
chance again.

A cigarette slid between the thin lips when she looked up,
the hand reaching for it smooth and clean. He had them
manicured, Grace said. Manicured. All that Englishness
and the house and the smoothness of everything about him.
He had no children. The idea made her suddenly angry,
furious. The match flared, the soft hand cupping the flame.
He had no children. But that was a terrible thing to say to
anybody, blame them for not being your father. It didn't
even make sense. The spent match fell and sizzled momentarily on the damp grass. She knew she was blushing. When
he started to move away, his profile fading through the trail
of smoke; when it was that split second over the edge of too
late; then, she knew. She knew what she should have asked
all along. What was *his spit?* This thing she was, just his
spit? And forming the question, she suddenly suspected the
answer. It was something too terrible to know about,
something nobody would say to you even if you asked, even
if they understood. She watched his back, the smoke drift
towards her from somewhere in front of where he was and
knew she would not say, she could not say that question. It
was the only question but not possible to ask. She could not
speak.

Felix scratched his ear.
    Getting maudlin in my old age. I just wanted to know if
you were happy. You are happy, aren't you? Does it make
you happy being here, love?
She opened her mouth, hoping, but nothing came out. He
stroked her hair then moved under the trees. She knew
when he spoke his voice would be changed.
    Ought to do something about these too.

Her eyes prickled.

All this bloody fruit. Ought to pick some of it. Waste otherwise.

Yes, she said, a long sigh. It was her own fault. The moment was gone now anyway.

What do you say?

She said nothing.

Pick some of this? We could manage just the two of us. He was talking about the plums, making an offer. It was ungrateful to keep him waiting like this, as though she didn't care. She tried to look as though she cared.

I'll get something to put them in if you like.

Maybe, she said.

The sound of her own voice a surprise. He looked and waited.

Maybe what? Not scared after yesterday, eh?

No. Just maybe. Maybe it's a good idea.

She didn't know what it was supposed to mean either. The butt-end of the cigarette wormed on the grass under his shoe and he breathed out the last of the smoke.

Too much of a fankle getting the ladder. We'll just see what we can reach eh? Just us two. Bugger ladders. And he laughed, his teeth yellow under the shadow of the trees.

Chips and eggs, bread and butter, jam, chocolate biscuits. Grace was still unpredictable so they kept the noise of the cutlery low. There wasn't much chance of playing the records or TV or anything. She'd put the nail-varnish on too and nobody had noticed, Duncan starting already with his road maps and muttering motorways. She and Grace tidied up silently while the men moved to the sofa, talking routes and place names. After the table was cleared, Grace looked at her watch and yawned. Eight o'clock already. She wouldn't be surprised if everyone else was tired too. She wouldn't be surprised if they would be going to bed soon. There was still packing to do after all. Senga got the one game of rummy before the cards needed to be packed up as well. The men were still playing with maps as the girl shut the door.

Beams through the ceiling. Worn red carpet and cream edging on the wood. Glass-eyed photos. She knew while she tried to absorb the details for the last time it didn't matter: what she would have to say about the house tomorrow would not be enough or not the right things. She never noticed the right things. The photograph halfway up the stairs, for example. 1944, RAF Bisley; the twelve young men still looking foreign and smiling at nothing. Stupid uniforms, the war. A lot of men talking about planes and guns, things that had nothing to do with anything. Nothing important. *They're all the same, football and fighting and drink. Motorcars. Wee boys. Bloody men.* Then she was embarrassed, alone on the stairs and embarrassed as if somebody had heard it out loud. Her mother didn't know everything. Maybe a lot of men were like that but not Felix; opening doors and helping you in and out of the car. He washed the dishes and did shopping, gave you chocolates and ran the bath, called you pet, sweetheart, love. Grey faces behind the glass, tilted hats and blobs for eyes. 1944. A lot of them would be dead by now. She hurt her eyes trying to see a resemblance to someone she knew. They say you get tearful when you're tired. Tired and overwrought. High strung. Laughter echoed from the living room as she went on up.

The mascara no one had noticed washed down the basin after the toothpaste, spit and soap. The lilac nails would have to wait. She rinsed her mouth again and went up to her room. Bottles and bits of make-up from the dresser, cards and presents from the market, creased clothes, books, the things she stood in. No point being neat: they'd all go straight in the machine when she got back. Another reason for moaning. At least it was your own place; you had a right to be there. And it would be all right leaving, as long as they didn't have to hang around a lot with the goodbyes at the door, all that hugs and kisses stuff. It wasn't comfortable. They never did it any other time and it always made Duncan's face swell up. It would be good if they got up early, just off and away. She closed the case and the curtains then sat on the edge of the mattress. The photo of herself at the bedside said SENGA, JOCK'S GIRL. Jock's girl. Her mother never even said his name. Just your father; just his spit, his bloody spit. The nightie was packed away as well. Just like the thing, undoing clasps and raking through stuff that was already away. The nightie was no great shakes either: terrible state. She kicked the case aside again, reaching her arms up to put it on. The cloth tumbled over her bare legs, the hem swaying to her knees. Then a noise like wood cracking, somewhere close. She straightened the sleeves, listening.

Only me, pet.

The handle turning so the shadow of the door inched across the rug.

Are you decent?

She looped the loose shred of lace fraying off the sleeve inside her hand just in time.

All right eh? as he came inside, round-shouldered, as if the ceiling was too low. All right? Didn't get much of a chat tonight, did we?

She smiled.

Nice holiday, pet?

Yes, lovely. It was lovely.

The nightie felt too short, dingy. He would know it hadn't been washed all week because they hadn't done any washing. He coughed and moved a step nearer.

Got something for you. That's why I came up just now. Going to give it to you tomorrow but, one thing and another.

A slim red case, held out as an invitation to look, not to speak but to look.

Something I hope you'll have.

She was going to have to take this thing, open her hand and take it. He would see the cuff, that tatty lace.

Thinking how I'd never given you anything before, nothing particular. Never got round to coming up when you were smaller, didn't see you as much as I maybe should have eh? You or your mum.

He slid a fingernail along the gold rim of the lid, prizing it up.

There. Doesn't make up for lost time, but it's yours anyway.

A string of beads on faded red velvet.

Your Aunt June's, long time ago. Pearls, love. Just seed, but pearls all right.

She could feel the look through the top of her head. Her toenails were purple, glossy with varnish. Common. Sweat beaded under her arm.

Don't have to say anything, pet. Just take them. Take them for me, offering the box across. She couldn't lift her hand to take it.

To remember this old man by eh?

He was standing too close. Knowing she wasn't able for this, that she didn't know what to say; grating the fragment of nylon against her palm because she wasn't able to do anything else.

Lovely. They're lovely.

The pearls lay on, misshapen in the low light. Terrifying.

They're lovely.

The box between them, too much that refused to go away. She couldn't even thank him properly, her nails sinking into the skin of her palm, the other hand that refused to take. Terrible. It would be terrible if she cried. Eventually, the box retracted. He settled it over on the bedside table, still open.

Well.

That dullness in the voice. She knew she had disappointed him.

Get you to bed, then. Big day tomorrow.

If there hadn't been the need to hide the painted nails, holding down her nightie with the one fisted hand. Things sticking in her throat she would never say. She could see the photograph of herself through the crook of his arm, squinting up into a black-and-white sun as he leaned to smooth the top sheet over her chest.

Night, pet.

All she had to do was say Thank you, touch him. Sheets tugging where his hand sunk into the mattress at her side, warmth seeping through to the hip. He leaned to kiss her forehead, a haze of wine and smoke from his mouth, then back again, sitting and looking.

Sleep tight.

Sleep tight.

The skin of his cheek magnified, the depth of creases and thread-veins, unavoidable eyeballs coated with pale yellow film. And she realised he had meant what he said, asking her to remember this old man. And he was, he was an old man. Pictures of him at home were turning brown. Her father's brother. She might never see him again.

Don't cry, love. Don't.

his lips parting as the breath slid out.

Cry.

Slipping.

She was reaching out to him when something started slipping. Not the covers but a hand, his hand moving closer and beneath the quilt. He was looking down into her face and touching her through the nightie while her body locked, knowing and not knowing at the same time, letting the hand search over the chest to cup one breast.

Give your uncle a kiss. Goodnight kiss.

Goodnight kiss hissing like escaping gas. The cotton slid on her legs and the headboard rocked as he pulled closer, dipping the bed with shifting weight, the dry fingers on her skin. She knew she wouldn't shout. No matter what happened she wouldn't shout. The headboard tipped the wall. Sudden and hard, the noise pulled the room too close, too real. The hand stopped, rested on her thigh through the cloth. Single strokes of the bedside clock getting louder. Then his voice, overhead.

It's all right, everything's all right, pet.

Almost a different voice. The quilt relaxed as he sighed.

You know, I used to take photos of you to work and show the boys. Wouldn't believe I had a niece so pretty, your age. Surprise, you coming so late. Your dad said you were a mistake. Mistake. But just fun, just fun. You could have made the difference to our Jock. Just like him. But you know the really telling thing is the eyes. Never heard our Grace say it but your eyes are just your mum. Just Greta looking at you. Haven't seen your mum for too long, years and years. Could have had a good life, your mum. But kept too much to herself. Too proud to ask for help, wouldn't take it. Too bloody deep. I had a soft spot for your mum. Best legs in Scotland. And you're going to be just like her. Wanton little thing.

He lifted the hand from her nightie. She closed her eyes, not able to breathe. Something tipped her shoulder.

Pretty as a picture eh?

He waited for a moment then took his hand away altogether.

Shhh. There there. All right. I don't mean anything.

She couldn't turn, couldn't speak.

Everything's all right.

The bed creaked and rocked as he stood up. He bent for a kiss and changed his mind, hovering while she turned away, ashamed. The sudden wallpaper and its smeary roses, her lungs quiet and sore. A ghost where his hand had been on her breast.

Shouldn't take things to heart, love. Mistake.

The door clicked open. He put out the light and waited a moment in the soft grey filtering from the hall before he spoke.

Goodnight, sweetheart. Sleep tight.

The strip of gritty lace torn inside her hand.

There was the shouting from downstairs, two or three times. Finally, the footsteps. Grace, a word retracting inside the woman's open mouth.

Is the case ready? Is it?

She moved a step closer. The lipstick was too thick.

Oh dear, she said. Deary dear. I thought you weren't ready and here you are, ready all the time. Sad. That's what's the matter eh? You can always come back and see Uncle again, back another time. Got folk worried. Just a wee bit sad eh? Come on then. Up you pop.

She clapped her hands against her knees and went to pick up the case, backtracking for something on the table. The velvet box.

Look what you nearly forgot. Silly Billy. Your good present.

The girl didn't look round.

Come on. Your Uncle Duncan's waiting.

She lifted the case.

Come on.

She reached for the girl's hand and it was easy then. Wanting to move away from this woman and her toad-skin touch. Too fast. Her reach for the box was clumsy and the box lid, still open from last night, snapped shut. Three or four beads pattered onto the rug, pinholes staring up like tiny eyes. Grace swooped right away.

For chrissake lassie. Never do anything without a song and dance. Look, you see to that and I'll take this away down. Two minutes eh? She slotted the single pearls inside the red box then smoothed back her hair.

Two minutes.

A watery smile.

And not have me come back up, eh?

The box shut on the bedside cabinet, the vanity case beside the bed.

The car ticked over, getting louder as she walked down and past the glass frames. Felix was looking up now, growing taller till he was head and shoulders above herself and blocking the way. She could not meet his eyes. Grace's stage whisper behind her back: Wee bit upset. He reached and brushed his old man lips to her cheek and she tried hard to smile. Duncan was waiting at the door with the camera. He took a picture of the three of them coming out, heavy with cases. There were only four shots left and he wanted to finish the film.

One with Grace and her brother, cheek to cheek.

Senga and Grace stiff as toy soldiers at the front door.

Felix and his niece, arm in arm.
Then another, waving at the lens.
They grinned wider with every click of the shutter.

More kissing. The gravel under her shoes. She walked down the drive, her lungs filling as though they would never stop. Duncan took the vanity case. She watched him clear space in the boot, pushing aside two boxes of plums. A present. There was open blue above the trees and the square of green. Grace came, waving backwards as she pushed inside the car, then they were all waving, the car tilting down the drive. Leaves scraped along the side-windows as the carcass bounced off the pavement onto the road. As the car swung straight, a floury face appeared over the top of the bushes, blotted of features. The girl kept her head up, trying to see his eyes and waving because she was going home. Her other hand felt stiff round the narrow box in her pocket, clutched tight in case it should open and she missed the last sight of him. Grace was sighing and rummaging for maps. Duncan started whistling 'Clementine' as the stink of plums began rising from the boot, thickening behind sealed windows. It went on rising all the way North.

valentine

I hate February.

There is no natural excitement about the second month of the year. Valentine's Day makes me embarrassed.

Despite me, the card is always there on the table when I get up, a boxful of something padded with hearts on the front and a poem that I scour with my eyes, trying to get below the surface and feel what it was that made him choose this one, which parts of it are closest to what he would say himself if he ever said things like that out loud. Only he doesn't. People don't, he says. That's what you buy the cards for.

> *You know that you will always be*
> *The one who's everything to me:*
> *Your eyes, your smiles, your heavenly touch,*
> *Mean, oh my darling, oh so much.*

Sometimes the poems don't rhyme.

> *One word is my essence of you . . . For ever.*

We two . . . are One.

This morning the Valentine is roughly A4 size with a baby blue background and gold border, two rabbits on the front. The rabbits have inflated faces, cheeks all swollen up like they have mumps and the bandages fell off. You can tell one is a lady rabbit because she has longer eyelashes and a pink bow round her neck. He has buck teeth. Nonetheless, their whiskers intertwine. Inside, it says:

> *I never thought that life could be*
> *As wonderful as this*
> *You mark my hours with happiness*
> *There's splendour in each kiss*
> *And tho it's true I sometimes fail*
> *To say what's really true*
> *At least I have this special day*
> *To tell you I love you*

My eyes fill up.
They really do.

I watched a tv programme once about how they made movies. One of the sequences was about tear-jerkers, how they fix them up to get you weepy. They demonstrated by showing how even a really terrible script – about a couple on the verge of divorce, in this case – could have music and stuff added in such a way that you'd still get hooked: nomatter how implausible, banal or shitty the thing was, the programme claimed they could still make you fall for it. So I made up my mind while I was watching that I'd use the information the programme was giving me: I would see the devices and not be manipulated by them. I stared out the rising melodic line with plaintive oboe counterpoint, sat steely through a barrage of soft-focus rose-coloured filters, single tears glistening on flawless female cheeks and smirked at the swooping crescendo of synthesised strings. I could see how it all worked and was managing to be really world-weary about it all. Then they did something hellish. Just when you thought you'd survived intact, a door behind the couple opened, flooding the foreground with white light and a child on crutches pushed himself forward out of the aura calling *daddy* in a tiny, reedy voice. It was ridiculous, of course. I saw it was ridiculous. Of course. But the bastards hadn't warned me it was coming. I just keeled over on the carpet and gret buckets.

Conditioning. Give me a cue and I play ball.

This is my valentine, the only one I get.
I kiss the first letter of his name, smudging the signature he has written in blue blue felt tip and underlined twice, imagining where his skin has traced over the card.

Blue marks on my lips in the bathroom mirror.
I stick the card on the top of the tv before I go out to work.

Stella has heart-shaped sandwiches for lunch. She says she bought the cutter to make heart-shaped sandwiches as a surprise for Ross when he opened his piecebox and she thought she might as well cut her own like that while she was about it. She opens one out to let me see. Perfect pink hearts of ham, the grain of the muscle severed clean at the edges of bread. No butter. She is on a diet. For Ross. He told her she was getting fat. I imagine Ross in his factory, opening the piecebox she has prepared and trying to hide what he finds. If he can't hide it then he will talk about Stella as though she is stupid: tell the boys maybe not

overtly, but tell them anyway what a liability she is, what
an embarrassment. Some of the boys he explains to haven't
shaved that morning. Others have tattoos. They're all glad
it isn't them with the sandwich problem. Ross eats the
sandwiches anyway, the shapes of the hearts hidden inside
his hands, just enough to bite poking through. And the boys
laugh, irrespective of deeper, more ambiguous emotions.
Maybe they want their women to be as little girl cute as
Stella. Maybe that's why they laugh, encourage Ross to do
the same behind her back: they're worried their women
don't love them enough to do something that bloody
ridiculous. Stella looks up and asks me if I got a card. Her
mascara is in blobs all along the bottom rim of lashes. Stella
is hopeless with mascara.

Of course, I say.

Boxed?

I don't tell her I think it's a waste of money. She'll think
I'm a killjoy or else I haven't got one and and I'm lying and
being sour.

I've not had mine yet, she says. It'll be there when I get
back with the roses. Yellow roses. Always gets me yellow.
Romantic and just that wee bit different.

She sinks her teeth into the bread, shearing half-moons
clean through the ham centre.

A big softie.

I suffer a sudden need to get out of there and brush my
teeth. Otherwise I will walk around all afternoon with egg
mayonnaise rising up the back of my throat like drain
emissions. I leave trying not to hear the noise of chewing,
Stella mashing her hearts to paste.

We leave work in a gaggle of five and squash into the
same car. After twenty minutes or so, the tower-blocks
poke into view. You can see ours from the road, blue towel
hanging out the skylight. They drop me off and wave, glad

of the extra space. I wave too till they're out of sight then start running. I run because I am wearing his jersey and need to get it back in the drawer before he comes home. If he finds out he gets moody and says I put his jerseys out of shape. He says I punch tits in the front, as though my breasts are leather darning mushrooms. I run up the stairs with the key on a keyring he brought me the week I moved in: tiny, delicate keyring with a white porcelain fob and my initial in gold filigree. I tried to keep it safe by leaving it in the drawer with my earrings but he got huffy. I bought you it to use Norma, he said. So I use it, knowing one day I'll have to tell him it's lost. The door doesn't feel secure when you open it: loose on the hinges. I keep meaning to do something about it but it causes bad feeling: if I pick up a hammer he thinks I'm trying to prove something. He's right. I'm trying to prove the door needs fixing but he won't buy that. He'd rather I asked him. He'd rather I nagged. Like his mother.

I'm always first back. Last out and first back. That means any mess that needs facing is how I left it so mine to clear up. Curtains not even drawn. On the way to open them I bump into the Moroccan table he carried all the way back from Fez which does not respond to cleaning as we know it, then reach and pull. Lots of stour on the sills and a clear view of the binstores for the whole block appear together. Over the binstores today, a flat stretch of sky is rising beyond the tops of the other buildings. Between the two furthest tips you see hills. Birds perch on the tv aerials before they wade back into the thick blue paste, settling on irregular air currents from the launderette vent. The polarising stuff in the window always makes the view look nice: bright and cheery. It's the thing I like best about the whole flat. I sometimes watch the clouds up here for hours. Not today though. Today I choose to tidy up. Behind my

back, two out-of-date papers opened at the tv pages, a jar
of brine with no olives left inside and an empty silver poke
of posh crisps need cleaning. Chili with a dash of lemon
flavour. Wee flecks, orange-dusted mosaic chips, tip out
when I pick it up. I brush the slurry with the side of my
hand, gather the debris. Share he said, we'll share. I get rid
of the bits and take off his jersey with one hand, haring for
the bedroom.

GET THEM OFF. YO. Catcalls and whistles. GET
THEM BLOODY OFF DARLIN.

I'm in the bedroom waving his jersey out the window
when I hear this yelling but it's only the guys from the
bakery. They keep up the catcalls and I ignore them. We've
done this umpteen times. No sign of the car. The jersey
must look like a bloody flag, though. Maybe he wouldn't
need to be this close to see it, a red rag, giving away my
every move. But I wave the jersey out the window all the
same, its scarlet sleeves catching and flicking bits of paint
off the frame like giant dandruff while the guys whistle and
roar some more. YO. I hope it will cool down and lose the
smell of me. I don't know what I smell like but he says it's
distinctive. He says he knows when I've been in a room.
GET THEM OFF. I leave traces behind.

The immersion light goes on when I press the switch:
dependable. It's an expensive way to heat water but at least
this way there'll be plenty for him coming home, and if
there's plenty of hot water he'll have a bath before he thinks
of doing anything else. Like opening drawers and raking
through his jerseys. He works in a glass office and sweats
when it's sunny. That's all I know about what he does. That
and the lunches: he always tells me what he's had in the
canteen. Good grub, he says, subsidised. What stumps me
is what else he does in there, what it looks like. I imagine a
glass office, maybe slotted into the middle floor of five, him

sitting at a drawing board and trying not to notice while the
sweat burrows like insects through his armpits, the thick
furze at his crotch. There are stains in ovals on his back and
where the arm seams join. All the seams of his clothes seep.
His tie is slewed to one side, top button on his shirt undone
showing the hair at the base of his neck. Every so often he
moves one leg behind the other, widening his knees to let his
body breathe. His skin bristles with the slow movement of
sweat beads. He frees the watch strap and rubs the damp
wrist, goes back to what he was doing. Usually I imagine
him holding a pen but I'm not sure what he's meant to be
doing with it, what he's writing. Maybe he isn't. Maybe it's
a pencil and he's drawing. I don't know what he does all
day. When I ask him he says it's not interesting: he doesn't
come home to talk about work. I know it involves pens
though. He's never done pinching mine. Sometimes he's
there from eight in the morning till after midnight.
Whatever it is, it takes up lots of time.

Other times I imagine him walking along a sunned-out
corridor, one hand balled into the right trouser pocket,
jacket slung over the opposite shoulder, watching his feet as
he walks. Occasionally, he kicks something on the floor
that isn't there, a mimed football tackle that pulls back its
power at the last minute. Just working off a little energy.
When people go past in the corridor he nods and keeps
going. Maybe he's going to the canteen and that's why he's
so relaxed. The canteen has glass doors that slide back
automatically when he's within inches of slamming against
them but he doesn't flinch or slow down at all. He knows
this place like the back of his

Oops.

Shirt on the floor. Didn't see it this morning.
I pick it up, breathe deep. His clothes are always nice to

touch, aromatic because he's so clean. Even things he
touches smell nice. I slip the jersey into the second drawer,
shaking it a bit so the layers of things in there resettle. Mine
are in the drawer above his. My things smell of deodorant.
I shut the drawer and stick a tee-shirt on over the bra, then
head for the kitchen. A half-eaten bit of toast I left on the
work surface hits the bin, door to the still-open food
cupboard slamming shut. At least tonight I don't have to
think what to make out of two tins of tomatoes, pickles,
anchovies and yards of herb jars. I don't need to think at all.
We are going out. I'm just thinking it would be nice to sit
down for five minutes, maybe make a cup of tea, enjoy the
sun coming through the tee-shirt making goosepimples on
my arms when for some unacccountable reason I turn
round, zero back in on the living-room and find one more
thing to tidy away. Another paper I missed first time round.
I've been working all day but that's no excuse for
sloppiness. Plenty of women work all day and have kids and
a man to run. My mother tells me I don't know what tired
is. So I pick it up: not consciously but something makes
these decisions for you. I don't normally bother with
newspapers but I read this. It says SUICIDE PACT FAILS.
Underneath, a story about two pensioners who went out in
a car, doused themselves in petrol then ran the thing into a
wall at 60. They both survived. Not intact but breathing.
Ten miles or so up the road to where I am sitting reading
this. A kind of village with an open park and lots of trees.
Ten miles up the fucking road.

    The sound of car brakes shakes me free. Car brakes in the
parking area six floors down. He's home.
    I imagine him, winding up the nearside window and
collecting his *Evening Times* from the empty passenger seat,
reaching into the back for the jacket he'll dangle from one
finger to come upstairs, sauntering with his eyes crunched

up because his hair needs a cut. He'll be walking upstairs now with his eyes screwed small, maybe resting finger and thumb of one hand on either side of his nose, trying to shake off tiredness, happy to be back. My heart jumps when I hear the sound of footfalls coming closer and when he appears on top of the landing, all my nerve endings blister. I can't help it. I'm crazy about him. Wholly and terminally, raddled with love.

He appears and I smile, meaning it.

He walks in smiling back, presents spilling from under his arm.

I get flowers, something chocolate (usually heart-shaped) and a bottle of wine, dry white. The wine is a compromise. He prefers red: I prefer sweet but he can't bring himself to stroll into Thresher's and ask for that. He's got pals in there for godsake. Also the white is a tradition from the days we didn't know any better, the days we used to stay in and have lazy sex all night after we'd eaten my speciality with the packet of frozen prawns and strawberry mousse, a magazine recipe that claimed aphrodisiac properties though in a self-deprecating way so you knew not to take it too seriously. My only speciality. It recurs. The magazine page is spattered with pink bits, fatty blobs that show I have been that way before but I keep it all the same.

Not tonight though. I'm not cooking tonight.

I nod at his card, waiting on the sofa. He opens it while I watch, then sits it on the tv next to mine. They both threaten to fall off, not designed to sit upright: too full of satin and foam. Anyhow, he seems to like it. We kiss. The tips of our tongues touch.

I've not had time to wrap it, he says, fishing something

else out of the poly bag. A flat, black box. I give him an oblong box covered with stars. We open them at what is meant to be the same time but I'm holding back. I know what he has since I bought it but I want to see his face. I'm just like Stella. He always looks the same when he opens something from me: pleased and shy. It lasts till he works out what the folded cotton really is. A pair of thermal drawers. He holds them flat in one hand, not wanting the legs to dangle, thin and empty, where I can see.

Very funny, he says.

I know something about the present has disappointed him. I interpret that he'd rather I was interested in what I've been given. Already I'm tearing the pale blue tissue, trying to rustle a lot so he knows I'm thrilled. One of the pieces between the layers touches my hand, soft enough to make my skin feel it's melting. I pull out something shiny, red nylon with a black panel, splay pieces on the settee. It's a suspender belt and bra, a pair of knickers trimmed with fluffy stuff; like tiny feather boas. Our faces look much the same then. Neither of us knows what to say. The evening is in jeopardy so we pretend this isn't the case at all, just float in separate directions and begin getting ready for going out. We haven't got all night.

The water is cool but okay. I fill my bath up to the mark he hasn't washed off after his and lie back, getting sad at the sounds of him getting ready elsewhere in the house. What he has to put up with, me being such a hard bitch and everything when he just bought me a present. After all, it's the thought that counts.

The fluffy stuff sticks to my skin cream. Two strands like ferns adhere to my upper thigh. I don't look in the mirror but it seems to fit as much as this sort of stuff ever does and the feather bits don't bumphle the material as much as you'd think. I dress fast, looking over my shoulder and listening, hoping to christ he doesn't come through. Maybe I want it to be a surprise.

The restaurant is somewhere we've been before: intimate concern run by two Italians with Scots accents. The waiter gives me the obligatory smile when he helps me to my seat, tells me I look nice and I smile back. Can't help it: I'm so bloody eager to please. He sits opposite, managing his own chair, and leans towards me in an anticipatory way. He likes good food. We get mildly drunk. Through the dessert and coffee we start sharing the looks that indicate sex. A particular kind of sex. I run my hand along the inside of his trouser leg with one hand under the table and he has to squirm while his brandy is being poured, barely able to stay seated while the erection forces a hump in his trousers. My hand shifts. Watching his face trying not to flicker when the waitress asks him if he enjoyed his strudel gives me a thrill of power. I'm making this difficulty, I'm altering his behaviour and it means he wants me. He wants me. I need to feel that's what it means.

On the way home, I hook the three-inch heel of one of my shoes onto the dashboard. He looks twice, undoes his fly as the car decelerates then stops the car and fucks me in a layby till the car windows run like rain on the inside.

I get more excited by this kind of display than I'd be prepared to admit when I'm sober.

Afterwards, I blush hauling my breasts back inside the feather and satin contraption, ashamed for something I can't quite pin down. He clears the inside of the windscreen with the back of his jacket sleeve and looks at me. I keep my eyes on the roof vinyl, listening. Sirens. I can hear sirens, far away like remembered noise, too distant to be definite. Maybe there's an accident someplace. I ask if he hears it and he says no. He says I imagine it and maybe I did. I get maudlin afterwards, volatile. It's what I'm like.

The parking space waits for us, a dry oblong on the wet concrete behind the Chinese. The launderette grille hangs on visible strands of condensation, dry ice. When we get out of the car, our breaths appear too, making low fog over the bonnet. There will be frost tonight. At the foot of our steps, I find an empty box and I fold it carefully for the bins rather than do it tomorrow. He doesn't notice these things. His collar flashes white semaphore from the top of the steps and I hear him reach for the keys. He opens our door and goes inside. This is our home, how we live. He is in there taking off the tie and loosening the trouser band, trying to feel relaxed. We have already had sex. Further touch is unlikely. I stall at the foot of the stairs, not wanting to, then hear his solution. Dirk Bogarde being earnest about something in a late-night movie. We always have the tv. Tonight it has cards on top.

> *And tho it's true I sometimes fail*
> *To say what's really true*
> *At least I have this special day*

I can always go into the kitchen and make tea.

Up the stairs, my turn to lock us in for the night. The sound of actors speaking on tv, my heart bursting with wanting to give more, not knowing what it is, how to give it. And sirens. I hear the sirens he thinks are not there coming closer.

where you find it

Nobody kisses like Derek.

First sight you think he's got no mouth, just a dry slit in that dry sheet skin, lips that don't look like they'd sustain much at all, like worm husks, little worms rolled flat with no juice left in but you'd be wrong. When Derek kisses he opens his face so wide you think he's choking on something, like he's swallowing an apple or maybe there's one stuck in his neck, like he's bringing something up from somewhere deep and you open up too. You can't help it. He prises you apart like you're in the dentist's chair and you *know* you're being kissed. You know what he likes? He likes his tongue buried and moving around in there, foraging into all the available recesses. You can feel the wee cord that keeps his tongue on stretching, pulling up from the soft veiny mass on the floor of his mouth, tightening to its limit like it might uproot. That cord is in there all the time, folded up like a fin or stray slice of tissue left on a butcher's tray, like something loveless left over from ritual surgery and on most people that's how it stays. You'd never suspect. When Derek kisses, though, you get a share of everything, you get it all. Sometimes it's scary like there's an animal between us, an engorged mollusc trying to get out: other times it's like he's sucking me in, drawing me inside him so I can't breathe but manage. I never push him away. That reflex thing where you think you're going to throw up? Even if he pokes the back of my throat, the bit that's sheer like a toad's belly, his tongue stiff as a nun's ringer it just never happens because it's not that kind of thing, not like a punter sticking his dick there the way some of them do, some of them not even careful, not even bothered if it hurts or anything, not bothered about your vocal cords or anything it's not like that. It's wonderful, the way he wants you to feel all of him in there, the root of this other tongue with taste buds bristling studding up like braille saying I AM KISSING YOU NOW so I have to make room for my own interior, pressing myself out of the way and against his teeth, finding out the peach fur in the distant corners of his molars, my tongue-tip caressing the places no-one sees. I love that, love it, love knowing all his secrets, even those bits of him, bits he doesn't see. Bits he doesn't even know exist. I love having no option, no choice. When he lifts those big square hands out of the blue, tangles his fingers up in my hair and tugs so my neck tilts for him without my sayso and just injects himself, without warning, I get dizzy, sick, weak to my water. That he'll do it anywhere, even in the street just hold me, squeeze me like an orange and take what he needs; that he can't wait for me, he just can't wait at all. There's no woman wouldn't love that. Tell me there's a woman wouldn't love being wanted that way, a way that doesn't hide itself, a way that can't be shy. He doesn't want to fuck me. He doesn't even want to touch me anywhere else. Kisses are what I'm for he says. They're our thing, how he keeps me in line. I wouldn't let any other bastard do it, not even if they ask, not even if they're good looking or offer extra, I don't care. I'm all his. All Derek's.

Good kissers don't grow on trees. It's worth bearing in mind. You don't get everything in this life, girl, count your blessings. Remember the things he can do with his mouth.

sonata form

A few stands, those coffins they put cellos in, the odd coat and sports bag. The flowers were there too but not him. She checked the wee toilet, the shower cubicle. No drips, nothing. It was just one of those things about being with Danny. People came and got him. They walked by the rank and file sticking their fiddles back in cases and zeroed in, even if he hadn't had time to wash yet, to change out of his soaking shirt. She'd seen him taking off his concert trousers, unpeeling the cloth off his legs, steaming like a horse and they just came in anyway, exchanging pleasantries as if he didn't need time to do even that by himself. She'd seen him zip hairs out by the roots doing himself up blind, maintaining eye-contact and a smile rather than say anything. Tongue biting. You had to do a lot of tongue biting in dressing rooms.

Over on the practice piano, two bus tickets, a chewed pencil. His teethmarks. Mona put it in her bag with the spare she'd brought in case he needed it then draped her coat over a chair-back, the shoulder-bag out of sight beneath it. No point carrying stuff you didn't need. His coat wasn't on the stool where it usually was. She looked around, scanning. It was there in an empty box in the corner, the tails junked on top with the lining showing. Crimson lining. Everybody else had grey but not Danny. You always found them no problem: in among all the other castoffs, Danny's tails were something else. Mona looked at them, the Ribena-coloured splash and black wings falling onto the floor. At least the poor bugger had had time to change his jacket. There would be women through there very disappointed. She went over and fixed it so it wouldn't crease, smoothed the arms flat. A few hundred quid's worth lying any old how. On the way out, she shut the door carefully behind her.

After ten minutes of blind alleys and droopy paperchains it was there like you couldn't miss it. People were spilling out the door, trolleys of drink rolling in. Every so often, great baboon-howls about nothing evident would roar out of the interior then fade. The second-desk double bass and big blond guy who played the trumpet walked in, doing their bit as players' reps. Some people actually liked it, Danny said. They liked the free food, especially this time of year. Eric and Simon were there too, hovering around the open door, peering in: Simon with a bunch of something and Eric not wearing his specs. They came sometimes but seeing them was always a surprise. Simon turned then and saw her. They walked over with their arms wide, smiling the same way. She knew they knew. You could tell by looking at them. Simon rubbed his cheek against hers, gave her one of those lightweight hugs he did. You just got used to them starting when they were finished. They were good hugs anyway. She told them it was great to see them and watched them go coy.

Well, she said, you got your money's worth. Was he great or was he great?

Oh you, Eric said. He rolled his eyes. Never mind him.

No, Simon said. We want to talk about you.

Let's have a look at you then, Eric said. He held her out at arm's length and looked meaningfully at her belly through the black frock. They all did. There was nothing to see yet but they all did it anyway. It was pleasantly embarrassing. Simon said he thought Danny was playing great just for the record and they laughed. It helped. Another few minutes of when's it due and how well she was looking. Things were just starting to get easier when Simon braced up, looked down at his wrist. Sorry, he said. They had to rush, wouldn't come in this time: too much stuff to do, she knew how it was.

Ivor Novello for somebody's party, Eric said. But we need the money.

Simon stuck the bunch of flowers into her hand. Give the maestro our love, he said. And tell him these aren't his.

Mona cuddled them into the crook of an arm. Roses. Not for Danny. She didn't know what to say. They left walking backwards and blowing kisses. Mona watched them, waving, knowing they knew they wouldn't have gotten in anyway. Friends didn't. These dos weren't for musicians at all, not even the ones who'd been playing. She heard the main door batter back on its hinges, knew they were irretrievably gone. The draft made the corridor chilly. Her cardigan was back in the dressing room but she had no idea how to get back there. There was nothing else for it. She put the roses down carefully on an empty trolley, ran a hand over her stomach wishing it showed more and walked inside.

Danny was on the other side of the room holding a wine glass and an empty paper plate in the middle of a huddle of women. It was where he always was at these things, what he was always holding. She nodded to let him know not to stop what he was in the middle of and just took her time.

Mona liked looking at Danny and you only got to look at
somebody properly when they were distracted, not
knowing you were watching. You got to read things they
didn't necessarily know they were telling you. Right now,
he looked that way he did when a concert was over and he
thought he'd done ok. Self-conscious, shagged out and
radiant. She knew that look from other places as well: it
always meant something good. He was close now, close
enough for familiar cosmetic smells to reach, a deodorant
and aftershave cocktail. She reached for the plate from his
hand without asking, took it over to the buffet table and
stood in line with the men already there, loading up with
fish and meat, lumps of mayonnaise-thick salad. Getting
the nosh was Mona's thing: it gave her something to do.
Cutlery in paper napkins, bowls, oval-shaped plates and
glasses. Most of the table was glasses. The salmon had eyes
in this time. It looked up at nothing, pink musculature in
tatters.

Best bit eh?

A man with a tight tie reached past for a sheet of ham. A
waitress with silver-coloured prong efforts was holding a
slice out for him but he didn't seem to see her.

Best bit, he said. Where they wheel out the eats.

He rolled the ham into a tube, popped it into his mouth,
offered her a plate then saw she had one already.

That's the girl, he said. He waved his fork in a cheery
kind of way and strolled along to the next tray, chewing.
The waitress still held the same bit of ham out but someone
else got in first. Mona didn't want it anyway. She walked
further up, found egg sandwich triangles, some cheese: the
only vegetarian stuff that wasn't salad. They always had
loads of salad at these things. Danny couldn't eat salad after
concerts. It gave him the shits. He always had bad shits
before concerts with the nerves and everything and it hung
on. He probably wouldn't eat the sandwiches either but she

would take a couple anyway. Just in case. She back-to-backed them on the plate, lifted a glass of something orange and picked her way back through. Danny wasn't looking in her direction but he didn't need to. His smile changed. It stayed in place for the woman Mona could only see the back of but it knew she was coming over.

Her son played, she was saying. Who knew maybe one day professionally she only wished she'd thought to let him come along you could have told him to stick in you don't mind if I call you Daniel. Then Mona got over and interrupted.

Hi, she said. She pushed the plate between them.

The woman with the son stepped back, followed the length of the arm to Mona's face.

This is Mona, Danny said.

Mona put her juice down on the table edge offered the freed hand for shaking. The woman with the son made a very big smile.

Lovely, she said. Lovely.

She didn't take the hand though. Some women didn't. Danny claimed his plate and looked hard at the shapes on it. Mona knew what he was thinking. He was thinking they never gave you real food at these things but not saying, pushing the triangles about with his eyes down. Mona let her arm drop, picked up the glass again. She smiled too.

So, she said. Enjoy the concert?

My goodness yes, she said. Yes yes. Who wouldn't have? Mona nodded.

I was just saying to Daniel here I'm *such* an admirer.

It was said for Danny to hear and he knew. He'd seen it coming and turned away just in time. A woman in a black strapless thing who'd been waiting for just that moment had got him as soon as he'd shifted his footing. Mona and the woman with the son looked at each other again. The woman coughed, looked at her empty glass, back at Mona.

Sorry, she said. Heather. She almost pointed at herself, thought better of it. I don't know who you are.

Mona, Mona said.

Of course, she said. Of course. And you're . . . are you a fan too?

No, no. Mona was no good at this kind of thing. She could hear herself being no good at it. I just live with him.

Oh, Heather said. The hand without the glass fluttered up to her neck. I should have known, shouldn't I?

No you shouldn't, Mona said.

I didn't even know he was married. Just didn't occur.

He's not, Mona said. He isn't.

Sorry?'

Married. We're not married.

Yes, she said. A studious looked crossed over her face. I see. It must be lovely anyway. She turned and smiled at someone over her shoulder. Jean?

She looked behind her. Three women looked up. The two talking to Danny didn't.

Jean? It was louder this time. There's someone you have to meet here. Come over. Come and meet . . . um . . .

Mona, Mona said.

Daniel's wife, Heather said.

All three came over. Mona held out her hand again. Two responded this time. Mona said her name to each of them to be on the safe side. She had to ask theirs. Jean, Carolyn, Stephanie, they said. They all had lovely teeth.

You must be very proud, Jean said.

I know I would be, said Carolyn.

Oh yes, Mona said, very proud.

He plays so beautifully. We were just saying, weren't we, girls? Jean opened her eyes wide to take them all in. Just saying we could listen all night.

We were not, Carolyn said. We were saying how good looking he was. Tell the truth, Jean.

You'll get me hung, Jean said. All right, I admit it. We were talking about more than the playing if I have to be brutally honest.

Good looking, Stephanie said. *And* gifted. You're a very lucky girl.

I expect you know that too, Mona, eh? Carolyn winked.

Oh yes, Mona said. Certainly do.

They laughed this time. Sort of giggled. Mona's glass was needing refilled.

I envy you, though. All that beautiful music going on all the time under your own roof, friendly terms with Wagner and Mendelssohn, the *Moonlight Sonata* raging away next door. Jean sighed. It must be marvellous.

Well. Mona looked at her. He plays mostly contemporary these days. More Maxwell Davies than Mendelssohn. Folk who're still alive kind of thing.

Sorry? Stephanie looked as if she hadn't heard right.

Beamish, Weir, said Mona. Nicholson.

Never mind, said Jean.

What's it like, though, living with that kind of creative talent? Living with it? Carolyn's eyes got bigger. It must be terribly romantic.

Oh you get used to it, Mona said. You . . . um . . . cope.

Maybe Mona is a musician too, though, said Stephanie. Creative people often team up with other creative people, the shared sensitivities and everything. I bet you're a musician too. Am I right?

No, I'm not a musician, Mona said.

She couldn't see Heather any more. Her voice was still there though, the word *sensual* rising and fading back into the continuous buzz from somewhere else.

Shame, Carolyn said. Still it's probably just as well. Somebody needs to be the practical one, able to do the organising and things. She took Mona's glass and put it on a passing tray, served them both another. Sorting out his music and concert clothes and so on.

Did you see his fingers? Jean looked at Stephanie. They're solid! Solid muscle!

Really? Stephanie looked horrified.

They're *huge*. Literally. Bulging. People don't think about it as a physical job do they? But there you are. Literally bulging.

I bet he's impractical though. Carolyn again. Creative people are famous for it. I bet being close to that sort of person has its downside.

Well, Mona said.

Not good with time-keeping I bet.

Well. Mona wasn't sure she should be saying this but she said it anyway. He doesn't dust or anything. I lift a lot of socks up.

It is though isn't it? Jean was fiddling with her hair, drawing her fingers through it, separating the lacquered sheets. Physical, I mean. Does he train?

Mona could hear Danny's voice close enough to whisper to. That's my job, after all, he was saying. That's part of what people pay me to do. Someone must have asked him how he remembered all those notes. A man laughed as though the answer was a joke of some kind and there was the sound of a hand slapping a back.

No, Mona said. He doesn't train. Unless lifting beer-glasses counts.

Jean laughed and shook her head as though Mona was a real wag, a card. Good for you, she said. Haha. Good for you.

They all smiled at each other again. Something had reached a natural conclusion. Mona looked into her orange juice and Stephanie and Carolyn began a slow drift in the direction of the buffet table. Danny's voice, further off but still clean as a triangle, was asking where the toilets were.

Well, Jean said. It's been a pleasure meeting you. She was turning away, not sure how to make the break without feeling she was doing the wrong thing. And that *charming* husband.

Mona smiled, nodded.

And tell him, Jean stage-whispered, that lovely man of yours, tell him he's *wonderful*. Flashing aren't-I-awful eyes before she faded further off. Behind her back, Mona saw Danny heading off out the door. One hand in the pocket, raking for fags. Mona kept smiling till Jean turned away.

The buffet table was crowded now, mostly women: more empty glasses dotted round the place than full ones. Mona thought about going over and couldn't be bothered. Up too early again, bed too late, Danny haring about with an iron before breakfast. Getting here. You got out of practice for being out: rusty for dealing with people. All they knew was work, when you thought about it: Danny in his room all the time with the bloody piano, crashing away till midnight depending what else he'd had to do that day, her trying to write at the kitchen table till godknows. They hardly knew how to deal socially with each other never mind other people. And then there was the dizziness, the waves of nausea that washed up these days. What she wanted was a lie down. There was a chair over on the far side of the room with no-one near it, just a man looking out the big bay window. The chair looked soft and Danny wouldn't be long. The man looked ok too: preoccupied. Safe. She was just about to go over when something touched her back.

A man was standing behind her with a wee book of some kind. It wasn't a concert programme, just a book.

Sorry, he said. Didn't mean to do that.

He had very pale skin, freckles on his scalp. That's ok, Mona said. Just don't do it again.

It was meant to be funny, light or something but he just

looked at her and didn't say anything. His eyes were
watery, filmed over. He looked not well.

Sorry, she said.

No, he said. I am. My line.

Right, she said. The watery eyes kept looking at her.
Mona gesticulated towards the chair. Just . . . um . . .
heading over here then.

What d'you think of this lot? he said. He rustled the
booklet between his hands. Lot of money to run an
orchestra.

Mona looked at him. Maybe he hadn't heard her. Maybe
she hadn't heard him, the wheezy voice needing to be
listened to harder to get more of a gist.

People don't think about where it comes from, he said.
Money.

The chair was still free. Mona could see it. The man was
looking out at the night skyline.

Dependent on things they know nothing about. He wiped
his mouth suddenly, the white end of a hanky disappearing
back inside the jacket pocket. Parasitic. The whole thing.
All parasites.

The feeling in Mona's stomach was intensifying. It told
her she wanted to get away but she couldn't think how.
How to do it refused to occur.

The people who come to concerts. Ignorant. Like everybody else.

Mona waited.

Am I not being interesting enough? he said suddenly.

No, Mona said. She said it without thinking. No you're
being. You're being what you're being.

People who come to concerts, he said again. He looked at
the floor.

You're not the kind of people who come to concerts,
then?

Oh yes, he said. Wife likes them. Women do. His eyes

scanned the parquet. I'm also the director-general of this outfit. It's sort of expected.

Something like a wince moved over his mouth, faded out. It was hard to tell whether he didn't know she hadn't a clue what he was talking about or simply didn't care. He kept looking down.

Right, she said.

They stood for a moment saying nothing.

Not a musician yourself, are you? He rolled the sore-looking eyes towards her briefly, lowered them again.

No, she said. You're safe there.

He made the half-smile. No I'm not, he said. You're a sympathiser. I can tell. I know you're thinking I'm a fool. A Philistine.

Oh?

You sense it, he said. Like a smell.

Mona had had enough. She didn't want any more of whatever this was. Not tonight.

It's what's wrong, he said. What's wrong with the whole country.

Mona said nothing.

No servant class.

Mona looked suddenly at him. She couldn't help it. She stood very still, just looking.

Given up our servant class. Self-evident that's no good. You look at the great civilisations and you'll see: give up your servant class and it all goes to hell. Too many people who don't know anything. They're not getting the proper guidance. Not getting a job where they're given reliable instruction. What are they supposed to do?

Mona didn't know.

Express themselves, he said. They go about expressing themselves.

He waved the paper limply, scanned the room. They had stopped looking at each other.

Doesn't build pyramids, does it?

Pyramids, Mona said. She kept watching him, the ironic smile or whatever it was, twitching at the corners of his mouth. Pyramids, she said again. There was nothing else in the room to attach to. Not a thing. The man near the window had moved away and you couldn't even see the streetlights from here. She watched black sky for a while. Then spoke.

My mother was a servant, she said. She was in service for eight years.

So was mine. The shape of him at the corner of her eye not budging. Interesting we should have that in common.

Stephanie was there suddenly, fussing.

Do you want anything Archie? He never eats properly. She raised her eyebrows, the pencil lines moving into mock-furious arches. I need to do everything for him.

She wiped his lapels and took the booklet out of his hand. He just stood there, letting her and Mona saw for the first time what it was. A score. He'd been in at the concert, if he'd been in at all, with a concerto score. Without it to hold onto, his hand started shaking. It trembled over the slit of his jacket pocket as though he was trying to pull out a stuck scarf. Like he had Parkinson's or something.

Go away, Stephie, he said. He was doing his smile, shifting the top lip. It occurred to Mona he might have had a stroke. She looked over at Stephanie and Stephanie smiled. Very gently.

Go away, he said again. She went.

Well, Mona said. She could see Danny at the door now, the travel bag over one arm, waving for her to come. Her coat was there too. Well. It's been . . . whatever.

Yes, he said. It has.

He reached to take the empty glass from her. He held onto it when she passed it to him, drew her nearer.

You despise me, don't you? he said.

It was just the same tone of voice he'd used all evening: even, disinterested.

I can see that too.

His eyes looked coated.

I don't know you, she said. She let the glass go. I know nothing about you. Of course I don't despise you.

You know the Koechel number of that concerto? The one they did tonight? The tempo for the second movement?

No, Mona said.

Thought not, he said. Neither does that young man.

I have to go now. She said it quite definitely, quite sure. She wanted away from him: this dying individual with his score tucked under his arm, thinking Mozart had written an instruction manual just for him, a set of tips on form. If she didn't go soon she'd say something and let Danny down. It was his do, not hers. This was Danny's work for godsake, not hers. Goodbye, she said. She walked away without turning round, hoping she had sounded calm. Jean and Carolyn weren't anywhere. Heather was dancing. Only Stephanie waved.

Christ I thought you were never coming, he said when she got out. He was pacing from foot to foot like he was frozen. Come on then. I'm dying for a fish supper.

Mona took Danny's tails on their hanger, her own coat.

You got your flowers? she said.

He hauled the tulips from under the sports bag, hers too. The roses. Mona had almost forgotten about them.

Don't tell me, he said. Simon said they weren't for me.

Mona nodded.

I told him you were pregnant. Did you tell him as well?

Mona looked Danny hard in the eye, put one hand on his shoulder. The cloth of his jacket was warm, grainy.

Danny, she said. Her stomach was tight. What was the Koechel number of the concerto?

Eh? he said. He stopped bouncing.

The K number. D'you know it?

Four-six-six, he said.

Mona looked at him.

Look, you don't spend months with a piece, seeing it every day without knowing the Koechel number. I can give you the date of the first performance as well if you like. Eleventh of February, seventeen-eighty-five. And his dad was there. Not that they've got anything to do with anything but I'm throwing in extra free. What kind of question's that supposed to be? Koechel number?

Danny, she said. She pulled him closer. He smelled of cigarette smoke, aftershave and sweat. A man after his work. Danny, tell me our child will not have to play the piano for a living, Danny. Tell me.

He looked at her hard, his eyebrows tangled up. Mona kept her face dead straight.

Mona, he said quietly. I haven't a clue what you're talking about. Not a clue.

I know, she said. Are you going to tell me anyway?

No, he said. Of course I'm not.

She knew that too.

Can I assume the daft questions concluded? He smiled when he said it but he was getting fed up with this, whatever it was. He wanted his chips and he wanted them now. Mona said nothing. Danny flexed his hands. Come on, Mona. It's perishing in here.

He stopped for the plastic carrier, the straps of the overnight bag. The blond trumpet-player came out the reception room rubbing his temples.

Thank god that's over, he said. He nodded in their direction. See you in the pub ok?

He walked off, shaking his head, down the corridor after his case.

Mona watched him. When she turned back, Danny was

standing, the weight of the big bag digging a groove into his shoulder. He was fit for the road.

Ok? The take-away on the corner. We'll catch the pubs as well if you're quick. He smiled like the sun coming out, kissed her cheek and started walking.

Mona watched Danny moving towards the night air outside, his flowers under one arm. Her wrist was sore, the hanger with the tails biting into her fingers. It was so bloody heavy. She looked down at the thing, the stubborn crimson lining, hearing the sound of his footfalls recede. Monkey-jackets they called them. Livery. Faint laughter was drifting from behind the closed door. Danny walked on ahead, two bunches of flower-heads bobbing under his arm. She hadn't even told him how good he'd been, how proud she was of him. His work. And that, she realised suddenly, was what she very much wanted to say. Yellow tulips still fresh beneath the artificial light.

I love you, Danny.

It was exactly what she wanted to say.

a night in

The door gave on the third shove. Stevie said it hadn't even hurt his shoulder.

There were workmen's things dotted about over the floor, boards rolling with strings of stour the size of carpet bales. We had seen the bales from outside, the shapes of them showing through the scaffolding by the light they hung on the gables overnight and hoped they might be insulating stuff, something we could use for covers. Just dust, though, fluff and unplaceable debris. Stevie kicked the nearest and it scudded away like a fish scouring the bottom of a tank. Like something living. Near to, the planks were plaided with squares of brightness from the security light outside, regular shapes crayoned thick blue. Their footprints became apparent as we walked: tyre-prints from the rims of work-shoes, a freestanding cast of someone's sole in mud, deep enough to hold water. We found an empty beer can, cigarette cartons, rags of newspaper. Nothing else. The lamp with the cable, a wire grid over the bulb, might have been a warm thing but we couldn't get it to work. Even if we had managed, it would have been too risky, drawn the attention of foremen or other people doing rounds,

neighbourhood watch people maybe, checking. At least
with the light not on we'd be all right for a wee bit longer.
Cold maybe. But dry. Stevie put the thing down when he
realised and stood up, fished in his inside pocket. He did
one of those slow smiles at me. I could hear it, even in the
dark, the sound of some kind of pleasure buttering his face
before he lit them, three single matches one after the other.
They all blew out. There was no glass in the windows yet,
just open holes. Holes in every wall. He held up the fourth
match to the ceiling to get it out of the draught so it stayed
lit. I saw two shadows dart the length of the boards from
under our feet and, on either side, the skeleton of the
building flaring, flickering up like flame. The vertiginous
height of scaffolding, the weight of this structure that hung
over our heads.

The first time I'd seen anything like that, what keeps a
house standing. I remember thinking how special it was. A
privilege. We were seeing something intimate, something
the people whose home this would become would never see
or even think about. Cats had walked through here, bedded
down in the dust where they felt safe. Birds maybe, insects
would have pitted into the unplastered brick. And us. They
would never know about us, what had passed through here
before their occupation: the way it had looked rolling with
ersatz tumbleweed, the windows gaping like torn posters
off motorway hoardings. The wind flapped the plastic
sheeting, the scaffolding whining like someone asleep,
wrestling with dreams and I knew it for sure, for dead
certain sure. We had been here and they would never have
a bloody clue.

At least I wasn't alone. I tried to remember that when the
match died, leaving everything darker than before. I wasn't
alone so it wasn't frightening. We both stayed still, maybe

thinking the same thing, till the filter of light from the safety lamp outside started to make a difference again. I remember seeing the shapes of my feet inside the wet shoes, flexing my toes to make them feel more real. The space opening out beside me that was Stevie moving away and whistling. I watched him walk across the boards, the back of his coat glittering with sunk-in rain. It'll do he said, squatting down in one corner: It'll do. And he opened out his coat. He held open his coat till I came towards him, letting me know it was all right. I looked at him, the dark patches where his eyes would be, trying not to shiver, looking into the still space inside the house that gave nothing away. And he started singing. Not words, not the kind of tune you could recognise, but singing anyway. That's what he was doing when the lightning came. I was walking towards him and he was singing, opening out his coat for me to come when the flash lit everything up with sore white light. Rain from nowhere heavy as running on the roof and the single snapshot of this place that would be a room, Stevie in one of its corners, waiting for me. He pulled me tight towards him then, folding me up inside the damp material. And we looked together out of the window space, the place that would be shut up with glass, waiting for thunder.

test

Rustling.

Shoes through dry leaves. Through crisp pokes.

There was someone in the room.

Large hands were uncovering something from inside brown paper, carefully. There was someone moving around in here, thinking her unconscious. Lying prone in the halfdark, Mhairi stiffened. The too-close wall was making goosepimples along her arm, her nerves bristling. Like her skin was contracting, trying to make less of itself. Under the covers, the tee-shirt was rucked to her waist. She was half-asleep, belly-naked. Prone. The sound came again, tickling the hair on the back of her neck. The crackle of someone unwrapping a claw hammer. A length of cable.
Cheesewire.

Mhairi held the same inbreath in her lungs, waiting, till her ribs started to hurt. Nothing happened. She waited some more, listening. There was nothing to hear but her own heartbeat, the slow whisper of air down her nostrils as

she metered the outbreath it wasn't possible to keep back.
HELLO? she said. Her eyelashes were separating. HELLO?
Whatever it was, she wanted to meet it on good terms. And
her eyes were open.

Curtained halfdark. The air looked grainy, full of hidden
spaces. She ran her eyes over surfaces, into corners: the side
of the washhand basin, the blur of telly, the daft ceramic
nativity set she'd insisted on hauling all the way south, its
hardly-any-watt bulb still on. Green figures on the dresser
blinking 7.15 7.15 7.15 were the only thing moving.
Nothing else. Nothing discernible anyway. She sat up,
checking, trying not to feel the curdled something-or-other
slopping like brandy in her stomach. Her bra was digging
in, underwires biting the top of her ribcage. But she wasn't
for taking it off. Those shooting pains when she tried to do
without the damn thing, even for a couple of hours, were
worse. Like a heart-attack gone wrong. The big girl's
burden, Patrick called it. Haha Patrick haha. It was sore
though. Her head too, thumping like a radio in another
room. There was paracetamol somewhere but godknew.
Mhairi imagined getting up and looking for it, putting the
wee chalk circles in her mouth, that taste like bile writhing.
The stink of bacon didn't help. Bacon, sausages, toast done
on one side and eggs. The kitchen right under her room: you
could smell burnt pig fat if you put your nose too close to
the wallpaper. Mhairi thought about Mrs Easter down
somewhere under her floorboards, frying eggs: mucous
coatings over pale yolks, bubbles in the whites. Like
diseased crocodile eyes. Christ almighty. At least there was
no axe-murderer as well. There was no sound at all. No
coughs or running water, no belt buckles clanking; that
quietness of razors against stubble that meant the men in
the next room were still around. Nothing. Godknew what
time they started on building sites, why the guys who
worked over the road stayed here. Being away did that: it

made you realise there were a million things about how the world was ordered, tiny, necessary things about life you knew damn all about. Things your grandfather never told you. He'd given her the nativity set, though. Just Mary and two wise men, a shepherd and a sheep but it had been complete once. Melchior had got stood on, the crib was empty and godknew where Joseph was. But it made her feel safer or something. Mhairi looked at it, smiled. And smelled the bacon again. She turned away, swallowed hard a couple of times. There was nothing for it. She'd have to put on the telly.

Mhairi stretched, pressed the button with her foot. White almonds reared out of the screen and turned into three tortoises chasing a rat. Cartoons. Mhairi didn't like cartoons. Even as a wee girl she hadn't liked them, except Dumbo. She couldn't remember who'd taken her to see it. It wouldn't have been grandad. But she remembered the film fine. The thought of Dumbo reaching for the big elephant's trunk through the bars of a cage could still make her eyes water. Not the stuff they put on these days though. Godknew what they were meant to be about, what weans saw in them. She let the turtles run for another minute anyway. Then a man and a woman came on, pretending to be chummy over cups of coffee. After the news, they said, have WE got something for YOU: the men who've been skinny-dipping in the Serpentine since January the first, the woman who's just given birth at the age of fifty-five and a new hard-hitting report that claims more children are likely to turn to suicide at this time of year than at any other. The man lurched forward out of his comfy chair, looking hard at Mhairi. Join us after the news when our phone lines will be waiting for your Festive Fallout Heartbreak call. Mhairi turned to sort out the pillow while he said the number and the news tune played. When she turned back, the eyes were there. Those big eyes that only very young children have. There was another fucking crisis in Bosnia. Little girls with scarves over their mouths in the snow, dusty white feet poking out of stained carpet coffins, women greeting. There were always women greeting. You couldn't hear them because the report was dubbed over the top of the film but you could see them all right. There would be a full report later. After that, a missing toddler found buried in an open field, a woman raped by a SAFE HOME AT NIGHT taxi driver, a drug-ring in Staffordshire and Tiger the dog. Tiger had been saved from a disused well shaft with only minor cuts and grazes. Tiger was ok. Mhairi turned the sound down and went over to the washstand.

The tube was flat. Sucked dry. Mhairi forced what was left inside onto the brush and threw the wasted container in the bin under the sink and something crackled. Something familiar. Slowly, she looked down. Under the individual milk tubs, paled-out tea-bags, kirbies, tissues, clumps of shed hair, the sandwich containers. Clear moulded plastic with the sticky label still intact. She reached forward, the brush angled in her mouth, touched the empty triangles with one finger. They crackled. Twice. Then again without her touching this time. The burglar/rapist/nameless intruder. It was a sandwich tray. The thing she'd said HELLO to, hoping politeness would make it less inclined to do real damage. HELLO for godsake. It was a sandwich tray. Mhairi straightened, brushing her teeth hard, acknowledging her own eyes in the mirror. Another grey hair right in the middle of the fringe. She pulled it out, spat, rinsed, shaking her head. HELLO for godsake. On the way past to the wardrobe, the folded jeans, she switched off the holiday commercials playing steel guitar to the empty bed and opened the wardrobe.

It wasn't cold and the men from the site didn't yell. Mhairi walked with her head up. A girl, maybe fourteen or fifteen, with no jacket and crutches was there just beyond the grass verge, hovering on the kerb for the sign to change. She could see her quite clearly: the first carefully placed step onto the road and the car coming round the curve of the park. The car accelerating. The lights had to be against him but he didn't seem to be slowing down any, just keeping coming. Mhairi was wondering if she should shout when the girl stopped. She stopped on the crossing with her arms at her sides and watched the thing coming towards her. Mhairi stopped too. At the last minute, the car swerved, brakes squealing at the white line. The tyres bumped the pavement as it stopped. And the girl was fine. Still there, absolutely fine. Mhairi watched the driver's window roll down, the man in the passenger seat turn away while his pal started roaring. The girl swivelled on the crutches and walked on, step for step, to the other side. As if she couldn't hear.

Stupid bitch, he yelled.

Nothing.

You could've caused a bloody accident.

From the other side, she turned back briefly. Prick, she said. Then walked on under the trees. By the time Mhairi reached the crossing the guy was back in his seat, combing his hair. Stupid bitch, he said again, loud enough for Mhairi to hear. Then drove off. He left behind a fresh skid-line, black rubber tread against the grey asphalt. There was no-one else on the whole stretch of road. Mhairi ignored three green men and checked the road umpteen times. Just in case.

The park wasn't really. Only a few hankies of grass, a dozen trees with warty-looking branches. It took no more than two minutes to walk through going slow. She could see

the mall sign now, star-shaped fairy-lights still showing
between the bare branches, SALE notices shouldering into
view beneath. This morning there were buds as well. Tight,
unidentifiable, but definitely buds, the sky behind them the
colour of a medical card. She'd liked this walk from the first
day: five minutes across the green and two sets of lights,
then down the pedestrian area to the gallery. She didn't
need to be there at all now. Her stuff was all set up and
Debbie did the selling but she liked to call in every day,
rearrange the brooches a bit, hang around and talk.
Watching folk try on the things she'd made was good,
having folk know who you were when you walked in
somewhere. Like you belonged. Even not meaning to go till
later, this was the way she was walking. Besides, the best
shops were near the gallery, Patrick and Maureen's presents
still to go. Maureen was easy: she liked anything that was
ear-rings. One of the other silverworkers in the exhibition
had promised her a pair in exchange for a pair of Mhairi's.
Patrick was harder. Tapes were always the wrong band or
the subject of HOW COULD ANYBODY LIKE THAT
CRAP monologues and clothes were too dear. Anyway,
she'd look. Then buy him beer. It was a pig to carry back
but you couldn't go wrong with Patrick and beer. Then
grandad. Didn't drink, didn't smoke, didn't read or use
aftershave, didn't play cards, dominoes or football. He
didn't play anything. Christ, Patrick had said the first time
she told him about him, he sounds like a right miserable old
bastard; is he the Pope? and Mhairi had smiled but not
properly, not meaning it. She was thinking. She was
wondering, mibby for the first time, what other people
thought. If it was the way she was talking about him or if
he really was a miserable old bastard. He made his garden
sculptures and drove his taxi, went to the spiritualist church
and tried to send messages to Mhairi's ma and grandma.
That was what he did. Sum total. Since he'd packed in the

fishing boats, he'd more or less stayed at home all the time. He didn't even watch tv. Anyway, it made him hell to buy presents for. The worst was the Christmas she'd given him tarot cards and he'd chucked them in the fire. Mistake. Keeping it simple was safest. Socks. He had drawers full of socks, the bands still on. It would be nice to get him something he'd really like but godknew what it was. More and more, especially now she'd moved away, he acted like presents were a waste of money. Something he wouldn't thank you for. As though you were a fool for trying to get him something nice. Mibby Patrick was right.

The shops were there now, the rest of the arcade stretching down the hill, rack outside Jezebel and sale labels visible all the way up the street. JEZEBEL in dayglo green, dripping, and underneath, her shoes. Cuban heel, suede, scarlet. She walked by them every day, imagining Maureen looking at them, talking to her as though she was off her head: they're dear, they're a funny colour, they're hopeless material, get something *practical*, Mhairi. Maureen was keen on *practical*: there was never any arguing about what it was and those shoes weren't. Patrick would be more succinct. He'd tell her they looked like something a tart would wear/had she paid for them/they must have seen her coming. That said, though, he'd like them fine. Grandad wouldn't even see them. He'd never been to Glasgow for ages. These days there were lots of things he didn't know. The fact her hair was a different colour for one thing. And short. And Patrick, that she and Patrick weren't just in the same house any more, they were in the same room. The same bed. He was funny enough about Patrick's existing near her never mind anything else. Mhairi stood still for a long moment, looking down the slope at the shoe racks, imagining the feel of suede under her hand. Wicked, gorgeous, wonderful. And not really for her. They were all

quite right. She didn't need them. Nobody did, she supposed. A wave of nausea washed at the back of her throat.
What she really needed wasn't shoes, it was indigestion
tablets. There was a decent cafe just over the road, the door
open and waiting. What she really needed right now was a
sit down.

Five servings of milk. She slipped them into her pocket
out of eyeshot of the woman serving along with four sugar
sachets and a couple of teaspoons for good measure, then
sat down at the window with the hot cup. Other wee odds
and sods were still in the bag from yesterday but it paid to
think ahead. Mrs Easter never gave her enough for the
amount of tea she was drinking down here. And postcards.
The postcards were still in there as well, not written yet.
There was nothing to put because they phoned all the time.
Every night so she didn't have to go out alone to a callbox,
making sure she was keeping herself safe. Trying to tell
them things that made it worth their bother wasn't so easy.
It was hard to say what it was like at all, the difference being
away. They didn't know the people she'd met, what the
names meant when she used them. Maureen always
laughed in the right places but Maureen did that. Even if she
didn't know what the hell you were talking about. She
always laughed in the wrong bits. It made Mhairi feel
awkward and embarrassed, as if she was talking another
language badly. Describing the New Year thing with
Debbie and Frankie, going out for a meal, staying on in the
restaurant with five Algerian waiters behind the locked
door, drinking godknew what to bring in the bells and
singing Pavarotti hits in different languages and kid-on
Italian. Total strangers. Debbie with the purple hair who
made necklaces out of shells. Frankie wearing Lycra shorts
and a rubber swimming hat with roses round the ears.
When it came to it, though, Mhairi couldn't remember why

it had been so good, couldn't tell it right at all. Patrick was the worst. He'd listened till she stopped then there was a silence on his side of the phone.

So what did you eat then? he said eventually.

Something with lentils, Mhairi said.

Oh? he said.

Egyptian Pie.

Oh?

Debbie said they called it that because it tasted like sand.

Should have had an omelette, then.

Yes, she said.

She knew Patrick was waiting for her to say something more but she couldn't think of anything. They'd done his gig in Edinburgh, Maureen's night in with her mum. She couldn't think of anything else.

So, he said. You had a good time?

Yes. She felt apologetic saying it. Yes.

Great. A long pause. You had a good time.

Maybe he'd hoped she'd need more encouragement or something, more reassurance she was fine elsewhere. Maybe he got a shock hearing her not needing it. And it *was* shocking somehow. How fine she felt. How perfectly all right. And she had missed him then, in the callbox near the bus shelter where the same two drunks hung about every afternoon asking for money: the hiss that might have been some form of loneliness coming down the wire. On the other hand, mibby that was just sentimental nonsense. Patrick always said she read too much into things, exaggerated what he said to suit herself. As though he thought she was trying to trap him, make him admit more than he felt. Maybe she was. Anyway she didn't want to start hiding things. She'd tell him about the evening the gallery staff had planned for her last day and hope he'd be pleased. Four days more. Then she'd be back, Glasgow Central by half eight. He'd be out with the band and not able to meet the train but he'd want to know. He usually liked to know. That was what she could put on the postcard, then. She put the cards next to the saucer, foraged in her bag for a pen. It came out with pink mush all over the tip. Lipstick. The top off the bloody thing again. The card she'd been saving for Patrick was wearing it too – a sheeny pink blob over the bit where his name would be. Imagining his face, lifting it from behind the door. He'd think she'd kissed the damn thing before she'd posted it and think she'd gone off her head. She dabbed the mark one more time, laughing, knowing it wouldn't shift.

The chemist was next to the post box. By the afternoon, there were queues at all the tills but right now was fine. Two walls of tissues, floor to head-height. Different colours or sizes, for make-up and sneezing into, pocket-size, travel-size, man-size, menthol, baby-soft: umpteen ply and pastels, Noddies, Postman Pats. Two walls. Mhairi took the cheapest and looked round for the sandwiches. They were visible from here but she didn't want to walk over. Not yet. Thinking about fillings was making her feel sick. She held the edge of the nearest counter and waited for it to subside, sweating. The caffeine, maybe. These places were always too hot. Another wave reminding her how much alcohol she'd drunk last night. There was a seat near the prescription counter, there behind the cotton wool and sterilising fluid. She knew exactly where it was. Behind the pink and blue boxes. Mhairi flicked her eyes in their direction, not sure why it mattered not to be seen. She'd spent half an hour there yesterday, gone out without buying. This time, the dizziness was more pressing. She walked over, sat on her heels holding the nearest shelf. It was daft to feel embarrassed. But the prices. Jesus. What was there in a Pregnancy Testing Kit that justified that kind of money –

more than half the price of the too-dear shoes? She looked at the side, the words in clean white lettering.

Contents: two phials of testing solution (with lids),
two colour tablets, two indicator wands, dropper, instruction sheet.
ACCURATE FROM THE FIRST DAY OF THE MISSED PERIOD.

The clinic said to wait another three weeks when she phoned, they'd have preferred six. Mhairi thought she hadn't heard right, the accent or maybe a bad line. But it was right enough. Six weeks. She told them she wasn't here that long and they said it wasn't their problem. She hung up. Now here was this box, telling her she could know now. Tomorrow morning. Before she went home and had to look at Patrick, work out how to be. She looked at the package, the price flash on the shelf. A purple anorak sleeve reached over her head. It took something from the shelf, retracted. The woman who owned it, a girl maybe, was standing behind her, reading one of the boxes. No make-up and her hair pulled back like that. She looked about seventeen.

Doesn't matter which one you lift, does it? she said. They're all complicated.

Mhairi smiled. Expensive as well.

Sorry?

Mhairi felt noticeable suddenly, shy. They're dear, I'm saying. Pricey.

The woman laughed. You think we could wait. Not as though you don't know soon enough eh?

She put the box back into the rack and walked away, bumping the wire basket off her thigh. It was full of babyfood. She walked back to the checkout carrying it, collecting a pushchair to wheel it through, a huge infant in

a snowsuit plumped up like an inflatable doll inside it. Its
wee eyes peered out, not blinking. Mhairi hadn't a clue how
old it might be, had no way of even guessing. Its mother
maybe expecting again, half Mhairi's age by the looks of
her, and here was Mhairi with no information on certain
vital subjects at all. Vital female subjects. She looked down.
Boy-blue cardboard, tidy graphics: a clock with a quarter of
its face shaded off, a hand holding a phial. It wasn't just the
money. The jewellery had gone well. She had sold stuff
here, more than she would have at home. There ought to be
enough for one-off extravagances. It wasn't just money at
all. It was the thought of having to pee straight into a tiny
glass container early in the morning, measuring out with the
dropper then the waiting, lying back on Mrs Easter's green
candlewick, trying not to look at the LED numbers not
changing, trying not to think about what this might only be
the beginning of, how many more samples and testing could
come next. Then taking out the indicator. Taking out the
indicator. It was still too hot in here. And the black
aftertaste in her mouth. Whether she felt this way from her
suspicion of what might be true or. Or what. It was hard
even to imagine the word. Pregnant. Suddenly the girl-
woman was back, reaching for the box she had put back
earlier. She looked at Mhairi and shrugged.

Well. She shrugged again, looking caught out. You do,
don't you?

Her sneakers squeaked as she walked away.

Mhairi looked at the package in her hand. She stood up,
carefully. One knee cricked, needing oiled. The things
inside the box shifted with her as she limped towards the
till.

Outside was better. Still not wonderful, but fresher.
Mhairi stood at the postbox, the polythene bag over her
arm, catching her breath. To look busy, she fished the cards

out of her bag, pushed them through the slit. She imagined
Maureen and Patrick picking them up, knowing whose
writing it was. Comparing notes. Four days. She would be
back in four days. The presents would have to wait though.
The thumping in her head was starting again, a heartbeat in
the wrong place. There were benches near the phone kiosk,
just a block further up. At the other side of the park. She
imagined herself walking into the kiosk, pressing her
forehead against the cool metal walls, her finger pressing all
the right buttons. Then. Then nothing. It was the wrong
time of day. Patrick was never in on Wednesday mornings.
He always stayed out after he'd signed on. Maureen was at
work. There was no-one to speak to. Except grandad. There
was an off chance there. Grandad. She walked till dizziness
threatened to make her fall then knelt where she was, the
bag at her feet. Breathing out and in slowly, counting. She
could see the phone ringing in the wee hall with the brown
wallpaper, the holy pictures still there with ancient bits of
tinsel left over from Christmas if he'd put any up this year
at all, the shore and the electricity pylons visible from the
tiny wee window. Barra shut for Wednesday and the phone
ringing out. Caitlin Sinclair pushing a pram with the bairn
in it she'd been too feart to admit to till she was in labour.
Dear god dear god. She couldn't phone him. Not with this
terrible danger inside her, the nearness of doing something
stupid and she didn't want to do anything stupid. Not
before she knew for sure. The best thing to do was wait.
Wait, go back for a lie down, and everything would be fine.
She'd hear them tonight: Patrick would phone and
Maureen would phone and she would listen to them in Mrs
Easter's kitchen, trying not to notice the smell of dead meat
laid out for the morning, their voices not knowing yet, not
treating her any different. And later, even when they did, if
they did, she'd still be fine. Fine. She might have to be finer
than she'd ever been in her life. For now, though, there were

simple practicalities. The cafe, the road and the park one step at a time. Mhairi looked up, gauging the distance. A face caught her off-guard, a face staring at her from the window of the shoe shop across the road. Her own. Just a glass reflection. If you refocused, employed a simple trick of the eye, it went away. All you could see were red shoes. She watched them for a moment then looked back down the mall. All that way to the chemist's and she'd forgotten the toothpaste. She sighed, sniffed, lifted her bags. Back at Mrs Easter's she'd make a list.

TOOTHPASTE, SANDWICHES, BEER, EAR-RINGS, SOCKS wrote itself in her head as she walked under the trees: a neat row in red biro, the handwriting she won gold stars for. At the other side of the park, the word WOOL appeared. WOOL. They said her grandad had used to knit, all the fishermen had. They'd wound oily wool round their big, gristly fingers, been self-sufficient, made their own jerseys. To hell with socks. She'd get him wool, take it herself and watch his face when he opened it; the surprise before he'd had time to control it. At least it would be some kind of reaction. Mhairi laughed till it started to turn into something else then stopped. Wool. His hands the way they were. He couldn't knit now even if he wanted to. If he ever had. She wasn't going to greet though. Greeting made you dangerous. It made you sentimental and that was no bloody use to anybody. Whatever happened, she wasn't going to give in. She wasn't going back to Barra, she wasn't greeting and she wasn't giving in. She had to remember that. She'd survive. People did. They had the capacity to survive. Another thing. She was going back for another look at those shoes. This afternoon, before some other bugger bought them. She'd write that down as well.

The trees were thinning out and the main road was

visible. Someone whistled, shouted over from the building
site. Mhairi heard but didn't look round. Prick, she said
under her breath. Prick. Black tyre skids snaked under her
feet as she walked over the crossing with her head up,
breathing deep for a lungful of fresh air. It wasn't fresh at
all, it was full of carbon monoxide. But it was fine. It would
do. Dear god but she wanted to hear his voice. Walking,
glass phials chiming at her heels, the sky blue as burning.

after the rains

think

it is too warm here and my heart is racing think where was I I was

in the bus shelter.

Dripping in there with the rest of them out of the rain.
It must have been shortly after ten because the bus to the Cross had just drawn up, the brakes still squealing and when they stopped there was a sound of nothing. That was what was different. I remember distinctly, the silence. The sound of people listening to each other listening. We peered, curled pieces of ourselves beyond the perspex, testing from under rain-mates for what it was. I watched an elder bush, the nearest of the seven planted by the council to represent nature on the estate. Its leaves dripped still. But I could swear the drops were less assured now, visible seconds lurching between one drop and the next as I watched. A child standing near me ducked and looked up, suddenly suspicious. With a muffled grunt that could have been apology, a large woman shoved by me and out into the

middle of the road to make sure for all of us. We watched
her stand there, face upturned. The slow, steady smile. In
that moment, we knew. It had stopped raining. After nine
solid months, it had stopped raining. Folk normally so
wary, so shy of ridicule it hurt, we blossomed. We cracked
jokes and spoke to perfect strangers, we embraced

like warm soup to remember it, the touch of human skin

while the bus sat like a ruin on the road. There was
laughing and cuddling and general pagan revelry. Some of
the passengers got off the bus and joined us as we emerged
from the shelter, one shaking a bottle of lemonade with his
thumb over the neck, spraying it like champagne. The
driver was out too. Even given the mood that was
remarkable since he was usually such a bloodyminded big
bastard. He looked, he saw, he made a hammy mime of
looking at his watch. Right, he said. The rain was off.
We'd seen what there was to see. If anybody's goin to the
Cross they better come wi me, he said. Some of us have got
schedules to keep. Nobody minded. We came, good-
natured to spite him: we drifted back. Then, as I straggled
on, I noticed something in the corner of the shelter: a wee
girl, huddling in on herself, keeking out between her
fingers. I watched her as the bus began to move,
indistinct behind too much hair. Something in my stomach
fluttered but that was all. Maybe I should have been more
curious, taken time. The bus picked up speed, though.
With the rest I let myself be taken and my excitement
eclipsed her.

The road itself was interesting now the rain had stopped.
Commonplaces became significant as we noted with
genuine feeling it was 'turning out nice' or 'taking a turn for
the better'. Puddles in the gutters seemed just as full but

elsewhere, tarmac was surfacing. You could see boys on the
crest of the road, in the middle of the traffic path, for the
novelty of standing there without water tugging at their
shoes. As we entered the town, a gang of youths were
kicking planks away. Everyone hated the planks. Stretched
kerb to kerb by selfish old people too afraid of the road
tides to attempt crossing without them, they caused
accidents, cost limbs, the lives of children. It was like a
blessing, a sign of something better to come to see those
boys kicking the planks away. Someone sang a hymn. The
rest of us pointed and waved, rubbing with cuffs at the
windows streaming with our too-close breath, the damp
smoking from our clothes. Talk seemed abnormally loud: it
wasn't just that we had more to say, but that the noise of
drizzle no longer deadened everything. Too much for some,
maybe. Too soon. A few near me were in tears and a low
groaning could be heard from the upper deck. I thought it
had nothing to do with me. I thought it would pass. When
the bus stopped at the terminus, I left without giving it
further thought.

Only half an hour later, the sky had lightened consider-
ably. Offices and shop windows were framed with workers
looking out. I could see rows of them from my bench at the
corner of the pedestrian precinct. I was

what was I doing?
just looking too looking up I was

looking up when suddenly, without warning, the sun
came out. A great rip in the cloud and there it was: one
whole, flaming presence. And with it came the colours.
Colours. With a catch of emotion, I realised how much we
had forgotten, how ashen everything had been for so long.
The low light, the constant smurr – we had encouraged it.

For some children, greyness was all there ever had been, was all we were entitled to. Now everything returned, yellows, greens, reds, oranges and wild blues shaming in their brightness. From all over the Cross came a sigh of relief and wonder. We realised how little we had fought. Yet the sun had come out. The sun had come out.

Those of us in the street found the windows of the television showrooms: we were, after all, only ordinary folk and untrusting of the evidence of our own eyes. For a moment or two, there was only a cookery demonstration, a chopping of knives. Then the first news flash. Words typed themselves over sliced vegetables as we watched. Letter by letter it spelled out what we had hoped. The sun had come out. Reassured, as though we knew it all along, we cheered. Laughter died away as a blender mushed solid matter to a pulp behind the printout. A huge pair of hands pulled the top off the glass canister, spilling its dark contents into a bowl before the food disappeared altogether and a man appeared, keen to explain with radiating lines and velcro symbols about the weather. He did that for five minutes, then read cheerfully from a slip of paper. Scientists were confident this was the end of the rain for some considerable time, he said. There would be a full report later and news flashes throughout the day. The Queen was preparing a statement. A picture of her shaking hands with the Prime Minister flickered over the monitor briefly. Both were smiling. Satisfied, we turned away from the tv and shone our faces upwards, crunching our eyes against the unaccustomed sky. I remember my scalp tingling, the back of my neck rippling with a warmth. On all sides, shop workers clustered in open doorways, filled their display windows with faces tilting towards the light. As if it had been waiting for this moment, a massive, seven-coloured arch appeared, pouring itself above the buildings and the town to prickle ready tears. We applauded. We applauded the rainbow and its promise. We were radiant.

By the afternoon it was hot. I hadn't moved much: the length of the street, a little shopping, then back to the bench at the Cross to watch the day unfold along with others who had the time. The streets were misty and dry patches had squared out on the paving. We remarked on the speed of the change of events, but not overmuch. It was enough it was happening at all. City bakeries sold out of sandwiches as people lunched al fresco. Bright dots of tee-shirts began to appear among the crowds. Sloughing off rain-clothes allowed us to look at ourselves afresh and become dissatisfied with what we saw. Those who lived close enough went home to change: canvas trousers, summer dresses, short-sleeved shirts with bleachy angles poking out. Some improvised, rolling up trouser legs in a jokey but serviceable imitation of Bermuda shorts, fit for the tropic the Cross had become. Almost everyone wore a hat, sunglasses or visor against the glare. More news flashes confirmed it: the country was in the grip of a freak heatwave. Temperatures were rising by the minute. The huge plastic thermometer in the travel agent's window bled steadily upward as we rolled up our sleeves and loosened collar-buttons. I went to the riverside walkway seeking cooler air.

cooler there
did I fall asleep? I must have slept
I slept and woke and

By late afternoon, the Cross was much less crowded. Many had drifted off out of the punishing light and gone back indoors to work. Novelty was passing. The crowd under the shade of the Co-op canopy were silent, merely

waiting for the bus home. The newsagent's on the corner
was shutting, the women who worked there clashing
security mesh in place, jangling keys into the stillness. As
they crossed the tarmac to the shelter, something pale and
smoky billowed out from under their slow-moving soles. It
took me a minute to work out it wasn't smoke at all. It was
dust. Dust rising up from gutters that had churned with
running water for so long. My head thumped. The heat and
windlessness of the street was surely intensifying. Workers
who had poked their heads from windows earlier to feel the
sun on their faces had long since retreated. I couldn't help
thinking of them in there – all that glass. A solitary blind
cord tapped listlessly against an overhead pane. Just then
the plump woman who owned the flower shop appeared at
her open door, wheezing and gasping, the effort of her lungs
making her very red about the face and chest in her short
summer frock. The OPEN sign swung behind her as she
fought for space among the carnations and dahlias. Some
other shops were near closing now there was no-one to buy
and a few individuals were lowering shutters, keen, I
supposed, to get out of the thickening air. The bus queue
swelled, sweating. The absence of the hiss of rain had left a
vacuum. Cars had quit long since and there was no thrum
of flies. It was sickly quiet. Seething. Something

something

was coming. A stretching sound, like a mass intake of
breath over our heads was its announcement. Then a low
rumble along the horizon, hollowing the ear: distant
thunder like men clearing their throats. Ready. It was ready
to begin. There was an earth-rippling crack and I looked up.
The rainbow was growing, inflating to fill up every stretch
of blue till none remained as a touchstone for the sky. At the
same time, a huge rushing sound spreading from ear to ear

as though some invisible hand were unzipping the hair from my skull. I threw up my hands for protection, seeing others doing the same, some falling on their knees. *Too late for that* . . . There were children too, the odd one or two dancing on the pedestrian walk-way while others were running or clapping their hands. *We are not all seeing the same thing,* I thought, *we are all of us experiencing something far outside the normal run, but,* and the thought horrified me in its obviousness, *but not the same thing.* A glance confirmed it: the faces around me, behind the glass, in doorways and on the road varied extremely. There was barely time to digest the idea when the sound, a terrible sound of high sudden screaming took all attention for itself. Heads turned to find its source. There, still struggling in her own front doorway, was the florist. She appeared to be trying to pull a shoot *no*

several green shoots she appeared to be trying to pull

several green shoots and leaves from her dress as we watched. More and yet more leaves burst out despite her efforts, and I realised suddenly they were not attached to her dress. They were attached to her elbow, to her arm. I looked harder. They were her arm. *They were her arm.* Greenery surged up her neck and into her hair, buds clustering in a pink halo all around her head. Huge roses ripened at her armpits and elbows; camellias and magnolias fanned out of her cleavage. Seconds or whole minutes, I could not say how long it took. When chrysanthemum petals began falling from somewhere beneath her skirt, the woman stopped struggling. Enough of her face remained however to let me see she was smiling. She was, I realised, welcoming the garden she had become. I felt a twinge of outrage, but as I looked again at the woman's smile and her pleasure, I was moved with compassion. I had to admire it too. The scent was overpowering. It carried all the way from the other side of the road.

In the commotion, we had not noticed a lesser transformation. Her assistant, formerly a girl of about seventeen, now a living display of hyacinth and spring ferns, stepped out from behind the older woman's shadow. At the next doorway, the grocer watched a cabbage foresting the front of his overall. He saw me gaping, hesitated, then pointed at it shyly with his ladyfingers, ears coiling with pea tendrils. The reaction of the crowd to his bravado was enthusiastic. Some cheered and one elderly woman shuffled over for a closer look, muttering endearments. From the back of the bus crowd, a check-out boy I recognised from Tesco's pushed forward to give himself room. The pregnant bulge at the front of his coat was elongating as he came, squaring out to make a trolley complete with front wheel to balance the projection from his body and toddler straps. He did not smile but lowered his shopping into it with great dignity. At the same time, the electrical goods manager of the Co-op displayed a shiny transparent door in the centre of his chest, eager for us to see the bright whorls of washing tumbling inside and receive congratulations on his achievement. All the while the sun grew hotter.

it is too warm here

My arms still cautiously hugging my head, I walked the length of the street to find some shade where I could more comfortably continue to observe. I thought I could see a pattern and wanted to watch it unfold. Though some might have longer gestation periods than others, the transformations would keep going. Loud snickering and the dull rustle of used notes emitted from the bookies as I went past: a squashy bundle emerged from the wool shop. Before long, it would be unstoppable. A whisper was mouthing in my head, half-formed. Perhaps I remembered the child in the shelter from the morning. Something like realisation prickled its beginnings up the back of my neck. I recalled the moaning I had heard on the bus, partial glimpses of things I had chosen to ignore. Without knowing why, I panicked. I ran round the corner, maybe in the hope of escaping, but something blocked my path. An enormous white grub spread the length of the pavement, bulbous tips waving in what looked horribly like appeal. Beyond this nerveless thing, a three-headed phantom groped forward on its hands and knees. Where features should have been was only tight, smooth skin, blanket-grey and eyeless. As another of its kind fumbled from the council offices, nail-less hands foraging for something to give it a sense of its bearings, I drew back, repulsed, fearing the thing it might touch would be me. In so doing, my back touched the wall of the Job Centre, rebounded again at the ripping cold of its walls against my shirt. Even in this heat, frost had feathered the windows and a faint haar issued from the open doorway. I knew nothing would come out of there. Then I was sure. There would be others like this too. Not flowers, not harmless eccentricities, but other things, terrible other things. At that moment, a pitiful screeching forced me to turn. I was facing the butchers'. The howling and the bloody trail at their doorway. The awful death stench and low weeping of children, childish voices seeping under the door of the church.

> I would not look in there
> I did not want to see

I began to run then. Faster. Curiosity pushed my glance down despite the urgings of reason. My hands were very pale and whitening still. Thinning.

They were stark white.

I kept on running.

waiting for marilyn

Rita's

Rita's

Rita's flashes backwards behind the net.

Multicoloured plastic strips shield a cavity in the wall
that isn't a door. They drift aside every so often, gusting like
plant fronds while you peer into the black hole beneath.
Nothing happens but you keep sitting, your hair in wet
rags, listening to what pass for love songs on some terrible
radio through the chalk-scrape of interference. Waiting for
Marilyn.

You never asked for her. Didn't, now you think, even
know what her name was till the third appointment but
that's whose you are. The receptionist says so: a child-
woman with black-rimmed eyes and the fringe like rotten
teeth, a breast or a target shaved into the stubble on her head
and a smile like a meat slice. Marilyn's, aren't you? the
purple stuff on her lips creasing. She smiles that way even
when you don't look. Especially when you don't look. It

means she knows. Even if you don't she does. You're
definitely Marilyn's.

Walk this way.

You follow holding the loose ties of the pinny they gave
you, not able to remember from last time how it's meant to
do up, hoping nobody's looking. Only one free basin.
Tomato-soup red and white checks appear in the mirror as
you hove into view, your hands the wrong way round tying
a double knot. Trying not to feel like someone's grandma, a
trattoria table, you sit, take the towel when it's offered, wait
as you're told. When you lower your neck down to where
the sink might be, the muscles in your belly take the strain,
levelling you backwards gently. The cold enamel bites at the
warmth under the hairline. It sucks like a mouth. But the
other feeling, a low excitement, carries on. Something that
might be called butterflies. Through the mid-Adantic
Glasgow dj roaring for Sonja's seventeenth CONGRATS
AND MIND HOW YOU GO OUT THERE SONJA,
through the start of a tune that files your fillings, even when
the shower touches first time. Through the repeated strokes
of cool water you can still feel it fluttering, swallowing like
a fish. The sensation of waiting. Waiting for Marilyn.

Nothing past the fringing.

The junior goes through shouting for Rita. You don't
know the junior's name but she washed your hair, wrapped
it wet inside the towel, twisting it too tight. You would have
said but she wasn't looking. She didn't speak either, just
walked you across the floor holding your arm like you were
frail or fragile, taking tiny, footbound steps to the middle
chair. The seat was burst, stitches big as bite marks over the
open red gash: a trail of wet dots tagged your heels like a

stray. You settled yourself over the healing plastic scar and waited some more. You wait still, watching the doorless hole gape and close, appear and fold itself away again behind the tease of strips. They nudge a little in the heat-haze while you wait, seeping, feeling the towel threaten to lose its anchor and fall to the floor. But you take a risk anyway, peer round.

On the left, the slatted muzzles of strung-up dryers grunt soundlessly behind two copper-coloured cans of spray. Net on a wire rope hides the misted window. On the right, four women ranged along the wallpaper stripes, frying. Under their electric drying hoods, wisps of silver and lilac stray down, making their faces pucker. Their hands turn pages, making dry sounds, louder than the radio. Half-price day for over 60s. She said that the first time: We don't get many youngsters on a Wednesday, easing a scarlet comb down the back of your neck: I'm lucky to get you. Drawing the wet strands past your shoulders, checking its balance, her hands tucking under the sleek sheets. Then someone behind caught your eye, watching, and you turned away, waiting for the scissors, her tug on separate tresses. You recall the thud of a curl on your wrist, its slithering coolness. Your breath drawing in.

ꙅ'ɒƚiЯ

The sign flashes on and off backwards from this side of the glass.

Same chip on the formica ledge.

Scarlet clamps, coils of cable snaking along the hairy floor, slit-faced socket boards in the skirting. But the plastic strips do not part. Anything that moved was only the junior, hauling one of the row out from under her smoked

Perspex. We're ready to take your rods out now, Mrs
Dixon. Mrs Dixon smiles and is easily led. The three
women left behind don't even notice. One is asleep: the last
merely holds a magazine, staring. It takes a moment before
you realise she has no option. She can't close her eyes
because the curlers under the hood stretch her skin too
tight. Water makes a sheen over her eyes, a runnel to the
cotton wool at the rim of the scarf. Someone slips past with
a mug of coffee that is not for her. She watches it, goes back
to the magazine. The phone starts and no-one goes. Mrs
Dixon says thank you three times through repeated,
unanswered ringing, the dj howling like a bitch in a shut
room. This is his ALL-TIME FAVOURITE, his RED HOT
TIP FOR THE TOP. You turn away, lower your shoulders.
Black rubber teats appear. They're attached to a hair-dryer
and you've no idea what they're for. You are still watching
them when it happens. Something clicks.

Metal against metal.

Marilyn is there in the mirror, mouthing hello. Your skull
tilting in her hands and Marilyn looking in the glass,
checking you over with her fingertips.

Right we are, she says, lifting a comb from nowhere you
can see. The usual? Marilyn lowering the scarlet teeth. Just
tidy you up a wee bit, then?

A tug sears then relaxes, burning at the roots.

Yes, you say, just the same.

And she smiles and concentrates, the tip of her tongue
appearing as she combs out your hair, wondering how
much she'll take off.

That much ok?

The burr in the voice when she settles her hand on your
shoulder to promise no more than an inch, you'll hardly
notice. Her breath scented with milk. No more than an inch.

She steps back to begin and you can see what she's

wearing today. Shorts and a loose shirt. Khaki. Things you wouldn't dare. Not knowing what to do with your hands, you watch her, Marilyn in army colours, raking her fingertips through the dead and drowned extremes of your being. It is you she handles with such seriousness, something you made from within your own body, opening the scissors carefully, bearing down and smiling to let you know it's ok. It's ok. Her familiar whisper. You're starting to relax when you see it. Something small glittering at the roots of her fingers. One finger. She sees you looking before you have time to cover up.

Engagement ring, she says. It's a real diamond.

The material of her shorts crushes against your arm.

I like solitaires.

A shear and flutter
Marilyn is cutting your hair.
Marilyn with her slim hand hooped to some absent man.

Yes, you say. You have to say something. I didn't think.

But you do. A man in this choking female interior. Greased-back hair and a square jaw, solid. What kind of man? A pale mouth swallowing one of Marilyn's tiny breasts. You can't work out what this is washing over you like iced water, whether you're jealous. Of whom. The backs of his hands wrapping her thin white thighs before his hips move. The cushion he would make of her. Hoping so loud you almost speak. I hope he's not heavy.

Sorry? she says. Half her face turns pale blue.

Sorry?

Marilyn's slip of a girlness wondering what it was you said. Is everything ok? And you say, of course, laughing to make it truer. Looking down to hide the blush that's starting, you see the shorts leg wide of her skin, the way the cloth lifts to make a tunnel at her thigh. Wide enough for hand to slip inside. Just talking to myself.

Big blue eyes that haven't a clue what you're saying. She smiles, her teeth perfect points, resumes.

The finger glitters as she tilts your head forward. A split-second of your own face, expressionless, appears as you go down, shutting its eyes again to wait for her touch on the nape of your neck.

The smug bastard on the radio keeps going,

Rita's

flashes backwards from the other side of the glass.

hope

The dark, the light, the dark.

The cartilage on either side of my little fingers. Blood bursting the capillaries in my nose rendering it warm. This is my face. My face. These are my palms on my cheeks like paper against more paper: four sheets. If I move them I will be able to see. I will be able to peek between first and second knuckle joint and see her. Still there. On the sofa opposite me, Hope. There is nothing surprising in that: it is where she always sits. Lies. Tonight she will most probably be lying down; lying down and not knitting. She will be lying down reading because it is the day her magazine comes. Every Thursday, the same magazine, one with advertisements and home decoration tips, how-I-coped stories. She reads it all evening, taking her time, snapping squares from a bar of chocolate. Other nights, she knits and watches tv: both at the same time. Tonight, though, she'll be lying on the sofa, sucking chocolate with her shoes off, the seams on the soles of her tights showing because this is her home. Home. A place you can unwind, let yourself go a little because you feel safe, in the bosom of your loved ones. A place you can be yourself. From where I sit, the magazine will obscure her face so I won't be able to admire it. What I will see are wisps of hair, her painted nails, tulips behind her head in a glass vase. I will be able to admire those instead. Red hair, red nails, red tulips with black hearts; concentric circles going round the handmade rug; Victorian washbasin on the windowsill; cottage prints, frills on the curtains. She uses decorating tips in the magazine so it's not money wasted. Doing things to the house gives her an outlet. She calls it that herself, an outlet. That and the poems. Hope writes poems. You need a hobby she says, hobbies are relaxing, they give you a sense of who you are and writing poems is hers. She encourages me in the same way, says I need a hobby too and she may be right. I work too much she says: working at home can do that. I work at home balancing other people's books. My own boss, hours I can fit round our life together instead of the other way round: all plus side, she says. Not only that but we have the constant reassurance the other is near. Constant. Not many people are so lucky she says, especially not people with children. We do not have children so we have the time to be truly together in a way most couples can only dream about. That is what we are doing now. The cats are in our bed upstairs and Hope is at rest in the sofa, reading her magazine. Though I can't see them, I know her poet's eyes are behind the cigarette carton on the back cover, glossing the promises of skin creams and home gardening tips, suggestions to improve her love life. Unless, of course, she has them closed. Even if my own eyes were open, I would not be able to tell for sure, not from this angle. I would, however, be able to regard her feet: vulnerable little feet inside nylon casings with blood-coloured nails glinting through the orange mesh. I would be forced to notice her nails match the tulips too. And if I looked down, if I turned my head, my own feet would appear. Slippered. On the rug. I peer through my fingers and there they are, my feet in blue tartan wrappers. I watch them double and blur, fade back into themselves again, my fingers pressing deep into the soft cave of my sockets before my eyelids reclose. They close because I cannot stop them. And the vision comes again: the same vista playing uninvited on the screen of my closed eyelids, the same vision every time. Mile after mile of empty rail-track, the moss on its sleepers deep as velvet. Mile after mile rolling between broken stone and sky. A place no train has passed for years or is likely to come again, where no-one will pass by, wave or turn to notice me. On either side, burned-out fields and wasteground that roll to the horizon are barren and roadless, a forgotten wild where no-one offers kindness, a meal on a clean tablecloth, a brow I can kiss. If I try I can feel the chill of the place slicing my coat, its scissoring wind: the almost palpable scour of sand between my teeth. And then, when I am on the verge of moaning aloud with pleasure, she catches me. She calls me back. Hope coughing. A sound she could not help but still. I press my fingers hard into the closed lids, trying not to know. The darkness, pain through the swollen skin. I push harder, heart pounding.

She coughs again.

Before long I will get up and offer to make tea. If I don't, she will come over. She will reach and pat my hand. Can't I be at peace tonight? Never mind. She will pat my hand, rearrange my shirt collar. I need more time off, she'll say. I ought to relax more. I smoke too much. I overwork.

On the other side of the room, I hear the crushing of the chocolate wrapper, the smacking of lips. Hope's sweet little mouth getting ready to offer me a kiss.

Sooner or later. I will have to open them.
Sooner or later I will have to open my eyes.

bisex

I worry.
Sometimes I need to hear your voice.

I worry. I phone.
You are often out when I phone.

I walk to the far end of the kitchen and hold the kettle under the tap, watch the red marker on the side rise on the fresh water. You could be shopping but not this late: a concert maybe, a show. Walking somewhere, backstreets under the streetlamps, the park no-one would go to the park at night, the middle of the town. I have no way of knowing. The pictures then, the sauna trying not to think the sauna. The kettle is half-full. Four cups. The sauna. I switch the tap off with one hand, bracing the muscles in the other for the weight of carrying, turn away from my reflection in the window, the rictus of polished jars behind the sink.

Three bags left. Three white purses pooling brown dust. That means six cups of tea if I'm careful. Six for one. I replace the blue and white lid so I don't have to think about there being less now and dowse the first square, fighting it back under with the stream of boiling water every time it tries to surface, then coax it with the spoon before fishing it into another cup for later. I'm running out of milk. Just enough so the tea turns cloudy auburn, seeping from the unmixed splash of white. Greyish white. The kitchen table, the hot cylinder between my hands. The sauna a disco or pub a pub always the same ones. Always. The same ones. Eyes closed, rubbing my mouth against the cup. Even when it burns I don't pull away.

You.

You reach across the table.

There is a glass with a slice of lemon, bubbles gathering like spawn along the rim. Your hand lays stripes on the frosted bowl. Your hand. It lifts the glass, settles it against your mouth momentarily, puts it back in exactly the same place. Holding a glass for no reason is what I do, not you. It's near an ashtray, stubbed with butts. Your hair is only just too long, blond creeper over the collar of your jacket at the back. At the front it makes spikes in your eyes. Between that and the smoke in here you can hardly see. Hair in your eyes, booze and no specs not even any sign of the specs. Little vanities leave you wide open. Regardless, you lift the glass again, sip. The way you swallow, jerk the plumbline of that maleness in your throat is smooth, practised. The way you settle the glass back, running your finger and thumb the length of its stem, watching it fizz.

My stomach dips.

Someone is pulling into focus behind the crook of your arm where it lifts, fetches a cigarette to your mouth. The

arm stays flexed, waiting for someone to offer a match. I
can't tell if you know he is there, whether you move
knowing you are observed or not. In any case, he
approaches while you strike and pout, inching the cigarette
for the flame the way I've seen you do it a hundred times,
eyes puckering up when you draw and his hand touches the
table. Your table. You peer at the nameless hand, flicking
your head to clear your vision, inhaling, blowing the match
out with the first breath of smoke. And you let him sit. You
raise your eyes slowly/blowing the match dead. You always
let him sit.

And I don't know. I don't know how you begin with
these men.

After the shared silences, the contact that implies nothing
and everything, messages that could be retracted as soon as
understood, after you approach each other, how the real
game starts. How you admit to each other what you are
doing, whether there is no need. Euphemism and hedging,
daring to meet his eyes for whole seconds, tipping your
tongue against your carefully white teeth. You play games
you would not begin to play with me, risking everything
and nothing, waiting for a sign. And sooner or later it
comes, though neither of you will be able to say afterwards
when that moment was or how it was reached. A change in
the temperature of the shared glances, maybe. Or he could
simply say it out loud. I don't know. I don't know how it is
decided, the rising to leave together, how you choose:
whether tonight it's you or him who stands up first.
Whether you have somewhere to go, whether you wait
while he finishes a drink and wipes his mouth or whether
you leave and he follows. His strange scent tracking you
down, maybe knowing somewhere warm and safe.
Whether it is only the bus shelter or back street, opened

coats and the press of concrete at your back. Whether you touch first or he does. I wonder and try not to think, thinking anyway. Either way, there are always folds of cloth. I always see folds of cloth.

Your hand stretching across the drapery of his jeans to his belt, your fingers lifting the buckle to slip the leather. Blond fingers, taut with muscle, white as mushroom stalks free the buckle and find the zip, a single nail running the length of closed teeth towards the tag to inch it down. Your lips part and your eyelids are closed. Already, your breath fractures as you reach inside. His fingers reach for your shirt buttons.

What happens then is less distinct. It's you I want to see. Falling blond, the fringe lapping the closed lids as his fist accelerates and your mouth opens, that catch in your breath. His lips cover yours, the scratch of stubble on your cheek something familiar, something fond. And I envy that kiss, this tenderness. The thick vein that I have trailed with my tongue courses inside his fist. It pulses for him. His grip stronger than mine.

And when it's finished, after you share a sameness with him and your hands lace, sticky, I worry about what it is you say. Whether you touch him the way you touch me. I don't want to think they spend the night, these pickups something stinging in the crease of my mouth these pickups and strangers. Yet I don't want to think of you alone. It feels terrible to think of you alone, smoking in cafes and bars, waiting. I do not want you to be alone. And I know somewhere deeper that's all you want too. What I imagine is nothing as real as that longing, as what you're really looking for. The thing that is not, will never be me. The feeling of coming home.

Should be more careful. Almost drop the cup.

It's cold now anyway, unpleasant to touch. Only fit for throwing away. I notice the crack on the rim when I cross to the sink, the red stain there. Little red trail against the eggshell blue. When I put my hand up to my face there's more. My mouth is bleeding. I rinse the cup, wipe my mouth, turn off the tap. Dark as hell out there: the guttering and dead leaves breaking off their branches. Steam growing from my breath against the pane. Trying not to think too much. Not to worry.

I need to talk to you.

I try not to reach for the phone.

peeping tom

I don't always see him.

The front door's quiet and I put the radio on the minute I get in so I don't always know he's back till he shouts. Then I turn the volume down, listen. Shoes clonking on the floor, the shiver of a shirt coming off. Bedroom. He's up the other end of the hall, in the bedroom. YOOHOO, I shout. I'm in the kitchen. He knows. I know he knows. He must have passed me on the way in but I like to shout anyway, be a presence. Now we both know where the other one is. Something comes back, an acknowledgement maybe. Either that or he's bumped into something through there. A kind of squeaky noise. I smile in case it's meant for me, turn back and get on with the pizza.

First pizza I ever ate was out of the Tally cafe at the corner of the main road, just across from Bobby's Amusement Arcade. We'd go in there after a night on the puggies and get a pizza supper between two. The big woman would chuck the pizza in the chip fat whole and it surfaced with the bread dough more or less transparent. Those days we had some kind of supper out the cafe every Saturday without thinking twice. Usually fish but with the occasional foray into the more exotic so eventually I'd tried the whole range: black pudding, chicken, sausage, hamburger, haggis, curry, chow mein, lasagna and pie. I only got the pie once. They got fried whole as well. The curry and chow mein were done in batter parcels like big spring rolls, envelope-ended. Godknew how they did the lasagna. I never heard anybody else ask for it but it was always there, on the menu board. Fryer Tuck's they called it. Fryer Tuck's. If there was any Italian connection they were keeping it to themselves. The chips were variable. Sometimes ok, other times slimy from the double wrapping, flaccid and sweetish with frying sweat. The longer you left them in their enclosed environment, the worse shape they'd be in when they came out. We got them anyway. Every time. It wasn't anything to do with the taste, it wasn't even that we were that hungry. Mostly it was to keep warm. I lived a long walk back from the stance, last bus and everything. He had to walk all the way back to the other side of town on his own. He always took me though, walked me home nomatter what the weather was like. If it was really cold, the fat congealed on our fingers, clung there like vaseline. I remember one night it was snowing, him holding a hand up to the streetlamp: five fingers splayed against the light, a thick fur of condensation round the bulb casing. He just held it there, sort of peering, clueless. He'd nothing to wipe them on. So I gave him something. I gave him me. Took his hand in mine and sucked it, all the salt and leftover slickness, one digit at a time. He knew exactly what I was doing. When I shoved him against the haulage contractor's wall just round the corner from Springvale Street he was ready. So was I. Dropped on my hunkers and took his prick in my mouth whole, one go. Sheer greed. I remember his breath turning to white cloud, spilling down over my shoulders. I can even taste him if I think hard enough, Roddy and leftover brackishness from the pickle skin. I have a memory like godknows. Ok it wasn't all that comfortable but it couldn't have taken longer than five minutes. Not long enough to get cramp. Afterwards, his jacket was pitted with pebbles from the roughcast, my knees rusted over with cold. He rubbed them till I could walk straight again and we went back, the two of us laughing like drains. My mother caught us kissing on the doorstep and acted shocked. Maybe she was. Mothers and daughters. There you go.

Tonight we're having pizza because he's in a hurry. I'm hoping he won't know the difference if it's yeasted or not. He's running a bath through there, drawers opening and shutting. He doesn't shout through or ask what's for tea. He locks the door.

How was your day? I shout through.

There's flour all over my hands, wee misty trails drifting down to the dark blue carpet while I'm shouting.

What? It's muffled through water noise and the layers of chip board. But he's heard me ok. Are you saying something out there?

I said, how was your day?

Fine, he says. How was your day?

So so. Well. Tell you the truth, some of it was terrible.

Yelling sends shock waves up my arms and a tiny piece of dough shakes loose. It drops from someplace I don't see and lands, a crescent in the night sky, on the dark pile. I look at my hands again, the dust filtering down.

I'm just going to wash my hands, I say. Ok? I'm making a big mess out here, then wait in case he wants to answer. All I hear is wee splashes. I go back to the kitchen with one hand cupped under the other, bolting the stable door. The flour just keeps felling through. Back in the kitchen I hear he's turned the tap on again, topping up. He likes a long soak.

Used to be as soon as I heard running water, I'd start shelling clothes. I loved getting in there with him, creaming up the soap then rubbing the lather from my hands over his shoulders and chest. We could spend ages, him making soap bubbles between my breasts while I dipped my fists under the water level, working till he poked out the water like a rhubarb shoot. After a while it was harder to find the time. New shift system and everything. I'M HAVING A BATH TO GET CLEAN FOR GODSAKE MOIRA he'd say I'M IN A HURRY. It wasn't just that though. I think he got shy because of this new stuff they started using on the plant, stuff that stank so he came home with it all through his hair, in places you couldn't imagine how it got there. He still left the door open, let me wander through and chat. I liked watching all that lean muscle, the way he could bend in the middle without triple rolls of fat appearing. Not long after he got on the overtime roster though, he took to snibbing the door. It was the only way to avoid temptation and anyway a man needs his privacy. You've all night to take baths, he says: some of us haven't. And it's perfectly true. He hasn't.

These days you get pizza topping ready made. It comes in jars with the garlic already in, herbs as well if you want them. You can get bases too but I still do my own. Even if it's just scone, my bases are all homemade. I put this one on a baking tray, stick on some of the jar stuff and add extra tomato, sliced yellow pepper, flakes of tuna. I'm just cutting a big chunk of cheddar for the grater when I hear the lock release, the pad of freshly-minted feet. He puts stuff like the filling out of After-Eights on them to get rid of the factory smell. He goes away through to the bedroom on these perfectly edible feet with one towel round his waist, another over his shoulders to catch the drips from his hair. His hair looks black when it's freshly washed though it's really ash

brown. It looks black at least once a day. I can see wee slices
of him from here, like a row of coins through the louvres of
the room divider, combing back the wet hair, laying out a
row of mousse and hair gel, deodorant, talc, aftershave. He
bends his knees to use the hair dryer, trying to see in a
mirror angled for my height. After a minute he goes back
through to the bathroom. Hiding. He knows I'm looking. I
go back round to the worktop and twist the lid off a jar of
gherkins trying to look if he's checking I've taken the hint
and something sears my finger. There's a cut, a clean white
incision fanning red threads through the whorl on my
fingertip. Cut myself and didn't notice. The evidence is
there, wee scarlet patches through the grated cheese when I
look. I'll need to do everything else with one useless finger
tucked into the palm. The plasters are in the bathroom.
Behind my back I hear the oven light change from red to
amber, the timer humming.

Fifteen minutes, I shout. Roddy? Your tea's up in fifteen
minutes, you hear? knowing he won't have. That door's as
good as soundproof. He won't have heard a bloody word.

After mine, I watch the news. It's what I always do.
There's something about the seven o'clock news that's
reassuring: the way it goes on for ages, does repeats of the
main bulletins to make sure you've heard it all as though
they really care. Jon Snow, all velvet voice and silk tie, tells
me about food mountains and the hard Ecu, his adam's
apple rising and dipping above a cool white collar. His eyes
are so blue they're not real. By the time he's doing industrial
streamlining, Roddy's voice slips over my shoulder in a haze
of aftershave.

Something smells good.

He means the pizza. I know he means the pizza. I turn
round ready to say, It must be you then, in a kind of sexy
way for a joke and he's not there. He's in the hall. His elbow

pokes out the junk cupboard, the rest of him in there wrestling to get by the hoover.

I've had mine. Shouting again. Yours is in the kitchen.

Sorry?

Pizza. I'm roaring. Your tea. It's in the kitchen.

Keep it for me ok? Hangers rattling. A thump. Christ, who put all this shit in here, Moira.

He's out the cupboard. The last word, that MOIRA, is louder so he's definitely out the cupboard.

Got the paper? There are jacket noises now, scuffling. Good movie on later. I saw it in the canteen.

Oh?

I forget the name of it now but it's a good one. You always say you've seen them but you haven't seen this. You should watch it.

What time?

Eh?

What time's it on?

Late. Late film.

Well. I don't know. I'm dead tired. Unless you want to see it. I had a terrible day.

Cmon Moira I'll not be in. You know fine. It's Tuesday. I'm never in on Tuesday.

Oh. When will you be home?

I won't disturb you ok?

When will you be home?

You won't even know I'm back.

Roddy? When will you –

The door clicks.

Beethoven. Not long after eight, the van comes round. The first eight of *Für Elise* buggered about to sound like a tune on a Waltzer but it means there are crisps and ice-cream, packets of fags if anybody's dying for them. Sometimes I'm in that state myself but not tonight. Not in

the mood for the queue. Anyway, hearing it reminds me to
pull the curtains, put on the wee lamp. Then I look back at
the telly. There's never anything decent on at this time of
night but I always flick through the channels just in case.
After a couple of goes I give in, switch off and start
rearranging furniture. It's not a big room but you can make
space: it rearranges fine. Some evenings I do that. I clear a
bit of space and do yoga. I wear black tights and a leotard,
leg-warmers. Used to yoga all the time only there was less
of me then. Moira, he would say, watching me stretch,
you're all woman. I still fit the same stuff but I only put it
on when he's out. Kitted up, I come down the hall again
avoiding the mirror, hooking in the dangly ear-rings blind.
I like to wear dangly ear-rings when I'm doing yoga. It
makes me feel more exotic, as though I know what I'm
doing. They brush your neck when you roll your head from
side to side, feel like someone's fingers. All the rooms off the
hall are in darkness. In the livingroom I put on the fire, sit
in front of the real-effect flames and select something for the
turntable. First thing that comes to hand is an old one.
Great Love Ballads of our Time. There's some crap on it
but at least it's slow crap. You need the right tempo for this
kind of thing, helps keep the heart rate steady. Annie
Lennox comes on, her voice all alone, then chiming bells.
Carefully, I put on the headphones. I turn the music loud
enough to block out my own breathing and I'm ready.

Steady.

I brace my shoulders so my chest pushes out, my stomach
in. The bass line throbbing through the carpet pile makes a
direct line to my crotch. Time to begin.

Kneel. Lean back till my hair starts folding under itself on
the fireside rug, lower torso from the hips, rest. Once that
feels ok, inch lower still, resting elbows on the floor to take
some of the weight before flattening my back against the

carpet. Rest. Legs bent double, feet cushioning my backside, I look down. All I can see are my breasts making roadsigns, twin humpback bridges. All woman. Rest long enough and the pain reaches one even note; disused muscles taking the strain, trying to accommodate. Then the last. I close my eyes for concentration then arch my spine, bracelet my ankles with my hands. I'm there. Bowed like a bridge, a perfect camber, I open my eyes. There's a man at the french window. Looking in.

Hardly anyone comes on the landing.
He knocks, hat dipping over the eyes.
A policeman.

It means only one thing.

1. They found a van covered with blood at the side of the road, a man several yards away. He staggered free and tried to reach a call box, one foot attached only by rags of skin. He's out cold but his diary gave them this address. The name in the diary is

2. There's been a head-on collision with a drunk driver. The drunk is absolutely fine. They tried to cut the other man out of his van but he's still there. They're having to amputate to free him so he can't be given anaesthetic. He's asking for someone called Moira at this address. The man's name appears to be

3. An overtaking lorry crushed a van into the crash barriers on the motorway. Every bone in the driver's body is broken. They don't expect him to last the night. There is nothing they can give him to reduce the pain. He screams himself out of unconsciousness and mutters our phone number every so often. He answers to the name of

4. To avoid a child on the road, a van driver swerved, skidded and drove straight into a tree. Smashed glass has made him unrecognisable and the steering wheel has pushed right through his ribcage. His eyes have been

Jesus.

Christ.

Before I've worked out how to do it, I'm out of position and racing for a dressing gown then I'm at the door. The policeman is calm. He says nothing awful. He even smiles. Routine checks madam, just routine checks. I'm catching my breath but so he doesn't notice, trying to look collected, calm. According to him this is a man's flat he says. So it is, I say, smiling back.

He just looks at me.

It is a man's flat, I say. I'm just a decoration.

He looks at me again. Pardon?

It's ok, I say. I'm being smartarsed, and he laughs. We both laugh. I live here too.

He comes in, sits down while I float back and forth with peach towelling bunched at my waist, leggings showing to the thigh. I invite him to take off his hat, brassy as you like. He wipes the single drops of rain off the brim with a slow, thick hand, sits back. He asks me to sit too. He's here to tell me something. There are Peeping Toms, he says. Three complaints from my block. I stop then, look directly at him. His raincoat smells so fresh it might be flowers. Big hands clutching the edge of the settee.

Roddy told me he wanted to be a songwriter. He couldn't play any instruments and wasn't learning any, but he wanted to be a songwriter. You would meet such interesting people that way, he said. Then he fancied lorry driving, cruising through the dark with hands steady on the wheel, watching the world with seen-it-all eyes, carrying explosives/nuclear waste/Yorkie Bars with slit-skirted girls thumbing lifts at the side of the road. Then he wanted to be an art student, a sound technician, a vet. He even wanted to be a policeman when he found out they got a house with the job. The apprenticeship at the petrochemical plant came up just when I was enjoying the idea of him in uniform. That's not now though. That has nothing to do with now. I can't think why I thought it. Right now, the policeman is talking to me. His notebook is tucked under his thigh. I raise my eyes slowly and tell him I've seen nothing. Nothing at all.

Anyone new in the area, recently? Hanging around the lifts or shops downstairs?

No, I say. Just in and out to work, you don't notice much. I wouldn't have noticed anyone old round here, never mind anyone new.

He nods, looks round. Nice flat.

Yes, I say. So my mother keeps telling me.

He makes a sort of smile, refuses an offer of tea. We say nothing for a moment while he keeps looking round.

Well, he says. He takes a deep breath in. Sorry if I called at an – eh – inconvenient moment.

I look down at the dressing gown belt, the big bumphle in the knot and try to look casual. That's ok, I say. Come again any time.

Right, he says. Haha. And he starts walking towards the door.

Sure you don't want tea? I say.

Quite sure, he says. You're very kind.

And before I know what I'm doing, it comes out.

There's pizza, I say. I hear myself saying it.

He stops, turns round. His eyes are dark brown.

Home-made pizza. It's just going to waste through there. You can have a piece.

I tilt my head.

If you like.

Two seconds. That's all it takes. And he's on the other side of the door before either of us sees how he got there. He looks back briefly, reminds me from the safety of the front porch if I see anything suspicious I'm not to hesitate to call.

I won't, I say.

He's already away down the stairs so I'm talking to the closed door. I tell it again for good measure.

I won't.

The headphones are still on the carpet when I go back through, playing to the skirting. I hold them to one ear. *When I Fall in Love,* Nat King Cole. So I put the damn thing off. Two cups, one untouched, go into the sink. I stick the uneaten pizza in the oven so it's there if Roddy wants it when he comes in, then close every curtain in the house. Tight. After that it's just me and the late-night movie, the livingroom light full on. I stare hard at the screen, trying to look totally absorbed, seeing nothing. All I can think about is some bastard up on the roof looking for gaps in the breeze block. Crazed with loneliness but jesus christ. The telly stays on till the dot appears, a silence then that horrible execution drum roll and the Queen on a horse. Somehow that's worse. It's worse than the silence, listening to the national anthem in the flat at night: like a setup from one of those films where some woman gets disembowelled with a tin-opener just when she thinks she's safe and sound in her own place. I read somewhere thinking like that is an easy option. Women these days should refuse to fall for that easy victim mentality it said. So I snap the red button on the remote control fast, brave nothingness instead. It's not better but it's not worse. I walk down the hall practising a brave face, refusing to be a victim. At least then I'll know if I'm raped and hacked to fragments I didn't give the guy any encouragement. I didn't ask for it. I want to be sure I took no chances on that score.

The bathroom is the only room with no windows. I undress in there tonight, put the dressing gown back on before checking the house again. I have to put the porch light on for Roddy: the hall is dark as hell. I go down it, patting the walls to find my way, stroking the sleek white plaster I'm so proud of. This is my home. A catch on the new estate. Everybody said so: seven power points in the livingroom and central heating. Central heating, my mother said. Don't know they're born these days. I think she was pleased. She never said things directly, my mother, nothing nice anyway but you knew. Don't know they're born. I remember she was standing at the far side of the stereo cabinet when she said it, rain-mate on. There were beads of rain caught between the folds of sheer plastic that did not fall. It smelled like clean. The whole place smelled like clean. She brought white sheets for a moving-in present, white sheets in cellophane. I'm remembering all this. I can hear the sheets for christsake, Roddy laughing. And suddenly it's all so clear, so sharp I need to stop and get my breath back. When I look up again I'm leaning against the wall, cheek squashed against the white surface. I'm embracing the wall and my face is wet. It only lasts a moment though. A moment then I'm fine, right as rain. I dust myself down just in case anybody was watching, reach for the porch switch. No faces loom from the dark, nothing sounds. I wipe my face with the back of one hand, tell myself I'm fine. Moira, you're perfectly fine.

Between the sheets before I take the dressing gown off. Funny how nervous you can get.

The rattle of his keyring comes eventually.

I hear him easing the key back into the lock on the inside, the tumblers being primed for the early start tomorrow. Then the hollow suckings of shoes being removed, stocking soles whispering towards the kitchen. The fridge hums when he opens the door, seeing what there is for late supper while the pizza sits ignored in the oven. He won't even know it's there. After a minute or two, he scuffles out of his clothes, runs water to wash and brush his teeth in the dark so he doesn't disturb me. He's always been thoughtful that way. He sighs, slips in beside me cautious as a cat then gently draws against my back, pressing his knees behind mine so we curve like spoons. It's warm; a good, good feeling. It's so good I want to turn, embrace him. I don't want to tell him about the policeman or the rotten day I've had, just hold him. But I can't. Instead I pretend to roll in my sleep, touch his hip lightly with one hand, hoping he'll reach back. He's wearing his underwear.

Sorry, he says. Sorry, too tired tonight.
He turns away, pushes his backside against mine.

Before long, I hear him snoring gently, mouthing empty air.

My eyes are wide open, watching for Peeping Toms.

babysitting

Something he can't see hurts.

He kneels on the floor to pick up the fallen shell of flying saucer and it bites into his knee, making a noise. A soft, spreading crack. Wondering if it was bone, your own bone maybe being drilled into by something very small. He lifts the knee to look and it's sugar. Little clear cubes sunk up to their middles, the skin pushing them out again with stretching over the kneecap. Skin is like that. Mushy. Things get stuck in it. Gads. The sugar bounces out of its burrows, skites on the lino: more of it scattered over the rest of the floor. It would be Allan did that. Allan in at the packet again and spilling it. A white trail coming out the cupboard to here proves it. Tommy watches it with his eye all the way. Where it stops is just sticky powder. The place the knee was seconds before. A drift of it silts in at the wood under the sink as well. And something else. Something with legs. A wispy black thing moves threads of itself against the skirting, a bead-string of a body rising up then away again, back underneath. He looks till his sore eye starts to nip but it's definitely away, just slivers of biscuit and crumby stuff left, papery shapes that onions leave all over the place. You see more things down here. Things you don't really want to

see all that much. Anyway the knee isn't sore any more. It's
got holes in. Pock marks. Most of the sugar has worked its
way out without him even trying. He picks out the last bits
with a nail. This filthy nail, black-rimmed where the horn
separates from the quick, the loops of fingerprint grey. The
blood bruise is still there. Going yellow. At least it isn't a
cigarette burn. They go brown.

Tommy?

A whine and a sniff is coming closer. The boy on the floor
doesn't move.

Tommy?

The last bit of sugar gouges itself out the knee as the sniff
blossoms out, rounding the hall corner. Allan.

Tommy?

Allan with his voice breathy, just the same. It never
changes, the way he says your name, whether he thinks he
knows where you are or not, not even when he finds you.
He always sounds as if he's going to moan about something. The warm bulk of the wee brother sends out signals
and Tommy knows what he's going to say. Starving. Is it
teatime. It's what he always says. Yesterday he kept it up till
they went and took some of the money for penny things:
toffee straps, licorice ropes. Flying saucers. Allan ate them
all in a oner and his face was black. The other day he was
behind the settee with four sweetie cigarettes and it was
ages before you found out where he'd got them. Finally he
said David Armstrong from up the stairs gave them to him
through the letterbox and you had to take them off him and
fling them in the bin. He shouldn't have been taking things
from David Armstrong. He was told not to take things off
anybody. David Armstrong was bad enough. Him putting
stuff through the letterbox was worse, though. Tommy
didn't know why but it was definitely not good. He had to
prop a chair in front of the door to stop the flap going up
again or Allan opening it from his side and shouting

through. Being so wee, you had to watch him all the time. Putting the chair there and just giving him a battering every so often was easier than trying to talk sense because he was too wee to do what he was told and be trusted. Even obvious things like not talking to Mrs Morrison. You just didny talk to Mrs Morrison. She just got you into trouble. Somebody kicked her door once and she said it was Tommy and dad told her to fuck off and then you caught Allan talking to her. She was a Nosy Old Cow and she gave you gyp. He'd been told but it had taken the leathering to get it through. Allan just hadny a clue.

Tommy?

Allan is there, fat inside the doorway holding an empty crisp poke. One leg of the trainer bottoms up at his knee and the sock needing pulled up.

Is it teatime Tommy?

A flake of crisp falls off the corner of Allan's fat mouth and in with the rest of the bits on the floor. His nose running, coating his top lip. Sometimes you want to thump Allan for nothing. He just gets on your nerves. Anyway Tommy gets up. He peels his knees off the lino and sees the sugar again but he doesn't say anything. He just starts walking. He walks through to the hall, past the living room door and through to the bedroom window, listening to Allan follow him. Allan's feet skiffing off the carpet. When Tommy stops, he does too. Just stands there clueless, crumpling the crisp poke over and over in thon irritating way while his brother looks out.

The sky is grey and pink.

No streetlights on yet but too hard to see right inside the house any more. There is a time when it is harder to see before it gets easier and it is that time the now. When it gets darker, the orange sifts in from out there and you don't need to put the inside lights on at all: you can see ok without

them. Anyway they only ever go through to the livingroom
and the telly is on in there. You can see it fine without lights
or anything. He can hear it, still going full bung, making
shouting noises and car brakes through the wall. Tommy
can hear it fine. But it wouldn't be a good idea to stick Allan
through when he went out for the tea. He didn't like it, being
on his own with dad through there. He does it all right if you
force him but not without a carry on. So Allan will have to
come too. Quicker in the long run. Tommy shuts his eyes
and thinks about going out into the hall. About holding out
one hand backwards and not having to wonder where Allan
is. He is just always there, ready to take it. He will drop the
crisp poke and fit his hand inside and let himself be taken.
It's what Allan does. He needs watching.

David Armstrong looks like a ferret and hunches his
shoulders up, looking over. He kicks the wall where the
chippy is, holding a bag in the one hand. Maltesers.

How were you not at school the day?

David Armstrong talks like a lassie and nobody plays
with him. He was never done out on his own, looking for
folk. Tommy feels the eyes and refuses to look up, the
crinkle of the sweetie bag in the other hand and keeps a
good grip of Allan. David Armstrong always has something
for eating but you're better off without it. Anything you got
off David Armstrong was not good. Him and his mother
both. You were better to tell them nothing. He would have
given the sweetie cigarettes to Allan and then told his
mother they'd been taken off him. He did things like that.

How no though?

The face a melted doll and the eyes watching. Able not to
eat and just wait. He made you sick. One time they dug his
rabbit up after it had been in the ground a week to see if it
was any different and it wasn't only the eyes were kind of
white and his mother caught him and he said it was Tommy

and Allan. He said they made him do it and started greeting
and that made his mother think it was true. You took
nothing off him if you could help it. Tommy flexes his hand
tighter, Allan's bone thin and hard through the cloth and
soft flesh and he whines. He doesn't pull though. He whines
a bit with the soreness in his arm but he doesn't try to go
over. At their backs, David Armstrong shouting Fuck off
then. Soft as rotten fruit.

Inside the chippy is warm. It is always warm and smells of
food. Mrs Mancini sometimes gives Allan a free pickled
onion. This time she just looks. She looks at Tommy and
twists the salt shaker.

    You two here again, she says. Her face isn't right. Bertie,
these two are here again.

    Mr Mancini looks over the top of the glass cabinet, thin
straps of hair over his scalp. His face boils over a cabinet
full of black puddings then goes away. Tommy holds up the
three coins. Maybe they think he doesn't have the money.
Nobody takes it. Nobody is looking because they are
talking to each other, words he can't hear right: Mrs
Mancini saying something about it being the umpteenth
time, you wonder where the hell it's coming from the two
of them twice a day and Tommy knows something. They're
talking about him and Allan. And that doesn't feel good
either. They should just get the food and get out. He wants
to get back up the road and jam the chair back where it
belongs. The back of the door is not safe when they're out
like this. He wants home.

    Fish supper and an extra bag.

    He hears his own voice being sure about what he wants.
Then they might get it and get out. Nobody can stop you if
you have the money.

    Fish supper and an extra bag.

    Mr Mancini says something about nothing to do with

him and the frying spits up. Tommy lifts his eyes. Mrs
Mancini's hair appears over the top of the cabinet, the pink
overall shifting into place behind the counter. She gives
them a look.

Ok boys. Fish supper and an extra bag.

Her lipstick is a funny colour and doesn't smile. She takes
the ladle out the pickles and stares at it. The chips come and
she wraps them staring at where Mr Mancini must be. She
picks up the newspaper bundle and reaches, still looking
away.

See and say to your daddy I'm asking for him boys ok?

Ok. Allan is looking at the newspaper parcel, saying ok
to Mrs Mancini. She claps eyes on him and stained teeth
show. Marks on her teeth like a vampire.

You need your face washed young man, she says. See and
wash his face if nobody else will.

The pink thing she wears moves when she leans, handing
over the bags. Tommy nearly takes it then remembers
sauce. Look at him Bertie he's completely mockit. He's
filthy. Tommy doesn't listen and asks hard for sauce. She
looks. She reaches to take the parcel back.

I don't know, she says. I don't know. A couple of
chancers.

Fat fizzes up and more fish hurl themselves into the
display case. Mrs Mancini holds out an opened palm for the
money.

The house always feels colder after you've been out.

Tommy shivers through the shirt and reaches for the
switch. Hard greasy plastic. It is not like real light that
comes on. It makes things look sore. The wrapped bundle
in at his chest, burning, he walks through to the kitchen.
Hot vinegar hurts his nose. Allan follows close enough to
tip the backs of his heels, the rubber bumpers of the trainers
touching. In a minute there will be whining about wanting

his bag. But there is something about the idea of washing his hands, cleaning Allan up a bit before he eats. He wants to make sure Allan looks ok. He puts the bags to one side of the sink where Allan can't reach and looks for the wet dish cloth. It isn't there. Tommy looks and the whining starts. The cloth isn't there. It isn't there because it's in the livingroom. The sound of the telly playing music and Allan starting to reach up for the bundle on the drainer. After. It'll have to be after. If Allan starts up now it'll be more bother than it's worth. Tommy watches the newspaper start to slide, Allan's face change as it falls into his grasp. He tears a bit off the end of the parcel and it nearly cowps. As soon as he gets the chips he'll want a drink. You were never done with Allan. He was always wanting something. They were nearly out of lemonade as well.

Cmon you. Cmon.

Tommy makes up his mind. He takes the chips before the whole lot falls and the greeting gets worse. They're not eating off the kitchen floor.

Cmon.

Any minute and the wail will start. But all he has to do is go through, look like he means it. Allan will follow. He always does. He runs.

Blotches.

The telly throws grey blobs over the inside of the room, shifting all the time. The sour smell. He holds the bags up to his nose for the vinegar stink off the newspaper to make it ok. And it is ok. It's always ok after a minute or so but you always notice the smell on the way in. Allan stumbles in grizzling then shuts up when he sees unwrapping going on. He never notices the stink. He never notices anything when he's hungry. Tommy hands him the extra bag and a piece of fish off his own. The fish is cool enough to tear easy without hurting your hand. Allan watches the trade of fish, bits flaking onto the carpet, then picks his bit up and sticks it to his mouth, chewing. Tommy knows what he forgot. Biscuits. There are no biscuits left and hardly any lemonade. Stuff just keeps going done. There's no sauce. It doesn't matter just now though. Just now, there are chips and sauce from the shop. It'll do. It'll have to.

From the far side of the divan, father's legs flash patterns: the news making spider webs. It makes the legs look as if they're moving but the feet are in exactly the same place. They never move. He might leave some chips in case though. Tommy bites the fish, looks down at the carpet. It looks as if it's moving as well, heaving about like the sea thon time they went the holiday, like something's living in it but it's still not time for the light yet. There are things you don't want to see when it's on. The yellow colour that keeps just getting yellower for a start. It is definitely getting darker since the start of this. Allan coughs suddenly and bits spray out but he keeps chewing. He's ok. The fat fingers glisten as the adverts change. After. He can get Allan through for a wash and into bed. It's getting too cold sleeping in here anyway, even with the two of them. That'll have to stop as well. After he's done with Allan, Tommy will come back through. He wants to sit for a bit. He needs to check for money in the pockets anyway. He wipes grease off his mouth, flicks his eyes away. It isn't nice to think about, raking the pockets. Having to touch him. It makes his mouth stop working, the chip mush in his throat stick. But he can make it quick. Then just sit, sit in with his own dad and maybe talk. Ask if he's ok. There's no point doing it out loud these days but he does it anyway. Even if he never says, you want to ask.

Inside the wrapper, the chips get colder. You see the fat on them going stiff. You know you don't want to lift his eyelids though. Touch the skin thickening there. You don't want to know the colour of his eyes.

someone had to

Blue eyes.

Right from the start her mother said, from the word go that was what people noticed. Took after her dad, she said: those big blue eyes, that LOOK on her. Not blinking. Fixed.

People sentimentalise; children and animals it's what they do. She may not speak much but she knows EVERY WORD YOU SAY. Her mother said that. Kind of thing you say about spaniels. Biddable things. Pets. They sentimentalise. It's easier than looking, REALLY LOOKING, seeing what there is to see. Little pinpoints, little drill holes. Sucking you in. Knowing what they're doing. Knowing EVERY WORD YOU SAY.

I tried. I gave her a fair chance. Took her out with the rest of us, the whole family so to speak, she had outings, money spent. Not that she appreciated it but she got it all the same. She never relaxed somehow. Difficult, withdrawn. Never said THANK YOU FOR TAKING ME WITH YOU UNCLE FRANK. Never said anything much at all. Never see that in the papers. Clumsy, awkward, a social EMBARRASSMENT. Shyness they called it. They said she was SHY. I lived with it remember, I was there. Nobody else bothered then, nobody else even LOOKED but I DID. If they'd looked they'd have seen but they chose not to. Left it to me. I was the only one who saw what was coming. And I saw all right. I saw it every DAY.

I'm not an unreasonable man.
I argued.
I said to her mother YOU need to do something about it she's YOUR kid SHE NEEDS SEEING TO before things get out of hand. I told her it wouldn't do. LET HER KEEP GOING THE WAY SHE'S HEADED I said and we'll ALL BE SORRY. That STARING all the time like I'd done something wrong. Those silences. They're unnatural in a girl her age, I said, and that WATCHING ME. WATCHING. Like I'd no right to say what was what in my OWN HOME. I said Linda that's how it STARTS how ROT SETS IN. It needs pinching out at source. DUMB INSOLENCE is the WORST KIND, the WORST I said and you're her mother. You just let her DO IT. She has a NEED TO DEFY I said, a need to set you against me, Linda, out of JEALOUSY I said. SPITE. You have to harden your heart for your own good. For HER good. I ONLY HIT HER WHEN SHE'S NAUGHTY I said, it's not SOMETHING I ENJOY. Look I said LOOK at least with me she KNOWS WHAT WILL HAPPEN. If she keeps STARING like that she KNOWS what the CONSEQUENCES WILL BE. She's the oldest I said she ought to be an EXAMPLE. You can't keep on threatening her with something she's not scared of. All right I said. Have it your own way. If you can't I will I said she WON'T EAT with us any more. If she won't learn one way, she'll learn another. She'll COME ROUND QUICK ENOUGH when she's hungry. Go sparing rods and she'll SPOIL. You'll destroy any chance we have of TEACHING HER ANY RESPECT. She'll thank us for it in

the end. So I put her in the corner and she went. She knew I meant what I said all right and she went. But it didn't stop. You know what she did? Just stood there. Stood there stock still and WATCHED us eating, WATCHED US, you couldn't think straight, so you couldn't enjoy your food. None of us could. Why SHOULD I turn my back in my own home I said SHE can FACE THE WALL I said but it was just the same. Stubborn. HOURS she could spend, HOURS in the same place staring at the SAME PLACE so you knew she was doing it to get on your NERVES. Don't push me Kimberly, I said. I know what you're doing you don't fool ME. But she pushed. It was in her nature. A NEED TO DEFY. So I put her in the cupboard it was only for an hour or so and it was for ALL OF US I said I AM NOT LOCKING THE DOOR LINDA I said just putting the light off till she sees some SENSE you've got to be cruel to be kind I said but it was still no good. Quiet as a mouse for the first hour or so, the first couple of times then she starts again. She starts WHINING. WHINING. That's what she did. This noise in the cupboard like a collared bitch, getting louder and louder and plainly CALCULATED TO ANNOY. Even when you opened the door you warned her STOP THAT NOW KIMBERLY DO YOU HEAR ME she just kept WHINING pushing her back into the wall, knowing and INVITING IT JUST THE SAME keeping STARING to see if she was HAVING AN EFFECT. I said to her mother I said LINDA she KNOWS what she's doing. I wouldn't put up with that from YOU I said you go giving in to her now and godknows where it'll end. SOMEONE has to mean what they say I said and you starting up won't help all the time this whimpering going on in there, proving something, turning the screw. LINDA I SAID DON'T MAKE ME SHOUT I said. I don't want to have to force you. BUT SHE'LL STAY IN THERE TILL SHE'S SORRY. Somebody HAS TO BE consistent I said KIMBERLY

THAT'S YOUR LAST WARNING and she knew I meant
it. She knew all right. The whining stopped and I shut the
door I said YOU'LL GET OUT WHEN YOU PROVE YOU
CAN BE TRUSTED and I went to read my paper. You can't
let these things get to you. But the next thing we were in
bed when it started the next thing it beggars belief but
it's true she started SCRATCHING I swear with her
SCRATCHING DO YOU KNOW WHAT SHE DID? She
CLAWED THE CUPBOARD DOOR with her NAILS SHE
CLAWED THROUGH TO THE WOOD. Don't tell me
that's NORMAL scraping her NAILS on the PAINT till
they bled you can't tell me that is NORMAL FOR A SIX-
YEAR-OLD CHILD. THEY KNOW THE DIFFERENCE
BETWEEN RIGHT AND WRONG. STOP THAT
KIMBERLY I said that NOISE like RATS like it followed
you to every room in the house I was calm I said STOP
THAT KIMBERLY till it was more than FLESH AND
BLOOD could stand. JESUSCHRIST LINDA I said it's not
even as if she was MINE WHAT MORE AM I EXPECTED
TO DO? You switch the tv louder and you still know what
for, you still KNOW WHAT SHE'S DOING. So the last
night it starts and I said DON'T PUSH ME KIMBERLY
down the hall I pressed my mouth to the door I whispered
DON'T DO IT PLEASE. I said PLEASE. I begged. And she
just KEPT GOING. And that was it.

I put my hand on the doorknob.
I turned the key.

She was sitting next to the hoover. STAND UP
KIMBERLY but she didn't. And I hit her NOT hard not to
begin with but she just LOOKS not even FLINCHING
when you TOLD her what would happen so I did it again
STAND UP KIMBERLY curling in a corner NOT EVEN
TRYING TO STAND UP just watching while I shook her,

I lifted her up put the cigarette onto the skin of the wrist it was MEANT TO BE A LESSON all she needed to do was say she was sorry to STOP not knowing when to STOP the nape of her neck blistering the INSIDE OF HER black mouth open not saying a word just WATCHING while I DON'T TELL ME IT'S NORMAL FOR A CHILD NOT TO CRY OUT.

I SAID TO YOUR MOTHER I SAID SHE'S LET YOU OFF WITH MURDER. THIS IS ALL YOUR FAULT I said and our eyes met.

So it was me.

I told her to run the bath but she wouldn't. So I did it.
I filled it with boiling water. I put on the kettle. Someone had to.
Someone had to do something.

I ran the bath. I lifted her up.

Those big blue eyes still staring up like butter

wouldn't

melt

a proper respect

He said her mother would have to know.

There are forms. Forms of consent she has to sign.

His mouth hardly moved.

Bit of a paradox, I suppose. If you went on to have the child and it needed an operation of some kind, you could sign for its treatment. But not for your own. Not for this.

Apart from her in his leather chair, hardening his doctorness like lacquer. It was just how it would be. Her mother would have to know. Alice turned away, knowing the colour of his eyes anyway: the same old scars scratching their way out from under the papers on his desk, familiar stains on the wall rising like continents from the wash of blue. It hadn't used to be that colour. Brown maybe, sage green, but not blue. Nothing light. The ceiling was new too. That tiny wee room up there. It would be full of boxes and godknows again, ladders and no people. No human beings. She could feel it up there now, through the fresh plaster and different paint, pressing down over their shared space like a grudge.

Home.

A cold attic room at the top of the stairs, single-bar heater on all summer.

Home.

There was nothing else on offer for a woman with no job
and a wean in tow, a woman who had voluntarily left her
man. Mary Quant, permissive age, the pill maybe, but not
in Motherwell. Not here. They said he liked a drink right
enough but whose man didn't? She'd a hellish tongue on
her. If he drank over the odds, he probably needed to: if
he'd hit her it would be nothing she hadn't asked for. Jimmy
McCardle was all right. Folk had seen him hanging out
washing for godsake, so it would be her fault all right and
anyway she left him. Her own mother wouldn't have it
either. You picked him, she said, putting her mouth that
way. It was you wanted the bugger. Anyway, there was no
room and she was past the age where she wanted a wean
running all over the place. So they went to the doctor's
asking for something for the nerves and something for the
angina and she had nearly cried when he gave her the prescription, was there nothing he could do? And the doctor
gave her a hankie and showed them the upstairs room.

A boxroom store.

Reeking of cardboard, no running water; a thick green
curtain on a wire to serve for a door.

A place no-one would knock.

It could be plumbed he said; something, he waved at the
doorless gap, something more suitable rigged up. A wash-
house, an outside toilet back-to-back with the builder's
yard, a tap. He pinked up when she asked how much. It
wasn't a question of money, he said. She needn't think of it
that way. Some light cleaning duties, the corridors, offices
and the surgery to keep things on the right footing, that was
all that was needed. Alice remembered looking up, the bulb
with no shade. There was nowhere else. Three nights on
somebody's livingroom floor, the two of them wrapped in

the same blanket and they moved in. Cardboard boxes, a
suitcase, the settee and the wardrobe. She carried the trike
herself. All the way past the downstairs doors, the bell
threatening to bump off the too-narrow stairwell and draw
attention to itself, shhh for goodnesssake shhh over and
over even though there was nobody else there. He'd said
after surgery. He'd been quite clear on that. Her mother's
voice saying shh anyway.

There was a lot of that: a lot of keeping quiet and being
good. People came Monday to Friday. They waited in a
coughing line to clock in with Mrs Beaton in her wee
cubicle, the name-badge and the white overall on, signing
folk in and giving them tellings off if they were late. They
would take the tellings off back with them and sit down,
staring at the brown gloss paint till their turn behind the
shut door. Sickness, sputum, sniffing weans. Alice kept out
the road and played on the drying green, the building-site,
the graveyard. If it rained, there was only staying in with the
radio too quiet to hear right, looking out the window. A
paper shop, a bus queue, a barber's with a stripy pole. She
could watch people going in underneath without looking
up, came out looking just the same. After five, the big storm
door got shut over. You could hear the tumblers all the way
up the stairs, know it was ok now. You could come out. By
quarter past they'd all be away and the two of them came
down instead. It was always dark in the surgery, not just the
mahogany and walnut. It felt like somewhere you weren't
allowed even when there was nobody else in it. The surgery.
The sound of it. The doctor's special doctor place, where
people came to be cut into. That was what surgery meant.
Not to run, not to shout, not to touch. You knew that
somehow from the smell anyway, the stink of bandages and
chemical things, the lavender polish her mother put everywhere. You knew it from how things looked, things you

couldn't imagine the half about: kidney-shaped metal bowls, empty bottles, black rubber worms in coils on the high shelves, canteens of medical cutlery in leather cases lined in velvet, slim metal probes up to their necks in purple pile. Not to touch. Watching the stuff in case it moved, in case it knew what you were thinking, Alice followed behind her mother's skirt, a rag duster balled tight into one fist. Sometimes, though, the phone would ring and she'd go to answer it. She'd go all the way through to Mrs Beaton's reception bit, leave Alice alone through there with warnings but leave her all the same and the badness would start. It was a terrible thing, the badness in Alice McCardle. It needed watching. Her mother was never done telling her but it didn't get any better. It got worse. In with stuff she'd no business touching like that, it could do terrible things, make her touch things she'd no right to. Left long enough, she'd even reach up for the silver spikes and hooks, the shiny probes in their velvet case. Shafts roughened like files, the glass-smooth tips. One had a mirror in a circle, like something dentists used. You could see yourself in it with the nose too big, face ballooned up and ugly as sin, eyes staring. One sound, one creak of wood under someone's shoe-sole and they'd be back where they belonged so fast not even Alice knew how she'd done it, her face fixed so nothing showed. Not a thing. There had been a mistake only the once, when something had fallen, she couldn't remember what. But she remembered what happened: the brokenness and her mother shouting, her mother crying out of nothing and the crying was the worst. The crying was terrible, the worst thing in the world. Alice hadn't run again, just been careful as hell. She learned how to control her face.

The way she was doing now.

She could see it reflected in the same sickbowls, blurry

against the chrome. The black case of instruments wasn't there though. She looked over the doctor's head, back down again. When she turned back, he was looking at her. He had asked her something and now she was making him wait. He sniffed and said it again, clipping the syllables.

I take it you haven't told her?

Alice looked at him. She said nothing.

You haven't told her.

If it had been a question before it wasn't now. Alice didn't know what to say. She was suddenly queasy instead, a cold wave pulsing at the back of her throat. The idea of a breath of fresh air, of going outside, just for a moment. But there would only be the waiting room queue, the bus stop beyond that. Carbon monoxide fumes, the men outside the barber's staring over, then the coming back in. Coming back in. She breathed deep through her nose instead, looked hard at the grey weave of her skirt.

I see, he said. He wrote something on a piece of paper, stared at it looking tired. I see.

No you fucking don't, she thought. But not out loud, never out loud. The fuzz from the light behind his head was making her dizzy, her eyes were starting to nip. Crying was not an option, though. It never had been. Besides she still owed him something: that first appointment with her missing period and kid-on confusion, letting him ask how was her mother keeping and was everything fine at home, letting him work through umpteen stabs at what the trouble was till the joke about gymslip mothers and her face giving it all away. And she hadn't said anything but his smile slipped and he knew anyway. No she wasn't sure she was pregnant but the possibility was what seemed to get him most. It still made her embarrassed thinking about his face, the stiff way it had gone looking at her, letting this something he didn't want to know settle. Four days later, hardly able to hear for ice cream van and weans running home, she

called from the kiosk outside the school and he said she
better come in again. She knew what it meant, was there
with the school tie on before the place shut, polythene bag
of books under one arm. He had a lab report on one side of
the desk but didn't show it to her, just told her to sit down,
told her what she already knew. He looked at a space
somewhere between the two of them and spoke to it.

You can't possibly know what this means, of course.

He kept looking at the space. Alice wondered how he
knew what it meant, how he could be so sure she didn't but
said nothing. Her throat was too tight for saying much
anyway. His face got dark. It got redder.

Well, he said. His voice was louder than it had been.
Where do we go from here, young lady?

Alice kept her eyes down.

What, for example, do you see as your prospects for you
and the child?

Alice tried. She didn't want to have to say anything and
irritate him more than she was doing already. But she could
make no sense of the question. Child. *Child.* There was
nothing she could make it mean. He waited a bit then spoke
again, the words *father job marry* coming out his mouth, no
more connected than anything else. Till it clicked. He
thought she could have it. He seriously seemed to think she
could have it.

I can't, she said. I can't do that.

Can't? He looked straight at her. It's a bit late for *can't*
now.

Alice sat up in the chair, looked straight back.

No it isn't and I'm not having it. I'm not. I can't.

They were both confused now, taken off guard. The
doctor looked at his blotter.

Well, he said. He had other patients waiting. People who
had not created problems of their own choosing. People
who were genuinely sick. People he would much rather be

seeing at this moment. He opened the door without looking at her. It wasn't till she was back in the corridor, listening to the echo of the closing door, her own heels off the gloss walls she felt the dizziness, the damp prickling over the surface of her skin. By the end of the street she had to sit down and doing that the word came to her. Abortion. She wanted an abortion. She walked all the way back to the scheme planning it, making it right: some medical fiction for the few days in hospital, D&C or somesuch. She didn't know what it was but girls her age had them. They were things nobody asked you about so that would be it, over and done with. There would be questions though, him trying to put her off. There were always things you had to prove to doctors. But she would manage. Up the stairwell with the lift not working and the stink of catpiss making her break sweat again, opening and closing a fist in one hand. Whatever it was she had to do or say, she would manage and nobody need be any the wiser. Her mother wouldn't know. Jesus jesus. Alice rested her head on the roughcast at the side of the front door. She could hear the tv on inside, gunshot and sirens. The channel changing, singing. Her mother must never know.

She went for the next appointment with pages of the *Home Medical Companion* learned by heart, could have drawn diagrams of bits she'd never known she'd had before if she'd needed to. He was readier too, though. He did all the asking like it was an exam but that was only to be expected. And she was good at those. School got you trained up for that kind of thing no bother. She was fine, saw everything coming till the last one.

What about school work?

She looked at him. It related to nothing she could think of. There was no way of knowing what he wanted, no time to wonder.

It's fine, she said. I like school. I'm good at it.

He shifted onto something else and told her to come back two days later. A day and a half of still not knowing, feeling for something moving inside that didn't. She kept away from school, walked down by the railway embankments, went home at the usual times to keep in her room. Her mother was pleased. She heard her out the back door, hanging washing. *She's in studying, Isa,* laughter. *Canny complain that way*. Alice kept her head over the book, not reading at all. Back at the doctor's desk, she watched him wash his hands, dry them with a towel She watched the towel while he sat down, wondering if it had been there before, if her mother had laundered it once. What else she would have to do for this man.

Well, he said. Well. He was looking at her very carefully. We have to make a decision soon.

He took a cloth handkerchief out of his pocket, dabbed his nose, leaned back.

I can't conceal from you this is a very difficult one.

No, she said.

Physically, there's no reason why you shouldn't have a healthy baby. He looked at the hanky, put it back in his pocket. No reason at all.

Thinking about the hanky was making the back of her throat work. She kept her face straight and still, breathing shallow. The doctor clasped his hands, settled deeper into the leather.

But. He arched his eyebrows. We have to think about other things too. You're a bright girl, they tell me. Would you say that's a fair assessment?

Alice said nothing.

The school say you've a chance of good passes later this year. An excellent chance in fact.

She looked at him.

So, he said. So.

Alice kept looking.

You spoke to someone at the school? About my exams?

He looked momentarily confused.

You spoke to someone at Braehead High?

Yes.

Alice looked at him till her eyes hurt. She looked at him till he knew there was something wrong. The hanky reappeared, went back to his nose temporarily. It was filthy.

I sought the advice of another professional person, he said. This isn't the kind of decision a responsible person can –

Who? she said. Who spoke to you?

The tone of her voice was a surprise to them both. Not sure, he waited. Then his voice seemed to be coming from far away.

Young lady, he said. He cleared his throat. You need all the help you can get. The school are prepared to say you should be given a second chance and I am satisfied to take that on trust. And if that doesn't suit you – he shook his head – I'm at a loss to know what you want.

Yes, she said eventually. Thank you. She could hear her breath coming through her nose, short catches. Yes.

He picked up a pen, rustled some papers.

It's not over yet, by any means. We'll need the agreement of the consultant and so on. But things can begin to move forward at least. We can't, after all, afford the time for the kind of social niceties you might prefer.

No.

Something was past now. They were moving on. Alice started rocking gently. Things were going to be all right. When she got out of here, time to think, things were going to be all right.

I'll come with you now, if you like, he said. Get it over with. She'll have to know sooner or later.

She almost smiled at him.

There are forms, he said. Forms of consent. Things she has to sign for the hospital.

It was only then she realised. She realised who he would explain to, where he was proposing to go. As she was meant to. After all, they said she was a bright girl. He could see it in her eyes and the terms were not unreasonable. What if the lassie was sixteen, the signature not necessary? The letter of the law was not the point. He was the doctor. He was an old family friend and the woman ought to know. He held out the forms.

Townhead Road flats is it? The same number?

The same number. The lift not fixed. The smells and those words painted up the stairwell. She couldn't hide any of it. Not a thing. The chair scraped when she stood up. The doctor opened the door.

the bridge

They left the boy with the painted eyes behind and made for the door. She glanced back while they paid at the till, watching to see if he was moving yet but he wasn't. Not so much as an eyebrow. Nineteen, maybe, his hair gelled into oil-slicked feathers, peering through that mess of green eyeliner at the sugary Formica as if his life depended on it. He'd been sitting that way since they came in: through their two coffees and Charlie's brandy, the same slumped shape and fixed stare, the cup beside him untouched. The same way he was now, in fact. Just a wee boy for crying out loud. She heard Charlie opening the door beside her, the sucking sound of seals being broken. He stood holding it, nodding for her to go first, its weight braced against one arm. She flicked her eyes in the boy's direction again, knowing he wouldn't be any different, hoping anyway. Then back to the open door. It wasn't a real choice. You didn't start things you couldn't finish, create expectations and just fuck off. That was the worst thing, the worst thing imaginable. Sometimes you just had to let well alone. She ducked under the waiting arm, telling herself that was just how it was. You had to believe that or you went crazy. Sometimes the only thing you could do was nothing at all.

Outside was cold. That thick dark way it went in the city and freezing. The wind would be coming off the river. He liked it here at night, he'd said: the water, the lights and the skyline. Cmon Fiona, he said, I've been in all day; the fresh air and everything, talking her into it. Then somehow they'd walked for a million miles and ended up at the cafe. They might be going there now, though. His hand swung next to hers as they walked but she didn't reach for it. Only knowing him this short while, it seemed the safest option. The most prudent option. It wasn't the easiest. Even here, walking down this perishing backstreet she could feel it: the wish to touch. Not just to take his hand but to caress him, to run her hands under the leather of his jacket and over his chest, feel his heartbeat warm against her mouth. His perfectly smooth, hairless thighs: the white slither they made moving between hers. Trying to control the thing, to keep walking in a straight line thinking this stuff was making her feel dizzy. Well, that and the fact they'd hardly slept: the ages they'd spent draining the same bottle, repeating the same exchanges about the same people before he'd finally shown her the spare bed; a further age of silences, reluctances to say goodnight and mean it before he'd gotten in beside her. Then, after the sex and the crying – it happened to some women sometimes – waking on and off through what was left of the night to find this other body: those long, pale arms cradling her shoulder, the crisp scent of his neck when she breathed deep. But that wasn't here, in an open place and sober. He was, after all, someone she hardly knew. Meeting every so often because you'd been to the same art school and you were friendly with their sister wasn't the same as knowing somebody. She'd always admired his stuff, written once or twice saying as much, not expecting replies. Then the chance sighting, his shout across the pub on his last visit home, *if you're ever in London* etc. Probably drunk. Probably thinking she'd never take it up.

But she had. Now this. This whatever it was. This melting in the gut when she looked at him. This unanticipated, sudden, shocking, lust. On the other hand, maybe it wasn't lust at all. Maybe she was just tired, suffering from weakness of a more banal sort altogether. The pavement had narrowed now, Charlie walking ahead beneath the streetlight. She watched him – the width of him under stretched leather, the pale drift of skin against the collar's edge – feeling an involuntary muscle clench inside. Tired was bugger all to do with it, the muscle said. If he got in beside her tonight, tired was the last thing she'd be thinking about. Tired would wait. If, though. There was certainly an if about the whole business. If if if. Oily stones scuffing her boots, rags of litter. He turned the corner, jacket creaking as he dug his hands into the pockets, and kept walking.

The bridge was there without warning: right there as she turned. Charlie had started up already, his shoes making flat coffin-thumps on the metal plates. Good shoes, decent soles. He hadn't seemed the walking type and neither he was, much. But he needed to get out and about at night, he said: get the paint stink out his nostrils, observe. The railing was bloody freezing. Gloves would have been good but neither of them had any. Godknew how Charlie managed in this weather. He was so fucking thin. She'd had a notion to make him a big pot of soup this afternoon, soup full of barley and rib-sticking things that would last a few days but she hadn't. He didn't seem to need much of a pretext for acting touchy, making out he was being patronised. Katrin called him twisted. On the other hand, it was possible he wouldn't even have noticed the soup, nomatter how much she'd made. He forgot sometimes, his word: forgot to eat. She'd taken him in some rakings out the fridge at lunchtime and he hadn't bothered. She'd eaten both platefuls herself, watching him paint. Three hours without it becoming boring, without conversation, feeling privileged to be there. Maybe feeling she was learning something. Veins like rope on his forearms. She was thinking about Charlie painting, the sexiness of his total absorption, when she almost fell over the man.

None-too-visible but there all right, a man folded into the corner of the platform, legs splayed over the studs of iron sheeting. Fiona could see an open-necked shirt, no socks showing above the rim of canvas shoes, an open cardboard box and a sign with something written on it. I NEED MONEY. The colour of the bridge lights made everything look blue, unwholesome but you could read it if you looked hard. I NEED MONEY. Of course he did. And she'd nearly fallen over him like he was so much rubbish. She had change somewhere, though. Lots of it. Groping in the shoulderbag found two receipts, a postcard, bits of Polo wrapper needing flung away. The man looked up as she riffled for the purse, a glint of eyeball through shadow. Warmth was inching up her neck like creeper, unstoppable. The A-Z, an identity card, godknew what else. Then it dawned on her. She'd left the purse behind at Charlie's place. The man coughed, whispered thank you. Before she had done anything. He was looking at her too, both eyes taking her in. Thank you. Fiona looked back. The accent, the straight stare. It was the same man. A couple of years ago now, but still recognisable. She'd been waiting in what was left of the fog outside the pictures and he'd come out of nowhere, aiming straight for her. She'd thought he was going to ask for the time, was lifting her wrist to tell him till she realised he was keeping coming, till he was far too close for comfort, and he was whispering. I have no money. She remembered standing, the wrist uselessly upturned, a scent of alcohol and some kind of medical stink. Noticing he wasn't wearing a jacket and doing nothing. He'd had to repeat himself increasing the volume and slowing down as though she was foreign or daft. MONEY. CAN YOU GIVE ME SOME MONEY? English public school vowels throwing her further. She remembered saying Sorry? like a halfwit and him looking, drizzle spangling on the tips of his hair. I. HAVE. NO. MONEY. MONEY. UNDERSTAND? Rubbing his thumb against the next two fingers, feeling empty space before he opened his hand. She had looked at the hand, soft and plump beneath the dirt. A beautiful hand. All she found to fit in it was a couple of small coins and one of them, she saw when she looked again, one of them was Irish. Thank you, he said. Voice up a notch or two, precision sarcasm before he kissed her. He kissed her mouth, made a wet patch that smeared onto her cheek as well, looked hard into her eyes. Thank you very much. And she had stood and let him. Hadn't moved. Refused to meet his gaze but hadn't shifted at all. They must have stood like that some seconds before he went. Just a shadow of him beneath the pillars by the time she was able to move herself, touch the ghost he had left on her face. Now here he was again, angled against the metal girders at her feet. The same queer sense of shame. It was the same man.

From somewhere far away, a light snapping sound. Fiona looked up. On the next level, waiting on the first step of the walkway, Charlie was cracking his knuckles. He was looking down, wondering what was keeping her. Quickly, without having to think about it, she reached for the note in her back pocket, the twenty she'd drawn from the bank machine to tide her over on the journey home tomorrow. It sifted out easily, open and warm. Then, hoping neither man would notice that's what it was, she dropped it in the box. Sorry, she said. Sorry. She ran up the remaining flight still saying it, this time for Charlie. Sorry. Thank god it was dark. Charlie noticed nothing, though. Just gave her one of those half-smiles he did, raised his eyebrows. And walked on.

She reached the top out of breath. Charlie was already staring out over the water, the river beaded with lights.

Look at it, he was saying. Look.

He sounded pleased. Behind him, white neon furred with mist. The view was St Paul's, city blocks, a skyscraper reflecting the water, the odd boat tugging on a rope. Beyond, a slab of indistinguishable shadows threaded with car lights.

London, she said eventually. It looks like London.

He laughed.

Well, it does. She was smiling back now, easier. You tell me what else it looks like then.

He said nothing. They waited side by side, letting the silence sift back. It was ok, this silence. Not chummy exactly but not hostile, just needing to thaw out a bit. She looked at him sideways.

You like living here?

I don't know. He breathed out, the exhalation turning to smoke over his lip. Depends what you mean by *like*.

She shrugged her eyebrows. Just you sound . . . I don't know . . . as though you're admiring something. I thought you sounded fond for a minute.

Ah. He sounded as though he'd just found something and was amused by it. Do I Feel I Belong Here, is that it?

Maybe, she said. I suppose so.

No, he said. The word came out like a silk scarf. Nooooo thank you.

Maybe he just didn't like talking about himself much. Some people didn't.

I'm stuck with Glasgow, she said. Only place I know how to work the buses.

She laughed to let him know it could be a joke if he liked. He didn't.

I like it too, though, she said. Glasgow I mean. When I'm there I take it for granted I suppose but coming back on the train or something, there's a kind of . . . relief. I don't know whether that counts as a sense of belonging but it's there all right.

He looked as though he was listening but didn't speak.

I don't think a sense of belonging is such a bad thing, really. Maybe that's a kind of couthy thing to say, not very sophisticated or cosmopolitan. But I do.

She was talking too much.

So, she said. What about you?

A boat on the far bank was nosing continually in the same direction, sucking grey weed towards itself from the river wall. Charlie said nothing.

What do you think? she said.

No, he said. The sound of his voice was a surprise. No. I can see what's here is nice to look at but it doesn't have anything to do with me really.

His eyes were fixed on something miles away. Fiona tried to see it too, working out what he was talking about. It took her a moment to realise he was still answering the first question. He must have been thinking about it while she was wittering away about Glasgow and only just come up with an answer.

I suppose I feel something for New York because of the Art School, he went on. I did all my growing up there and it kind of . . . kind of sticks you to somewhere. Coming back was – he tailed off, shook his head. Horrible. That's the word. Fucking horrible. But that's finished. I don't have any friends there any more. He looked at her briefly out of the corner of his eye. People I know but not really friends.

You must have somebody, she said.

Katrin had told her he was married out there. There was even something about a wee boy but she couldn't remember all that well. It was all a bit personal and a bit vague to start pushing for answers about that though. Charlie said nothing.

Somebody you write to even, phone now and again?

He shook his head.

The bridge was shoogling, rattling beneath her feet. She hadn't realised trains came by this close. When the noise level was low enough she tried again.

What about back home? D'you not have friends there either?

Home, he said. You mean Scotland? Bloody Greenock for godsake?

He was smiling now, big generous grin, rocking back and forward on the rail and looking down at the water.

Well, you are aren't you? Scottish, I mean.

He snorted, said nothing.

Is it the word you don't like? You don't feel Scottish, is that it? Give me a shout if I'm getting warmer.

He snorted again, keeping her hanging a moment longer.

Well, he said. A long drawl before he warmed up. Well, sometimes. Not often but sometimes. Mostly when other people provoke it though. In the States, for example: they'd ask you stuff, stuff they expected you to know – politics and history, current trends in the Scottish cultural scene kind of thing. Recipes even. I didn't know. He laughed. I didn't care. It was like they couldn't get a handle on that at all. All this banging on about my heritage. *Heritage*. Poor bastards hadn't a clue. Scottish culture jesus christ.

He shook his head in a manner indicative of disbelief.

I used to tell them they'd been misinformed and pretend to be Irish. At least they've got a fucking country. Less embarrassment all round.

Fiona said nothing. His outbreaths were audible in the stillness. When he spoke again, his voice was measured. It was very, very calm.

No. I don't want to belong to any of that thanks. *Being Scottish*. He took a quick swig of air through his nose. At least if you live in London people take you seriously. I don't think I want to belong to anything. Except art maybe, my work.

She could see a stain of paint on his knuckle, a night colour that might be red in sunlight. It might even be blood. Further off, an ambulance was sounding, weaving between unseen buildings.

I know what you mean about Glasgow, though, he said. He laughed. Scared of the big bad world out there. Some folk are uncomfortable anywhere but in a rut, I suppose. It serves a function.

The stained hand clutched the railing, relaxed despite the chill. She watched it for a while then turned her eyes up to his face. He was swaying slightly, a cloud of condensation like an aura round his head. He looked very young somehow. The skin on his cheeks flushed, his eyes shiny and pink-lidded. Maybe he was trying to wind her up. Maybe he was trying to sound surer than he felt and it just came out that offensive, arrogant way. Maybe he was high on something.

Well, she said, cagey. It seems to suit me.

He smiled again, looking at her now. A generous, sensual smile. She dropped her shoulders a little more.

I wouldn't like to live here anyway.

He said nothing.

It's nice and everything. Not intimidating. London's just a collection of wee towns really. It's all the different bits coming together that is the best thing about here. She breathed in deep. But it can get so . . . well . . .

He cocked his head. So *what?*

It can get awfully . . . cozy, you know. The seat of government, the critical establishment and all that. Just it must be so easy to get . . . sucked into those kind of priorities down here and think it's the world. That they mean something more important than they in fact do.

His smile had gone.

Cmon Charlie, this place can be a helluva rut as well. You don't have to look far. Wee elitist games and who knows who, the right accents, faces fitting. That stupid insider mentality. You know fine what I mean. London isn't the Big World at all. It can be a beautiful place, a seductive place. But it's never struck me as particularly important. It's also as parochial as get out. Don't kid me on you haven't noticed.

I wouldn't know he said, turning away. I don't have the same need to react against it as you obviously do.

React against it? React against what?

What you call the establishment. Insider mentality. I've better things to do with my time than get het up about that stuff. Like paint.

His hand slid off the rail and up inside the jacket cuff.

Establishment. Jesus. Very sixties.

She could see he was frowning and waited, silent, in case she made it worse. Volatility went with talent, they said. Maybe it did. Maybe Charlie was tortured by stuff going on in his brain, great thoughts or something and it made him snappy, volatile. Maybe it was just how it was.

People spend too much time on things that don't matter, he said. Where you belong and stuff. What difference does it make?

He sounded very sure but at least he wasn't huffy. She waited to see if there was more to come.

I got homesick once, he said. The year I did in Berlin. Now my German's pretty good, right? I could understand the sense of humour, the references. I knew most of what was going on but I never talked much. Not with the people from the art school, even other places. They thought it was because I wasn't up to the language, the patois and so on but it wasn't that. I knew it wasn't. I just couldn't be bothered.

The thin metal sheeting was shaking again. Another train.

Do you know what I mean? Just there wasn't anything I
had to say about any of that stuff: people's kids, who said
what to who, who was having an affair with who, buying
furniture and getting a wee place to stay – it was all so . . .
I don't know. I just couldn't see what was meant to matter
about it all. It was all so bloody ordinary.

The last word swallowed off inside engine noise, the click
of resettling wheels. He kept looking at her, the blond hair
rimmed with silver from the neon, his eyes with those rings
that needed sleep. Inside the sound of the train passing, he
looked like his bones would splinter at the slightest
pressure, shatter like eggshell. And he didn't know. He
didn't know how not well he looked. How child-like.

Maybe that's all there is though? she said. She said it very
gently. He looked over, his eyes wide. I mean what's
ordinary is what's universal, isn't it? That's where the
biggest meanings are.

He kept looking at her.

Aren't they?

Jesuschrist, he said. He laughed. Jesus. If that's true I
might as well jump off this fucking thing now.

She wanted to touch him but this was not the moment.
She could ask something though, make some kind of
contact to stop him digging the trench any deeper. The train
was past, silence expanding. It should be now. He beat her
to it though, made a kind of laughing sound, air hissing
over his teeth. He tilted his neck while he did it, staring into
the black sky.

D'you know what I think?

No, she said.

I think. He paused. I think. I think the less time I spend
with people the better I like it. People are always a waste of
time in the end. They don't think, don't prioritise their
fucking lives. People *wear you down*. At least painting
makes something. See, my trouble, Fiona, my trouble is I'm

too observant. I *see* everything. If I didn't order some of it on canvas, I'd go round the bend. Art *makes sense*: people *don't*. And I know what I'd rather spend my time on. Any day. Any day.

Neither of them said anything for a moment. She looked out at the skyline, trying not to feel whatever it was that was hurting her chest. Anger, maybe. Whatever it was it was getting bigger.

Too fucking observant, he said again. People like you don't know how lucky they are.

Look, she said. She said it very slowly. I don't think *sense* attaches to anything intrinsically. But you can't seriously be telling me people don't matter.

He said nothing.

Cmon. You're saying for real that people aren't worth anything?

Nothing.

Ok. This supposed Life and Art debate: this notion you're somehow above *ordinary* living order to be an Artist and Life is for the lower orders or something – it's all crap. Maybe male crap, maybe just elitist crap but definitely crap.

He was smiling now, still not looking at her. She didn't know whether she was saying something funny or he was trying to annoy her.

It's worse than crap, it's a con trick, Charlie. If there's no Life there is no bloody Art is there?

And what's Life then? he said.

Talking and interchanging, the raising of weans. Getting by. Behaving decently towards other people. Love, I suppose. If you don't attend to that, you attend to nothing. Love, Charlie.

My god what was wrong with her? This monologue and that word suddenly coming out. She shouldn't have used it, not used a word like that. Not to Katrin's big brother, to someone who could paint the way he could. Not to Charlie. She had to slow down, care less. Try for lightness.

If there's no Life there's no Art. Discuss.

He didn't laugh. Just looked at her, his face blank. It was terrible not being able to embrace him though, make sure things were all right. His hand still lying there on the metal rail, nails flecked. A man who forgot to eat. A man who had kissed her awake.

Was it a mistake coming away from the States then?

Her voice had gone that soft way, like a psychiatrist. A doctor in a film.

He shrugged. I don't miss anywhere. A place is just a place.

The disappointment was unexpected. But unmistakable. It wasn't till she felt it stuck in her chest like cold pudding she knew what she'd been doing. All this time. She'd been wanting him to say something else. A question, maybe, something that wondered what *she* cared about, her work or something. Only he'd never seen her pictures, never asked her to send any when she'd offered. And anyway that wasn't really it at all. What she'd really been wanting was more humiliating still. Some kind of sign, something as trivial as a compliment. An invitation for tonight, that's what she wanted: some kind of possibility opening up between them. She flicked her eyes up to see if he knew somehow. He was hunting for something in the inside pocket, oblivious.

I suppose I don't feel I belong anywhere either, she said.

It was impressively matter-of-fact.

Not till something gets me angry.

He was smiling properly now, feeling better for just having found whatever it was he'd been after. It was fags. A packet of fags.

Unreconstructed Romantic, eh?

She watched the smile widen, his hand slip into the trouser pocket, looking for matches.

You need to pick your fights, Fiona. Look after number one a bit more. Too bloody soft, that's your trouble. You're too bloody serious about the wrong things. You mind Alison Sime? She could paint. She could really paint. You know what she's doing now?

Fiona looked at him, the packet he'd unearthed secure in one hand.

Two kids and the glory of motherhood, that's what she's fucking doing. Not painting. Not bloody making a name for herself. Women's priorities. He shook his head. The things they do to themselves. That's where women always fuck up, you know? Sentimentality. What your lot need to do is realign your priorities.

She knew it wasn't really him. Even while it was happening, she knew it wasn't him that was making her feel so terrible. It was her. If she hadn't got him so riled up, hadn't pressed all the wrong buttons, he wouldn't be saying any of this. Everything was in jeopardy and it was her fault. Even knowing, she hung back, reluctant to acknowledge the fact it wasn't coming right, that saying anything else was just going to make it worse.

So, he said. Here endeth the lesson. Will we get going?

He had lit up, the thing glued to his lower lip as he spoke. He couldn't understand what was keeping her standing at the railing. They moved together, without touching. They drew close at the top of the steps and without thinking, she asked for a kiss. His proximity made it seem natural. He said No. Just one word. No.

A piece of scarf, a rag of cloth was tied to the rail on the way down but the man was gone. No man, no box, no wee sign. Charlie didn't seem to notice. Fiona looked out over the scrub at the side of the bridge but there was no sign.

Know something, Charlie said. He was buoyant when they got to the bottom. I meant to say when you were doing your mile about Scotland and belonging. Your name, Fiona, it's not Scottish. It's not even old. P. G. Wodehouse or somebody made it up. He raised one eyebrow. And you're telling me about con tricks eh?

He laughed all the way to the tube station.

After the waterside, the tunnel light was harsh and yellow. They avoided looking at each other on the way through. By the time they reached the ticket machines he had become restless, less self-contained. He muttered something about wanting to explain, nothing more. The explanation, whatever it referred to, didn't surface. They sat with one empty seat between them on the tube back, not talking. Soon they'd be back at the house. Maybe it would all be sorted out there: something simple would be said and the tension would lift. Or break. Whatever it was tension did. Maybe the whole thing tonight was a misunderstanding, a nonsense they'd laugh about later. Maybe it was PMT or something. Godknew. The train shivered round a corner and into another station that wasn't theirs. He was playing with the cigarette carton, eyes shut, miles away. She stared at the route map, its circles and interconnecting lines. Another three stops to go. There was an off-licence on the way back, the corner just before his place. She could go in and buy a bottle of something, a bottle of something usually helped. They'd get in and Charlie would fetch the gas heater, make them both something warm to drink. They might sit on the big double mattress on the floor to drink it, move close. Closer. Just three more stops. Further down the carriage, a drunk was trying to stand, preparing to come in their direction. Soon, she hoped, maybe very soon this cold feeling in her chest would go away.

tourists from the south arrive in the independent state

They touched down four hours late and the luggage hadn't arrived but they didn't mind. These things happened. Even in the most sophisticated of places, these things happened. They spent the time they might otherwise have spent minding in a cluster at the carousel, willing it to start, nodding to clusters of Islanders left over from internal flights. Trying not to stare overmuch, the sight of decent wool knitted into such awful jerseys. They chose instead to listen, feeding their ears on those thick, near-Slavic vowels, now and again, an almost-familiar word crunching with consonants. There was a distinct Eastern Bloc snubness of pronunciation when you attended carefully, really something less harsh than one had been led to believe. Only there was no Eastern Bloc now. No Cold War. The way of the modern world, the forgings of proud independences etc. It was best to welcome it all as a Good Thing. They looked up keen then, prepared to smile their warmest smiles for these people from a colder, possibly even nobler, climate. Odd that their countries being formally separate now should make them feel so much closer, so much more tolerant. Smiles were the least they could do to salute the fact.

The Islanders weren't looking. They had huddled together, lighting a single cigarette and passing it on. They did not smile back. They didn't even notice. And that was perfectly all right too. Of course it was. Gauche to force contact in any case, patronising. They were a people whose history had led them to be wary and rightly so, rightly so. The red-head closest shouted something and gestured with his hands. He had the richest accent. They listened carefully, relishing cadences they recognised from tv documentaries, the odd series. *Taggart, Para Handy.* Catching themselves whispering sample phrases for the feel of it in their own mouths, they almost blushed.

A noise like an industrial crusher sounded suddenly close, making some of the group start. The indigenous group didn't flinch or even turn round. Perhaps they knew it was only the carousel. A first battered carpet bag was already coming through, string and bits of insulating tape binding a rip on the material. Someone who had not plumped for new cases after all. It went round unclaimed. Though they kept their eyes on the luggage vent, nothing more appeared. Not yet. Not for a while perhaps. The Islanders had begun passing round oatcakes and a page of a concertinaed newspaper. Racing Tips. So unperturbed they were laughing. They waited coughing, riffling in pockets for things that weren't there. Some wandered to the pinboards inexpertly attached to the walls, the single poster left intact with its patterning of trees and water. Lock Lomond perhaps. Lock Ness. One torn banner had nothing left but its words: THE BEAUTIES OF ROYAL DEESIDE against a ripped edge. An irony, perhaps, a joke. The conveyor kept turning with nothing on the belt.

When they looked back, something was missing. It took a moment to register: the Islanders had gone. Four douts, one of them still smoking on the tweed-coloured tile, and an

empty IRN BRU bottle were all that remained. The luggage
had arrived. Whatever the Islanders had had to collect was
gone, leaving the tourgroup's flight bags and cases, the odd
rucksack piled in a crumbling mountain behind the only
trolley. They had no sooner begun to gather them together
when someone appeared, a shout and an arm waving from
the double glass door. THE BEAUTIES OF ROYAL
DEESIDE slid past for the last time as they walked into the
clear night air.

Outside smelt of faulty incinerators and fish suppers. A
faint undertone of malt. The arm that had waved belonged
to a thin man in shiny trousers and no jacket despite the
cold. They noted he had not shaved either but he smiled
and pointed to a bus half-mounted on the paved area. An
old bus. He kept pointing till they made for the single step
up onto the platform, helping the heavier among their
number inside where the seats were pleasingly whole and
covered with tartan flocking despite the strong tang of
nicotine and spilled alcohol. Still, everything seemed very
clean. They were sure it was all very clean. They were still
settling when the bus started without warning, elbowing
heavily onto the road, and the interior lights switched off.
Some thought about asking to have them switched on
again then thought not. It might have showed a terrible
lack of something, lack of awareness of the need to
conserve energy. In any case, the driver had put the radio
on: something jolly on an accordion. And with the lights
off it was possible to see the wide streets much more
clearly. Wide streets and long stretches of wasteground.
They noted a pile of rubble that might well have been
something impressive once, something important. Then
more wasteground. Eventually, the streetlamps came into
view. By their light, hoardings with unreadable
exhortations became visible, graffiti under the bridges.

Doubtless the work of dissidents, though whether of dissidents before or after recent events would be impossible to say. The driver's high nasal whine joined in the radio-singing only he was talking. They did not recognise the words but he was pointing at something, possibly a landmark of national significance. They peered out of the windows, rubbing holes in the condensation already gathering there, saw nothing but late-night neon, a stretch of warehouses closed for the night behind shutters. A flyover spanning a shimmer that might have been water. On the other side, streets broad and lonely as ship canals stretching to the edge of the sky.

When the bus finally tipped them out at a too-big hotel, it was snowing. They fetched their own things from the belly of the bus because the driver did not, nodding to reassure there was no assumption he was at fault. They had hesitated only to be sure, aware of the fine line. They walked inside then, cold and getting colder over the thinning Black Watch shag pile to a high reception desk. Behind it, three women wearing suits and 2 am faces waited under clammy electric light. The sign on the counter, PASSPORTS MUST BE SURRENDERED ON RECEIPT OF KEYS NO TICK, made them uneasy but they did not quibble. They were tired. Zips fizzed cautiously, careful not to break the quiet; they booted baggage through the dust drifts towards the desks. The passports were new, a different colour and awkward to find. Somewhere to the right, the sound of football on tv veered blurrily close then swallowed off again. The women waited patiently, sucking dark lips. Still foraging, they tried smiles but did not hold them long. It was better to keep eyes on the reflections of their own shoes on the dull tile, the mosaics on the far wall. Blue with white webbing.

The river Clyde, the wonderful Clyde.

The woman behind the counter had sung it. She stopped, took the passport.

The Clyde, she said. You'll have seen it on the way from the airport.

A passable Standard English except for the phrasing. Behind her, representational water flowed down the wall in tiny squares while she looked from passport photo to face and back again, her mouth tightening at the corner in an attitude that resembled amusement. They tried to think that was not so. It would just be tiredness playing tricks, the mild paranoia of new places striking home. And they were indeed. They were very tired.

Now they held pink hotel cards, keys. Behind a square-edged pillar, the LIFT sign, handwritten, appeared. Something to walk towards. They shuffled inside, six at a time, watched the red numbers on the way up, left without speaking. They wanted only to find their respective rooms. Alone and quickly, tiptoeing past the sleeping janitor in his den, they pursued the numbers on their keys. None knew when breakfast would be served, or where. No-one had offered or said. Those who had learned any prior to the trip had not used their patois. They did not want to start now. Without help, they found the right doors but the locks were resistant, reluctant to give in. They persisted, they muddled on, twisting their wrists and fingers in the hope that the next turn would be all it took. But now, fifteen floors high in the New Independence Hotel, glimmers of admission that things were not all they had hoped for were undeniable. They slumped then, leaned against the cool walls, gathered strength. They tried not to think about the possible quality of guest soap or toilet paper, whether the curtains would close. The inevitability of a monster tv in one corner. That the sound of bagpipes and that single word shouted from streets distant would not go away. It was impossible not to sigh.

Yet behind the closed eyelids, they hoped for better things. Perhaps the door would surrender next try: the room that opened before them might be cheerful, modest and clean. They would walk inside, close the old day out, leave luggage where it fell and tumble onto the freshly-turned sheets. The Kelman novels they had brought for atmosphere would wait or be used, spines cracked open, to place over weary faces to keep out the morning light. When it came. And it would. It would certainly come. Morning always did.

The shout again, the same expletive. A sound like an owl.

Hooch.

Hooch.

But for now they were still in the corridor, keys hard inside their fists, yet to comply. They heard others in adjoining corridors sigh too, the thud of shoes against unyielding wood. It was three am. And they thought how understanding they had wanted to be.

How generous. How tolerant.

How kind.

he dreams of pleasing
his mother

The blue dress flickers like a cold flame.

She was walking along the edge of the road, one foot dragging a little but her pace even, without hesitation. Making for the truck. The truck was the biggest thing apart from the sky: vast red body buffed hard as mirror, radiator gills burning like magnesium flashes. Dazzling. The sun must be high, up there. It had to be though he couldn't feel it. If he looked carefully there was heat-haze, wavy lines moving over the solid machine up ahead, making it ripple, but no warmth or sound, no rush of air on his cheek. Maybe he was behind glass. He looked without moving his head, casting his eyes side to side whilst keeping his body rigid but it was impossible to tell; not without stretching out a hand and giving himself away. To show any form of fear would be self-defeating. There was no room for wrong moves. Even though there was no-one else, no-one else visible anyway, you couldn't be too careful. People were surprising. And there was always the possibility of being watched from control boxes, the whole road being monitored by cameras. She was still there, coming steadily down the kerb. He screwed up his eyes, peering to see her face, read it for clues of some kind. She was still too far away. He realised then he had been wondering if she knew anything he didn't, if she had even set this up somehow. Terrible thing to think about your own mother but that was what he did sometimes, the kind of bad bastard he was. He kept watching her all the same. She seemed no closer but things were clearer somehow. He could tell things he hadn't been able to before. The dress, for example. It wasn't a dress. It was a two-piece: one of those skirt and cardigan affairs she liked with a string of black beads. His mother did not own black beads, they weren't the kind of thing she wore, but there they were, double-looped on her chest. Maybe they were new, a present from someone. It would please her if he noticed them and made some remark. Even at this distance he could tell she was smiling, giving him a hint. A big smile. So big it made her teeth look longer, whiter. Almost unnatural. The skin on the back of his neck bristled. Maybe they weren't her teeth at all. They could be false, capped maybe. Or. He felt dizzy thinking about the or but he was thinking it anyway. Or they were the teeth of some other animal entirely. He looked at it hard, knowing even as he did it there would be no way to tell. Because if it was a beast, if it really was some terrible thing with terrible powers the likes of which he could only begin to guess at, it would have done the disguise properly. Dear god dear god. The need to struggle to remember to give nothing away, to remember not to run. He warned himself against being a child and a fool several times, keeping his face impassive. It helped to remember the pain in his head was not visible and the rest of his face was good at obeying orders. If he had learned nothing else, he had learned that. Eyes refocusing, forcing his brow smooth. Now he'd pulled himself together, she looked fine. The smile was perfectly normal. He toyed briefly with the idea of smiling back, rejected it. If it looked forced or too eager, wrong somehow, it would ruin things.

Whatever happened, he knew he better not mention the animal idea, not even as a joke. Shame caught his chest just thinking about it. If she knew what he'd been thinking, if she knew what went on in his head, if she even suspected. The shame pressed harder. And she would, all right. She'd notice. She noticed fucking everything. But things were ok now. They were under control. She hadn't shown any displeasure so far, hadn't really shown any sign she'd seen him at all. That being the case, it was entirely possible he was invisible and all this worry was for nothing. Maybe that was it. Maybe he just wasn't there. Cheered, he turned his head up, let his shoulders relax. The sudden fear invisibility could be construed a major fault occurred and was pushed away. No need to get paranoid.

She stopped walking then.
Level with the red cab, she stopped walking.

She waited a moment, brushing the skirt sleek with one hand, preparing and he could not help but feel a flush of pride. Mother. She always liked to look neat. She looked up at the cab and reached for the handle, stretching. One foot rose to the black platform and he saw she was wearing her best shoes, the ones with ankle straps and the little cuban heels. He concentrated on watching the shoes in case her skirt rode up when she hauled herself onto the step. That would feel unpleasant, voyeuristic. He looked hard at her foot. The foot was so clear he was sure the face would be too and he was right. Mother's face. She was wearing a touch of powder and lipstick and looking into the cab interior with something approaching delight. It was definitely her though. He watched her steady herself then launch upwards, the familiar head and blue two-piece cramming themselves into the cab, the mouth-parts of that great red beast perched on the road ahead. When she reappeared, high off the ground behind the windscreen, she looked smaller somehow. Like a woman he didn't know. He wondered if he should shout, give her some kind of warning he was here after all. Then her features creased, the smile returning, and he knew his warning was not something she needed at all. She was perfectly fine. Putting on her crash-helmet, a bullet-shaped dome with a full-face shield. She didn't need him for a thing.

He watches the woman he knows to be his mother vanish behind the polarised visor, her fingers secure the clip at the neck. Her ring finger glitters before it drops out of sight. He knows that ring. The mark she made on his face when he was six is still there, a light score. That was an accident, though. She always said it was an accident. That ring doesn't come off. They will need to bury her in it, he thinks. No-one will ever see it again. His nose is running now but her hands offer nothing. They are still out of sight. They are out of sight because she is turning the ignition. The sides of the truck quiver. Exhaust fumes cloud the chromium sheen of the radiator muzzle but he hears nothing. Even when he puts out his hand, there is no glass. No bars, nothing. He really must be here. He must.

When he looks down he sees feet. They are wearing his shoes. Half on the grass verge, half on the surface of this road that might be a motorway though he has seen no evidence, no other cars. Maybe they would still come. The vibration he could feel, the trembling, had to be caused by something. His feet – they can be no-one else's – stand on tarmac and earth. There are no flowers between the green blades. When he begins to walk – it is the only thing he can think of to do – the shoes stay put. Of course they do. The clothes are only trappings. It is him she is here for. Keeping his expression still, measured, as though he knew all along, he walks carefully over the cold asphalt in his stocking soles. He is dimly aware he does not want to do this but tries not to notice. Stray stones and shale, step after step, he just keeps going to the white centre-line. He stops. There is a hole in the sock-tip, a rag-nail poking through. Noticing chills him. It chills him hollow. It reminds him he cannot put off knowing what will happen now. He stares at this sign of his body's existence, his knuckles whitening. Then looks up.

The juggernaut grins.
Coming and going like a red mirage, settled on its hunkers.
The scarlet and silver casing, the deep, black treads.

He lifts his head then, the whole heavy weight of it, levelling his eyes to show he is not afraid. The juggernaut sighs, releasing brakes. She would be doing that. Her hand. And now they will be resettling on the wheel because the tyres are beginning, rolling slowly forward. He swallows, wondering if she can see him yet, if there is a chance he will be able to make her look directly at him. Maybe when she is closer he might even be able to make her hear. The new beads. If he has time to mention them, say how nice they look. She might smile then. She might even reach for the brakes. His throat is dry. A vein in his neck is pumping blood. It keeps doing it.

Ahead, in the thick, still air of this place he does not know yet has been all his life, the truck is growing larger. He flicks his eyes to the road behind, hearing the other cars, other engine sounds growing louder. They might well reach him before she does. The curve of a bonnet perhaps at hip-height: whether metal or rubber will make contact first. He has no way of knowing how much it will hurt. But he knows he will not move. Not now. He would just wait here till she came: nomatter what condition he was in when she arrived, he'd be here. To see if this time it would be different. He wanted to see if he could provoke compassion. But even if he couldn't. Even if she didn't look or acknowledge him at all before the wheels bore down, he wanted to know he'd given it his best shot.

He tilted his chin, catching the last of the sun. He had good bone-structure. And he very much wanted to be beautiful. For her to be proud. Beautiful, deliberate, dignified, he waited for his mother.

last thing

we were
coming

   coming back from the pictures with half a packet of
sweeties still coming round the corner at the Meadowside
with Mary saying she was feart to go up the road herself
Mary is feart for everything but so I said I'll take you
because I'm bigger than her the film thing we'd saw at the
pictures that Halloween thing wasny really scary I don't
think but Mary saying she hated all the screaming the big
knife was horrible one time her brother pushed one under
the toilet door she said and told her to slit her wrists but
he's not right Billy he works a place they make baskets or
something he's not right in the head so I said I'll take you
up the road offering her a sweetie it got stuck to the back
of her teeth and she was laughing kidding on her mouth
was glued shut and she couldn't talk only make these
moaning noises because her mouth was all stuck together
when this shape a big kind of shadow thing started it
came out of the close at the corner of the main street right
where the streetlight is at the corner a big shape coming
out and turning into a man he was only a wee bit bigger

than Mary so maybe he was a boy really and he said

I've lost my mate

just like that he said and away back in again away in the close he had come out I just looked but I couldn't see him but he was definitely there you could hear him saying it again in there I've lost my mate only a wee thin voice with no body now but you couldn't see maybe he was round the back garden or something and I thought he must be lost too the man maybe not from here with him speaking funny the way he did not knowing you didn't wander about in people's gardens this terrible idea of being lost and maybe not knowing where you were and not being able to find the person who had come with you like losing the only thing you understood and I went in Mary was kind of hanging back she didn't like people she's an awful feart kind of person Mary she gets rows from her mother for talking to folk she gets rows for just being there but I went in away after the sound of the voice that had lost its friend and was maybe lonely I went in after the voice and I couldn't see him at first it was too dark too

dark off the main road and I didn't like it was too dark I couldn't hear anything any

more and I was nearly shouting for Mary to come too it was frightening expecting to go in and help somebody and suddenly they weren't there to be helped and it was like a dark tunnel between nothing and where she was out there so I was about to shout her when something

some thing wrapped it

self around my neck I didn't know just felt the tilt backwards and couldn't work out why I was unsteady on my feet till the thing went tight in my neck like a piece of pipe or something it was blocked a stuck thing poking into where I needed to breathe and my legs going soft like they wouldn't be able to hold me up I just went like a dolly

because I got a surprise not knowing what it was till I was
being dragged backwards back

       wards away from the road the streetlight out there
the yellowness kind of slipping further away because
somebody some body was dragging me by the neck a man
he said YOU'RE COMING WITH ME but his voice wasn't
right like he was choking or crying maybe something was
wrong it was definitely the man saying YOU'RE COMING
WITH ME and he shoved one of his hands up under my
jersey I could feel the big shape of his hand sort of pulling
my jersey under my jacket and going up onto my belly and
it made me stop and breathe wrong it was so unexpected his
hand there then he pushed me round the edge out the close
altogether against the wall so then I could feel the wall
being crumbly thon way plaster goes after years with the
wee bits of moss growing through it crumbling through to
the grey stuff underneath you think it would have felt
scratchy but it wasn't it was just this stuff disintegrating
under where he was pushing me back against the wall so it
was hard to keep breathing right with his hand pushing
under my chin so all I could see was the sky a funny colour
with the orange off the streetlight making wee grains in it
like off milk but right then right that minute something kind
of turned in my head something kind of clicked and I
wanted to look him right in the eye

  it was what I really wanted to do I wanted to
  just see his face just
look him in the eye he was pushing my face so hard my
nose was running he was hurting my wrists but I kind of
pushed my head straight till I could see because I wanted to
see his face I wanted to stare at him he was cutting off where
I was trying to breathe and know I just wanted him to know
to see me and know what he was doing the noise of Mary
greeting from the street out there I could hear her in the

place by the close mouth Mary a terrible coward and not
even sure where I lived and even if she found it I was scared
she got a row so would I for being out I could get a row easy
for there being marks on my neck maybe hit I wondered if
it looked like lovebites or hit for not being back on time the
face of the man rising a single eye in enough light to glisten
seeing me watching him and thinking it will make a
difference if he can see me so I looked at him

right into his eyes I looked right at him
keeping
   my sights

   clear

   and

still

not flu

A whisper. Peter's voice, muffled through the layer of hollowfill, a word in the unknown tongue. Bloody Dutch.

Rachel peeled her face out the pillow, turning towards more light than was bearable. A magnesium flare on the dressing table mirror. He'd opened the curtains again. The duvet was too close, one stiff corner shoving against her lip. She shifted to avoid it, making one hand an eyeshade against the closed lids. It didn't help much. Tiny silver-red beams, cloud linings the colour of fresh blood, filtered through the spaces between her fingers, the tang of overnight sweat from her open palm nipping the soft-boiled whites till they watered. Bloodshot. That was how they felt: covered with tiny red threadveins. All burst. The sounds were still going on in the other room. She could hear them quite distinctly: a polythene bag opening and closing, taking surreptitious ages, then muttering. She listened hard but the words were indecipherable. Not understanding didn't mean they didn't filter through, though. The two of them thinking they were being so careful, thoughtful, trying not to wake her up. Lying like this magnified things, made them impossible to blank out. Even so, she knew fine she ought not to be doing it. Listening to folk behind their backs. Eavesdropping, they called it. Well, that's what Enid Blyton books called it. She couldn't think of any other word. Eavesdropping. Bloody disgraceful. Rachel closed her eyes again, shifting the hand that had covered them over an ear instead, trying to behave. The other hand had surfaced from beneath the sheet, she used it to rub a sore place just behind the hairline. The roots there thick, greasy. Needing washed. One eye opened, found the clock. Five to five. It was always five to five. Over a week now and she still hadn't replaced the fucking batteries. Rachel moaned, moved to sink her face into the pillow again when another sound made her stop short. Knife noise, the scrape of stainless steel off cheap china. Her cups, her knives being passed hand to male hand in the kitchen. The bastards were making breakfast.

The flash of anger caught her by surprise. Unpleasant surprise. Rachel opened her eyes, making them water. The man was a guest for heavensake, a foreign guest. He was here because he'd been asked, because he'd been invited. It was her had asked him. He was simply making his breakfast, doing as he was told and making himself at home and there was nothing wrong with that. Nothing wrong with speaking Dutch, either – what else was he supposed to speak? It was meant to be the point. Peter's other language. It was for Peter. English didn't feel right in his mouth any more, he said. After eight years in another country no wonder. That beautiful, choked way he spoke, accent so overlaid with the different tongue it was hard to tell where he belonged. Edinburgh born and bred and that silly cow in the delicatessen over the road thought he was South African. Sud Afrique? he'd asked one day, twisting the pitch up on the last syllable like a parrot. He'd said it every time since. It drove Rachel cuckoo but Peter just laughed. He was never out that shop. Other ways, though, other ways he just wasn't settling back at all. He fretted about his Dutch going to waste, his pass-for-the-real-thing idioms rusting. So it was *her* that said it, her idea: ask one of your mates over, it's your place too now and he smiled that way that made her stomach slide like sand. A carnal sensation. Less than a week after, when he said Marc was coming, the feeling came again only this time closer to the lower intestine. Someone she didn't know would be sharing their living space for a fortnight. More food and electricity, having to put a camp bed up in the living room every night, whether he would leave his stuff lying all over the place, whether it was rude or bourgeois to care. And Dutch christ christ Dutch. Peter just smiled when she said she was scared. Once. Then he'd gone back to his blueprints, his notes in the margins. There was no-one to blame but herself, after all.

By the time they were standing at the airport, though, clutching bunches of tulips she wasn't sure weren't a joke, it seemed better. It seemed better because of Peter's face. She'd never seen him look so something. Radiant, maybe. Happy. Helping to look for someone she'd seen only one bad photo of; relieved, for some reason, when he looked less like Peter than she'd expected. Even if she had made an idiot of herself blocking a whole planeload of folk trying to get by, even if she had felt surplus to requirements, it didn't matter. Watching Peter exchange kisses with the other man, seeing his pleasure, made the apprehensions petty and mean-minded. When Peter gathered her in too, making a three-sided embrace, she knew it for sure. Nomatter what the guy was like. Marc. Nomatter what Marc was like. Everything would be just fine.

Laughter.

Rachel's back stiffened, her ears pricking. In the other

room, the toaster popped, ejecting both barrels: a single
word emerging from a blur of giggles. There was no other
word for it, they were giggling. Her eyes were closing again,
one hand rising to her temple. She pressed the warm skin
there, feeling the skull beneath push back. Bone under flesh,
resisting like eggshell.

It must have been 4, something like 4 am. She had woken
with his breath in her ear. A half voice, not making words
she could turn into meanings yet. Peter saying something. I
don't know what to do. She had thought it an intimacy, the
depth of dark and the heavy scent of him next to her, maybe
a tenderness, and she had turned, expecting the weight of
his hand to fall on her breast. A kiss, perhaps. Her nipples
had tensed, waiting. But he didn't reach. He didn't touch
her at all. The sheets were cold, he said. He whispered. The
sheets were cold. And she had fumbled her hand towards
him, finding something cloying, clammy. The sheet on his
side damp enough almost to be called wet. Something was
wrong. It was not an embrace at all. I don't know what to
do, he said. There was a moment of nothing before he
repeated it. He didn't know what to do. It was happening
again.

Thinking about moving jesus trying to open her eyes. The
air inside the room thick as raw meat. Just breathing it in
was an effort. She heard him sigh again, the sound vast in
the stale blackness. She should have forced him to take
those bloody vitamin things. He'd not liked her going on
about them but she should have forced him all the same.
Now here it was again, another night of this broken sleep
and sweating. Four nights in a row. Not ordinary sweating
either but rivers of the bloody stuff, his skin in spate. She
dragged her hand back from the sheet and lifted her head.
Christ, the dizziness, a kind of spiralling soreness behind the

eye sockets. It got worse as she hauled into a sit then pushed off the mattress to stand. The blackout curtains left no light to see by, none at all. She found the door anyway, banging her shin on something hard, not able to keep her eyes open for longer than seconds at a time. But she had to do something. The least she could do was get him some clean sheets.

The hall was cooler, the press door opened first tug. The two sheets she expected to see were right at the front, the smell of that fabric stuff rising from traps in the fibres. A smell like peaches, almost soothing. She'd put stuff in the machine specially. They weren't ironed but they were fresh. She bundled them in her arms like a child and went back through. This time the bedside light was on, Peter was standing up. Trying to stand up anyway. She could see him, through half-shut lids and a mesh of eyelash, pulling something on over his chest, tugging it down, hardly able to keep his balance for heavensake. She dropped the clean linen without saying anything and peeled back the duvet ready to dismantle the damp mess underneath. It wasn't easy. She'd made the thing up too fussy: hospital corners, wee games of nursemaid. Now it was a bastard to pull apart. He was suddenly beside her then, reaching to help, blue veins visible through one ghostly wrist. She squinted sideways but there was no comfort in it. He looked exactly the same as the other nights. Terrible. Eyes heavy and skin taut over the high cheekbones, his lips chalked out. He shouldn't be trying to do this. He shouldn't be standing up, never mind anything else. But she said nothing. Trying to tell him how to look after himself always caused more problems than it was worth. It was virtually done anyway. She let him tug the last bit free and dump it with the other castoff already on the carpet. The undersheet was stained and damp too, she touched it to make sure. He caught her eye and they stripped it away, all without speaking. Three sheets to take through to the washing pile. Peter didn't sit down though. He just kept standing looking at her. It wasn't till Peter sighed again that Rachel realised it wasn't the tired kind of sighing at all but another kind that had something to do with her and looked down. She was naked. Hauling the bed apart like a thing possessed and stark, seal-belly naked.

I've no dressing gown.

It hung there, not explaining anything. She wasn't sure why she said it, why it sounded so much like apology. She often slept naked, at least often in summer. Other times when there was a likelihood of sex. A wish for sex. And this wasn't summer. A confused embarrassment was spreading over her skin, some kind of shame she couldn't place. From the corner of an eye, she caught a glimpse of herself in the mirror, a lump of marbled lard. His bathrobe was here somewhere: she'd seen it in a heap on the floor before she had put the light out. It was still there now she looked, behind the wicker chair leg. She stooped to pick it up, trying not to wonder whether it was right side out, whether he would mind. Whether it was even sanitary: it was probably hoaching with his flu germs, bacteria and microbes and godknows. It didn't matter though. It didn't matter a damn. She wanted to cover herself up before he sighed again, before she did anything else. She shouldn't be barging about naked with a strange man in the house. Not that Marc looked at her much but that was beside the point. Other people's sensitivities and so on: it might have offended him to hell. The belt was in a knot now, a solid knot. When she looked back up, Peter was angled against the bedside, exactly where she had left him. Shaking. His whole body shaking, the clean tee-shirt he'd put on already patched with dark under the arms.

Jesus Peter. Are you ok?

He said nothing.

Put the heater on or something. Sit in front of the heater and get warm a minute.

He didn't look at her but crouched down on his hunkers, reaching for the socket. Rachel watched him feel for the switch, press it once, his neck sheeny with drying sweat. There wasn't a damn thing she could usefully do. Except maybe make up the bed again, hope they both got some sleep, wait for the thing to pass off. Maybe that was all it needed: a decent night's kip and they'd be fine. She turned away from the sound of the fan, the soft billowing of overheated air, heading back to the press for the third sheet.

The shelves were empty. Nearly empty. Just a torn thing like a sleeping bag liner crushed at the back. It was all there was, though. This morning's wash was still up on the pulley: there was no point even checking it. She lifted the torn sheet and went back through not looking. That was what did it. She knew even before the pain registered, a dry sharpness shooting from the ankle, she knew it was her own fault. If she hadn't been rushing, preoccupied, whatever it was she was being. But she had. Her shin and the bedside cabinet collided again, the same shin, the same place. The kind of pain that got worse after initial impact.

Jesus she said. Jesus jesus.

Peter wheeled, looking anxious. She made a sharp intake of breath, the soreness hugging the bone now. Fuck fuck jesus. Then there was another noise. A slow hissing. Shhh. It was Peter saying Shhh.

She looked at him, still clutching the ankle, not sure.

Sshhhh. He looked desperate. For crying out loud, Rachel. All that noise, banging into things.

What? she said.

You're so bloody clumsy. So bloody. He waved an arm limply. I don't know. Can you not be a bit less obvious for once and just. His voice died back, breathless. Just calm down.

Neither of them moved or spoke for a moment.

People are sleeping, he said. His shoulders slumped. Sleeping.

He didn't say anything else. Just clasped the rim of his tee-shirt, hands cupped where his genitals were beneath the cloth before his gaze broke and he looked away.

Rachel straightened up, taking her time. Peter was there on the other side of the bed, his face the colour of separated milk. She looked at his face, the curve of his back. He wasn't well, he was missing sleep. They both were. It wasn't the right time to start asking questions now, be angry or hurt. It wasn't the right time to say she felt the two of them blocked her out all the time and it wasn't just the language: it was the different mealtimes, shut doors when they stayed up in the evenings or worked together, heads close over blueprints and drawings. It was a lot of things. He seemed to be between them all the time. Even now, in the middle of the night changing the sheets in her own bedroom, the bastard wouldn't go away. It was something to do with Marc, this embarrassment of Peter's, his saying she was – what was it? – too obvious. Too *there,* was that what he meant? The time the two of them had gone out to some pub when he arrived, the way Marc smiled when she asked to come too: she wouldn't like it there, it would bore her and she said how can you be sure and he smiled again. He just knew. Now Rachel thought she knew something too. The reason he hung around the house so much, why there was no time they were alone except when she and Peter were in bed and even then he was semi-fucking comatose with sleep or drink, too tired to talk, too tired for anything at all. They hadn't made love since that man had been here. They hadn't even embraced for christsake.

Shhh.

The low insect drone of the fan heater stopped. Completely. Peter had slid back down onto his heels, still shaking, and switched it off. It was impossible to tell if he had silenced her again, if she had imagined it. In the bloom of silence, Rachel looked hard at his back, the skin tight over his spine. This terrible yearning to touch. He wasn't well. He had woken her up saying it, not knowing what to do. And for three nights she'd been fetching sheets and stripping beds because she didn't know what to do either. And still they soaked through. Because it wasn't flu. It wasn't that kind of sickness. It was something between the two of them, something between the two men. She knew she was shaking too now only it didn't show. A bead of sweat glistened on his jaw, melting into stubble as he stood up, facing her. Eye to eye. He would not understand if she touched him now, if she took his face in her hands and kissed him. Hard.

Sorry, he said. Almost inaudible. Sorry.

It wasn't the right time. Not the right time at all. She shrugged, looked down. The sheet was there in her hands. She took a pace back and snapped it wide, a white billow over the mattress. Peter stood up and moved to the other side. Their hands started smoothing then, putting the thing to rights. The Dutchman moaned, turning in his sleep. Rachel and Peter went on making the bed. They would make the bed, go back between its sheets and not sleep. He would sweat. It would not be possible to comfort him because of the burning, his skin burning up and needing peace and calm. Her touch would not allow him peace. It would make him worse. And she would lie next to him, trying not to come too close.

She must have slept, finally, on the edge of her side of the mattress. This cramping in her shoulders, stiffness up the

back of her neck. Maybe not well, but she had slept. And
still he'd managed to be up first, pulling the curtains, getting
on with things. Making breakfast. He laughed then. She
heard him laughing, through in the other room. His head
tilted, his neck bared. He'd have fixed something for him
and Marc, the way he had every morning, not mentioned
his waking in the night. When she went through, there
would be general jollity and making light of things, gentle
protests she was being fussy and overprotective – you know
how women are. She heard him laugh again: Marc, his
voice rising as he laughed too.

Rachel lay as still. As still as.
Keeping her eyes shut. There was nothing she wanted to
see.

It was time to get up.
Time to get up and tell herself not to be difficult. She
would tell herself not to be paranoid and get out of bed.
She would wash her face with cold water to make it look
less hellish and smile when she opened the kitchen door.
She wouldn't ask if he'd taken the vitamin C, at least
not immediately. After a couple of minutes though, she
wouldn't be able to help herself. Very soon now, she would
get up, defying lost sleep and godknew what else. She would
butter toast, make a joke of herself dosing him with fizzy
health supplements from a wine glass, and smile some
more. It was all she could think of to do. Her head crushing
tighter. Knowing it wasn't flu.
It wasn't

flu.

proposal

Shit

zeroed through two walls and into her ear, bloomed there like a bomb.

The way his voice could do that, just find her out: through precast concrete and pebbledash like a heat-seeking missile, straight through solid structures. The windows not even open.

Shit
coming closer.

Then the door sprang off its catch and a blur of what had to be Callum shot by the back of the settee. She knew it had to be Callum because of the way the air displaced, shifting out his road. Also he spoke. It's only me jesus crying out loud there's birdshit all over the fucking car for godsake, before the door slammed back again, him outside, her in. The reverberation of his voice hung on, palpable. Irene imagined if she sat very still, screwing her eyes up, she'd be able to see it: wee lines radiating from the space he had occupied then abandoned, like in a cartoon. She waited till whatever the lines were made of melted then got off the settee. It was ok. It was always ok. Just Callum, that excitable way he got – in the cupboard and out of it before you even had time to turn round. He would be outside with his polishing cloth again, quite the thing. She imagined him scouring, lifting the rag with wee daisies he'd made out of an old sheet. He'd lift it up and glare at the wee daisies for not trying hard enough, then press them back down hard, scouring till the windows gave in. Spotless, like they weren't really there. The way he liked them.

Irene? Five minutes ok?

A dunt at the door, feet on gravel, car locks freeing and slamming. He'd have a heart attack before he was thirty at this rate. She was never done telling him and he was never done kidding on he couldn't hear. Irene couldn't blame him. Nagging, you called it; what husbands gave in evidence they were Not Understood when they spoke to strange women in pubs. What they couldn't talk to other men about for fear they'd be thought less of. She lifted the empty glass on the coffee table, looked into it. If she didn't take it through, rinse it now, there would be a ring of dried-out sherry welded onto the bottom when they got back. Everything else was done: cases out, sockets switched off, doors pulled over, the curtain arranged so it looked not shut and not open at the same time. She glanced across at the kitchen, back down at the glass, then raised it, tilting her head back for a last drop that didn't come. What did was a clear picture of the corner of the ceiling. Those marks up there. They were definitely getting worse. Not just dots and maybe-not-there-at-all things but noticeably greynesses, widening out. A piece of wallpaper was lifting from the border as well, something blurry, fungal maybe, creeping out from underneath.

Irene? Cmon. It's now or never.

She put the glass down on the mantelpiece, reached for

her bag, draped the strap over one shoulder without taking her eyes off the ceiling. The car horn sounded. Twice. Irene bounced the keys in her hand, still looking up. Then turned her heel quickly and opened the door.

Callum wasn't in the car. He was staring at the guttering and pointing.

Look at that, he said, Look.

The gutter was glutted with chicken bones.

Bloody dogs at the bin bags again, he said. You think folk would feed their own mutts. Look at it. Terrible. He rubbed his hands together and looked up then, smiling. We ready for the off?

Irene looked at him.

We got everything?

Callum, she said. She hoped it sounded irritated.

He looked back, blank. Not playing.

How come knowing whether we've got everything's my area of expertise, exactly? Why's it my responsibility?

His eyebrows had sunk. He hadn't a clue. Irene tilted her head to one side, sighing.

Yes, she said. Yes. We've got everything.

He went back to the smiling, the mild abrasion of his palms. Irene poked her arse and one foot inside the car, keeping her knees as together as possible. The dress rode over her thighs anyway, a pale triangle of knicker showing through the crotch of her tights when she sat down but she said nothing. It was one thing being fed up with the weeness of the MG but another being sarky about it. He was quite right: the so-called witticisms about sports cars and penile length were no longer funny. Besides, the frock wasn't his fault. He might well have suggested she wear the damn thing, said if he had the choice he would wear a dress now and again, but it was her that had put it on. Anyway, dresses were better for you. They didn't give you thrush and compression marks the way jeans did. He was right about that as well.

Hey look, he was saying. He was pointing at the floor. New rugs.

She saw things like red toilet seat surrounds, black letters chasing themselves under her feet. HERS. HERS HERS HERS HERS HERS in an endless loop. Callum's had their own railtrack. HIS HIS HIS HIS HIS.

Two for the price of one, he said. He was turning the ignition and looking over, thrilled to hell. Good eh?

He stroked her leg, laughing, his mouth wide open. Irene couldn't think of the last time she'd seen him in this kind of mood. Laddish. Like a wee boy. It was more than the new rugs, more than the daftness he'd bought them for. He looked over at her then, his eyes shiny: a look that said she was a thing of beauty, a joy for ever. It was the frock. It didn't matter how crabbit she was being, he was loving seeing her in the bloody thing. They were going on holiday and she was wearing a frock. Irene looked at the smile, at Callum behind it.

There's paper coming off the wall in the livingroom, she said. I told you it needed redecorating.

He shook his head in a manner suggestive of astonishment, one side of the smile widening.

I don't know, he said. You're unreal, you. He shook his head again, good-natured, flicked the indicator switch. He laughed out loud. You're un-bloody-real.

Callum's mum was in the kitchen surrounded by smells of spitting meat. Callum ducked to avoid a mobile that hadn't been there before. Lavender bags strung on garden twine, tiny pink bows all down its length.

You've arrived, she said.

No lipstick yet but her nails freshly varnished, pearl-white hearts. Their tips cramped what was left of a cabbage

tight against the chopping board, pale green shreds falling
in layers to cover the design of little girls in mob caps. She
gazed down at the cabbage like the Virgin Mary, keeping
slicing. Callum picked a single sliver off the board and held
it near his mouth. He always took something when he came
in, posed with it till she gave him a mock slap on the wrist
so he could do his look of mock outrage. It was a routine.
Irene watched them do the whole thing.

When's the dinner ready then? he said. I'm starving.

O you, she said, O you, and rolled her eyes.

There was a recipe for rack of lamb on the pinboard. The
cardboard horseshoe with a sprig of heather was coming
loose. Cousin Angela's wedding favour. Her eldest must be
six by this time, Irene thought. Six at least.

Is he not terrible? Mrs Hamilton said.

Irene asked if there was anything she could do. Mrs
Hamilton said she'd give her a shout. It was what she
always said. When the shout came, it would be to come and
get a basket of bread that was already sliced and carry it
through. It was all a shout ever meant. She always asked
though. Through the connecting door, the tv was running
Tom and Jerry. The news would be next. She watched it till
the tune started but didn't go through. Callum never liked
her doing that. He liked her to stay with them in the kitchen
even if there was nothing she was useful for. He was
anxious about it now, looking over while pretending to
rummage in the cutlery drawer, exclamation marks
showing between his eyes. Irene nodded to let him know it
was ok. He poked his thumb into the air to show her he was
pleased and went back to the rummaging while Mrs
Hamilton lifted their jackets, carried them out to the hall
cupboard. The soft sound of receding fur mules, Callum
crashing out cutlery in fours.

There were two geraniums on the sill: no withered leaves,

no fallen blooms. Beyond them, Irene saw Callum's father working, making holes in the dark garden border soil. His hair had been cut, the temples shot with more grey. She watched him reach and ferret forth something from a plastic bag, something with roots that would fit the hollow he had just cleared with his bare hands. Dirty but fine boned, the wrists narrow. They had worked for a security firm for twenty-four years, those hands, gloved in leather: the rest of him swathed in navy, a helmet with a full-face visor. Irene watched him work, forcing his fingers into the soil and wondered if he'd ever battered the hell out of somebody during those twenty-four years; gone queer-bashing or studied the reader's wives or Dutch porn the other boys kept stashed under the seats of the van. It was entirely possible. He wouldn't have enjoyed it or anything but it was still entirely possible. He was looking round for something now, failing to see it. He stood up instead, wiping his hands along the seams of the trousers he wore for the garden and would wear to the table too. On the edge of the lawn, she could see a pair of garden gloves, the plastic tie unbroken. The ones she had given him for Christmas. To George xxx. Untouched. He strode over them, careful of plant shoots, heading for the house.

The door opened. Mr Hamilton stood on the top step of his own back door, knocking mud off his boots, a loose lock of hair falling forward over his brow as his feet struck the stone. He nodded to Irene, inscrutable. Callum came back through from the livingroom and opened the fridge door.

Aye aye. He spoke to the freezer compartment.

Aye aye. His father nodded again, eyes focused in the general direction of Callum's feet. All right, then?

Callum looked above the white door rim for a moment, a kind of confused smile coming with him. His face was pink.

Aye fine, he said, the smile stuck. Like he'd been caught doing something naughty. The eyes of the two men met by mistake for a moment before Mrs Hamilton opened the serving hatch. The peach-coloured lipstick she was so fond of, the one that made her mouth look like it had been squeezed out of an icing bag, moved.

You've a clock in that stomach of yours, it said. ESP or something.

George bashed his foot one last time for luck and closed the back door. What is it then? he said. He didn't look at her.

I don't care what it is, Callum said. Just get it on the table.

Mrs Hamilton looked at them. She looked at Irene. I don't know, she said. Her face plump with happiness, delight even. The things you've to put up with in this house.

Mr Hamilton started washing his hands.

It was cabbage, potatoes, cauliflower and carrots. The basket of bread went in the middle: the big plate of roast something, last. The roast always sat next to George because George always carved it. It was George's job. He cut the meat and put it onto plates. Irene's was always first. She took her plate, told him it was fine. Callum took his, looked down at the meat and said, We're going to Belfast.

Silence. Irene looked. She knew from the way the words were hanging over the dinner. The bugger hadn't told them. He'd said he would and he hadn't. It was the first he was telling them now. Mrs Hamilton looked at George, looked away again, held a big spoon of carrots out for general inspection.

Your daddy grew these. What do you think?

Very nice, Callum said. Lovely.

Irene wondered when the fork would come over. Callum usually pinched her meat and gave her his vegetables. He did it particularly when he was trying to be charming. The

fork didn't come though. She heard George put down his
knife, the silence stiffen up.

When? He said it very slowly. When's this then?

Callum kept his eyes on the salt shaker, poking it as if the
holes were blocked. He shoogled it a couple of times.

Soon, he said.

Oh yes. You're going to Belfast, then. Soon.

Callum put the shaker down. Mrs Hamilton settled back.
Everybody got everything they want?

When's that then, George said. Soon? What's that
supposed to mean? What for?

Soon. Irene knew from the way he said it he was looking
at her, wanting her to look back. Soon, ok? Soon.

He chewed something as though it was burning his
mouth, swallowed.

Soon, he said. Tomorrow.

George looked straight at Callum then back at his plate.
His mother doled out cabbage.

For goodness' sake, she said.

Callum ran his finger along the blunt edge of the knife,
back again. He didn't look at her.

You never tell us nothing, she said. It's terrible. Is it a
holiday or what? It's terrible.

George made a noise like clearing catarrh and
swallowed.

You could have stayed at your auntie Pat's if you'd let us
know. I don't suppose you've contacted her either. Eh?
Contacted Pat?

Not yet.

Ha. There was a note of genuine pleasure in George's
voice, triumph or something. Irene heard it. Not yet he says
ha. I didn't think so. Not yet eh? Ha!

His knife scraped against the white ceramic.

Stupid, spending money. You could have stayed at Pat's.
Dunno what's wrong with you, boy. Got secrecy like a

disease. He sniffed. I'm taking it on trust you know what you're doing, boy.

Callum.

His mother's eyebrows had collapsed like a swing bridge. Not holding bowls or spoons any more, she looked bereft, lonely. Even her back slumped.

Honest, it's terrible. If you're away a holiday you could just say. I don't know what you're like that for, son. She looked like somebody had punched her.

You'll miss the big meeting as well, George said. He mumbled. You won't be here.

Not even saying, though. She looked at her husband. He was cutting a potato. You'd think we were bad to him or something. You'd think we were – then she couldn't think what else they might be and stopped. Irene looked at Mrs Hamilton, the way she tried to meet the gaze of people who would not look back. For six years she had been calling her Mrs Hamilton. Now, suddenly, she wanted to call her something else.

The carrots, she said.

Callum turned. They all did.

These carrots here. They're very nice. Wilma.

Everyone had stopped eating, nonplussed. Then George's face melted.

Course they are, he said. Grew them out there. Organic what-you-call-it. Organic methods. Good for you.

His teeth, clean marble slates, showed briefly. He'd never had a filling in his life. Wilma held out the blue dish still half-full of orange discs.

Here. Her voice was full of something. Have some more, she said. There's plenty.

Belfast, George said. I don't know. But it was better somehow. It was definitely better. Callum raised his eyebrows so only Irene could see, keeping his head down while he slipped his fork over and stole the last slice of her meat.

Oh you, his mother said. Under the peach-coloured smile, the real colour of her lips beginning to show. Oh you.

There was the eating of pudding, the clearing away, the settling of dishes in the sink.

No don't you do them, she said. Away you two through and watch tv.

Singing came through the hatch with the water noises, wee bits of ABBA and godknew. George went to get his roses done before the sky clouded over. Irene and Callum had two cups of tea, a Hitchcock remake and *Songs of Praise*. The usual Sunday afternoon.

George missed the chips and cold meat and Callum doing the washing up. Callum went out to the shed to fetch him in when they were leaving. They all stood on the front door step except Irene. There wasn't room for four. Mother and son kissed, she on her toes, fingers tipping his shoulders as if she might keel over reaching so high. Father and son didn't. They didn't touch at all. George came down the step for Irene though. He leaned forward, brushed her cheek with his mouth pursed. Nice in that frock, he said. Should wear a frock more often. Then he stood back and smiled. He had a beautiful smile, George. They both had beautiful smiles. Callum looked like both of them whether he smiled or not. You could see it without even trying.

You taking that thing? George pointed at the car. You serviced it then?

Callum got in, rolled the window down. It's fine, dad.

Fine for a heap of junk. Bet it won't start first time.

It did. Callum stuck his head out the window, triumphant. His father smiled again: unstinting, clean. He waved.

See and have a nice time, Wilma shouted. She waved too.

George and Wilma smiling on the front porch, forearms ticking like metronomes. They kept doing it till the car was out of sight. Callum relaxed into the driving seat, changed gear.

Heap of junk, he said. Cheeky bastard.

Three EXPECT DELAYS signs were evenly spaced along the approach to the shore road. The shore road was usually ok. Sunday nights it was hardly ever busy at all. Tonight it was a risk. Callum took it anyway. He weighed the possibilities and made a decision. After ten minutes or so with no trouble, he relaxed. Irene didn't realise till he did it he'd been anything else. He put his hand on her leg, patting it lightly.

Ok?

Irene said nothing.

The patting became a long stroke, knee to thigh, back down to rest where it started.

What time we due at your mother's then?

Ten.

She knows we're coming?

Of course she knows. I told her not to make up the spare room. Told her we'd do it.

Callum's hand cut off at the wrist by the black jersey, white against the orange tights. Irene stared at it.

Callum, she said. She paused, choosing the right words, the moment. How come you never said to your folks about us going away? The hand moved back to the steering wheel. He looked in the rear-view mirror, back out front again, checking something. He checked it for ages.

Callum I'm asking you a question.

I did tell them. They must have forgot.

Irene levelled her eyes on his face. Callum. You didn't tell them.

I did.

No you didn't.

I did.

Irene sighed. Callum blushed right down to his neck.

I did. They must have forgot. Honest.

Callum. She bent his name into a hillock. He looked at her out the corner of an eye and sighed.

Ok ok, he said. Ok so I didn't tell them. I own up it's a fair cop guv I'll never do it again. Satisfied?

No I'm not satisfied. I know perfectly well you didn't tell them. I don't want to know *whether*, Callum. I want to know *why*. *Why* didn't you tell them?

He drove, staring hard at the road. His chin disappeared.

I just didn't want any hassle.

What hassle?

The twenty questions thing. You know what he's like about the car, telling me what I should be doing and all that stuff. You know what he's like, Irene.

You could have told your mother. Her voice was down to its usual octave again, coaxing. Cmon. You could have said to her on the phone.

He sighed again.

There was nothing stopping you.

What difference does it make eh? It's ok now. They weren't bothered.

They were so bothered. More to the point I was bothered. Me, Callum. *I* was bothered.

Aw cmon Irene.

Cmon nothing. I *was*. They must think I'm a rude bastard, that I was in on it or something.

In on it? In on what for godsake? I'm twenty-two for christsake Irene: I don't need to tell my father everything I bloody do. Am I supposed to be asking for permission or something, is that it?

That's a complete side-issue, Callum, *completely* beside-the-point. The point is not about asking permission: the point is you told me you *did* and you bloody *hadn't*. You *hadn't*.

So?

So you gave me misinformation. You made me look like an idiot and/or an accomplice and I don't like it.

Oh for fucksake Irene.

Don't fucksake me, Callum. You did. Either they thought I was in on not telling them, on not giving a toss what they thought *or* they've picked up the fact you never tell me what's going on half the time either. I don't like it. I don't like not being told what's going on. It's embarrassing.

Callum snorted.

It is. It's humiliating. I don't like being shown up in front of folk like that. Especially not your parents. It's controlling and humiliating and I feel belittled by it.

Belittled. He said it like it was a foreign word. Belittled?

The car was slowing down, tacking behind a queue of others. Yellow lights were flashing up ahead somewhere. Callum pulled up the handbrake. The creaking died away.

That's ridiculous, Irene. That's the most ridiculous thing I ever heard.

No it isn't.

Yes. It. Is.

Irene turned to the side window. Outside was getting dark now, the sea washing with nothing to glitter off. She watched it come and go in the half-light, mist gathering in the corners of the window.

I don't know why you're doing this.

It was a very measured voice. She turned round. Callum was shaking his head, holding the wheel with both hands. The car was rolling, almost imperceptibly.

Oh for godsake. She sighed. Are we going to play a you-started-it game?

Silence. Big silence.

Look. Irene breathed heavily down her nose, rubbed her

temples hard. Ok. I'm doing this badly. What I'm really trying to say is you don't need to be so . . . whatever it is.

I don't need to be so what?

Manipulative, Callum. That's what you don't need to be. Telling lies about trivial wee things then getting annoyed when I find out. Like I'm not supposed to let on I've noticed.

He pulled the brake back on full, his mouth set.

Me. I tell *you* lies? I tell you *lies?*

Ok maybe it's not lies. Evasions then. Is that a less contentious word-choice?

He said nothing for a moment, just glared at the windscreen. Sometimes. He said it like the first number in a countdown. Sometimes, Irene, you can be a sarcastic cow.

That's as may be, she said. But you're still doing it. You're avoiding the issue, steering the conversation away from what I'm trying to say.

Which is?

Which is – her voice was getting louder again, hard to keep control of – which is, Callum, you telling me you'd told your folks when you hadn't. The issue is you controlling information and not telling the truth.

I do tell you the truth.

You tell me the truth?

Yes. I do.

Ok. You tell me the truth, then. Tell me it now. I'd like the truth about this meeting, please.

What meeting?

This meeting you won't be there for. Tell me about that.

Callum said nothing.

That's all I know, there's some meeting and you won't be there – and I only know *that* because your dad said, only there was other stuff going on at the time. Now there isn't so you can tell me. What meeting? On you go.

I don't know. I don't know what he was talking about.

Irene looked at him. She kept looking at him. Callum

intensified his gaze on the nothing that was behind the windscreen.

Are you being serious? she said.

Eh? He screwed his face up as though something was annoying him, as though he was concentrating really hard and not able to hear her. Eh?

I said –

Callum sounded the horn suddenly, leaning hard on the middle of the steering wheel.

Look at this carry on, he said. Look. Bloody road works eh?

Irene turned away. She banged her head off the side window. Then she did it again. I give up, she said. She exhaled very slowly. I. Bang. Give. Bang. Up. Bang.

Her hair had brushed a gap in the condensation. Through the streaky mesh, she could see the shore wall still there, the mission rock behind it. ETERNITY. She could see it quite clearly: the paint luminous at this time of night. Nothing else, not even the sea. Just the rock and its message, a present from the holy rollers who prowled the seafront with a bucket of whitewash every summer. They had cookouts and things, sang hymns. ETERNITY. Irene looked at the letters, the gaps between them. She was wondering how often they did it, repainting the same thing to keep it clear, whether they came at night to keep the whole thing a kind of mystery. Maybe you were meant to think god had done it, or something. Then it clicked. George saying All right? that way, Callum going coy. The conversations she'd heard father and son having umpteen times and thought were just one-sided. It clicked.

You've joined the Lodge, haven't you? she said. You've joined the bloody Orange Lodge.

She turned and looked at him. He was looking back at her, his face flushed.

No wonder you're fucking embarrassed. She was staring at him so hard her eyes hurt. Christ on wheels Callum. The Orange Lodge.

Callum's mouth was open but nothing was coming out. He looked caught. Scared. Ridiculous. For no reason, without seeming to want to, Irene started laughing. A steady through-the-nose snort. Callum looked away quickly, crunching into the wrong gear, back out again. The car in front had started moving. Callum let the motor inch forward, closing the gap carefully but the engine was revving. Irene didn't drive but she knew it didn't need to rev that hard. The laugh had died away now, stopped as fast as it had come. A string of red lights flashed on down the whole slope of the hill. The car settled on its hunkers again, rocking slightly.

He was still saying nothing, just sniffing. After a moment he made little coughing sounds, sniffing some more.

Jesus christ almighty, she said. She didn't turn round, just kept staring down. The pattern on the frock rose and fell with her breathing, rose and fell. She watched it, waiting. Then looked up. His eyes were very shiny, trained on the tail-lights ahead.

Dad put my name up, he said. I thought I could do something he'd like for a change. That's all. Doesn't matter.

He rubbed the bridge of his nose, wiped one side of his face with the back of his hand. The other held on to the steering wheel. It held on tight. The insides of the windows were steaming up again. The car was completely still.

What are we doing, Irene?

His voice was so soft, she hoped for a moment he hadn't spoken at all. He had though. She said nothing waiting.

Everything, he said. Everything is up in the air all the fucking time. Can't even visit my parents these days without something, some bloody thing . . .

He ran out of words and leaned forward on the steering wheel.

Look. I wasn't trying to keep things from you. Honest.
I'm not trying to do anything, just get on with a normal life.
That's all I want. I want us to have a normal life for
godsake. You and me. That's all I'm trying to do.

And all I want is to be let in on things. I want you to stop
making decisions for me.

He sat up again, glared at her.

It's still the engagement ring isn't it?

Irene said nothing.

You just can't let it go, can you?

Irene said nothing.

Ok, he said. I confess, I confess. I did a terrible thing: I
bought you an engagement ring. Yes, I know I should have
asked you first. I know I shouldn't have told anybody we
were getting married before I asked you either. I know I
know. I said I was sorry. Most women would have
managed to find something flattering about it but there you
go. I have to say I'm sorry. So I did. And I am. And I'm still
getting this shit.

Irene said nothing.

Jesus christ Irene, what are you wanting me to do
though? I don't go on about what you've done. That affair
you had, that bloody John guy or whatever his name was. I
don't keep dragging that up. I've tried to put it behind me.
We need to put in a bit of effort for christsake, move
forward. You don't fucking try.

Irene said nothing.

What are you thinking?

Nothing.

I know what I think.

Nothing.

I think we should get married.

This time she groaned. He just kept going.

I've asked you often enough. If we got married things
would be different, all sorts of things. You'd see.

The engine purring, a stink of damp dog. Looking down, the short blue hem, her legs swathed in orange mesh. Tights. She was wearing tights because. Because. The words HERS HERS HERS coursing under her feet. She could think of nothing to say.

Please. His voice was clear and sure. All you need to do is show willing, Irene. That's all.

He swallowed, didn't look at her.

I don't want us to go off the rails again.

After a while the car in front started to pull away, this time more definitely. Callum reached for the glove compartment, took out the cloth and wiped the inside of the windscreen clear. Irene took it from him, their fingers touching briefly, and finished the rest. It was her job anyway. Slowly, he released the handbrake. Callum's big, competent hands. Like George's. Just like his dad's.

What time did you say we were due at your mother's then? he said.

The side-window showed nothing. Irene rolled it down, watching the glass level fall, breathing deep. Ozone and pitch black. That's all there was. The sea was out there somewhere but only in theory. There was nothing of it visible at all. She had a notion for a moment to ask him to stop, pull the car over so they could go outside, walk for a bit on the sand. But the line was moving. They were inside Callum's car going to her mother's to spend the night ready for the morning ferry. She'd be waiting for them now, watching tv and wondering where they'd got to, nipping in to check the big bed with the top sheet turned back. Everything would be waiting. Irene tucked the cloth away where it belonged, spoke to the windscreen.

I told you already, she said. Ten. She's expecting us at ten.

We're going to be late, he said.

Ahead, the motorway lights, official apologies on reflective metal. Cars picking up speed.

six horses

I

Eve is reading.

After three days' climbing, they still did not know each other's names. Eve sees two people, a man and a woman, peering over the edges of scarves, mouths muffled against rock dust. In this way, dusk falling, they became separated from the rest of the party. Speechless, unsure of their bearings, they climbed deeper hoping to hear an echo of the others from a nearby chamber. Eventually, they reached a soft place in the rock, a shelf already giving under their boots: crumbs of shale and pebbles at first, then the ground dissolving, separating from itself with such languor neither of them thought to move out of its way. A light ripping sound of fibres parting, and they fell, not far, into a narrow tunnel underground. A fine deposit gusting up from the floor, twisting in the light of their helmets like smoke and filling their nostrils with a taint like gunpowder; acrid, dry. The walls shone dimly with hematite and coal. Thrown together, listening, they waited till the dust settled back around their feet. Then, soundless lest the vibrations disturb the rock overhead, began walking. After only a short distance, the roof angled sharply downwards. They could no longer stand upright but kept going. At the end of the tunnel, they found a tumulus, a swollen belly in the wall covered with lichen. He ran his palm over it, found it warm. The texture of dried peat blocks or matted earth. They exchanged glances only once then began, pulling with bare hands till the bulge opened suddenly, a hole big enough for the lamps of their helmets to shine through. Inside, spectral in the white beams, they saw a horse. A horse whole and standing in a sealed tomb. The man couldn't help himself. He stretched his hand. One touch. And the beast was no longer there. Vanished, crumbled to powder. It was no longer there. He is glad she (he puts his mud-caked hand inside hers, squeezes tight) was with him or he might have thought the whole thing a dream. Eve reads the scientific explanation, an irrelevance. What matters is only this: a man and a woman looked at nothing with a faint trail of smoke through it, a roomful of mist where a horse had been, then looked at each other. Knowing they would never be strangers again. Eve clutches the paper like hair, looks across the room.

2

Listening, the timbers of an unread book creaking under his hands, he keeps his eyes steady. The headphones, she knows, are not to keep the sound in; they are to keep it out. If she listens hard she can hear music but it's distant, an echo. On the other side of the street, workmen are scaling scaffolding. Behind his back, they lean against the monkey bars, peer across to see if she is watching. His book falls, unnoticed, from his lap. A boy in a yellow helmet, a tattoo of Pegasus winding round one arm, hangs smiling by his boots from the sky.

3

Another cigarette. He lights up, draws; the tips of his fingers amber. He picks winners while she picks up the phone. There is no-one at the other side. She'd rather go home tonight, she says. Tonight she won't stay. Cab and a train, he says. This is serious. Smoke trails over his lower lip, spills over the newsprint picture: its black and white eyes, the bit between its teeth.

4

The tunnel goes on. Blackness hurling past the window, reflecting her features on smeary glass. People don't die for lack of love, she thinks: at least no-one dies. Except children. She looks at the eyes in the window pretending to belong to someone else. For a split-second, she sees what he sees: a woman with an alien face flaring on the tunnel wall before it gives way. The wall disappears taking her with it and the tunnel is over, past. Her ears fill with quiet as a rabbit makes a ghost of itself against the scrub. Closer to, a luminous shape rears out of the wash of grey. Grazing.

5

It is the room she left but not the same. Still cold, but tiny
things look warm, look open to touch. That someone else
could be here did not seem impossible any more. It's all
right, she would tell him. We're not children. He wouldn't
be listening. He would be looking at her. Dark-drown eyes.
Outside, past the advertising hoardings, the washed shore
wall, white horses rising on the crests of harbour waves.

6

They have not had too much to drink. He takes off his shirt, his shoes; loosens his belt. The last layer. Thick twine over his sternum and belly widens out into black ferns, an upturned V at his crotch. His penis is so pale in the half-light she can't help her mouth being drawn like a butterfly, a moth. She has only known fair men, has not been prepared for this dark texture, this hardness, the scent of this skin. She wonders till his hand stretches for her hair, then stops wondering altogether. Eve, he says. He says her name. In the morning, she finds five long strands from his head, a cache of pubic crescents, a single eyelash. Faint trails on the white cotton streaked with a henna of coming menstrual blood. It is the room he left but not the same. Her head is full of rockfalls, coal-dust phosphorescence, melting horses.

www.vintage-books.co.uk